MOTHER OF SPADES

LUCK GODS SERIES BOOK 2

J. GABRIEL GATES

Steed Publishing and Media, LLC
Michigan
Steedpublishing.com

Book Cover Design by Steed Publishing. Interior illustration by Etheric Designs

1

———

AGGIE

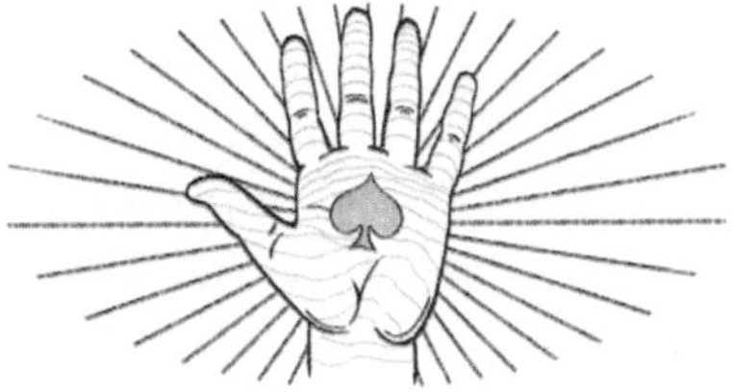

Falling in love is like blazing down the highway on a motorcycle, blindfolded. Wind in your hair. Horns blaring. Deadly obstacles whooshing past unseen as you blow by them on your way toward an explosive and uncertain bliss. Nice metaphor, right? Except in my case, I was literally speeding down the 696 freeway on a motorcycle. I was literally blindfolded. And I might literally be—*eek!*—in love.

Jack Valentine rode behind me, his strong arms wrapped around my waist, his lips tantalizingly close to my ear as he gave instructions.

"Stay relaxed, Aggie. Don't think too much. Just open yourself and let the charm flow."

Charm. Luck power. Did I mention Jack and I are both demigods with the power to control chance?

I felt heat in the palms of my hands as the pips—glowing heart-shaped marks—throbbed with power. I slowly twisted the throttle, and the engine roared louder, speed building. But I was still in control. Tires screeched as cars lurched out of our path, our luck causing the drivers to glance in their rearview mirrors at just the right moment to react and keep us safe. I leaned slightly left, and we drifted to avoid what must be a vehicle in our lane. It just felt like the right thing to do. If I were lucky, there would be no semitrucks in this new lane for us to smash into. And I was lucky.

I felt it then, an inward tug, an urge. I extended my arm, opened my hand, and released charm, which felt like a pleasant burning in the palm of my hand. There was a shriek of tires, the bleat of a horn, the sound of cursing muted by engines and glass.

Jack laughed.

"What?" I shouted back at him over the rush of the wind.

"That driver was gawking at us. You helped him look away just in time to avoid rear-ending the car in front of him."

Using our power to help others makes our charm increase. *The work,* we call it. I felt the result now, more charm rising like a surging tide in my veins.

"Our exit is coming up," Jack shouted over the wind. "You ready?"

My breath caught in my throat. I was so *not* ready. My dad died in a car accident on the freeway—while I was in the car. If anything filled me with unmitigated dread, this was it, which was probably why Jack had chosen this particular stunt for the culmination of my training, the gateway between my being a newbie luck god and becoming a full-fledged member of the Valentines. Jack had been prepping me for weeks. I couldn't let him down. But...

I felt my heartbeat in my ears, a relentless drumming, and I counted the beats *one, two, three...*

No, I admonished myself. No matter how scared I was, I was not going to let those old OCD compulsions cripple me today.

You're a goddess. Fearless. Powerful, I reminded myself.

But I was also Aggie. And Aggie was flawed, flawed, flawed.

"No counting," Jack said in my ear. These days, he seemed to know me as well as I knew myself, which was almost as scary as the test ahead.

Physics was my jam. I could calculate the amount of speed and force necessary to kill a person in any number of gruesome ways. But the amount of charm needed to prevent that death? That was far harder to quantify, and there were no good textbooks to teach it. Believe me, I looked.

How lucky would a person have to be to survive wiping out on a motorcycle at ninety miles per hour?

This lucky, I thought. *Ditch the bike and use my charm to keep us from dying.*

Go!

Only I couldn't do it. Even after everything I'd been through, everything I'd overcome, I was still freezing up. Tears of frustration welled in my eyes, wetting the blindfold, and I blinked them back ferociously.

"Six?" Whenever he was being stern with me, Jack called me by my rank. When I didn't answer, I felt him sigh, his broad chest rising and falling against my back. "Fine, I'll do it."

Before I could protest, he wrenched the motorcycle's handlebars. The Ducati jogged sideways, shooting out from under us. For an instant, we were a pair of projectiles flying down the highway in midair. My stomach flipped with panic, but my reaction was automatic from my training. *Relax. Tuck. Roll.* All within the invisible halo of my flaring charm.

I was tumbling, skipping off the pavement like a stone across water, then hitting the pavement again and rolling—in a lucky move—to my feet. I ran for a few steps, spending the last of my momentum, before my feet ground to a halt on the roadway. Reflexively, I bent, catching my breath with my hands on my knees, my body quivering like a leaf. After a moment, I became aware of a sound rushing toward me, a rumbling of air and the earth as powerful as an onrushing hurricane. I turned, slipping off the blindfold to see a semi thundering toward me.

I didn't try to dive out of the way. Didn't run. There wouldn't have been time. I just raised my hand, flared my charm, and shut my eyes. There came a shriek of tires and an agonizing squeal of brakes that seemed to go on far too long. A puff of acrid wind buffeted my face.

I opened my eyes to find the chrome grill of the semi three inches from the end of my nose. Its trailer had jackknifed sideways, blocking the freeway, and irate drivers behind it were slamming on their brakes and honking.

I grinned. *Wish I could watch that in instant replay. Eat your heart out, Neo.* I thought of sharing that particular quip with Jack, but he was extremely remedial in his nerd lore and probably hadn't even seen *The Matrix*, which was... *Wait. Jack!*

Like a counter punch, the thought struck, knocking all elation out of me. What if Jack wasn't okay?

I looked right, to the windswept shoulder. No Jack. I looked left, to an impact-snarled guardrail. No Jack. If possible, my heartbeat sped even faster. *One...* I counted my tremulous breaths. *Two...*

"Jack?" I called with rising panic over the honking horns, the humming traffic. "*Jack?*"

He appeared then, walking up the highway to emerge from behind the hulking semi. Both hands were opened toward me, the red heart-shaped pips on their palms flared bright. I caught a wild, scared look in his eyes before his usual carefree smile returned. Could it be he was just as scared for me as I was for him?

If so—*eeeeeee!*

"Let's go!" he shouted. "Before the cops show up."

The semi driver was shouting something rude at me, but I ignored him as I ran to Jack, leaping over the snarled and smoldering wreckage of the discarded motorcycle. We ran up the embankment at the side of the freeway together, crashing through the tall grass hand-in-hand and laughing like a pair of wild kids.

❧♡♤◇♧☙

The Valentines mansion was a posh, luxurious French-style mansion located lakeside in a nice neighborhood (or should I say a *lucky* neighborhood?) in suburban Detroit.

Upon our arrival, our fellow Hearts mobbed us to congratulate me on completing my training. In order of rank, there was the lovely Latina badass and my sometime nemesis, Ten. Her ponytailed hunk sidekick Cobe was our nine. My sweet buddy Mina was our eight. British boxer Walter Whitman, A.K.A. Dubs (who looked more like Wesley Snipes circa *Blade II* than the famous grizzled poet), was our seven. I was the six, of course *curtsy*. Five had just returned from a stint doing reconnaissance on the West Coast, and I didn't know him very well. His name was Abraham, and he'd ascended to his rank after my trainer, Ari, had died fighting the Blackovers a few months before. His quiet demeanor made me nervous, but he seemed nice enough. Four was our angsty token French girl, Adelie. Three was Deuce, of course, one of my favorite boy-humans ever. Two was a new recruit, a tall, dark, brooding boy named Galen who had been playing basketball for Wayne State before Ten had found him. Having another Heart loyal to Ten come into the suit was likely bad news for me, since Ten had more or less hated me from the moment she saw me, but so far, Galen had left me alone. There were also King Michael and the ace, but neither of them tended to hang out in the kitchen and mingle with the rest of us.

Mina and Deuce were my two best friends in the suit, and as soon as they saw me walk into the kitchen, smiling in my shredded motorcycle leathers, they immediately went into a dance routine they'd been working on for the occasion. This was made hilarious by the juxtaposition between the two of them: Mina being an adorable waif who'd once led a K-pop group whose name roughly translated to *The Little Candies* and Deuce, who was hairy, husky, and awkward beyond belief. The dance reached its climax, which featured Deuce twerking while Mina spanked him—a sight which will doubtless be burned into my psyche forever—then the two sandwiched me in a big, claustrophobia-inducing hug, which had me laughing until my chest hurt.

"So, now you know how to crash a motorcycle," Deuce said, decoupling from Mina and slapping me on the back. "What's next? Barrel off Niagara Falls? Fist fight on top of a speeding train?"

"Actually, Jack here promised to read over some college essays," I said.

Normally, Mom would have been my go-to helper for school-related tasks, but she'd been working crazy long hours since returning to her job at Oak Hill College, and I'd been spending more and more time at the Valentines' house.

"Plus, I have to work on my MGIS submission," I added.

"What's MGIS?" Abraham asked. He was maybe the only one in the suit who hadn't heard me yammering on about it for the last three weeks.

"Michigan Girls in Science," I said. "It's a fifty-thousand-dollar scholarship that gets awarded every year to the girl with the best science project in the state, which is obviously me."

"You know we Valentines have more money than God," Ten said. "If you insist on going to college, just ask Michael, and he'll cut you a check."

"It's not just about the money," I explained. "There's a lot of prestige attached to it. This award can open doors to some of the nation's best colleges, many of which I happen to be applying to."

Ten rolled her eyes, which seemed to be her default response to anything I said or did.

I turned to Jack. "So, shall we get to work?"

In the interest of one-hundred-percent transparency and to avoid being labeled an unreliable narrator, let me disclose that I was also hoping to make out with Jack pretty intensely for about half an hour before getting down to other business. But he gave me an apologetic half-smile that I'd come to know all too well and held up his phone.

"I just got a text from Seemor. He's gotten reports of shimmers over by the lakeshore. It's probably just peri coming through the rift on run-of-the-mill business, but I need to make sure."

I tried not to look as pouty as I felt. "You want me to go with you?"

"That's okay," he said. "Those essays and science projects won't finish themselves. I'll be back soon to give you a ride home."

He came close and squeezed my hand, which was the closest we came to PDA in the Hearts house common areas since Ten happened to be Jack's jilted ex-girlfriend. I was loath to let go of his hand for so many reasons. Because I really wanted to go upstairs with him. Because it made me very nervous when he went out on missions like this alone, which he did all the time. And simply because I wanted to keep him close. But he pulled away, smiling in his disarming, absent way as he snagged a small sandwich (there were always snacks at the Valentine house) and made his way to the door.

As it slammed behind him, Deuce sidled up to me.

"If you're looking for help with your project, I'm something of a girl scientist myself," he said.

Normally, Mina would have joined me too, but she was talking to Galen across the room—something I'd noticed her doing more and more often lately.

I smacked Deuce on the arm. "Alright, you big lug. Let's get our science on."

❦

Stepping into my bedroom in the Hearts mansion always felt a little like walking into a fairytale. It held a canopy bed overarched by high ceilings with a large window looking out on Lake St. Clair. A wingback chair sat by the window, next to which stood a teetering stack of books I'd pilfered from the Valentines' extensive library. My reading had taught me a lot about the Luck Gods—about their history and the nature of their power. But it was like physics, in a way. The more I learned, the more acutely aware I was of everything I didn't know, and there were many mysteries in the world of the luck beings—the *peri*, as they called themselves—that I was dying to unravel. But I had some normal science and some typical senior-in-high-school stuff to bang out first.

Even though I'd spent quite a lot of time in Jack's room lately—*ahem*—this room still felt like a home away from home for me. In some ways, I was more comfortable here than in my bedroom at the apartment Mom and I shared.

I even had a pet: as soon as we were in the door, Hadron, the cat Deuce had gotten for me, slunk up, purring, and began rubbing himself on our ankles.

"Aw, hey, you big furball," Deuce said, his normally low voice going adorably high as he scooped up the kitty and sat on the bed, stroking him. "So, tell me about the mad science you've been doing, Dr. Frankenstein."

"Okay, check this out," I said, taking out my phone. As I pulled up the app I'd created, I felt myself lighting up, as only nerding out about science can do. "A couple of weeks ago, Hadron got out, and he must've been doing what tomcats do, you know, being social or whatever, and he came back with fleas."

"Ew," Deuce dumped Hadron on the bed and wiped his hands on his pants.

"Right. Kind of gross," I went on. "So I shampooed him with the flea stuff. Then, as I was rechecking him, I thought *there must be a better way to do this than trying to spot these tiny specks with my naked eye.* I mean, even now that I'm a demigod, my vision still isn't twenty-twenty," I said, readjusting my glasses.

"So..." Deuce prompted.

"So I invented this." I handed him my cell phone. "Go ahead, point the camera at Hadron."

Deuce zeroed in on Hadron, who lay on the bed languorously licking one paw. I leaned in so I could see the phone screen, too—close enough that I could smell Deuce's aftershave. He smelled like a grandpa, but not in a bad way. He smelled clean. Fresh. Wholesome.

The phone's camera took a moment to focus, the app took a moment to process, and then *voila!* a series of red dots appeared overlaid on the image of Hadron.

"Whoa," Deuce said. "Are those really...?"

"Fleas? Yep," I said. "Go ahead and check."

Deuce came closer to Hadron, zeroing in on one of the red spots, then moved the phone aside to look with his naked eye. After a moment, he reached down and picked a flea off Hadron and held it up in triumph.

"Nice!" he exclaimed. "How did you do it?"

Explaining how things worked was always my favorite part, so I paced as I spoke, dragging it out and being as dramatic as possible. "So you know there are cloud-based AI applications that are available to use for free?"

Deuce nodded.

"I used one of those and trained it on tons of pictures of fleas. First, I used pictures of fleas against white paper, then I trained it to pick them out in Hadron's fur. I also used other fur, so the app would be useful for other animals. I got a couple of fake fur coats, a couple of wigs."

"And gave them all fleas?" Deuce laughed.

"Right. Then I had to create an app to integrate the flea-spotting algorithm with the phone camera and make the red dots show up on the display, which was fairly simple, actually." I shrugged. "I only have the app for Android right now, though. I still have to make the iPhone version."

Deuce nodded in appreciation. "Dude, that's pretty brilliant."

"Brilliant enough for me to win Michigan Science Girl of the Year?" I asked, batting my eyelashes.

"I don't know that many science girls, to be honest," Deuce replied. "But I'd say you're the best one for sure. Poor Hadron, though. He's had fleas this whole time?"

"Yeah, he doesn't seem to mind them," I said, stroking Hadron.

"So what do you need help with?" Deuce asked. "And don't tell me you want to give me fleas . . ."

I shrugged. "I don't really need help with the Science Girl project. I have to revise the report a little bit, but it's pretty much done. The problem is I've been putting all my time and energy into this project, so I'm way behind on my college essays. I don't even know what to write about."

Deuce rubbed his stubbly chin. "Yeah, writing about pretty much any aspect of your life right now would make you sound certifiably bonkers, wouldn't it? Think of the essay titles... *How I became a demigoddess.*"

"*How my mom ate a shard of an obsidian obelisk and briefly became a supervillain,*" I said.

"How the power to control luck has impacted my ability to crush standardized tests." We both laughed.

"My boyfriend lured me into a magical cult, and I love it," I said. At the word *boyfriend,* Deuce's smile wavered, and I suddenly felt mortified. Not just because I'd called Jack my boyfriend, which wasn't entirely accurate as we'd not yet put a label on our relationship. But also because months ago, before Jack and I became —whatever we were—Deuce had asked me out, and I'd shot him down. I still caught glimpses of pain in his eyes when he was looking at Jack and me, but we both pretended to ignore it. Just like we both ignored the icy feeling that crept into the room now.

"Anyway..." he said stiffly. "You have some essays to write. How can I help?"

I picked up Hadron and dumped him into Deuce's lap. "I'll write. You shampoo the cat," I said, and gave him my most charming smile.

❤ ♠ ◇ ♣

I'd completed a first draft of my University of Michigan essay, and Deuce had washed and blow-dried Hadron by the time Jack returned. He looked tired and stressed as he did so often these days, but when I asked him what had happened, he only kissed my cheek. Deuce suddenly became very interested in petting Hadron.

"False alarm," Jack shrugged. "Probably some sprites or goblins smuggling contraband luck artifacts from the rift to Bartholomew Barth. Nothing to worry about. Come on, I'll give you a ride home."

I can't lie, I felt a tug of disappointment that we weren't going back to Jack's room for a while. We hadn't gone all the way in the carnal sense—I'll just put that out there up front. I'd never done that before, and in the beginning, there had been some trust issues. Mainly, I was mad he knew about the ace burning down my family home and hadn't told me the truth about it right away. Then there was my jealousy. Jack seemed to have a runway-worthy ex-girlfriend lurking around every turn. But Jack Valentine was hard to stay mad at. It was much easier to fall into his arms and kiss and forget than to hold grudges. But that didn't mean the things that separated us didn't exist.

All summer we'd gone through this cycle: I'd feel close to him, drawn in, the way we'd been on the motorcycle today. And then I'd feel him pulling away, growing cold. We were like a pair of rotating magnets going through cycles of repulsion and attraction. From a physics perspective, an arrangement like that could produce energy—a lot of it, in our case. But it also created friction. It was frustrating, dizzying, and at times a bit lonely. Right now, every cell of my body wanted to be drawn close to him. But he was right. Mom would be getting back soon, and I got so little time with her as it was that I liked to be there when she was home.

Deuce dumped Hadron into my backpack, which was his favorite mode of transport, and I thanked Deuce for his help. He gave me a hug, and when we pulled back, he met me with another of those sad smiles.

"Watch out for fleas," he said.

"Watch out for... girls," I said, then cursed myself. I'd been flailing for something clever to say, and that's what came out. Clearly, even being a demigoddess hadn't made me immune to being awkward.

"Girls?" Deuce said, perplexed.

"You know. Girls can be sort of infectious. Like fleas. And they can be scary, right?"

Deuce grunted. "You have no idea."

"Don't worry." Jack grinned. "Deuce might face a lot of dangers, but too many girls is not one of them."

"Har har," Deuce said as we departed.

"That was kind of mean," I said to Jack when we were down the hall and out of earshot.

"What?" Jack said.

"Saying Deuce can't get girls."

Jack laughed—loudly.

"What?" I demanded.

"Deuce is a Valentine. We're the fair suit. The lords of love. I was just making a joke. Deuce could get any girl he wants. Well, any mortal girl."

When I thought about it, Jack was right. Even though Deuce was one of the least smooth and least—I don't know —*polished* members of our suit, all the Valentines were infused with so much luck it made us supremely attractive. Guys at school even fawned over me, for cripe's sake! And I'd seen plenty of girls giving Deuce the side-eye when we were out in public.

"It's Deuce who stays away from girls, not the other way around," Jack said.

"Maybe he's not into girls," I mused. "Maybe he's... into boys."

Jack chuckled. "If he were, I think he'd dress better."

Neither of us speculated further on Deuce's reasons for staying single.

We took a luxury car from the Valentines' ample stable of fancy red vehicles. As we sailed along the freeway, I watched Jack. Was he my boyfriend? It was true that we'd never applied that title to our relationship, but the way he acted, the way I knew we felt toward one another, made titles irrelevant. *Boyfriend.* That word—along with every sidelong glance I stole at him—made me feel like a shaken-up can of pop, fizzy inside and ready to explode.

I'd never had a real boyfriend before (card-carrying nerds like me who snort-laugh on the regular and make up songs about the periodic table of elements for fun rarely score high on the "I want to date her" list, it turns out). But the main thing that stressed me out was: *Jack was Jack*. Perfect blond hair, perfect blue eyes, perfect veins running along each perfect bicep. A perfectly roguish grin. A perfect quip always ready on the tip of his deliciously perfect tongue. All that *perfect* made me nervous, because in my experience, *perfect* never lasts for long. It left me waiting for the other proverbial shoe to drop. Over and over, I'd had to remind myself there was no other shoe, and now, as our delirious summer drew to a close, I felt like I was finally accepting my good luck. Jack was Jack. He was real. And he was mine.

Darkness had fallen by the time we pulled up in front of the apartment Mom and I lived in, but her car was still gone.

"She's spending a lot of time out these days." Jack's observation was weighted with the suspicion all Valentines felt for my mom. She was technically a bad luck god. A Morbus. An enemy. The fact that she'd been captured and basically forced to take the mark of Spades made little difference to most of the Valentines. She couldn't have gotten the mark if she hadn't accepted it willingly, my dear frenemy Ten loved to remind everyone.

I understood why they were suspicious. When it came to generations-long animosity, the Valentines and the Morbus made the Montagues and the Capulets look like a couple of kids tussling over a beachball. But they didn't know Mom like I did.

"She's just obsessed with her new black hole experiment." I shrugged. "When she's working, she really gets sucked in."

Jack raised an eyebrow. "Black hole. Sucked in."

"Very punny," we say together—one of our little inside jokes.

"So I'll pick you up tomorrow for the Choosing?" Jack said.

That made me roll my eyes. "Come on. Everyone knows Michael is going to pick Ten."

King Michael—who didn't like me—was going to choose Ten—who *really* didn't like me—to become his queen at a ceremony early on a Saturday morning that I was supposed to get dressed up for. Nothing in the scenario appealed to me.

"Choosings are a flush," Jack reminded me. "That means required attendance for all members of the suit."

"I know, I know," I sighed, slipping my hand over his. "I guess if you'll be there ..." I fluttered my eyelashes playfully.

He brought my hand to his lips and kissed it. God, was it his luck that made those lips so soft? Or was it just Jack himself? I was just leaning toward him for a real kiss when a pair of headlights flashed across us. Mom's Honda sedan appeared, pulling into the parking lot and jouncing over speed bumps, coming toward us. She didn't seem to notice us—luckily—as she passed and stopped under the carport.

"Crap," I said. "Let's go."

We both exited the vehicle, darted across the apartment complex lawn, and crashed through the bushes to my bedroom window. Before I jumped to catch the window frame and haul myself up, Jack grabbed my arm, spun me to face him, and kissed me. A real kiss. Lips and tongue and breath and tingles. I felt every joint in my body unhinge, every cell of my being simmer to life.

Then we were apart. He boosted me up while I clambered through the window. I landed in a heap on the carpet, then turned and poked my head out to get one last look at him.

"Bye, Toby," I said. His real name was a secret between us, and I liked to use it to exert power over him, *Eragon*-style. He gave me a look. "Bye, Jack of Hearts," I corrected, keeping my tone equally flirty.

"Bye, Six," he said. "I'll get you at nine AM."

I couldn't keep the goofy smile off my face. "It's a date."

By the time Mom made it to my room, I'd traded my flashy, heart-patterned clothes for some flannel jammie pants, scrubbed the lipstick off my mouth with the back of my hand, flopped into my bed, and stuck my phone in front of my face. *Look at me, I'm a normal teenager.* A master of disguise . . .

The door creaked open.

"Bonjour, Parent," I said, impressed by how casual I sounded. Was it bad that I was getting so good at deceit?

Mom crossed her arms and leaned against the doorframe. She looked better than she had when she first returned from her captivity. Her face was less gaunt, and a little color had returned to her cheeks. Of course, being starved, imprisoned, and brainwashed by a sentient stone while simultaneously possessed by a bad-luck demon could do a number on anyone. That stone—a shard of the obelisk of Spades, still sat in her stomach, where no surgery could safely remove it. And she still had those bad luck Spade pips on her hands, although she'd gotten so good at hiding them that I barely noticed them anymore.

She's getting good at deceit, too, some cynical part of me said. But that was absurd. There were no secrets between Mom and me, not since her drinking had stopped. Well, except for my liaisons with Jack and the Valentines. Mom knew the lives of luck gods were dangerous, and I didn't want to worry her by letting her know I was hanging out with Jack. She had enough to deal with.

"Hey," Mom said. "What have you been up to?"

"Oh, you know. Riding motorcycles. Hooking up with wild boys. Risking my life."

Mom cocked an eyebrow.

"All on the pages of my trusty e-reading app," I finished, waggling my phone at her.

She gave a little snort-laugh and came to sit on the edge of my bed. "Really, you ought to get out sometime."

"This from the woman who spends every instant of her free time alone in her lab working on a science experiment. When are you going to let me have a look at it, anyway?"

"Soon," Mom said, patting my leg. "Like I said, I'm close to a breakthrough, and I want it to be a surprise. After that, I'll let you work with me on the final stages. I promise."

I gave my best dramatic sigh. Little did Mom know, I was grateful she'd been so busy. I secretly dreaded the day she would quit staying at the college physics lab until all hours—it would make it much more difficult to spend time with Jack.

She rose and stretched. "Well, I'm beat. I'm crashing."

"Okay. Hey, I'm going out early tomorrow," I said. "Molly has a shift at the library, and I promised her I'd help re-shelve all the sci-fi. It gets boring there without my sparkling wit to entertain her. Her words, not mine." It really was disturbing how good I was becoming at lying. But Mom would be dead asleep at nine in the morning. She'd have no idea who I left with.

Mom smiled. "Far be it from me to deprive Molly of your wit. Besides, how much trouble can a girl get into in a library? Permission granted."

"So kind of you, Parent," I said with mock formality.

Mom yawned again and turned to go, but I noticed something.

"Mom?" I pointed to a splatter on her shirt. "What's that?"

"Hmm?" She glanced down absently and picked at one of the spots with her thumbnail. "Huh... Oh, you know, I had pancakes for lunch. At the Coney Island. Must be I dripped some syrup."

"Must be." I forced a wan smile. "Good night, Parent."

"Night, Aggie," she said, already gone up the hall.

I sat staring at the doorway she'd just vacated, compulsively counting her footsteps as she disappeared.

Stop. You're just being paranoid, I told myself. *Mom is fine. She's herself again.*

But Mom was a luck god, just like me. All luck gods feel compulsions to do *work*, which increases their power. Good luck gods, the red suits, Valentines and Diamantes, dole out good luck. The black suits, Blackovers and Morbus, like Mom, spread bad luck. Mom swore that she had the Spades power under control, that the shard of black obelisk in her belly that whispered evil things into her mind had gone silent. And I believed her. I did.

And it was true, Mom did love brunch. So did I. It was a major Van Der Graaf family tradition, an incontrovertible fact.

But another fact nagged at me: I'd dripped maple syrup on my clothes more times than I care to admit. I knew what the stains looked like. And in this light, Mom's spot had a tinge of red that didn't look like maple syrup at all. It looked like blood.

2

AGGIE

The people who love to watch royal weddings and red carpet galas would choke on their pearls if they could see a Valentines flush. First, they take place at the Hearts' mansion, which as I may have mentioned is a decked-out and flawlessly decorated chateau on the shore of Detroit's Lake St. Clair. Everyone is impossibly gorgeous with that godly glow that only oodles of good luck can impart. And their clothes? Well, if an Armani designer got time-warped back to the middle ages and you gave him only super expensive heart-patterned fabric in every hue of red to work with, you might come out with the couture Valentines wear to their gatherings. Even I gave in to the spirit of the day and put on a heart-patterned ballgown, although I insisted on wearing my customary beat-up sneakers underneath. It was lucky I dressed up, because I had to stand next to Jack, who looked truly godlike in an impeccably tailored red suit with a black velvet collar.

Valentines were rarely all present in one place. Someone was usually out spying on the dark suits, recruiting sycophants (a.k.a. sycos—luck gods' human helpers who run the day-to-day operations of the suit), or jetting off to Monaco to meet with the Sylph Council—that sort of thing. But today, everyone was present when Jack and I entered the throne room.

Mina skipped up to greet me first, her short, straight hair dyed an electric red for the occasion. "Big day," she said, sounding so nervous she might actually be afraid she'd be picked.

Someone stepped up behind me and covered my eyes. "Guess who?"

As if anyone else in the suit talked in a mumbly British accent. "It's either Prince Charles or..."

I wheeled to find Dubs smiling behind me. "You crash any motorcycles this morning yet, love?"

"Not yet, but the day is young," I said. "What about you? You staying out of trouble?"

"Not at all, Sweet," he deadpanned. "I'm a Valentine."

The door opened behind me. Valentine training had hard-wired me to be aware of my surroundings, even here in the mansion—luck gods don't stay alive long otherwise—so I spun toward the sound. Ten swept into the room in a stunning sequined gown the color of fresh blood. I glanced at Jack, a bit jealously, to see his reaction. His eyes flicked to Ten then he looked away again immediately, not nearly giving her the full inspection her beauty deserved—which made me feel so grateful I took his hand and squeezed.

Before our last queen—Aubra—died, I had thought she was the perfect Queen of Hearts. But seeing Ten now, I couldn't help but admit that she was perhaps an even better fit. She was different than Aubra, to be sure. Our former queen had been sweet and warm, curvy and cunning. Ten, by contrast, was lean and cold and severe, uncompromising. Where Aubra was strawberries and cream, Ten was ruby and steel. But the old Hearts' history books all agreed that the most important attribute in a queen was strength, and Ten certainly had that. She was poised. Tenacious. And probably the best fighter, strategizer and charmer in the suit. I still hated her, mostly because she still hated me. But part of me was grateful that she was going to be our next queen.

"Hey, Ten." I curtsied as she approached. "Or should I say, Your Majesty?"

She gave me an icy look. "Don't reference a promotion before it's been bestowed, Six. It's bad luck. Not to mention bad manners."

No matter what, I always seemed to say the wrong thing when it came to Ten. It was a knack, I guess.

"See? Just what a queen would say." I gave her a toothy smile and let her pass.

Jack squeezed my hand, a friendly reminder to shut up before Ten broke my nose. But she'd already drifted to the far side of the vast, marble-floored hall to join her crew. Cobe, Adelie, and Galen all greeted her with what looked like reverence, especially the young two, Galen.

The fact that the king had let Ten choose Galen was another irrefutable sign that he planned to pick her for his bride, everyone agreed, since picking new recruits was traditionally the queen's role. I had my own evidence that Ten would be the pick; I'd seen Ten and the king kiss once, before he killed his former wife to protect Jack. But I had been spying, and that kiss was sort of a secret.

A paper airplane sailed in to land at my feet. I knew who'd thrown it before I knelt to pick it up, but it was more fun to play along. I unfolded the paper to read:

. . .

Gift Certificate:
Good for 1 handcrafted latte
and inane conversation about pop culture
topic of your choice
to be redeemed in Valentine library.
Your devoted personal barista,
The Deuce

Deuce jogged into the room wearing a red velvet tuxedo complete with an ascot. The pants were comically short, and the shirt was stretched so tight on his husky frame that the pearl buttons strained. When he spun around, I saw that the suit coat had tails.

"Oh no!" I laughed.

Deuce shrugged. "Well, if his majesty King Sourpuss demands we dress up, I for one am going to do it ironically."

He raised a hand and hailed Ten loudly from across the room.

"Hey Ten! This is probably my final time to give you crap before you're royalty, so I just wanted to remind you: Jack dumped you. And you are not a nice person."

Ten flipped him off without pausing in her conversation.

Jack smacked him on the arm, but he was shaking his head and laughing.

"What?" Deuce said. "If she's going to hate me, I want her to hate me completely. That way I know where I stand."

"Deuce. Bad idea, man. Did you play with fire when you were a kid, too?" Jack said. "Stick your fingers in electrical sockets?"

"He's not Deuce anymore," I reminded Jack. "He's a three now. We should call him Bruce Trés or something."

Deuce gave a dramatic sigh. "Naw, it's fine. Everyone is used to calling me Deuce now. And people call Galen Galen, not *two* —so it's fine. I accept it. I'll be Deuce forever. It's probably karma. I'm sure I was Genghis Khan or something in a past life."

"Don't be so hard on yourself," I said. "I'm sure you were Marilyn Monroe."

Jack shuddered. "That's a disturbing thought..."

With a loud *click,* a pair of doors at the far end of the room swung open, and all the chatter hushed as King Michael entered. He wore a red fur cloak and a golden crown with a ruby the size of a silver dollar set in its front. The only sound was his footfalls as he took his place in front of his throne. He paused, then glanced at the queen's throne, which sat conspicuously empty.

Michael always looked a little like a stone gargoyle to me. He was lanky and pale, his long gray hair swept back from a brow that always seemed creased with frown lines. As much as I disliked Ten, I almost felt sorry for her having to marry a crusty old jerk like him.

Still staring at the empty throne, Michael cleared his throat, and the silence deepened, a nervous hush tinged with expectation.

"We all miss Aubra," he said, his voice hoarse and low.

I glanced at Jack. Jack had told me Michael's secret: Aubra had died in our battle with the Blackovers, yes. But it was Michael who pulled the trigger. And the ace, that mysterious old matriarch of our suit—she had ordered him to do it. Seeing Michael feign sorrow over his wife's death when he was the one who killed her made me hate him even more.

"She was special to all of us," the king went on. "The heart of the Hearts, you might say. In her time, she led our suit well.

But we are entering a new era. Our ancient enemies are rising again. Alliances are shifting. The future is… uncertain.”

His faded gray eyes ranged over all of us in turn, making me cringe.

I noticed Mina, who stood next to me, fidgeting nervously with her skirt. It occurred to me again that he could pick her. As an eight, Mina was high ranking. Plus, she was adorable. Smart. Tough. I'd certainly pick her over Ten. *Ick*, the thought of Mina with Michael made me shiver with repulsion. But what about Adelie? Adelie was relatively weak, and she didn't seem terribly interested in power or political intrigue—or anything really, except fashion and money. But maybe the king wouldn't want a strong queen. Maybe he'd prefer someone passive who he could push around. *No. Everyone knew it would be Ten. It* had *to be Ten.*

The king's dramatic pause filled the room with tension so strong it almost crackled like electricity. Hardly aware that I was doing it, I flared charm—not because it would influence the king's choice, but purely out of habit. The warmth on my palms was nice, like having two handfuls of sunlight. *Don't pick Mina,* I thought.

Michael cleared his throat, and the suit held their collective breath.

“Here, in the presence of our entire suit,” he said, “I hereby fulfill my ancient duty, with full support from our exalted ace. To be my bride, to be your new queen…”

Ten stood a little straighter. Mina tensed. Even Adelie looked attentive and on edge.

But the king's eyes flicked to me.

“I choose Aggie.”

3

AGGIE

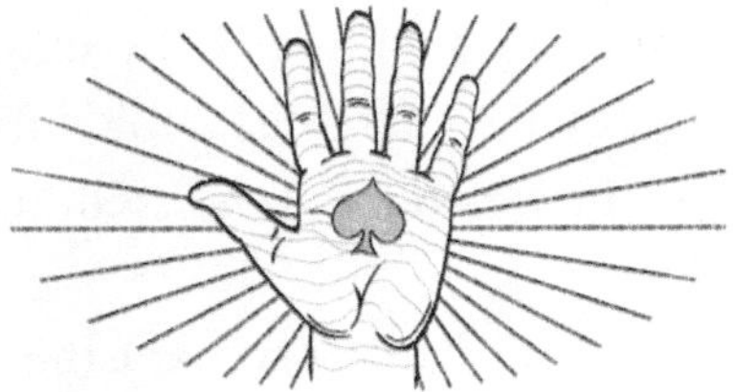

Have you ever watched one of those disaster movies where an airplane's hull gets breached and everything—air, napkins, people—gets sucked violently out into the void of the sky? That's what it felt like now, only no napkins fluttered or plates flew. Nobody screamed. Nobody moved or spoke or breathed. But the air definitely got sucked out of the room. One by one, heads turned until everyone was looking at me. I realized that I was supposed to say something, but my mouth felt stuck shut. I swallowed and my throat gave a dry click. Jack squeezed my hand, prompting me, only I didn't know what I was supposed to do. I'd never expected to be picked; I hadn't studied up on the process. My first impulse, to scream *no* and elbow my way out of the room, definitely seemed incorrect.

"Go stand next to him," Jack whispered, letting go of my hand and nudging me toward the dais where the thrones sat. I floated forward, unaware of my legs moving beneath me, until I stood next to King Michael, facing the assembled Valentines. Every face I saw held an expression of carefully cultivated neutrality, except Ten's. She wasn't frowning exactly, but her eyes could have burned me to soot.

The king took my hand and I had to force myself not to jerk away from him.

"According to custom," King Michael said, "we will meet here again in three days for Aggie to announce her acceptance. Then, the queen trial may begin."

Michael looked at me, but I couldn't meet his eyes.

"Dismissed," he barked, and everyone shuffled out of the room without so much as a whisper between them. Only Jack remained, watching Michael and me expressionlessly.

King Michael sniffed, nodded to himself, then turned to go back the way he'd come.

"Why?" I asked. My throat felt so tight that hardly a sound came out, but he must have heard me, because he turned back. "Why me?" I pressed.

The king fixed his gaze on me, his eyes like bits of chipped flint. "Some decisions are beyond even a king's control," he said. Then he turned and left.

❦

That evening, I lay in bed next to Jack, staring up at the ceiling of his room. It was one of the smaller rooms in the Valentine mansion, but still luxurious, with vaulted ceilings, exposed beams, picture windows, and a large TV. It had been a home away from home for me all summer. But in this moment, even Jack's bed with its butter-soft sheets and its sweet Jacky smell felt unsafe. I'd been asking questions for hours, trying to learn everything I could about what was happening and what was expected of me. Jack had remained patient enough to keep letting me rehash the same territory, but at some point in the conversation, he'd risen and was now pacing like an agitated animal.

"So the king expects me to accept him," I said, recapping what Jack had already told me for the bazillionth time. "And if I do, the ace will send me out on some dangerous quest to prove my womanhood or something."

"The queen trial," Jack supplied.

"And if I actually succeed and survive, then what's my prize? I get to spend eternity married to Michael."

"And you'll have the power of queenhood."

I rolled my eyes. "Like I care about power."

"Maybe you don't," Jack said gently. "But the king does, and he's the one who chooses a queen."

I shook my head, frustrated. "Why would Michael want to marry me? He knows I hate him."

"The ace," Jack said simply. We'd been over this already. That was what Michael's cryptic final words to me had meant. The king would probably have preferred to choose Ten or Mina or even Adelie, but the ace had ordered him to choose me instead. Just as she had brought me into the suit as a six rather than a two, as was customary.

"But why?" I railed. "What's so special about me?"

"Well, your charm is exceedingly strong," Jack said with infuriating calm.

"That was just from my mom's dark matter machine," I said. "If anyone had stood in that polarized field, they'd have just as much charm as me. Or more."

"Maybe," Jack said. "But you did a pretty good job of destroying that machine, defeating your possessed mother and preventing the world from being overrun with jinn," he pointed out. "Which would have tipped the balance of luck toward bad and basically made the world a terrible place for a few generations to come."

"Yeah, I guess I did do that," I allowed. "But still. He could have picked Ten. *Ten*."

Jack slunk into the bed and slipped his arms around me. "Sure, but then what would we call her? Queen Ten? That makes no sense. We already have Deuce Trés, for God's sake."

I laughed in spite of myself, then thumped him on the shoulder in frustration. As usual, it was like whacking a cinderblock.

"I'm serious," I said. "This is a man who killed his ex-wife. What's he going to do to me when I say no?"

Jack's smile fled. His eyes held mine—those eyes like staring into a summer sky. Like falling upward.

"I think you should say yes," he said.

I must have reacted like I'd been slapped. I blinked. Stiffened. Wriggled out of his arms. "What?"

"It's not like a normal marriage," Jack said. "At least, it doesn't have to be. You've read the histories. You don't have to kiss Michael or hold his hand or even touch him. There have been plenty of king-queen matches that had nothing to do with romance and everything to do with power."

I was on my feet now. "So you'd be okay with that? With me *marrying* someone else?"

He hesitated, a rare expression of surprise crossing his handsome face.

"Not that I expect to marry you," I added quickly. "That would be crazy. I mean, not *crazy* . . ." I pressed my hands to my face in utter despair. This wasn't coming out right. Nothing about this day was going right. Jack came to me and tried to peel back my hands to look at my face, but I pulled away from him again, counting my steps as I retreated across the room.

"Aggie..."

"No!" I shouted. I couldn't help it. "Why didn't I see this coming? Everyone warned me about you."

He recoiled. "What?"

"*Jack only cares about power.* That's what everyone said. And I was a fool. I believed—" My throat closed up. I tried again. "I become queen. I have more power. And you have me. That means you have more power. That's the idea, isn't it?"

"Aggie—" he sighed.

"You're buddies with the ace. Did she come to you in your dreams and tell you that I was going to be her pick for queen?"

Jack paused. It was just the briefest flicker of hesitation, but it was enough to smash my heart like a hammer.

"She did," my words came out a breathless whisper. "You knew!"

Jack had been going on rounds on his own all summer. He always had an excuse for not bringing me along, and I trusted him. When I asked about his quest to unify the suits, his responses were always vague and noncommittal.

Don't worry about that.

I'm not thinking about that right now.

It's too dangerous for you to get mixed up in, Aggie.

You can help me when the time is right.

I'd assumed he'd put his plans on the proverbial back burner. Or that he was leaving me out of things in order to keep me safe. But maybe neither of those things was true. Maybe I was just a chess piece that he'd left sitting on my square until he was ready to move me.

"Aggie." He reached out to touch me again, but I jerked my arm away.

"Don't," I said. "I'll find my own way home."

Then I was out of his room, slamming the door behind me. *Don't look back.* I commanded myself as I rushed down the hall. *Don't give him the satisfaction.*

But I couldn't help it. I did look back, part of me hopeful

that he'd be running after me, an apology on his lips, an explanation ready.

But the hallway was empty.

Technically, as a member of the Valentines, I could have taken one of their many fancy cars any time without permission, but my hands were shaking so much I didn't trust myself to drive home. I could also have used my leprechaun key, with its ability to whisk me home in ten magical seconds. But traveling via the leprechaun underground weirded me out; I didn't like doing it too often. And the truth was, I didn't want to be alone, either. Mina offered to drive me, but she was playing video games with Galen, and I didn't want to interrupt. So I texted Deuce.

He met me in the garage two minutes later, and as we pulled out into the clear Michigan twilight, I saw him glancing at me out the corner of his eye, probably noticing the lines of dried tears streaking my cheeks. For a guy known across six continents for an inability to keep his mouth shut, he did a pretty admirable job, but finally, I broke the silence and explained to him why I was so upset. He stayed quiet again for such a long time, I started to think he was annoyed with me. But at last he said, "It's hard being caught between duty and desire."

I laughed. "Did you read that on the back of a historical romance novel?"

He sighed, and I could tell I'd hurt his feelings. Obviously, he was trying very hard to say the right thing. The problem was, there was no right thing.

"Look, I know Jack has a lot on his mind," I said. "But the idea that I could marry Michael—and that Jack would *want* me to . . ." I shook my head.

"I'm sure Jack was just—"

I held up a hand, the glowing pip on my palm momentarily bathing the car in red light. "Don't," I said. "I know Jack is your friend, but just don't defend him, okay?"

We rode in silence until we reached the exit for my house.

"Actually," I said, "can you take me to the college instead? I want to see my mom."

"She working late?" Deuce asked. It was 8 PM, which might be late for most people, but wasn't late at all for Mom. She was a night owl anyway, and lately she'd been working until two or three AM regularly.

"She's always working late," I said.

Deuce looked concerned, just as Jack had when the subject of Mom came up. But the Valentines had taken possession of all the pieces of her previous machine, the one that had caused so much trouble, and there was no way she'd be able to re-create it without months of effort gathering unusual instruments and rare materials. Plus, Mom had had me scrub the math on her latest black hole experiment. It was legit. And it was brilliant. Once it was finished, she might finally get the recognition in her field that she deserved.

"Don't worry," I told Deuce. "She's teaching four classes and doing lab work. She's too busy for mischief. And I'm keeping an eye on her."

The car slowed to a stop beneath one of the massive trees that gave Oak Hill College its name, and we sat together for a second, listening to the sound of the wind stirring the treetops. As I groped for the words to say goodbye, I realized that this might not just be *goodbye for now*. It might be *goodbye forever*. Obviously, I wasn't marrying King Michael, and what would happen then? Would I still be welcome at the Valentines' mansion? Would Michael have me banned from the house? Would I be thrown out of the suit altogether? For all I knew, he'd send an assassin after me. He'd killed Aubra. What would keep him from doing the same to someone as insignificant as me?

As it turned out, I didn't need to come up with the right words. Deuce pulled me into a hug, and I felt the tension in my shoulders melt away, surrendering bit by bit until I was perfectly relaxed.

"I'll give you this much," I sighed. "You give some excellent hugs, Deuce Trés."

"Yeah," Deuce said. "Hugs are my moneymaker."

The Oak Hill campus was always a little spooky at night, what with the 19th-century stone buildings and the vast, gnarled oak trees. But since the duel with my possessed mother here a few months ago, it felt worse. I couldn't look anywhere without remembering jinn swooping around like monstrous, blood-thirsty shadows or Blackovers and their violent sycos marching across campus like an apocalyptic circus parade. The Zune science building, where Mom's old dark matter machine had been built, sat vacant, surrounded by flapping yellow caution tape until the damage our battle caused was repaired. (Fortu-nately, no one had witnessed our fighting. And if any of it was caught on surveillance camera, whoever saw it must have decided not to share it with anyone—probably because it looked like something out of a Harry Potter movie and they didn't think anyone would believe it was real.) The new tempo-rary location for the science programs was a newer building on the other side of the green, and I made my way there now.

I sighed as I stepped into the bright light of the lobby, releasing a pent-up breath full of nervous energy. Then I galloped down the stairwell and into the basement level, where Mom's new physics lab was. Since I hadn't seen her new project yet, I was a little nervous about barging in now—mostly, I didn't want her to be mad at me for ruining her surprise. I couldn't take being in a fight with her and with Jack at the same time.

But when I tried the door to her lab, it was locked.

I paused, perplexed, and checked my phone. There was no *I'm coming home early* text from Mom. And this was definitely the right door. The room number was 0314; I'd noticed it when she first showed it to me, the day she'd gotten her job back. And I'd never forget the first three digits of pi.

Maybe she did head out early. Maybe she planned to come home and surprise me. She was my mom. I should trust her. I shouldn't snoop. But suspicion stole over me, a cold prickling like spiders crawling over my body. Could Mom be re-creating the machine that had caused so much trouble in the first place, even though the Valentines took all the pieces?

No. No, even if she wanted to, it had taken her years to build it last time. And she *didn't* want to. I believed her when she said she was doing well. I had to believe her because the opposite was too scary to contemplate.

Still... it wouldn't hurt to take a peek and confirm.

I took out the golden key that hung on a chain around my neck. I really did hate passing through the leprechaun underground. There was something creepy about their tunnels, and it was disorienting to step through a doorway in one place, walk through a hallway, and step out someplace miles away. But the upside was that locked doors were not a problem. The key flared in my hand, filling the dim hallway with golden light, and this time when I turned the handle, the door swung wide. Instead of opening into the lab room, though, it revealed a short tunnel with walls of rough earth, like the insides of a grave. I walked through it, and at the other end, I found a door identical to the one I'd just passed through. It was surreal.

Stupid weird leprechaun magic.

I opened this door, too, my heart beating fast with trepidation. The room beyond was dark, but still, for some reason, I called out:

"Mom?"

I suddenly dreaded what I might find in this place. Mom had spent almost every waking minute in this room over the past few weeks. What if there was something terrible inside, something that proved that despite her telling me every day that she was okay, she wasn't? The dark pips on her hands weren't nothing, the evil black shard of obelisk in her stomach hadn't gone silent. That was my nightmare, and I could barely force myself to reach out, groping for the light switch in the darkness. My other hand slipped inside my hoodie to the hilt of my ever-present knife.

Click. The lights went on.

Whatever evil thing I was afraid to see, I didn't see it.

Normal signs of Mom's presence—old gas station coffee cups. Half-completed crossword puzzles printed up from *The New York Times*. Dog-eared books. Three-ring binders full of data. Bins of parts and materials. Moldy cartons of Chinese takeout—those weren't here, either.

The room was completely empty.

❦

I took the leprechaun underground back home, but Mom wasn't there, either.

So I baked some brownies, fired up my laptop, and killed a few hours playing an online role-playing game that I hadn't had time to mess with in months. Sure, I should have been working on another college essay, but my brain felt like it had a fuse burned out, and it was nice to space out and smash some baddies with Lollie, my she-ogre avatar. But I had to stop when I found myself counting my kills. Nothing brought back those OCD compulsions like worrying about Mom.

I spent the rest of my evening either pacing or doom-scrolling on social media until, around one in the morning, Mom came home. She slouched in the door, laden with a purse, a satchel full of papers, and her ever-present water bottle.

"Oh, hey Aggie," she said. "I'm surprised you're still up."

She'd been looking better, I'd thought, but now as I eyed her more closely, concerning details emerged. Her hair was a little wild. Her fingernails were broken and dirty. I forced myself to lounge on the couch and give her a breezy smile.

"Hey, Parent. What have you been up to?"

She unslung her bags and set them down by the door. "Oh, same ol'. At the college, working on the experiment."

"Oh," I said. I realized in that moment that I'd been hoping she'd be ready with a valid excuse, a logical explanation, something. Her lie opened a trap door, and it felt like my heart was tumbling out of my chest. But I managed to stay outwardly calm. My poker face was improving, apparently.

Stripping off her jacket (black leather, I noticed. Did she use to wear so much black?) Mom sat beside me and helped herself to a Pizza Bite, the last cold remnant of my lonely dinner.

"Yep. Busy, busy. Those black holes don't make themselves," she quipped.

"No," I agreed. It was all I could do to keep my smile from becoming a sob. So much for confessing that I'd been spending time with the Valentines or talking to her about my problems. I couldn't say another word without my voice breaking. Instead, I got up, hugged her tight, then hurried off to bed, counting my footsteps as I went.

4

AGGIE

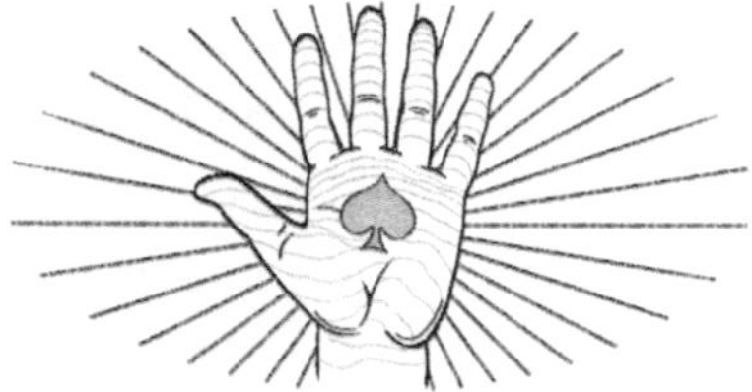

"**G**irl, you seem distracted. You okay?"

I blinked out of my reverie. I sat in the high school cafeteria, surrounded by the chirpy chatter of the popular girls and the monosyllabic grunts of the jocks at our table. It was Claudette speaking to me, my childhood best friend turned nemesis turned friend again. Or my syco. I wasn't sure what our relationship was these days.

Mina had warned that relationships with non-demigod friends were likely to get weird as my powers played out, and she was right. Before becoming a Valentine, I'd pretty much been a nonentity at school. If I had been any more invisible, I'd probably have been able to walk through walls (if such a thing were possible, given the known laws of physics in our universe, which I should be clear—despite the weird vagaries of luck magic—they are not). But as soon as I got those heart marks on my hands, the perception of me at school changed overnight. People started to sense instinctively that I had power, that luck followed in my wake, and they gravitated toward me, did me favors to keep me happy so they could be around me more, and eventually would do almost anything to stay in my good graces, to remain close to the source of their good luck. It wasn't a conscious thing, I don't think. But I have a theory that people are subconsciously drawn to good luck-charged people and objects and unconsciously repelled from bad luck ones. Evolutionarily speaking, that sort of an instinct makes sense. Someday I'll do a study to try and figure out if the phenomenon is real and how it works in people's brains, but for now, we'll call it an anecdotal observation. Anyway, suffice to say that I was once a dorky outcast and am now a dorky popular girl, with Claudette and her entire cool-girls' clique under my thrall. Not bad for a summer's work.

Now, boys were always asking me out (girls too, actually), kids were always complimenting my clothes or my hair, always asking my opinion on their social media channels, or wanting to partner with me on group projects.

It should have been a dream come true for a tried-and-true nerd like me, but the truth was, I didn't take much satisfaction in it. If I weren't a goddess, I'd be just as invisible as I was before, so what did that say about the people walking around adoring me? And what did it say about me that I accepted their fake adoration as if it were genuine?

The only thing I really enjoyed was doing *the work*—using my power to help other people, which, in turn, made my charm power increase. The work felt good. Amazing, really. Like a drug. I assume.

"Aggie?" Claudette waved a hand in front of my face, getting my attention.

"Sorry," I blinked. "What?"

I glanced across the table. My best friend Molly was bunched up with the other girls from our cool-girl posse, making kissy lips as they took a selfie. She and Claudette were the only ones who knew about the whole *me being a luck god* thing and, unlike me, Molly had no qualms about using my newfound luck for social gain. She'd also taken to wearing designer clothes and fancy makeup and getting her hair done at a fancy salon in Royal Oak. I still hadn't figured out how she and her mom were suddenly able to afford such luxuries. She claimed the money came from a promotion at her library job, but I suspected it had more to do with the new guy—or guys— her mom was dating, one of whom was apparently pretty rich. I hadn't pushed her for information. I knew she was embarrassed by her mom's antics, and I didn't want to make her feel bad. Besides, she'd share the truth with me eventually. She always did.

"I *said*, are you coming to the Fall Fest after school?" Claudette asked.

Fall Fest was a carnival thing the teachers put on every year in the gym. I'd manned the robotics club booth freshman year but had bowed out the last two years to concentrate on my schoolwork. The truth was, with everything else going on, I hadn't even remembered it was happening.

"Oh. Uh, maybe," I said, then turned my attention to Molly. "Hey Molls, a word?"

Molly glanced at me, looking a little irritated to be pulled away from the giggle fest with our cool new friends. She poked her phone with a finger.

"Aaaand posted!" she said, eliciting a squeal from the girl crew. When she saw me standing, she rose and followed me into a quiet corner of the lunchroom.

"I need to run a scenario by you," I said. "Some serious luck god stuff."

"Uh oh. What's up?"

I raked my fingers through my hair. "Ugh. Where to begin..."

As briefly as possible, I explained about King Michael selecting me as queen and about Jack's response.

"So, are you going to do it?" Molly asked.

I gaped at her. "Marry Michael? Of course not!"

Molly drummed her fingers on her chin thoughtfully. "I guess you *are* too young. It wouldn't be legal."

I rolled my eyes. "It's a luck god thing, not a civil thing, so the legal part doesn't matter. But that's not the point. King Michael is super gross. And evil. Evil adjacent, anyway. And I— Jack and I—"

Molly gave me an admonishing look. "Jack and you what?"

She'd taken it as her friend duty since the beginning of my dating Jack to prep me for an eventual end to the relationship by sharing such pearls of wisdom as *players play*, and *you can't change a bad boy*. She hadn't gone so far as to tell me *Jack is out of your league*, but she knew I felt that way, and she hadn't done much to dispel the feeling.

I knew she was just trying to protect me, but all along I couldn't help feeling like she didn't really understand Jack. Or me.

Now, I felt like maybe I'd been the one who didn't understand. Honestly, what could Jack possibly see in me that would make him want to stay with me forever? That is, unless I offered him access to more power. Queen-level power. Maybe Molly was right. Maybe to Jack, I was just a pitstop. A plaything. True, I'd missed about twenty calls from him and gotten just as many unread texts since we'd parted ways last night. But what did that prove? That he loved me? Or that he loved the idea of me being queen?

"If you were queen, you'd be super powerful, right?" Molly pressed.

I shrugged. "Well, yeah."

"Think about what you could do," Molly said. "Right now, as a six, you run this school. As a queen, maybe you could run the country. You could be president. Think of all the science you could fund. Goodbye, climate change. Hello, Mars colony."

I cracked a smile. "That would be pretty cool," I allowed.

"Hell yeah it would," Molly said. "President Van Der Graaf."

"That's a mouthful," I said.

"Then President Valentine," Molly said.

I nodded in spite of myself. It was a fun dream. But it was also supremely irritating that Molly would take Jack's side.

I started to respond, but I saw that Molly was distracted by something across the room. I followed her gaze to Braden, the cutest boy in our school, who'd entered the lunchroom with some of his friends, all of them rollicking and jostling one another like a pack of dumb puppies. I glanced back at Molly and caught a glimmer of longing in her eyes—and maybe hurt, too.

Back in the spring, I'd made the mistake of using my heart power to make Braden fall in love with Molly. He had chosen Claudette in the end, and despite Molly swearing she was okay with it, I still caught her staring at him sometimes.

"So you think I should—?" I started, but she'd already broken off our conversation and was sauntering up to Braden. She said something, and he and his friends laughed. Seeing her walk away like that stirred up some old loneliness in me, the pain of being an outcast. But something else immediately distracted me from the bad feeling.

As Molly and the boys walked toward the table where Claudette sat, I noticed something out the window behind them. A flicker of movement in the woods outside. But it wasn't a normal movement. It was like a shimmer of a mirage. The telltale sign of a peri, a luck being.

I bolted across the room, out the exit, and into the underbrush where I'd seen the shimmer. The knife I kept concealed beneath my hoodie glistened in my hand as I drew it and scanned the woods for movement—and found it. Another distant shimmer, receding fast. I chased it, my feet pounding as I huffed for breath. What would I find if I caught up? Assassin? Spy? Or—

My body slammed to the ground. Pain throbbed in my forehead. I untangled myself from a snarl of sticks and sat up. A dead tree branch had fallen on me. What were the odds that a big branch would break and fall right as I was running under it?

One in fifty thousand, probably. It was no coincidence.

It was bad luck.

Someone had been watching me. Someone with dark-suit powers. I groped for my knife among the fallen leaves, picked it up, and stood, scanning for my enemies.

But the shimmer—and whatever enemy had made it—was gone.

5

———

MOLLY

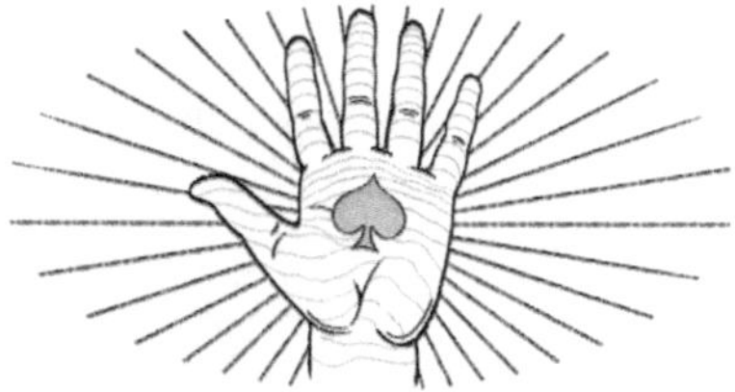

"Mom!" Molly called, dumping her backpack onto the floor and taking a few steps into the foyer of the townhouse she and her mom, Lauren, shared. Molly had an appointment to get to and didn't plan to be here for long, but even though her mom had officially gone off the deep end, she still felt some residual need to keep her in the loop about her whereabouts and her activities, mostly out of habit.

The place was a mess. It looked like a family of raccoons lived here, what with the carryout food containers piling the kitchen counters, the unfolded laundry jumbled in the middle of the living room floor, the dirty dishes piled in the sink with a small swarm of fruit flies hovering over them.

She heard laughter and followed toward her mother's

bedroom, dreading what she might walk in on. But the door was open, and her mom stood next to the bed wearing khaki slacks, a flowery top, and a sun hat. A suitcase sat open on the bed and Lauren was folding clothes and placing them inside. A man lounged on the bed with his arms crossed behind his head. A second man sat in the oversized chair in the corner, looking at his phone. The one on the bed was younger, perhaps mid-twenties, with a wispy mustache. The other was probably in his mid-fifties with a graying beard. Her mom's boyfriends. Molly knew their names were James and Mel, but despite meeting them several times, she didn't remember which was which. And frankly, she didn't care to know.

"Molly!" her mom beamed when she caught sight of her.

"What are you up to?" Molly asked warily.

"Packing. For Palm Springs. You remember."

"Uh, nope," Molly said. "First I've heard of it."

"Oh," Lauren said, going back to her packing. "Well, we're taking a little trip for a week. James surprised us."

"Sugar daddy," the mustached young man on the bed teased Mr. Silver Fox in the chair, who smiled back at him.

"We could get another ticket," the bearded man—James, I guessed—suggested. "The desert is a wonderful place. Very cleansing."

"Well, I have school. Besides, I wouldn't want to get in the middle of," Molly gestured vaguely to the three of them. "All of this."

Lauren wheeled on Molly and put a hand on her hip. "Don't be snide, young lady. You've promised to support my lifestyle."

"And I will," Molly said. "I think polyamory is dope. Do your thing. I just don't want to be like—all up in it. I mean, how would you feel if I had boyfriends chilling all over the place in here like it was a Roman bathhouse?"

Mel chuckled.

Lauren scowled. "I would be relieved if you had a boyfriend, actually. Since I met these two wonderful men, I've been happier than ever. Especially happier than I was—"

"With Dad," Molly rolled her eyes. "I know, I know. With each new dude you snog, your revenge gets closer to fruition. Except guess what? Dad is remarried. He doesn't care about you or how many guys you hook up with. He doesn't care about me either, for that matter."

Molly's mom sniffed as tears rose to her eyes. Mel—the young one—came and put a comforting hand on her shoulder.

"I don't understand why you always have to be so cruel," Lauren said primly.

"It's not cruel, Mom. It's reality," Molly said.

This was always her mom's trump card. Cry. Play the victim. Meanwhile, if it weren't for the extra money Molly was bringing in, her mom's quest for personal discovery would already have left them homeless and destitute. Molly was so profoundly sick of all of it.

Now, her mom was wheeling, throwing the rest of her clothes into the suitcase in a dramatic frenzy and zipping it up clumsily.

"You know, I was having a great day. I was excited to go and immerse myself in the energy of the desert, and now I feel like you've ruined it already. Ruined it by attacking me with your judgment, just like you always do."

She roughly hoisted the suitcase and stumbled toward the door with it until James hurried to her side and unburdened her.

"Okay, Mom. Start a fight. Whatever makes you feel better about abandoning your daughter for a week. Were you even going to leave me any grocery or gas money?"

"I—of course—where's my purse?" Lauren made a show of looking around.

Molly held up a hand, stopping her. "You know what? Don't worry about it. You're not the only one going on a journey of personal discovery, Mom. I've got my own money. My own life. And one day you're going to look around this pigsty of a condo for me and I'm going to be long gone."

"You're just mean," Lauren blustered as her two boy toys comfortingly patted her on the back, escorting her out of the room.

"Bye," Molly called after them. "Enjoy cleansing yourself in the desert."

When the front door slammed, Molly thought, *Yay. I don't have to deal with her nonsense for a whole week.* But she felt a little like crying, too.

Never mind all that. Molly had more important things to deal with than Mama drama. She had a meeting to get to.

❦

The Diamantes occupied the penthouse of a downtown Detroit skyscraper. It had taken weeks before Danusia, the Jill of Diamonds, who had secretly taken Molly under her gilded wing, had given Molly access to the suit's headquarters, and Molly took her trust as a mark of pride. Now, Danusia's leprechaun thug Lorcan led Molly down a hallway lined with priceless paintings by Mondrian, Monet, and Kandinsky—well, not priceless. The Diamonds had bought the paintings, after all. As Danusia liked to remind Molly, everything had a price.

"So, how are our friends the Hearts doing?" Lorcan asked in his faintly Irish accent. Gold rings glinted on his fingers to match his gold teeth. A gold chain with a charm of a boxing glove hung around his neck. His arms and hands were tatted up, and he walked with a limping swagger, as if some invisible creature had glommed onto his ankle. A flat-brimmed Boston Celtics baseball cap sat on his head, tilted at a jaunty angle. He was pretty tall, too, and all in all, Molly thought he was kind of cute, in a dangerous, odd sort of way. But her life was crazy enough without adding a hookup with a leprechaun to the mix.

"The Valentines are fine," Molly said coolly. "And even if they weren't, I save my reports for Danusia."

Lorcan eyed her as he pushed the door open and let her walk past, out onto the veranda. "Another uppity lass. Fine, keep your secrets. Danusia will get them out of you. She always does."

Molly found Danusia lounging in an infinity hot tub that looked out on the city. A pair of large sunglasses masked her eyes and her long blonde hair was wet and slicked back like the hair of a goddess on some antique car's chrome hood ornament.

Molly sat on the chaise lounge next to the hot tub, and when she glanced down, she saw something sparkling in the roiling water. Probably real tiny diamonds. The Valentines surrounded themselves with hearts and the color red because it increased their charm power, according to Aggie. Ridiculous displays of opulence probably had the same effect on Diamonds, Molly reasoned. It was weird, but then most things about the luck gods were weird.

"So?" Danusia prompted without turning to look at her.

"I have news," Molly said. "Big news."

Danusia raised one hand from the water and examined her long, glistening fingernails. "Yes?" she said.

God, Danusia always sounded so prim and aloof. So fancy and British. Molly would have given her left tit to be half that cool. Well, someday, she would be. This was the first step on that journey.

She steeled herself, then said, "It's... it's going to cost you."

That made Danusia smile. "It always does. You'll get your envelope on the way out as usual."

"No," Molly tried to keep the nervous quaver out of her

voice. "I know one of your suit died fighting the Blackovers. I want their spot. I—I want to be a Diamante."

Molly had watched Aggie over the last few months. She'd watched as her friend grew more beautiful, gathered friends effortlessly, got a sweet new wardrobe and a dozen shiny cars and a mind-blowingly hot secret boyfriend. It was simple: Molly wanted the same thing. Molly and Aggie were alike. They'd always been alike. And if Aggie deserved to be a goddess, then Molly did too.

Sure, Molly had benefited from Aggie's ascension. She was one of the "in" girls now, and Aggie had hooked her up with clothes and stuff here and there (although most of it had hearts on it, *blech*). Molly had done well in her dealings with the Diamonds, too. She'd made more money in three months than her dad made in a year just for telling Danusia gossip. And Danusia, in a rare moment of empathy, had given her some crazy thousand-dollar Israeli skin-care cream that had all but cured her ichthyosis vulgaris, the dry, scaly skin that had been the bane of Molly's adolescence. But these trappings, these table scraps, weren't enough. She wanted it all. Aggie was a goddess, and Molly intended to become one, too.

And when she was a goddess? The first thing Molly would do was steal her eternal crush, Braden, back from Claudette. Then, her life would be complete.

At Molly's bold words, Danusia at last looked at her, but she didn't answer. The only response was the grumbling hum of the hot tub, the shush of the traffic far below. The silence went on for so long, Molly felt doubt creeping in. Honestly, why did she think this would work? Danusia would never make Molly Carpenter a god, not in exchange for information, not for anything. Danusia would just as soon drop Molly off the balcony. And who would even care if she did, except maybe Aggie?

"Oh, sweet little Molly," Danusia said, a note of pity in her voice. "It appears you do have one ingredient required to become a luck god: moxie. But you misunderstand our present power dynamic, my dear. I get information from many sources. I suppose you've rushed in here breathlessly to tell me that your friend Aggie has been selected as the next Valentine queen. Is that right?"

She already knew. Molly tried not to slump, but the weight of disappointment pressed down heavily on her.

"Don't fret," Danusia said, climbing out of the hot tub in one swift, lithe movement and swooping a glittering towel around herself, covering her tasteful white swimsuit and her perfect body.

Jesus, even their towels are stitched with silver thread, Molly thought. *I so want towels like that.*

Danusia removed her sunglasses, revealing a pair of eyes the blue of glacial ice.

"I once told you, Molly, that everyone has a price. Goddesses are no different. I can be bought, and the rank Two of Diamonds can be bought, as well."

Hope made Molly suddenly breathless. "I'll do anything."

"We'll see," Danusia replied. She went to a cabinet, opened it, and turned back to Molly, holding a sheathed knife. It was a gorgeous weapon, with an ornate golden hilt and a huge ruby for its pommel.

"Becoming a luck god is like gaining a whole new life, Molly. But nothing is free. To earn it, in this case, you must take a life." Danusia drew the knife and considered its glistening blade.

"Take a life..." Molly whispered. "Who?"

"The most dangerous luck god alive today. Fortunately, I believe you can gain access—with the necessary element of surprise."

Who? Molly wanted to ask again, but Danusia was already placing the charmed knife in her hand.

6

───

RACHEL

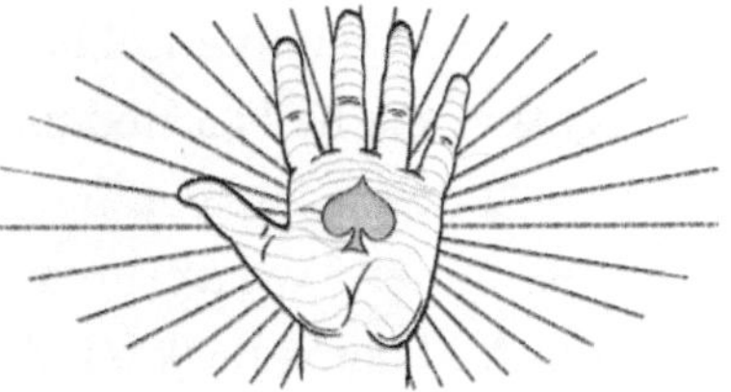

Rachel stood leaning on the podium at the front of the classroom, watching her students take their first quiz of the year. Like the Brownian motion of particles in fluids, Rachel liked to keep her quizzes random. Even before she became a bad luck queen, she'd taken a certain dark pleasure in watching students who hadn't done their reading when she slapped a quiz down in front of them. Their faces portrayed abject shock and dread, followed by acceptance, followed by earnest thought. The hope was that the unpredictability of her testing would cause her students to be prepared at all times and keep up to date on their reading and studying. In practice, it more often turned out like many things in life: the more successful ones triumphed even with the added pressure. The unprepared, under-motivated, and unlucky ones sank.

To the sound of scratching pens and the clicks and taps of computers, Rachel flicked through screens on her phone. Emails. Social media feeds. Text messages, including a particularly amusing GIF from Aggie that almost made her snort out loud. A student came up and asked a question, fishing for a hint, and Rachel answered artfully and sent the boy back to his seat to puzzle things out for himself.

God, it felt so good to be back at Oak Hill. The dusty, Pine-Sol smell of the classrooms, the creak of the desk legs scraping the floor, the sound of the lawnmower outside, the distant rattle and *oomp-ah* of the band practicing—all filled her with a sense of profound belonging. She loved the start of a school year on campus, too. The energy. The excitement. The anticipation.

It was doubly sweet that she had earned back her dream job after losing it. You never knew what you had until you lost it, they said. Well, Rachel knew what she'd lost. She never intended to lose it again. And being back felt divine.

Still…

When she'd been fired last time, it had been because of alcoholism, a dark mistress tugging her down a sorrowful path. There was a dark mistress this time, too, one ten times more potent than alcohol had ever been. She could feel it now, that icy sizzle of need pulsing in the palm of each of her hands, where the spade marks glowed like strange black-light tattoos. They were hungry, those marks. Always grumbling, nudging, clamoring for her to do *the work*. To visit bad luck on someone.

They were stirring now, in fact.

But Rachel knew how to deal with them. She'd figured it out. *The work* wanted her to do big bad luck things—stuff that would result in death, dismemberment, and large-scale suffering. But she'd discovered through a process of scientific (well, pseudo-scientific) experimentation that if she just made a string of less terrible things happen, the longing of the work was assuaged. Mostly.

But it was coming for her again, now. That need. That drive. It was hitting her, big time, and soon her hands would be burning so strongly there'd be tears in her eyes. She had to do something, or—

"Ms. Van Der Graff?" a boy in the front row mumbled.

"Hmm?" Rachel replied through gritted teeth.

"Can I go to the bathroom?"

"Yep," Rachel said.

The boy rose and shambled toward the door. The desire to make him piss himself struck her powerfully, but she held it in check like a wave of nausea. *Don't be cruel. That's not you,* she admonished herself.

Instead, Rachel looked out at the students, busy with their quiz. A few surreptitiously glancing at their phones. A few others, having given up already, napped with their heads on their desks.

What are you going to do, Rachel? a mocking voice said. It was the obelisk of Spades, that nexus of the Morbus' power which inhabited a stone which she'd literally swallowed. It lived within her now, forever whispering its venom inside her mind. *What are you going to do?*

The work. That was the answer, always. Because she was a luck god now, and luck gods did their work. There was no other choice.

And so, keeping her hands concealed beneath the podium, she opened them palm-out toward the students. Hex pulsed from the spade marks, like a sigh, like a song, like an orgasm, a sweet relief. At their desks, her students looked up as one in sorrow and befuddlement. One young woman burst into tears. A tall, pale boy rubbed his forehead and dropped his pen in frustration. Another student stood, ripped their test in half, and dropped it in the trash can on the way out the door.

Memory, the mind, the psyche, all were surprisingly subtle things, Rachel had learned. So much of success or failure, brilliance or stupidity, came down to the momentary vicissitudes of luck. Good luck. Or—in the case of Rachel the Queen of Spades—bad luck.

7

———

RACHEL

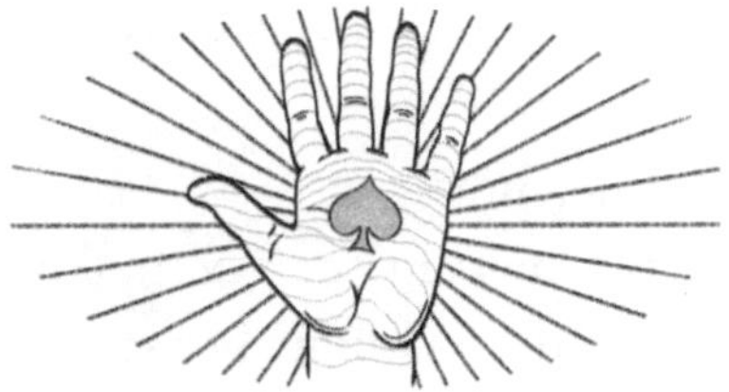

The sickening, meaty thud of a fist hitting a man's face; even after all the horrors she'd witnessed over the past few months, it still made Rachel wince. And yet she remained still in the shadows of the dark alley, watching as the larger man, Shady J or Shade, as everyone called him, loomed over a smaller man, who lay slumped against a brick wall. Shade's boys, a crew of six young men as raw and tough as iron ore, stood fanned out behind him. As Rachel watched, Shade yanked a gold chain from the unlucky victim's neck.

"Gimme that, punk. You know what? Give me your wallet and phone, too."

He stooped and rummaged in the pockets of the other man, whose only resistance was to turn his head to the side and spit a bloody tooth on the pavement.

"This isn't for me." Shade waggled the man's wallet in his face. "Nah. I don't get down with this petty shit. This is for my boys." He tossed the wallet to one of his friends, who caught it smoothly. "You put them at risk, man, by bringing this mess into our neighborhood. You sling, you better sling clean dope. None of this poison Fentanyl shit. My home girl Celia damn near OD'd on some of your garbage. And none of that meth you been bringing around, either. Whatever you sling it better be clean, and you best be giving me my cut. Your boss doesn't like that, tell him come see me. I got a long clip and a short temper. Now, you going to go call the cops?"

With what little strength the man on the ground had left, he shook his head.

Shade cupped a hand to his ear. "What? Speak up."

The man made a wheeze, like air coming out of a punctured tire.

"Not answering me, huh?"

Shade kicked him hard in the gut, making him jackknife, his body convulsing with something between coughs and sobs.

"This is my neighborhood, Slim. We run a clean game here. This is the only warning you get," Shade declared. Then Shade turned away, making his way up the alley, and his men fell in behind him.

Rachel stepped out of the shadows to block their path. She felt a strange thrill being here like this. How terrified she would have been in her old life, one woman standing alone in a dark alley at night with these seven dangerous men. But how times had changed in a few short months. The old Rachel would have been scared, yes. But now, she was the dangerous one.

Shade stopped, blinking with surprise, and his entourage halted with him. He was taller than she'd realized, and Rachel saw he had a spiderweb tattoo around his left eye.

"Yo, a soccer mom," he laughed, and the men behind him cackled. "What you after, soccer mom? Dope? Coke?"

"You," Rachel said.

Shade raised an eyebrow. One of the men behind him quietly took out a gun.

Rachel's heart rate sped up. It wasn't that she didn't feel fear anymore. Far from it. She was afraid all the time these days, but the thrill of it was something like doing *the work*. Intoxicating. Undeniable. Its own kind of dope, she supposed.

"You want *me*." Shade cocked an eyebrow.

"I want you to serve me. You and your men."

Shade snorted. "Serve you? Crazy white bitch. Get out of my face."

Just then, the gun Shade's man was holding went off, shooting one of the other men in the leg. He went down screaming, while the guy behind him said, "Damn, sorry, Mike. My bad. Damn!"

Shade wheeled on him, furious.

"I didn't even touch the trigger, I swear," the shooter shrilled, backing up.

Three of Shade's thugs stooped to tend to the fourth, but the other two kept their attention on Rachel. One of them drew his gun, but as he did, a spring inside it gave way, and the clip fell out. He bent to retrieve it, and the other man tripped over him. He went to catch himself and landed on broken glass. He screamed, holding his wrist and staring at the chunk of beer bottle protruding from his hand. The single streetlight that illuminated the alley sparked, flickered, and blinked out.

Shade tore his eyes from the pandemonium behind him to look back at Rachel. She was holding up her hands, and the glowing spades cast him in a wavering purplish light, illuminating the dawning horror in his eyes.

"What the hell are you?" he whispered.

"Wrong question," Rachel said. "The question is, what are you? And what will you become?"

8

JACK

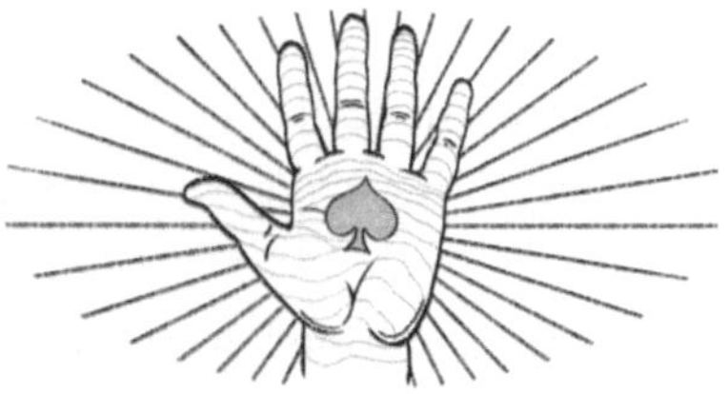

Jack stopped recording video on his phone and stepped back into a shadowed doorway just down the alley from where Aggie's mom and her new friends stood. He had watched with a sick sort of fascination, which ballooned into admiration as Rachel dealt with Shady J and his band of gangsters.

They called themselves the Woe Boys and were well known in the city. They were loosely affiliated with some crews that the Blackovers did business with, and in the course of doing his good luck work, Jack had cleaned up their messes and helped their victims more than once. The Woe Boys were the worst sort of people. Some criminals were motivated primarily by money. Others, by power. From what Jack could see, Shady J and his crew seemed to use money and power as an excuse to punish others. Jack doubted that even Thad, Marley, and the other Blackovers would traffic directly with psychopaths like these.

And yet Jack watched as Rachel spoke to them in tones too low for him to overhear. After a few moments, she walked away up the alley, and they followed her like ducklings trailing their mother. It was impressive. And incredibly disturbing.

Of course, this was only the latest of Rachel Van Der Graaf's exploits. Jack had been watching her for months now, had seen her perform one piece of bad luck work after another, some bad enough that it still made his stomach churn to think about them.

The Morbus, the absolute worst of the four luck suits, was re-forming despite everything the Valentines and the Diamantes had sacrificed to destroy them. Under normal circumstances, he'd have tracked them to their lair, called in all the red suits, and wiped them out now, exterminated them like rats before they had a chance to multiply. But this was no ordinary Morbus queen. It was Aggie's mom. Aggie, who believed she'd saved her mom and that everything was fine.

He'd debated telling her the truth. More than once, the words had been on the edge of his lips. And yet despite her wit and her intelligence, there was a certain innocence to Aggie that her trials with the luck gods so far had been unable to destroy. That innocence would die soon enough. No luck god stayed alive for long with unbloodied hands or an untroubled soul. But Jack didn't want to be the one to tell her the truth and snuff out the hopeful light in her eyes. Not until he had to, anyway.

Jack pressed himself back to the wall, held his breath, and charmed himself to remain unnoticed until the footfalls of Rachel and her new friends receded into silence. When he was sure they were gone, he stepped out and crept down the alley to where their victim lay broken and bleeding.

The work rose strongly in him then, and Jack knelt and charmed the man, holding both hands over him and letting light from the heart-shaped pips shine on him. The luck power subtly nudged the injured man's body to work more efficiently, to slow his bleeding, limit his swelling, diminish his pain, keep his cuts from getting infected. Healing always required luck. For someone injured this badly, their fate teetered on a knife's edge, and a little luck was often the thing that pushed them toward life—or death.

With the charm taking effect, the man slept peacefully. Jack felt the wages of the work, an increase of charm that ignited his body with warm, jittery energy and made light and power pour from the pips on his hands, causing them to glow brighter than usual. He took out his phone and called an ambulance, then waited with the unconscious man until he heard the wail of approaching sirens.

Just as he was about to steal off into the shadows, a voice, as faint as a fallen leaf skittering across pavement, called to him.

"Hey," the injured man said. "Thank you."

Jack nodded. "Good luck," he said.

Then he left, moving away from the sirens as quickly as he could.

I should tell Aggie, he told himself as he swung onto the main street, approaching his waiting motorcycle.

But not now. Aggie had too much on her plate. After her college essays and her Girls in Science thing were done, then he'd tell her, and they could decide what to do about Rachel together.

In the meantime, he had to make sure Ten and King Michael and the rest of the Valentines didn't find out about her. If they did, they'd ride in with the cavalry and kill Rachel—that or die trying.

No, he would just have to keep the secret. Watch and wait.

And yet every day he hesitated, the Morbus queen grew stronger.

Back in his room at the Valentine house, Jack lay down on his bed. It was strangely easy to fall asleep these days. At times, it seemed that all he had to do was close his eyes to be immediately transported into slumber. Every night he dreamed, and in every dream, the ace was there.

It was no different now. He took a deep breath, sighed it out, released his tense body, and then he was falling through the black veil between consciousness and unconsciousness.

In the dream, he stood in a primordial cavern. Cave drawings scrawled upon the walls by countless ancient hands spiderwebbed across the walls. In the center of the cave stood the red glowing crystal obelisk, nexus of the Valentines' power. And in front of it, her energy-charred arms grafted to the obelisk like a pair of tree branches, knelt a woman who looked more ancient than the rock walls that surrounded them. The ace.

"My boy Jack," she said, a sweet wistfulness in her raspy voice. "How goes our quest?"

Jack shook his head. "Not well. Aggie doesn't want to be queen. Her mother is consolidating power. We'll have to do something about her soon, or—"

"What have I told you about power, Jack?" the ace interrupted.

Jack gave a half-hearted laugh. "A lot of things."

"Aggie doesn't want to be queen. Her mother must be stopped. Two problems, yes? Where the weak see problems, the powerful see . . ."

"Opportunities," Jack sighed.

And he understood what he had to do.

9

———

AGGIE

The punching bag jangled on its chain as I hit it with another combination of blows.

One, two, three, four, five... no.

Working out was the one time when my OCD tendencies to count things always seemed to come out. I'd count steps while running, reps when lifting weights, even seconds when I was holding a yoga pose. It was normal to count sometimes during workouts, but I couldn't help feeling like it was a slippery slope that might lead me back to the worst days of my OCD. I always tried to stop counting when I caught myself, but old patterns are hard to break. Just ask Mom.

I shook my head, trying to clear it of bitter thoughts. It wouldn't do any good dwelling on Mom's failings. She'd disappeared on me numerous times when her drinking was at its worst, just after Dad died, and she'd lied about it plenty, too. After she'd gotten sober, there were the long nights she'd spent out at the V12 Casino, playing poker. I knew she was working to bring in enough winnings for us to survive, but it still left me with an eerie, lonely feeling to be sitting at the house for half the night by myself. She'd disappeared again when the black suits kidnapped her, and although that hadn't been her fault, the emotional scar remained.

But what was happening now... this new lie, this slow disappearance—it felt different.

Just finish your workout. One punch at a time... One, two, three —no! No counting.

"Towel?" The voice came from the empty air directly to my left and made me gasp.

The air shimmered and glitched as Seemor, one of the sprites who worked for the Valentines, unblurred into existence. I was pretty sure I'd never get used to the weird look of the creatures—think four-foot-tall hairless humanoid pug dog with antlers—and although all the sprites I'd met so far were weird and surly, Seemor was weirder and surlier than most.

He was Jack's go-to stakeout-slash-intelligence-gathering agent, which meant he was good at sneaking around. And he seemed to get a sick joy out of popping out of thin air and scaring people.

I snatched the towel out of his hand. "Towel with a side of heart attack. Thanks a lot," I said, swabbing off my sweaty face.

"Seemor, buzz off, man," Deuce said as he entered, carrying a pair of iced lattes. I had to hand it to him, Deuce's ability to show up at the perfect time with delicious coffee was unsurpassed.

"Oh, Deuceo my Deuceo, wherefore art thou Deuceo?" I said, in my best Shakespearean accent, batting my eyelashes and accepting the cup he offered.

"I ask myself that every day," he said with a wan smile.

"Seriously, you're amazing. Thank you."

We sat on a pair of rolled-up wrestling mats to sip our coffees while Seemor glitched and shimmered out of the room, still chuckling to himself.

"So," Deuce said after a moment. "Queen Aggie."

I gave him my fiercest glare. "Don't even start."

"It has a ring to it," he allowed. "Her Majesty Agatha Van Der Graaf of the House Valentine, First of Her Name, Queen of the Highschoolers and the Last Men, Khaleesi of the Great Detroit Suburbs, Breaker of AP Tests, and Mother of—"

"Iced coffee," I finished, and we both laughed way too hard.

When I'd wiped the giggle tears away, I found Deuce watching me thoughtfully.

"Seriously, where's your head at with this whole queen thing?" he asked.

I snorted. "There are so many choices. I could say *no*. Or *hell no*. Or *are you kidding me?* Or *absolutely not, I'd rather get shot out of a cannon into a pit full of venomous snakes*. Or just *no thank you*. The options are endless."

A smile curled one corner of his lips, an expression that gave him a glimmer of handsomeness. "Or you could say... yes."

I glared at him. "You didn't see the smackdown I was putting on that punching bag, did you? Otherwise, you'd be way too scared of me to say that."

"You scare me plenty," Deuce said.

"Did Jack send you in here to convince me? Because if he did—"

Deuce shook his head. "No. This has nothing to do with Jack."

"Then why?" I said, my voice rising in spite of my efforts to stay calm. "I thought you of all people would understand that... that..." I didn't know how to finish the thought.

"Aggie," Deuce said gently. "Someone has to be queen. Do you really want it to be Ten?"

I laughed. "Oh, I see. You're scared Queen Ten will get her crown and immediately shout *off with your head, Deuce*. She probably will, come to think of it."

"I'm serious," Deuce said, and he tried to look serious, too, as much as he could with that teddy bear face of his.

"I'm serious, too," I said. "Do I want Ten to be queen? I mean... I don't know. Ten is strong. She's smart..."

"—she's got anger issues. And she's not the biggest fan of Jack, me, or you."

"There's Mina," I said.

"Mina is great, but she's not a leader. Adelie is *not great* and also not a leader. Who does that leave?"

"How about you? It's about time we had a male queen. Huzzah for equality."

Deuce chuckled. "Sure, I'm game. But good luck convincing Michael."

I sighed. "I didn't even want to be a luck god. I just wanted to go back to my normal life with Mom. And if I couldn't do that, at least I wanted things to stay the same here. But everything keeps changing..." I shook my head, then looked at Deuce. Empathy welled in his soft brown eyes. "You'd really want to see me married to Michael?" I asked.

He bit his lip. "No. I never want to lose you," he said, then quickly amended. "I mean as a friend. Because of an unhappy marriage. But there's more than one way to lose someone, Aggie. I came in replacing a Valentine named Klaus, who died after the Battle of Siberia. Then we lost William, then the queen and Ari. Things do change fast around here—and it's usually because luck gods die. The more power you have, the safer you are. The safer all of us are."

I closed my eyes, steadying myself. This extra pressure was not what I needed right now. I'd expected Deuce of all people would side with me, that he'd never want me to become queen, especially if I didn't want to be. Now, on top of everything else, I was supposed to be his protector?

"Ten would protect us, Deuce," I said quietly. "She might not like us, but she wouldn't just let us die."

"What about your mom?" Deuce said. "Look, I hate being the one to tell you this, but the red suits don't trust Spades, Aggie. They never have and they never will. If Ten becomes queen, sooner or later she's going to take your mom out."

That evening, I sat on the bleachers in the high school gym as the Fall Festival played out around me. Antics abounded that should, theoretically, have been fun. There was a dunk tank where you could throw a ball at a target and try to dunk the principal in a vat of water. There was a face-painting area. Some carnival games. An obstacle course where a handful of rowdy jocks were showing off for one another. A popcorn machine—and various other stations that blended into a generally frivolous atmosphere.

The room was roughly divided between kids avidly participating and others who were lounging on bleachers or leaning against walls, too cool to have fun. Normally, I would have been down there throwing balls at old milk bottles and trying to win a stuffed monkey, but I had too much on my mind. Besides, it was fun to people-watch. Jared and Keegan, two boys I'd brought together using my Valentine love power known as Cupid's Arrow, were walking hand in hand, adorably eating caramel apples. Seeing them so happy made my pips fill with warmth, the pleasant feeling of the work flowing through them. At least I'd done one thing right as a luck goddess. Still smiling, I scanned the room again. This time, my attention landed on Molly. She was flitting from booth to booth and talking with our new cool-girl buddies, but wherever Braden went, she was never far behind. Was she really planning to make a move on Claudette's man? Or just amusing herself, I wondered. Only time would tell.

"Penny for your thoughts?" Claudette climbed on the bleachers beside me and sat.

"Oh, just..." What was I supposed to tell her? *Thinking about ways to avoid becoming a goddess queen?* My problems weren't very relatable. It was ironic, really. I had more friends in school than ever before. I was popular and doted on and desired, but in a lot of ways, I felt lonelier than ever.

"How's your mom?" I asked, changing the subject.

Claudette's mom had been injured three months before during the big battle with the Blackovers. She'd been pinned to a ceiling by jinn—shadowlike luck gobbling demon things. I'd rescued her, but not very well; she'd fallen on her head from twenty feet in the air. True, she had been working with the Spades obelisk and a handful of Blackovers to imprison and brainwash my mom, but I still felt bad about it.

Claudette sighed. "Better. She keeps saying head traumas take a long time to recover from, but I think it's just an excuse to make me do all the cooking and cleaning. How's your Girls in Science project coming?"

"Awesome. I'm totally going to win."

Claudette smiled. "Actually, I am."

For a moment, there was a contented silence between us, punctuated by the background chatter that echoed through the gym. Across the room, Braden's throw thumped the target, sending the principal into the dunk tank, and everyone screamed in triumph.

"Claudette," I said suddenly. "What would you do if someone offered you a position of power. Something that would let you do amazing things but that would change your life forever. Like... if someone said you could be president, but you'd have to break up with Braden."

She snorted. "You're really asking me that? Aggie, any dumb boy can hit the dunk tank target. But there can only be one lady president. At a time, anyway."

I frowned. Across the room, Braden was vigorously chest-bumping all his buddies—including Molly. "Bad example..." I said.

A basketball bounced up to us with a boy chasing after it. He was Landon Hughes, a junior. I didn't know much about him except that he was on the swim team and his dad owned a lumberyard or something. Was he pulling the old *let my ball bounce over to the girls so I have an excuse to go retrieve it* trick? I wondered. Or was he genuinely bad at ball handling?

"Hey, Landon," Claudette said.

"Hey," he said, but he was looking at me. He was quieter than Braden, but every bit as handsome. "Why are you guys sitting over here all alone?"

"So nobody will bother us," Claudette snarked.

He grunted a laugh and looked down at his feet. At least he had the good sense to look sheepish.

"I was just shooting hoops," he went on. "I thought if you were bored, you might like to play a game of horse."

Claudette raised an eyebrow. "Landon. Do we look like we were sitting here just yearning to play horse?"

He looked sheepish again, but I put my hands up in the universal *throw it to me* sign. He tossed me the ball. There was a hoop about fifty feet away, to our right. Without looking, I side-armed the ball, goosing it with a bit of charm. It flew in a wide arc through the air before swishing through the hoop.

"H," I said.

Claudette laughed, clapping.

Landon looked from the hoop to me, wide-eyed.

"Lucky shot," I shrugged.

He frowned, pointing at me. "Uh. Is your hand glowing?"

Indeed, the pip on my hand was flared brightly.

"Glowing tattoo. It's a thing," a familiar voice said, and I looked over to see Jack striding toward us. Like a movie scene when the star walks in, Jack seemed to snap into focus while everyone else became a background blur.

Landon stuck his hands in his pockets and skulked off after his basketball.

Claudette's eyes lit up when she saw Jack. "Is this the mythical boyfriend?" she whispered—loudly.

"And you must be Claudette," Jack said. "It's true, what everyone says about you. Your hair is very shiny."

Claudette ran her fingers through her hair self-consciously. "I also speak three languages, play piano, code computers, and dance competitively, but... yeah."

"If you'll excuse us." Jack turned back to me.

Claudette was clearly unused to being dismissed, but it only took her a moment to gather herself, rise with great dignity and great posture, and head off across the gym in search of Braden and the girls.

Jack looked at me with those blue eyes of a god, more vivid than all the rest of reality combined. Seeing him now, here, in the middle of my real life, was almost like seeing him again for the first time. It made my heart stutter its beat.

"What are you doing here?" I asked.

"I have something to show you," he said, taking my hand. "Come on."

AGGIE

We tore through the night on the back of Jack's motorcycle. Not the one we'd destroyed, of course. The Valentines had a multitude of vehicles and were always getting new ones. Something about thousands of years of collective good luck had given them a bank account so extensive it made money sort of not a concern.

But it wasn't the motorcycle that made me nervous. It was the way Jack was driving it: aggressively. Like it was a cannon and he was trying to use it to fire us at something. Despite the way he was driving and despite the fact that I was still really mad and hurt that he wanted me to marry Michael, I still couldn't quite stop myself from hoping this was a date.

"Where are we going?" I shouted into his ear. "Is it a surprise? Does it involve hamburgers?"

The fresh popcorn scent had been singing its siren song to me back at the high school, making me starve, then Jack had shown up and spirited me away before I could get some. Compensation in the form of a burger would only have been fair. But his only answer was to jog the bike left and accelerate, rocketing past an SUV that had been going the speed limit.

"This is a weird apology," I went on. "But I will accept remorse ice cream, if you're offering."

No response.

"If you can't tell, I'm hungry," I shouted.

My stomach did a barrel roll as Jack leaned hard and we listed to the right, taking the freeway off-ramp. When I saw the boarded-up houses, old factory buildings, and weedy lots strewn with broken glass surrounding us, my hunger origamied itself into a sick feeling in the pit of my stomach. This was no apology dinner date. Jack was taking me somewhere dangerous.

He confirmed my suspicion by pulling into an alley behind a row of rundown businesses and killing the motorcycle's engine. I knew better than to make any jokes now. Already, the feeling of hex was prickling at the back of my neck, and I felt the charm in my hands guttering like candle flames in a breeze. This was a bad luck place.

Jack took a chrome 9-millimeter pistol with a red grip out of the storage bin on the side of the motorcycle and handed it to me. It seemed to buzz and sizzle against my hand, the sign of a highly charmed weapon.

Jack could tell a question was rising to my lips. "You'll see," he said. "Just stay close."

I followed him to the end of the alley. On the corner, there stood a massive building of dirty, whitish brick about nine stories high. Its lower windows were boarded up and scrawled with graffiti. The higher ones were black, many of them broken —probably by boys with rocks. A faded sign on the side of the building read, "Templeton Hospital." I didn't like the look of the place. If I were driving past, I would have hit the accelerator. If I were walking past, I'd have crossed to the other side of the street. But Jack, of course, led us straight for it.

Ahead, a row of rusty steel loading dock doors stood out against the building's brick walls. Two of the doors were shut tight, but the third had a six-inch gap at the bottom, revealing utter darkness beyond. Jack went to this door and shoved it up. With a screech, it rose another foot. Jack boosted himself up and slithered through the gap, then offered his hand and pulled me through after him.

I stood, brushing the grime off my clothes, counting the brush strokes. *One, two, three... No.* I chastised myself. *This is no time for OCD shenanigans.*

Darkness seemed to press in from every side. I took a shaky breath and the air tasted musty and stale. Poisonous. Somewhere, water dripped in a maddeningly uneven cadence. *Dop-dop-dop, dop-dop. Dop.* I'd only felt an oppressive atmosphere like this once before, at an old Spades base. It hadn't ended well.

Jack opened his hand. Its faint red light was no match for the potent darkness around us, but as my eyes adjusted, its glow sketched the outline of shapes. An old wheelchair. A broken pallet. A doorway. Still, Jack didn't move. I'd learned this technique in my Valentine training, too. I could almost hear the voice of my trainer, Ari... *When you step into hostile territory, don't just charge ahead. Pause. Wait. Observe. And remember, it's not just your eyes that can give you information. Smell the air. Feel the ground—vibrations will tell you if someone is coming. Most of all, listen.*

We did. And I heard something, a sound so low I could barely separate it from the hiss of silence. It was a voice.

Jack nodded ahead and started walking. As I fell into step behind him, I slipped my knife free of its sheath and clicked my gun's safety off. Jack already had his dagger and gun at the ready. Forward we went, down hallways with walls streaked with mold and scrawled with graffiti. Our feet crackled on broken glass and splashed in dark puddles. We turned a corner, walked, turned a corner, walked, turned again, until I'd completely lost my bearings. *It's a labyrinth,* I thought. And in the myth, what was at the center of the labyrinth? A monster.

The voice was closer now. Jabbering. Low muttering. A sudden, strident curse. The ravings of an insane person. Some poor, mentally ill, unhoused individual had holed up in this sad, empty hospital. But why would Jack bring me here to see someone like that?

We rounded one last corner, and the corridor ahead opened into a large open space: the hospital lobby. We crept forward, weapons at the ready.

The first thing I saw was the birds. A whirling flock of crows, probably a hundred of them, made swooping circuits around the expansive space. Occasionally, one would caw and another would answer, but mostly they remained eerily silent except for the thump and rustle of their flapping wings. Here and there, a feather would fall, giving the impression of fluttering black snow. And in the center of this avian maelstrom, a woman stood facing away from us. She was tall. Dark-haired. Slim and square-shouldered.

She spoke in the same clipped and frustrated tones we'd heard from down the corridor. "I've *done* everything you *told* me to do, haven't I? So just tell me what else I'm going to have to do before you'll *let me go.*"

Thump. With a sickening sound of crunching bones, a bird hit a wall, fell in a puff of feathers, and hit the floor. It wasn't alone. I noticed, with rising dread, that all around the edge of the room were heaps of black feathers—dead crows. I winced as another hit the far wall and went spiraling to the floor.

"Of course I'll *want* you to let me go at the end of this, I'm in *hell*," the crazy woman snarled to her imaginary companion—for there was no one else in the room besides her and the crows.

We inched closer, improving our view. As I watched, the woman opened her hands. A dark purplish light pulsed from them, and two more crows smashed into the wall. As they did, the eerie light from her hands glowed brighter.

This was a bad luck god, doing her sickening work. And not any bad luck god. As she turned toward us, I saw her face illuminated by the evil glow of her pips. I knew who it would be. I'd known all along. But it still hit like a gut kick.

Jack was grabbing my arm, whispering something in my ear, but I pulled away from him, heedless, and charged into the room.

"Mom!"

To someone watching, our expressions must have looked like mirror images of one another. Bafflement. Horror. Hurt. Anger—all flashed across Mom's face in an instant. Then tears filled her eyes.

"Why are you here?" her voice was a growl within a whisper. "You shouldn't be here."

"I could say the same thing about you," I said. "You told me the pips weren't bothering you. The obelisk wasn't talking to you. You said everything was under control."

"I didn't want to worry you," she wailed. With a rueful glance over my shoulder at Jack, she added, "or your friends."

I looked back to find Jack with his gun aimed at her.

"Jack, put that away. She's not dangerous," I snapped.

He slowly lowered the weapon but didn't holster it.

I turned back to Mom, wary. "Are you? Dangerous?"

She looked away, her eyes tracing the drifts of broken crows. Each one was a bit of *work*. With each dead crow, her power had grown. But what was she growing her power for? What was she planning?

"It'll all be over soon," her voice was toneless, flat. "Then we can go back to... back to..."

Her eyes flashed down to her belly.

"SHUT UP!" she shouted at it.

Jack gently took my arm. "We saw what we came to see," he said quietly. "Let's go."

He turned me back toward the hallway where we'd entered—then stopped. All down the corridor, doors were opening and people were emerging from the hospital rooms. The first four were a red-haired woman, a boy younger than me, a tall man with a shaved head, and a young Black man with a tattoo around his left eye. Behind them, more people were emerging. Many were emaciated and filthy and looked like homeless drug addicts—but not all of them. One man wore what looked like an expensive suit. A woman wore a torn fast-food uniform. Most held weapons. A brick. A pipe. A board with a nail driven through it.

Mom hadn't been building a science experiment all these long, lonely nights. She'd been building an army.

11

———————

AGGIE

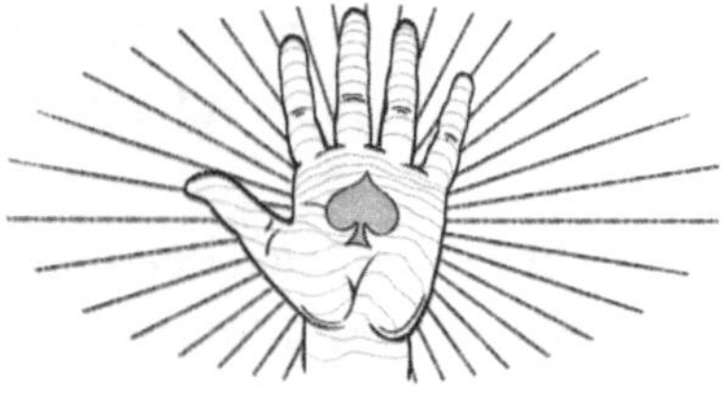

s Mom's minions encircled us, Jack shifted so that we were back-to-back, in a fighting position. But this was not going to be a fight.

"Mom, call them off," I said. "Come with us and we'll go to the Valentines. Maybe the ace can help you."

"No!" she shouted.

Hex pulsed from her hands. I felt it all through my body like a clap of thunder, and for an instant I swear my heart stopped beating. I knew from my training that the human body was a complex machine, each system balanced upon the others. A shift in chemical concentration, a disruption of the heart's electrical biofield, a small tear in a blood vessel—and bad luck could kill. This was a stark reminder of just how powerful Mom's hex was. She had queen power, and that was much stronger than the charm of a six—or even a jack.

Her sycos drew closer, ringing us in, their weapons at the ready.

"I have to finish my work," Mom said. "It's the only way the stone will let me go."

"What work?" I asked.

Her eyes met mine. She wasn't a different person like she had been when we'd last fought on the Oak Hill campus a few months before—when the jinni Invidia had possessed her. She hadn't been herself, then. Now, she was Mom. But there was so much anguish in those eyes. It was the look of a person whose soul was being torn in two. Behind me, I felt Jack move and glanced back to see one of the sycos swing a lead pipe at Jack's head. It was the sort of strike I'd seen Jack parry a hundred times in sparring, but again Mom's hex pulsed, and the weapon glanced off the blade of Jack's dagger and clipped his forehead. Instantly, a stream of blood poured down Jack's face.

"No! Stop this!" I shouted, but no one listened. Mom's sycos descended on us. At least a dozen lurched forward, and more poured out of the hallways that emptied into the lobby, swarming like rats.

Jack fired his gun and it exploded in a scattering of smoking metal. Hexed. He snarled, cradling his injured hand against his chest. Seeing him hurt and stunned, three sycos pounced on him at once, but he was still able to cut all three of them down with a spin and a slash of his dagger. More sycos still emerged from the halls, so many that we'd never be able to fight our way past them all. We had to face this problem at its source. I turned and pointed my gun at Mom.

For a second, she looked startled. Then she gave an almost imperceptible nod of her head.

"*You wouldn't dare,*" a voice boomed, vibrating the whole

room. I didn't have to look around to see where it was coming from. I knew. It came from *inside* Mom. It was the obelisk of Spades, speaking from within her belly.

Behind me, I heard the clash of arms as Jack fought off our attackers.

My hand, holding the gun, trembled. The Morbus obelisk was right. I couldn't hurt Mom. There had to be another way.

Above, a crow cawed and drew my attention upward. Above us was the skylight. Half the panes were broken—that must have been how the crows had gotten in. But the rest of the panes were intact. Not for long.

I poured charm into my gun, then aimed it upward. To shatter dozens of panes at once would require hitting the bracing at the center of the skylight. A very lucky shot. I charmed and pulled the trigger.

First came the booming report of the gun, then the glint and clatter of breaking glass. The crows, spooked by the gunshot and cut by the falling shards, dipped and dove for cover, swooping among Mom's sycos. They might have been an army, but they were no trained soldiers; some ran, others dove for cover, leaving Jack and me just enough space to flee. Back through the black labyrinth we sprinted. After a moment, we heard sounds of pursuit behind us. Shouts, footfalls, even a gunshot. But soon we'd reached the loading dock. Hardly breaking stride, we threw ourselves under the doors, tumbled out into the alley, and ran to the waiting motorcycle.

Jack fired it up, I wrapped my arms around him, and we shot off through the night, blowing through stoplights and tearing around corners. I hardly saw anything through the blur of my tears.

Before I knew it, we'd come to a stop in the garage of the Valentine mansion, where we both climbed off the motorcycle and looked at one another. Jack looked like something from a horror movie. Blood streaked his face. His left cheek was swollen and purple. Broken glass glinted in his hair, and a smattering of tiny cuts bled on his head and neck. His hand that had held the exploding gun was red, blistered, and cut in two places.

I couldn't see myself, but from the way Jack was staring at me, I guessed I must look almost as bad.

We both stood there for a long moment, trembling and catching our breath. I had so many feelings swirling around in me, so many thoughts sparking through my synapses that I didn't know where to begin. Thankfully, Jack broke the silence.

"I'm sorry," he said. "I wanted to show you, but I didn't know... she's so powerful."

I nodded, not trusting myself to speak without crying.

He put a hand on my cheek. "Something will have to be done about her, Aggie."

"I know," I whispered. "But if we tell the king and the others—"

"They'll kill her." Jack nodded. "I know. It'll have to be us, then. You, me, Deuce."

"But how?" I said. "With that obelisk inside her... and all those sycos... we barely got out of there alive."

"We'll need more power," Jack said simply.

I shut my eyes, trying with all my will to press back those tears that kept trying to come. I found myself counting the seconds that my eyes were shut. *One, two, three, four...* I would have loved to get to twenty-three, my number of completion, but I wouldn't let myself. Instead, I stopped counting and opened my eyes again.

There was only one way forward. I saw that now. I'd wanted to keep things the way they were, but that was a cruel joke. Everything was always changing. Things could improve, or they could get worse, but they were never going to stay the same. And the only way to make sure things got better—that Mom got better—was to have enough power to make it so.

I wanted to save her, yes. But I'd have to defeat her first. And to do that, I had to become stronger.

"Alright," I said softly. "I'll do it. I'll become queen."

12

AGGIE

I spent that night at the Valentine mansion. Deuce cleaned and bound our wounds while Mina made us some of her all-healing *dwaeji gukbap*—a Korean soup. Dubs and Adelie were there too, and we all crunched popcorn and watched movies in the mansion's screening room until late into the night, when exhaustion took the edge off my nerves, and I was finally able to quit counting the cuts within scenes or how many times the main actress blinked. By night's end, the movie, the company, the snacks, and the tiredness almost made me forget about Mom and all I'd seen. Almost.

That night I lay in bed next to Jack, wide awake despite my exhaustion, staring out the window at Lake St. Clair as it shimmered under the moonlight. Jack and I hadn't talked about where I was going to sleep that night before coming up to bed.

He hadn't even taken my hand. We'd simply walked together down the same hall and up to his bedroom in a fugue of wordless understanding. It was like that with us sometimes when things were good. We simply wanted the same thing, and it was to be together. There were times when we kissed, when we touched—and those felt tectonic. But just as often over the summer, there had been nights like this, where we simply lay together, silent and still except for our breathing, and existed. Honestly, they were some of the happiest moments of my life. And soon, they'd be coming to an end.

"I'm going to be someone's wife," I mused quietly.

Jack rose on an elbow and looked at me. Seeing him—his unbearable beauty—filled me with a trembly sort of ache that had all sorts of feelings wrapped up in it. Longing. Fear of loss. Suspicion, as if this moment were the result of some colossally elaborate practical joke. Even after being with Jack all summer, sometimes I still felt like an imposter. Who was I to lie in the bed of a god? And not just any god, but the Jack of Hearts? More to the point, who was he that he wanted to be with me? It all felt tenuous. Fragile.

"Someone's wife," Jack repeated quietly.

"How do you feel about that?" I asked warily.

He frowned. "I don't know. How do you feel?"

His evasion irritated me. "I asked you." It came out sounding more juvenile than it had in my head, like I was a little kid arguing with a sibling, tit-for-tat. I sat up to see him better. The faint bluish light shimmering off the water illuminated his blue eyes, making them seem phosphorescent. He was so lovely there, gilded in moonlight, that I couldn't help but reach up and run one finger across his stubbled jaw.

"I mean it. I really want to know how you feel," I pressed, almost begging.

I expected him to look away from me, but he held my gaze.

"Honestly, I don't know how I feel," he said. "I guess...

maybe when you've done what you have to do for so long, you forget how to feel what you're feeling. Because it doesn't matter anyway. Does that make any sense?"

I thought about it. I'd lost my dad. My house had burned down. I'd lost Mom several times and in several different ways. In becoming a Valentine, I could feel everything I'd been slipping away. School. Robotics club. Molly. Mom. Everything was changing, drifting, ripping apart. And had anyone stopped to ask how I felt? Did the vast, ever-expanding, ever-evolving universe care one iota about my feelings? No. No more than the sun cares if one human lies on the beach and gets sunburned.

"It makes sense," I agreed. "But I guess... I still wanted to hear that you don't want to lose me."

He looked at me. Usually, there was steel in his eyes. Something hard and impervious. But sometimes when we were close like this, together in the moonlight, the gates would open, the curtains would part, and I would see him. *Really see him*, vulnerable and naked, a soul as delicate as a dragonfly wing. As if he might at any moment laugh, or cry. Or kiss me—which is what he did now.

♡ ♤ ◇ ♧

The following day at noon, every Valentine stood gathered in the throne room. Sycos had decorated the already opulent chamber, hanging silken swag from the rafters and filling the room with huge vases of red roses, the rather too-obvious flower of our suit. I had once more struggled into my fancy dress and donned my high heels so I could match the pageantry of the rest of the suit, who looked ready for tea with the queen. Of England, not suburban Detroit.

The only one who knew my decision was Jack, and I could feel nervous tension percolating as I entered the room. Queens were extremely important to any suit of luck gods, and my answer today would affect the suit for a generation. Unless I died young.

As everyone waited for the ceremony to begin, I could feel the questioning glances coming my way. Mina and Deuce even lingered nearby, and I could tell they were both hoping for some whispered hint of my decision. I would have liked to tell them, but in truth, part of me still wavered. I knew I needed power to save my mom. But when the moment came, when the king asked his question, would my lips betray me? Would I lose my nerve? Would I actually be able to say, *yes, King Michael, I'll be your queen*, or would I simply be unable to do it, no matter what might hang in the balance?

After what felt like ages of nervous loitering, King Michael entered, looking haggard and weary beneath his glinting crown. He took his place in front of his throne, and the chatter gave way to silence. With a nod, he gestured for me to join him on the stage. I made my way onto the dais, using charm to keep myself from tripping on my fancy gown, and took my place in front of the dead queen's throne. King Michael gave me a smile that could have launched a snow flurry, then he addressed the suit.

"Valentines, we are gathered today for one of the most sacred rites of our suit: the choosing of a queen. Agatha Van Der Graaf, I have proposed that you marry me and ascend. It is an offer freely made, and the response must be freely given. What is your answer?"

I glanced across the room at the faces of my fellow Valentines. They were tense, rapt, and I could almost hear their thoughts, some praying for me to accept, others willing me to say no. Anything I said now would be disappointing to some, disturbing to others, hopeful for a few. And without a doubt, it would change the course of my life forever. I'd never made a decision like that, one that I knew would have a bearing on the rest of my life. Choosing a college was supposed to be the first one. But this choice was even bigger than that. There were no transfer credits in the world of the luck gods. No gap years. No masters programs or internships. It was an identity. Being Queen of Hearts wouldn't be something I'd do, it would be who I was. And the only way out, as far as I knew, was death.

Saying yes was terrifying. But the only thing more terrifying would be to say no because that would mean letting Mom go, and that was something I could never, ever do.

So I stood as tall as I could, trying to muster at least half the poise our traitorous Queen Aubra had shown—before Michael blew her head off. The hush in the room deepened to an electric silence. My gaze met Ten's; she glared at me with eyes of stone. Deuce looked like he might cry. I looked to Jack next, but I couldn't read the expression on his face. Now, as he had been so often over the past few months, he was a mystery to me. There were no answers out there among my fellow Valentines. The answers were within me.

I turned to Michael, stood straight, and mustered my most regal voice.

"I accept."

I expected to hear whispers, maybe gasps. Instead, everyone stayed stonily silent, which was maybe even more unsettling.

King Michael gave me a tepid smile that made my skin crawl, then turned to our fellow Hearts.

"Do I hear any challenges?" the king asked.

"I challenge," Ten said immediately, stepping forward.

This time, there were gasps.

I repressed a groan. Of course there was a catch. And of course, if there was a chance to throw a wrench in what I was doing, Ten would do it.

"Challenge? What does that mean?" I asked.

"It means we fight." Ten grinned viciously.

In the crowd, Deuce whispered something to Jack, who shook his head. I wished I'd spent the night in the library reading up on the traditions of Valentine ascension rather than snuggled up in bed. But it was too late for research now.

"Is that true?" I demanded of the king. "I have to fight her?"

"It is Ten's right to challenge," the king said. "But first, you must visit the ace and receive your queen trial. Should you pass it, then Ten will have the chance to challenge your claim."

I felt suddenly sick to my stomach. So even if I managed to survive whatever harrowing task the ace had in store for me, I could still look forward to being mangled by Ten. Fabulous.

I glanced once more at my friends. Jack watched, his face as expressionless as an iron mask. Deuce looked pale. Mina had tears in her eyes. And Ten looked like a wolf about to tear into a bloody snack. All I wanted to do was save Mom, but I realized now I'd been fooling myself. The truth was, I'd be lucky if I lived to see her again. But everything was already in motion, like a chemical reaction no extinguishing agent could quench. I would either emerge transformed and stronger—or burn up in the process.

The king offered me his arm. "Come, my bride. The ace awaits."

❧♡♤◇♧☙

Down the narrow back hallway I trudged, following Michael toward the ace's lair.

I'd met the ace once, when she appeared in the shell of my burned-down house and made me a Valentine, but I'd never seen her since. None of the Valentines were allowed to visit her without royal permission, and she apparently spent most of her days in some sort of weird trance state in which her mind melded with the obelisk of Hearts to help control the flow of good luck worldwide. At least, that's what the books I'd read in the Valentine library said. I'd never even seen the ace's room in the Valentine house, so I watched with interest as King Michael paused in front of an arched wooden door and took an iron key from his pocket. The door yielded, revealing a staircase spiraling downward into darkness.

"I would tell you not to be scared," King Michael said. "But when one is dealing with the ace, a bit of fear is wise."

"Great. Thanks," I muttered.

Down we went, our way illuminated only by the light of the king's glowing pips. They were bright, I thought. Much brighter than mine. That was the power of a king. Soon I'd have almost that much power myself if I could pass the ace's test. *If.*

Down and down and down we spiraled. Near the top of the staircase, the stairs were made of marble to match the floor of the hallway. As we descended, they changed to rough-sawn wood, then finally to stone, cut from the living earth. Just when I was starting to think the stairway was bottomless, it ended. Ahead loomed a stone archway. From beyond it, a familiar crimson light shone.

The king put a hand on the small of my back, ushering me forward. "Remember, Aggie, no matter how difficult the ace's test is, she has brought you this far for a purpose," he whispered. "She wouldn't have done that if she didn't believe you worthy."

"But... if I'm not worthy?"

The king's tiny, mocking smile returned. "Then you will die, and the ace will choose another."

On that cheery note, he led me into the ace's sanctum.

It was less a room than a cavern, the walls carved from what looked like white stone. I'd heard of salt mines running under the city of Detroit, and that's what this was, I guessed. Good old *NaCl.* It looked strangely beautiful in the quivering red light. The space was round and perhaps only fifteen feet in diameter. At its center stood the obelisk, a glowing crystal tower with strange glyphs carved into it. The ace knelt before it, her charred hands pressed to its surface, her eyes closed, her lips muttering—whether it was a prayer, an incantation, or pure nonsense I couldn't say, but it certainly wasn't English.

"Your Worship," the king said, bowing.

The ace ignored us.

The king cleared his throat. "Your Worship. I've brought Aggie," he said louder.

She continued her muttering, oblivious.

"Let me try," I said. Ever the teacher's pet, I'd come prepared. Stepping forward, I reached into my little purse and took out the ace's favorite treat, a small strawberry cheesecake tart wrapped in cellophane that I'd nabbed from the kitchen earlier.

"I brought you something." I held the tart close enough that she might catch a whiff.

Sure enough, her eyelids fluttered open. I glanced back at the king, trying not to look too smug.

"Agatha Van Der Graaf," the ace said, a note of fondness in her creaky, dusty voice. I was sure if three-hundred-year-old oak trees could talk, they'd sound exactly like the ace.

With what looked like considerable effort, she removed her hands from the obelisk. She took the tart from me, brought it to her nose and inhaled deeply. "I knew there was a reason I liked you," she said, and shoved the entire thing into her mouth. An excruciating minute passed while she smacked and licked her lips.

King Michael cleared his throat. "Your Worship, Aggie has accepted my marriage proposal and is ready to enter your queen trial."

The ace finally got the dessert down and looked from the king to me, her ancient eyes glittering with amusement. "Truly? A budding young flower like you is willing to marry this old barnacle? I thought you'd say no."

That made me snort laugh, but I quickly stopped myself. "I have reasons," I said with an uneasy glance at the king.

The ace gave a slow, knowing nod. "You do. Just remember this about power: for every problem it solves, it creates two more."

"Well... I'm willing to risk it," I said.

The ace pursed her lips. "But are you willing to risk *your life*?"

My hesitation lasted only a second. "Yes."

The ace's cloudy old eyes searched mine for a long moment, then she sniffed and smiled. "Of course you are. I knew that already. I just wanted to watch you say it. A great deal of life when you're old and wise like me consists of watching things play out that you already knew were going to happen."

"Sounds boring," I said.

The ace smiled and licked a bit of cheesecake off one of her fingers. "On the contrary, it can be very satisfying," she sniffed. "And I still get surprised, now and then. Very well. The queen trial. Listen well. There is a certain house in Nashville, Tennessee, that sits upon the bank of a river. A castle made all of stone, with a roof of copper. Inside, there is a chest, black with gold binding. You will find that chest and bring it to me. But beware. Both the house and its contents are well guarded."

"What's in the chest?" I asked.

"You'll see," the ace said with a haggard smile. "But do not open it until you've brought it back to me. To do so would be very dangerous."

I nodded to myself. "Castle in Nashville. Get the chest, bring it back, don't look inside. Got it. Can I bring someone with me?"

"No other Valentines are permitted to help in a queen trial. However, if you wish to bring non-luck gods with you, that is your choice."

I nodded, ready to leave, but the ace was looking at me strangely. She raised an eyebrow. "You have something you've been wanting to say to me."

She was right. There was something I'd wanted to confront

her about for months now. I'd convinced myself not to say anything today, because it didn't seem like the right occasion. But since she'd brought it up...

I bit my lip, then forced myself to speak. "You burned down my house."

At first, I'd thought it was the Blackovers or some other black suit baddies who'd destroyed our family home. But I found out afterward by watching the surveillance video that it was this sweet-looking, ancient woman.

"Why?" I demanded.

The ace flashed a mischievous grin. "Pass your queen trial, and I'll tell you," she said. "Is that all?"

Our eyes met, both of us illuminated by the eerie red light of the obelisk.

"Yeah. Why me?" I said. "Why not Ten, or Mina? What makes me so important?"

The ace's crinkled face grew hard.

"What is the importance of a match? A stone? A brick?"

I hesitated, confused, then shook my head. "None of those things are very important," I said.

The ace nodded. "Neither are you. And yet a match may start an inferno that burns cities. A misplaced stone could derail a train. A brick could dash in the head of an emperor."

I felt my frown deepen. "So I'm a tool? Is that it?"

She tilted her ancient head. "You're a scientist, aren't you, Aggie? You're not a tool. You're a catalyst."

I was almost afraid to ask...

"A catalyst for what? What are you trying to make happen?"

The ace's lips curled into a smile so dark it curdled my blood.

"That," she said, "is not for a catalyst to know."

I ran a trembling hand through my hair. "Fair enough. I'll do my best. But you should know, even if I pass this trial, I don't know if I can do whatever it is you think I'm supposed to do. I don't even know if I can be a queen."

"Being a queen is easy, my dear," the ace said. "All you have to do is smile with the world on your shoulders. You have three days to return to me with the chest."

I nodded. "Okay. And if I'm late?"

The ace's charred hands closed into fists, snuffing out their charm light. "There are only two possible outcomes of a queen trial, Aggie. Ascendance and death. You'd better get going."

13

—————

AGGIE

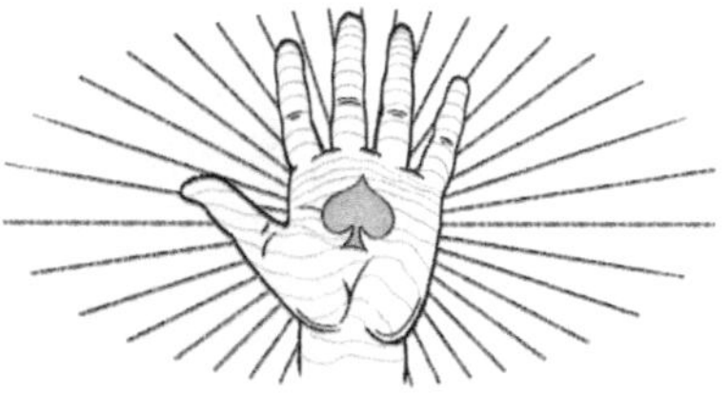

I found Jack sitting on the back deck, staring out at the iron-colored, choppy waters of Lake St. Clair, sipping an orange juice that smelled suspiciously of vodka. Deuce and Mina bookended him on the patio sofa looking somber, and I got the eerie feeling that I had stumbled into my own wake. Mina was the first to swoop in on me, snatching me into a ferocious hug.

"Oh, sweetie," she said, her face pressed against my neck.

Deuce also stood, leaving Jack the only one still sitting and brooding over his drink.

"So?" Deuce prompted. "What's the queen trial? You have to go arm wrestle Thad Blackover? Jump into the rift and yoink a hair from a goblin warlord's mustache? Beat down a—"

"Deuce," Mina interrupted his nervous chatter. "Let her answer."

"I have to go to Nashville," I said. "And get something. A... chest."

"Huh." Deuce rubbed his chin. "That doesn't sound too bad."

"It's got to be harder than it seems," Mina warned. "I heard Aubra's trial was assassinating the Morbus king."

"Right." Deuce nodded. "I heard about that. She lured him into bed then took him out with a garrote made of wire from Liberace's charmed piano, right? And had three fingers and a tooth broken in the process."

Mina must have noticed how not encouraged I looked, because she quickly said:

"But she did it. Aubra succeeded and became queen."

"Good thing the ace doesn't have you assassinating Morbuses," Deuce told me, "since the only one is—" he changed his mind before saying *your mom* and lapsed into an awkward silence.

Mina mouthed *shut up* to him, and he shrugged apologetically. Actually, I didn't mind Deuce's chatter. When I was nervous, I counted. He talked. In a way, it just showed why we were such good friends. We were alike.

I looked to Jack, who still sat gazing into his drink.

"What about you?" I asked him. "No comments? No jokes?"

He sloshed his drink to stir it for a moment before looking up at me. "Mina is right. A queen trial is always deadly. If the ace made it sound easy, that worries me even more." He took another gulp of his drink.

"But you still want me to do it," I said, my eyes narrowing.

I saw his hands tense on the glass and for a moment thought he might squeeze until it broke. "It doesn't matter what I think," he said quietly. "You've accepted the trial. You're in it, now. You either succeed or you fail."

I took a deep breath to steady myself. I knew exactly what he meant. Succeed or fail. Live—or die.

"Well, I've survived a Blackover uprising and an invasion of jinn. I think I can make it through this," I said, sounding a lot more confident than I felt.

"And we're coming with you," Deuce said, standing tall.

But Jack and I both shook our heads.

"No Valentines are allowed to help in a queen trial," Jack said. "Otherwise, I'd be packing instead of drinking."

"Well, it's good you got a head start with the booze," I said. "Because I need you to call Lorcan."

During the long trudge back from the ace's chamber, I'd been thinking about how to approach my trial. I couldn't bring any Valentines with me, true. But it would still be smart to bring some allies with me on my quest, my very own Fellowship-of-the-Ring-style crew. I had a pretty good idea who I wanted to include, and Lorcan was one of them.

My words finally stirred Jack from his depressed stupor. "Lorcan? That lowlife? You already have a leprechaun key. Why would you need him?"

I shrugged. "He helped me once when I was lost in Detroit, after you were captured by Bartholomew Barth. Besides, how many people do we have that we can trust?"

"Who says we can trust Lorcan?" Jack exclaimed. "He works for the Diamantes and hangs out with Blackovers."

"My queen trial, I pick the crew." I crossed my arms.

"Fine," Jack growled. "But you're taking Seemor, too."

"Already texting him," Deuce said, tapping at his phone.

"Not Seemor," I whined.

"Why not?" Jack said. "He's my most trusted—"

"Yeah, yeah, yeah, he's your guy," I grumbled. "But he's constantly popping up out of the blue and annoying people. The other day I was working out in the gym in my sports bra, and he just appeared and handed me a towel like some peri pervert."

"Yeah. He is a pervert," Deuce agreed.

"He's the best reconnaissance sprite we've got," Jack said firmly. "And I trust him."

"Fine," I huffed. "Seemor can come, but I'm bringing Lorcan, too."

"Deal," Jack sighed and downed the rest of his drink. For some reason that still wasn't entirely clear to me, leprechauns were more likely to show up when the person who summoned them was a bit sauced. "Lorcan! LORCAN!" Jack called.

It usually took Lorcan a few minutes to appear, but this time the leprechaun sauntered around a corner of the house right away, as if he'd been lingering there and listening the whole time—maybe he had been. When he saw the four of us, he crossed his arms and glanced around uneasily.

"Well, look at me. Summoned to the house of Hearts. *La-dee-da*. What's the occasion?"

"We thought we'd throw you into the lake and see if you can swim," Jack groused.

I gave him an admonishing look.

"First, I have a bone to pick with you," I told Lorcan. "Last time you were here, I did Cupid's Arrow on you and Queen Aubra. Something I'm not exactly proud of."

"Why not?" he scoffed. "Love is a beautiful thing."

"What did you do with her?" Jack asked.

Lorcan snorted. "What do you care? Didn't she betray you and sell you to Bartholomew Barth?"

"That's beside the point," I said.

"We respect women around here," Jack said. "Even traitorous ones."

Lorcan stood up straighter, looking affronted. "Respect her? I painted her toenails and recited poetry for her, you bloody hypocrites. I didn't take advantage of her. I loved her—more than I can say for you lot, who blew her brains out in the middle of the street."

"Alright, fine. Take it easy," I said.

"Is that what you brought me here for, to question my credentials as a feminist?" Lorcan blustered, red-faced. "I love and respect women more than the rest of you sots combined. I love women more than booze. More than fighting. More than gold!"

"Okay. We get it. You treated Aubra with respect," I said, then paused. "I brought you here to ask a favor. I'm going on my queen trial. I want you to come with me."

My words shook Lorcan out of his anger like a splash of cold water. "Why would you want me to go?" he demanded.

"That's what I said," Jack grumbled.

"I might need help," I said. "The Valentines aren't allowed to help me. And... and I don't have a lot of friends who aren't Valentines," I finished—why not be honest?

"Fair enough," Lorcan said, arching an eyebrow. "But why would I help you?"

I paused. I hadn't really considered that question. "We... could pay you," I suggested.

Lorcan laughed. "We've been over this before, lass. I work for the Diamantes, remember? No one outbids the Diamonds. Try again."

"We don't have to outbid them," Jack said. "Double dip. We'll pay you to bring her back from the queen trial safe. Then you can go back, tell Danusia everything that happened, and collect your reward from her. We'll give you a million in gold."

The leprechaun snorted. "Chump change."

"Three million," Jack said.

"Six," Lorcan said, "or stop wasting my time."

"Four," Jack said. "And don't pretend Danusia won't pay you three times that just to hear firsthand how the queen trial turned out."

Lorcan frowned. "You'd pay me to spy on you?"

"Bring Aggie back safe, and you can spy on us all you want," Jack said.

Lorcan rubbed his scraggly beard. "Still, queen trials are dangerous. What exactly would I be risking my hide to do?"

"You'll see," Jack said, but I chimed in, earning a dirty look.

"Travel to Nashville, retrieve a chest, and bring it back here," I said.

Lorcan's eyebrows went up. "Nashville... a chest containing what?"

I hesitated, glancing at my friends.

Lorcan scoffed. "You don't know? What a cluster. Look, I'm flattered you thought of me, but the thing is, I'm not the one you want."

I shook my head, confused. "Who do I want, then?"

Lorcan smiled. "This is a heist, miss. And for this heist, you'll be wanting the best thief in the world. My sister."

"I didn't know you had a sister," Jack said.

Lorcan snorted. "Of course you don't. You think I'd let the Jack of Hearts near my little sister? Not that she couldn't slice off your twig and berries and serve them to you on a platter."

"She sounds charming," Deuce quipped.

"Leprechauns are the best thieves in the world," Lorcan declared. "And Cleo is the best leprechaun thief."

"Great," I said. "Call her up."

Lorcan folded his arms again. "Sure," he said. "For another four million in gold."

Jack threw up his hands. "I told you not to call this guy. He's just trying to shake us down."

But I was watching Lorcan. There was something about his demeanor when he mentioned his sister, a certain light that crept into his eyes. He might be trying to get gold out of us, but he meant what he said about his sister.

"Fine," I said. "Four million in gold for you, four for your sister—if we succeed."

It wasn't lost on me that I was telling the truth. If I became the Queen of Hearts, I really would have millions of dollars that I could spend on a whim. Sure, the Valentines gave me all the money I needed now; all I had to do was ask. But being queen would be different. Mom and I would never have to worry about rent money again. Mom would never again have to beg for grant funding for her science experiments. Money wasn't the most important reason to risk my life in the queen trial, but it wasn't nothing, either.

Lorcan eyed me. "Well, what the hell? I like a good heist. You got yourself a deal, queenie," he said, then reached out and shook my hand, squeezing so hard I almost yelped.

"I'm in, too," a voice said, and Seemor glitched into existence next to Lorcan, startling him.

"Jesus's teeth!" Lorcan exclaimed. "If this rodent is going with us, my fee goes up to six mil."

"Leprechauns are always jealous of us sprites," Seemor said. "Because of our good looks." He ran a preening hand over his wrinkly face and beige antlers.

Lorcan snorted. "A head like that would look perfect stuffed on the wall of a hunting lodge."

"This is great," I beamed. "We're assembling our fellowship. Lorcan, why don't you get your sister? There's someone else I have to go recruit."

❧♡♤◇♧☙

I stepped out of the library restroom and emerged in the middle of a kids' story time. The reader, a woman with dreadlocks and a patchwork skirt, looked baffled when she saw me. Clearly, she was aware that no one had actually gone into that bathroom, and therefore should not be coming out of it, and I silently cursed the leprechaun key that hung on its golden chain around my neck. How come the stupid thing always had me emerging from bathrooms?

I smiled and waved to the kiddies, then slipped past and made my way to the circulation counter. A tall boy in a Detroit Lions jersey was scanning books and placing them on a cart. I craned my neck to look behind him.

"Can I help you?" the boy asked.

"I'm looking for my friend. Molly?"

He looked at me blankly.

"She works here," I clarified.

"Oh, that Molly. Yeah, she doesn't work here anymore."

That was new. Poor Molly! She loved her library job. What had she done to get herself canned? I wondered. If I knew Molly, she was probably making out with one of her fellow library employees, but I doubted it was this guy. If it had been him, he would have at least remembered her a little better. There was bound to be a logical explanation, which Molly would doubtless tell me when I saw her. Still, the whole scene gave me an icky feeling that reminded me of going to Mom's lab and finding it empty.

Of course, Molly was nothing like Mom. She didn't have a piece of evil obelisk living inside her as far as I knew, and she'd never lie to me. All the drama of the last few months was just making me paranoid.

I turned to go, then paused.

"Out of curiosity, how long ago did she quit working here?"

The boy shrugged. "I don't know. A few months?"

I frowned. So Molly had started having a bunch of money at the same time she'd stopped working at the library? I didn't really believe she was making all that money just from her job here but still, it was strange. One might even say it was fishy. But I didn't have time for sleuthing. I had to get Molly and get on the road to Nashville, because three days wasn't a lot of time —and the clock was ticking.

I fished the leprechaun key out of the top of my shirt. This time, instead of the bathroom, I went to the elevator doors, which were in a less conspicuous part of the building. I pushed the button and held the leprechaun key in my hand. When the doors slid open, they revealed not an elevator, but a long, brightly lit tube, like a tunnel one might see at an airport terminal.

It took me a few more trips through the leprechaun underground before I found Molly. I checked her house, the pizza place she and her mom frequented, and the Oak Hill College library before at last tracking her down at the bubble tea shop.

She sat at one of the booths with Bianca of the cool-girl clique, chatting about history class, but their conversation became a pair of greeting squeals as they caught sight of me. Ugh, Molly was even squealing like a cool girl now.

"What's up?" she asked once I'd extricated myself from both their hugs.

"I have to go on a road trip and I need my favorite getaway driver," I said.

"Road trip? Going where?" Molly said.

"A mission. A queen mission," I said.

Molly's eyes went wide. "You're doing it?"

I nodded, trying to look confident rather than grim.

"Doing what? I want to come!" Bianca said.

"Sorry," I said. "Top secret."

Bianca gave us a very practiced pouty face.

"I'll bring you a souvenir," Molly said, blowing her a kiss. "Promise!"

We bustled away, used the leprechaun key to make a broom closet into an exit, and departed.

We found the others waiting at the Valentine house where I'd left them.

"Christ almighty, where'd you go, Jupiter?" Lorcan griped when we reappeared.

I paused. "Wait. Can the key really take you to another planet?"

Lorcan glowered. "And here Jack talks like you're some sort of brainiac. You think you can go *underground* to Jupiter? Do you suppose they have doors up there?"

"Point taken," I said, then turned my attention to the girl standing next to him. She was a couple of inches taller than Lorcan and looked just a few years older than me. She wore a green jumper, a miniature backpack of black leather, and a pair of expensive-looking sunglasses. She had a mane of golden curls and a pair of curved daggers hung at her waist. At her feet sat a little boy who looked about six years old, playing a handheld video game.

"And you must be—?" I prompted.

"Bored off my arse," she said, in the same odd, not-quite-Irish accent as Lorcan.

"My sweet little sister Cleopatra, everyone," Lorcan said.

"Cleo," she corrected, then eyed me. "So, this is the future queen? She doesn't look like much."

"You should watch how you talk to her," Jack said, a quiet danger in his voice. "Heart queens have a tradition of lopping people's heads off."

"And I have a tradition of sticking daggers in pretty boys' backs," she said.

"I like her!" Seemor said.

The leprechaun girl glared at him with a look of bored contempt, as if he didn't even warrant a one-liner.

"And who's this?" I said, kneeling in front of the boy.

"No one," Cleo said, crossing her arms. "Don't talk to him."

The boy, for his part, kept playing the video game without glancing up at me.

"Is he... your son? Is he coming with us?" I asked, confused.

"Yes," Lorcan said at the same time Cleo said, "No."

They leaned together, conferring in low tones.

"We could use a good luck charm," Lorcan hissed.

"It's bad enough you dragged me into this," she said. "We're not risking him."

"We need every advantage if we're going to make it through this in one piece, sister."

"You want a lucky charm, go and pick your ass a four-leaf clover. The boy ain't coming," she declared, then pulled out of their little huddle. "And I'm not coming either. Unless someone babysits the boy."

Jack laughed and shook his head. "This is unbelievable."

"I'll watch him," Deuce said, stepping forward. "I love kids."

Lorcan snorted. "I know this guy. Look at his hair. He can barely take care of himself."

Deuce touched his bedhead self-consciously.

"Better if we bring the boy along," Lorcan finished.

"No, damn you," Cleo snapped.

"I'll help watch him," Mina said, kneeling and putting a hand on the boy's shoulder. "Hey, you like swimming? We could go swimming in the lake."

The boy looked up from his video game and nodded.

"Not to butt in," Seemor said quietly to Jack. "But I know this Cleo by reputation. She's not just a thief—more of a klepto-maniac savant. You don't want her little boy running around the mansion for three days. He'll probably rob you blind."

Everyone looked at the little boy again. He was skinny, with dark hair and big brown eyes rimmed by long lashes. He looked far too sweet to worry about.

"I think we can handle a kid, Seemor," Deuce scoffed.

Seemor gave a shrug that said *it's your funeral.*

"Enough," the leprechaun girl said. "You want me, you watch the kid. That's it."

"Fine," Jack said, ending the debate.

The leprechaun girl knelt next to the boy and tousled his hair. "Don't tell them anything, got it? And mind your manners." She turned her attention to Deuce and Mina. "He likes pizza bites. And Superman ice cream. But he hates peanut butter. And don't let him have the TV on at bedtime, or he'll be up until the wee hours. And no drinks after eight PM or he'll piss the bed. For a little man, he's got one hell of a bladder."

Deuce and Mina both nodded dutifully.

"Good," I said. "It's settled."

Deuce stepped forward. "I brought the Escalade around front. You're driving, right?" He tossed the key fob to Molly. "Lucky Charms here doesn't drive, and this squirt can't see over the steering wheel." He nodded toward Seemor, who chucked the core of the apple he'd been eating at him.

"If you could teleport across the world, you wouldn't bother with cars either," Lorcan grumbled. "Filthy contraptions, anyway."

"Yeah, but if you can't envision your destination, you can't access a door there, right?" Deuce said. "Kind of a flaw in your transportation system, greenie."

Lorcan shrugged irritably.

Deuce approached me, holding a small nylon case in his hand. He unzipped it, revealing one of his bird-shaped drones inside. "I'm sending Lorelei with you. I know you have a bad track record of crashing my drones, but try to take good care of her."

I took the case and gave Deuce a hug.

"Thank you," I said.

Mina gave me a hug next. "You got this, girl. Remember, use your superpower."

"Of course," I said, flashing a glowing heart pip, but Mina shook her head.

"No." She pointed to her temple. "Your brain."

I hugged Mina again.

Next, Jack stepped up to me. He held my weapons belt in his hands, my charmed dagger and gun hanging from it. He slipped it around my waist and cinched it tight, his hands slow in a way that filled me with longing. They'd gotten weapons for the others, too, while I was picking up Molly. Mina handed them out: a charmed knife for Molly and a pair of charmed golden brass knuckles for Lorcan.

"I'm armed already," Lorcan said, though he was admiring the knuckles.

"We expect you to keep our girl safe," Mina said. "If we could give you a tank, we would."

There was no need to provide Seemor with any charmed weapons; as part of Jack's crew, he was always armed to the teeth, and Cleo obviously liked to flaunt her daggers.

Mina handed Molly a bag of snacks she'd put together, and at last, all the preparations seemed to be made. There was no excuse to delay any longer. As everyone piled into the SUV, Jack approached me for a final goodbye.

So much had passed between us over the last few months that I felt like I finally understood what people meant when they said something was a whirlwind romance. That's what it felt like with Jack, like some great force of nature had gusted in and lifted me off my feet and spun me around. Everything in my life blurred. I felt dizzy, exhilarated, terrified, alive. I also felt, somehow, that if the whirling stopped, if the centrifugal motion let go of me, I'd fall, dropped from the sky. It made me afraid to be away from him. As I stood there looking at him, my impossibly beautiful boy, I realized our relationship scared me more than anything that might be waiting for me ahead on my queen trial. What would happen when we were apart, when our impossible tornado of bliss subsided? Would it be like a real storm? Would I find myself on my knees, the world in ruins, the source of all that turmoil blown away to gyrate through someone else's life?

I wished I could bring him with me. I wished I didn't have to let him out of my sight.

"One favor," I said. "Try to keep an eye on my mom for me?"

He nodded. "I promise."

Then he kissed me. It wasn't the sensuous, hungry kiss I'd come to crave from him; this kiss was delicate, ephemeral. Just the barest taste of his lips, as if he wanted to send me off yearning for more. And I did. He stepped back and held me at arm's length.

I love you. The words shot through my mind. But whether I was really feeling that way about him or just willing him to say those magic words to me, I didn't know.

14

RACHEL

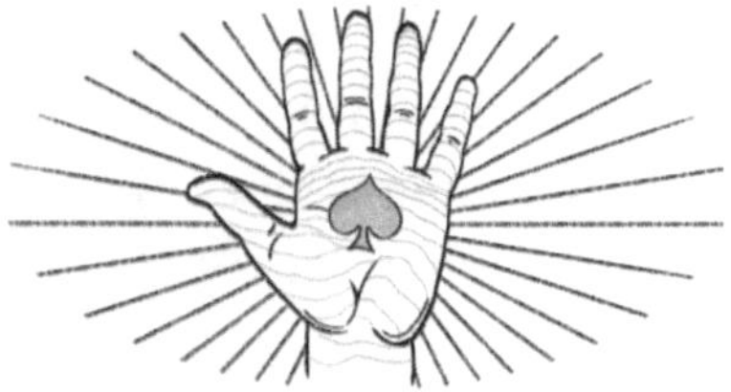

The brewery was closed. Still, as she followed her host through a production area full of huge steel vats and out into the bar, the sweet, yeasty smell of spilled beer permeated the place. It brought up memories of the worst days of Rachel's alcoholism, which made her uneasy. It should have been laughable after everything she'd seen and done as a Morbus that drinking a little booze should scare her, and yet it did. Even in the face of the torment she'd experienced and all the depravities she'd committed over the last few months, she hadn't relapsed and started drinking again. That was a tiny victory, at least. But it seemed like only a matter of time before she lost her sobriety on top of everything else, and being in a place like this didn't help.

The Blackover walking ahead of her pushed open the brew

pub's back door and led her out into the beer garden beyond. It was a ramshackle place comprised of sprawling, high decks, strange outbuildings, an amphitheater, an open-air bar, and an assortment of graffitied picnic tables, all surrounded by a wall comprised of steel grating, wooden beams, and chain link topped with razor wire, like a strange modern-day castle wall. In the center of it all sat a fire pit, casting everything in shivering shadows.

Rachel's escort consisted of four sycos and two Blackovers, one of them walking behind her and another leading the way, all heavily armed. She supposed she should feel complimented that they felt it necessary to treat her with such caution, but it also made her feel a bit like a prisoner. Which was exactly what she might become if this negotiation didn't go well. That is, if she didn't end up dead.

Ahead, a long table rested atop a raised platform. Blackovers sat along it, an abundance of pizza and chicken wings and pitchers of beer set before them, a spread as excessive as a medieval feast. The Club king was easy to spot. He was a mountainous man with shoulders as broad as a doorway and a black beard that would have made him a stylish Viking. He wore no true crown, but a band of iron circled his brow that was somehow even more regal for its simplicity. It said something about his leadership style, Rachel imagined. Unembellished yet unbreakable. The entourage came to a halt in front of the table, and the big king's dark eyes locked onto her.

There were two types of men, Rachel had found. Those who would glance away from a woman they found attractive and those who would let their eyes linger without hiding the hunger in their stare. King Thad was definitely the second kind, and she found her heart beating faster in spite of herself.

The other Blackovers were a varied assortment of rogues and misfits clad in iron and leather, looking like a post-apocalyptic motorcycle gang. Rachel scanned the table for the queen,

Carlotta, but saw no one who fit the description the obelisk had given her. The only females among them were a sharp-featured blonde with one side of her head shaved and a second woman so large she might have outweighed Thad.

They were a wild collection of characters, but it was the king who held her attention.

"Well," he boomed. "This is the new queen of the gravediggers we've heard so much about. Rachel, is it?"

She gave a single nod.

"We'll have to work on that," the king laughed. "What kind of harbinger of pain and suffering is named Rachel? It doesn't exactly instill fear in the hearts of your enemies."

And yet he will fear us before we're finished, the voice in Rachel's gut whispered. *Everyone will.*

"Come, Rachel the Terrible. Sit." Thad gestured to the seat opposite his, and Rachel sat. Thad picked up a three-foot-long sub sandwich and took a bite, talking as he chewed. "Our suits have been allies since before they started writing history down, eh? It's good for us to know one another. And trust one another. There's a lot we could accomplish together."

Rachel nodded.

"When the Morbus were wiped out in Siberia, we were worried. Fewer bad luck gods in the world means less black suit power overall. It weakened us, too. Of course, the Blackovers and the Morbus haven't always been friendly, exactly. No one is too friendly with the gravediggers—no offense. But we support your efforts to rebuild the suit."

Thad washed the bite of sub down with a gulp of beer, then looked at Rachel with narrowed eyes.

"You're a quiet one," he observed. "I like that. Not like these goddamn chatterboxes," he said with a vague gesture to his fellow Clubs. The blonde woman threw a chicken wing at him. It stuck in his beard, and he pulled it out and ate it, laughing.

"I've always felt," he went on, "that alliances work best when you start by identifying mutual goals..."

Give him nothing, the stone inside Rachel warned. *We are the ones in control.*

"So what do you want?" she asked Thad. The words came out sounding suggestive, and she saw a light of desire kindle in his dark brown eyes. He shifted in his seat and grinned.

"You're direct. I like that." He gestured down the table. "You might have noticed. We are missing a queen."

"I did notice," Rachel said. "What happened to her?"

King Thad's smile flattened, his face suddenly becoming cruel, impassive. "She made a mistake," he said. "A fatal one. But we miss having a queen. And I like your face, Rachel the Terrible. You're skinny, true. But we have enough beer and brats to put a little meat on that ass of yours. What do you say?"

Spit in his face, the stone inside Rachel hissed, but she wasn't ready to go that far. Not yet.

"I would not be queen of the Blackovers—" Rachel said.

"Why not?" Thad eyed her, twisting his beard with a finger. "Double the marks, double the power. True, combining suits has been banned for a few thousand years. It has been called an abomination. A sin. But whatever. We dark suits love our sin, don't we? Besides, it was done in the past, in ancient times, before the death of Uthule. Our ace says those times are coming again. Bloody days. Alliances will be everything. Merge or purge."

That last gruesome phrase stuck in Rachel's mind, the way a bit of gristle might lodge itself between a person's teeth. *Merge or purge.*

"You didn't let me finish," Rachel said. "I wouldn't be queen of the Blackovers but..."

Thad leaned in, hungry for her next words.

"I would be high queen," she said.

The huge man's face broke into a grin, then he laughed, and

his laugh became a roar. He slapped the table with his hand so hard that steins ten feet down the table jumped and spilled their contents. He wiped a tear from his eye with one thumb, still chuckling. A high queen, of course, outranked a king, and Thad's response to this impertinence would tell her a lot about him. So far, the laughing was a good sign. Far better than cold fury would have been.

"Damn, I like you, Rachel. Come on, be my queen. We have a motorhome in the back with a queen-size bed. Let's consummate this thing. I'll rock you like a battering ram, Rachel the Terrible."

"Tempting," Rachel said drily. Reflexively, she picked up the mug of beer that had been set in front of her and brought it halfway to her lips before realizing what she was doing. She set it back down, her hand trembling. That had been close.

You should drink, the stone inside her said. *It's rude not to.* But there was mockery in that voice. It knew exactly what it was goading her into.

"No," she hissed at it.

"What?" Thad said, frowning.

She turned her attention back to the Clubs king.

"You speak of building trust," she said. "There is a way you could gain mine. All I ask is a little gift."

"Name it," Thad said. "Anything."

And so Rachel repeated what the stone within her had instructed her to say before the meeting—about the object she needed Thad to obtain for her and where it could be found.

In Nashville.

15

AGGIE

oad trips with Mom and Dad were always the best. We'd stop off at a gas station and get an absurd amount of junk food. As we drove, Mom would DJ us though a historical tour of her favorite tunes from the 80s and 90s, with the special addition of Dad's surprisingly good and always hilarious falsetto singing. With Dad gone and Mom in her current state of partial erasure, the memories held an especially sweet ache now, as I replayed them in my mind.

Safe to say, my current road trip held none of the nostalgic charm I remembered from my childhood. Molly kept checking her social media accounts while driving. Seemor endlessly complained about the radio. (Apparently, sprites have a thing against music? He seemed to think recording a person's voice stole a part of their soul.) Lorcan was always either texting on his phone, snoring, or griping about how much faster the trip would have gone if we'd taken the leprechaun underground—which caused his sister to loudly remind him to quit being a wanker and shut his yap.

As for me, the accident Dad and I had been in, the one that had killed him, had permanently ruined highway travel for me. Yes, my Valentine training allowed me to speed down the road on a motorcycle blindfolded. But perversely, the danger in that situation actually made my anxiety better. I had to focus all my energy on my charm to keep from crashing. The effort required distracted me from my fears. Now, I was just *sitting* here. I tried working on my college essays, but everything else happening made it all but impossible to concentrate. After three disjointed paragraphs, I clapped the laptop shut and gave up. Without writing to distract me, all sorts of dreadful worries and grizzly crash-and-burn scenarios played out in my head, and I had to grit my teeth to keep from counting the mile markers.

There was also the tension with Molly. She'd lied to me about her library job, and I didn't know why. She probably had a good reason, I kept telling myself. Maybe she'd gotten fired and didn't feel like talking about it. Maybe she'd gotten a different job she was embarrassed about. Was she selling drugs? Stripping? Either would certainly explain her newfound wealth, but I couldn't quite believe Molly had gone down those career paths, no matter how good the pay was. Regardless, she hadn't been honest with me. It hurt my feelings and made me uneasy. The world of the luck gods was full of schemes, machinations, power grabs, and assassinations. If I couldn't trust my best friend, who could I trust?

Molly glanced in the rearview mirror, then shifted lanes.

"Look at these fools," Seemor said, gesturing in disgust to a billboard for an orthodontist featuring a smiling teen. "On the other side"—this was how the sprites referenced the mysterious place beyond the rift, where all peri came from—"people don't give away bits of themselves with photos and songs. Here everyone picks off a little bit of your soul, like a grain of sand lifted from a beach. Sooner or later, it's all gone. Just look at these *social media influencers*. What could be more foolish than to give away pieces of your own being in exchange for—"

"Quit yer nattering, sprite," Lorcan muttered. "Or you'll lose more than a bit of your soul, you'll lose the whole thing."

"Oh, go crawl in a hole and count your pennies," Seemor snipped at Lorcan.

"I've been videoing you this whole time, sprite," Cleo said. "Posting it now."

"You will not!" Seemor snarled, making a grab for Cleo's phone. She palmed his forehead and turned him aside, jamming his face into the back of my seat while laughing hysterically.

Molly glanced in the rearview mirror at the bickering peri in the backseat, distracting herself from the road ahead, which of course made me break out in a sweat.

"Kids, stop fighting, or we're turning this car around," I deadpanned.

"If only," Lorcan muttered, his words barely audible over the peals of his sister's laughter and Seemor's furious grunts.

It hit me then, a warm, urgent feeling in my hands. *The work.*

"Get off at this next exit," I said quickly.

"Humans." Seemor rolled his eyes. "Bladders like hummingbirds."

Molly took the exit.

"Hang a right," I said.

We were soon in a small town's commercial district. There were a few chain restaurants, fast food joints, a dollar store...

"There," I pointed at a supermarket. It was a company I'd never heard of before, and the building was modest, but a colorful banner slung along the building's front read *Customer Celebration Month*. It was early afternoon on a Saturday, so the parking lot was more than half full, with carts rattling up and down the aisles of parked cars.

"Shopping? Really? We're never going to get to Nashville," Seemor griped.

But *the work* was important because it strengthened a luck god's charm power. I had no idea what I'd face when we got to Nashville, but it was a good bet I'd need as much charm as possible.

"Are we here for tampons or gum?" Cleo said. "Cause I can hook you up, sister."

Molly had already stopped in the parking space I pointed to.

"I'll be right back," I said, climbing out of the car then jogging toward the store.

It was weird how *the work* operated. You'd get this feeling in your hands, then if you opened yourself up to it, your attention would get drawn intuitively to whomever you were supposed to help. So far in my reading, I hadn't found any neurological explanation about how it worked, and I'd vowed to study it someday.

Now, my attention locked on a woman and a little girl who were walking into the store ahead of me. They both had long, black hair coming almost down to their lower backs. Something about their gait was identical too, like the girl was simply a half-sized version of the woman. Mother and daughter. I fell into step behind them.

As I gained on them, I noticed the little girl's white sneakers were beat up and dirty. The left shoulder strap of her shirt had broken and was held in place with a safety pin. The woman's T-shirt seemed to be the uniform of a restaurant, but her jeans were stained and dingy, as if they hadn't been washed after at least a week of daily wear. I picked up on their conversation as I neared.

"But I want berries," the girl complained.

"I told you, sweetie. Berries are expensive," the mom whispered. "All we're getting today is a box of cereal. Come on."

Automatic doors whooshed open as we entered. I passed a cardboard celebration cutout, more posters and balloons, but I didn't pay any attention to them. My focus was on the subject of my work, the mother and daughter, as I tried to figure out what I was supposed to do to help them.

We passed through the entryway where the carts were kept and into the store itself. The mom grabbed a handheld basket and walked on, with the girl lagging dejectedly behind. I trailed them, flaring my charm.

Come on. Show me what I'm supposed to...

Suddenly, music blared. A cheer went up around me, making me jump. I flared my charm harder, my hand going to the dagger concealed at my waist. Then something bopped me on the head. A balloon. Dozens of them floated down from the ceiling. Store employees had gathered around me, clapping and chattering happily, but in the chaos, I couldn't make out what anyone was saying.

Finally, a man in a suit approached carrying a large, posterboard check. It was made out to *One Millionth Customer* in the amount of ten thousand dollars.

"Congratulations. You're a lucky girl!" the man in the suit was saying. Employees hovered around me, snapping pictures, making videos as the man handed me the check. "What are you going to do with the money?" he asked, smiling at me, then at one of the employees, who was taking a video of us on her phone.

I looked to where the single mom and her daughter stood, watching my spectacle unfold with sad, resigned eyes.

"I'm going to give it to them," I said, walking over and offering the absurdly large check to the woman.

She looked stunned as she took it, but the little girl jumped up and down shouting: "Yay! Berries, berries, berries!"

I walked out of the store with a smile on my face, the charm in my hands burning strong.

16

RACHEL

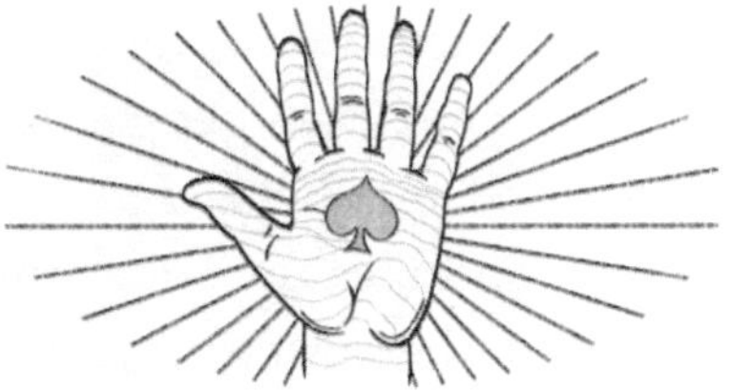

Rachel sat in a large chair her sycos had pillaged from a vacant house. It wasn't quite a throne, but it was made of heavy, carved mahogany, and though the cushions had been stained by years of dust and moisture, they were upholstered in rich crushed velvet. From this perch, she surveyed the heart of her palace—the lobby of the abandoned hospital. At her bidding, the broken glass and dead crows had been cleared away, but a miasma of death still lingered in the air, and the floor still glinted here and there with specks of glass the brooms had missed, sparking like bits of shattered diamonds. Her sycos lingered around her in various poses of repose, sleeping, chatting, playing cards, eating.

It was eerie how quickly they'd embraced this place as their home and her as their queen. But then, it should not have surprised her that lost people longed for a home or that lonely people longed for a family. That was what this was becoming, Rachel had come to realize. Her sycos acted like siblings to one another. Friendly. Fond. Sometimes jealous and competitive. And when they weren't calling her queen, these sad, lost souls called her mother.

That was one of the traditional titles of her rank, the obelisk had told her: Mother of Spades. But the symbolism of the name made her feel uneasy, too. Because spades were for digging graves; Morbus were the grave diggers, and their queen gave birth to destruction, desolation. And so her name had another meaning. Mother of Death.

Only for nine more months, she reminded herself.

And yet with all these people relying on her, it would make it harder to leave. Broken and sad as they were, her children had hearts and dreams. They were people. And now many of them relied on her for food and shelter and, most terrible of all, for their sense of hope and meaning. Plus, they relied on her power, which redirected the misfortune—which seemed to plague so many of them—away, onto others. The Mother of Spades had given a future to these bad luck people.

It was one of these children in particular who she watched right now: the one called Shade. The obelisk had drawn her attention to him, and she observed him with interest. He was a natural leader, that was obvious from the way he'd amassed his gang on the streets. But even here, his fellow sycos had almost immediately started looking to him when something needed to be done, gravitating toward him when they needed protection. Of the six young gangsters he'd brought in with him, four had departed—apparently finding Rachel's cult too weird a scene for their taste. The two that remained, Mo and Fitz were their names, seemed to be good workers and followed Shade implicitly—which probably contributed to the aura of leadership that surrounded him. And yet Shade kept himself apart, mostly. He was pacing now at the far end of the room, muttering to himself and shaking his head. Clearly conflicted about something.

He's an important one, the obelisk reminded her, speaking in her mind—such an irritating ability it had, to intrude on her thoughts. *He is one we must raise up. The time has come, but he will not accept his marks easily. There is someplace we must take him. Go, and bid him come.*

The obelisk was not in the habit of saying please, and if it wasn't obeyed it was quick to twist her insides painfully, a feeling as if the shard of stone were a fork and her guts were spaghetti. And so she obeyed. These days, she always obeyed.

"Shade," she called. Her voice cut through the chatter, reducing it to a hush instantly.

The young man looked to her, his brown eyes filled with some mingling of awe and dread and longing—the same way all of them looked at her—as he approached.

"Come with me," she said, and turned to walk away without glancing back. She sensed his hesitation. He was a strong-willed young man, a leader, not a follower, and it was against his nature to listen when someone ordered him around like a dog. And yet people listened to Rachel the god, even strong-willed boys who ruled the streets.

Without looking back, she heard his footsteps behind her.

She approached her car, which waited on the street. It was a long, black Mercedes. A few months back, the obelisk had told her she needed transportation that befitted a Morbus queen and directed her to a small office in Dearborn. The sign over the door had read Pathos Wealth Management. The man inside, Darby was his name, had looked more like an under-taker than an investment advisor, with his black suit stretched over a skinny, angular body and his mop of dark hair. The obelisk had introduced him as a loyal Morbus syco who oversaw the suit's finances. Darby had given her ninety thou-sand dollars in cash in a black carpet bag and had gone with her to the Mercedes dealership to purchase the vehicle. The salesman had taken the money and signed the car over to her without so much as a raised eyebrow. So far, Rachel had kept the car at the hospital and used it only for queenly business; she drove her old Honda every time she went home. Aggie was too smart to believe any lies she might tell about where she'd come up with the money for a fancy new luxury vehicle.

The young man, Shade, fidgeted as he rode next to her.

"Where are we going?" he asked, sounding uneasy.

He'll see... the obelisk inside Rachel said.

"You'll see," she echoed.

The obelisk directed Rachel down a side street and into a neighborhood where half the houses were abandoned—and the other half looked like they ought to be.

Stop here, the obelisk said, and Rachel pulled up to the curb next to a two-story brick house that was clearly uninhabited. Trash skittered across the lawn. Weeds jutted up from the cracks in a disjointed front walk. The top of the chimney had broken off, leaving a jagged spire that looked like a protruding broken bone. Tattered plastic covered the windows, and even that had ripped and now waved in the wind, like the shrouds of ghosts flapping goodbyes into the purple twilight.

"I ain't getting out," Shade said quietly, staring at the dashboard.

He will get out, the obelisk said. *Go around and open his door.*

Rachel did as she was told, walking around the car and opening the passenger door to look down at Shade, who sat slumped in the passenger seat like a truculent kid.

"Get out," she said, amazed by the steel in her voice.

"How'd you know about this place?" Shade whispered, still staring at the car's dash. She recognized what he was feeling, then. He wasn't being stubborn, and he wasn't angry. He was afraid.

"Out," she said again, more gently.

After a moment's hesitation, he did as she commanded, getting out of the car and taking a few unsteady steps across the sidewalk and into the desolate, overgrown yard of the empty house. At a spot a few feet off the home's cracked walkway, he knelt in the weeds and touched the ground with his fingertips. Rachel drifted over to stand next to him.

"I haven't been back since..." he said thickly.

"Since what?"

He sniffed. "You brought me here. You don't already know?"

His sister, the obelisk prompted.

"Your sister," Rachel said.

The young man shut his eyes and shook his head. "Damn. You read a file on me? You a psychic? What? You know what, never mind. I don't want to know."

His fingers closed on a tuft of grass, and he slowly ripped it out. It made Rachel think of tearing hair out of a person's head, which made her pips twinge hungrily. She shivered.

Without being prompted, she said, "Tell me about your sister."

Shade was silent for a long moment, kneeling there, staring down at the weedy ground. Just when Rachel was sure he wasn't going to answer, he said:

"She was my big sister. Natalie. Nat. She used to take care of me when my mom and grandma were at work, and they were at work all the time. She was like a mom to me. More than a mom, she..." He kept his head bowed, his face hidden by shadows, but the shuddering way he took a breath betrayed his emotion. "I was seven. She was thirteen. She was putting me to bed, and I'd left my favorite stuffed animal outside in the front yard. I was crying about it, you know, like kids do, saying I couldn't go to sleep without it or whatever. Being a brat. She went out here to get it for me... It was a stray bullet from the next block over. Some gang kids just showing off, trying to scare each other. The bullet... got her in the neck. By the time I realized she hadn't come back in... I went out front to look for her... she was just in a pool of blood, just lying in it. It was still gushing out, but every squirt was less than the last one. And I knew. I knew what that meant. I remember going to her. And my stuffed rabbit, she was still holding it, but it was soaked with blood. Just... soaked. I picked up my rabbit and held it and I just stared at her while the blood dripped onto my bare feet from the rabbit and I kept saying her name like Nat, wake up, Nat, Nat, Nat... only she just kept staring at the sky. All that blood..."

Shade clasped his hands together and Rachel knew he was holding the ghost of that stuffed rabbit, clutching it to his chest again.

"The cops came and looked at her," he went on. "They called my mom and Grams. I still remember them saying *one bullet* and shaking their heads. Like damn, just one stray-ass bullet. Just..."

"Bad luck," Rachel finished.

He looked up at her finally, tears glistening in his eyes.

"Yeah. Bad luck. This neighborhood is full of it."

"She died," Rachel said.

Shade slowly shook his head. "No. That's the worst part. Dying would have been better compared to how she is now."

Rachel nodded and took a step closer. "Shade, no matter how much respect you get in the streets, no matter how many friends or guns you have, the bad luck that killed your sister will always be out here. And some day, sooner or later, it'll get you too. You, everyone you care about. But I can help you, Shade. That's why you're here. I can give you power over bad luck."

He looked down at his hands, still clasped in front of him.

"I used to be like you," Rachel said gently. "Scared."

"I'm not scared," he said fiercely, but the haunted, wild look in his eyes gave away the truth, and he seemed to sense it. He looked away from her to stare at the empty house. Seeing ghosts.

"I used to be scared," Rachel went on gently. "But I'm not anymore."

He looked at her and his eyes narrowed. "Really. You're not scared of anything now?"

She met the boy's brown eyes and held his gaze for a long moment. "The only thing I'm scared of now," she said, "is myself."

This wrung from Shade a smile of bitter recognition. Being afraid of himself was something he understood, it seemed.

Good. You're getting through to him, the obelisk whispered in her mind.

Rachel held up her hands, letting that weird blacklight spill from her spade marks, onto the kneeling boy.

"You've been a victim in your life," she said. "And you've been the hand holding the gun. But I can make you the bullet's random trajectory. I can make you the moment the trigger is pulled, the angle of the shot, the breath of wind that makes a bullet find its mark—or miss. I can make you a prince of bad luck, Shade. It is the power of life—and death."

He shook his head. "Only God has that kind of power," he whispered.

"You're right," she said. "So be a god."

He looked up at her through the deepening twilight, a riot of conflicting emotions in his eyes.

Accept, Rachel willed the boy, her hex flaring. Because she saw now that the obelisk had been right, as usual. The boy was ripe and worthy. If he were to accept, that would be one more person besides Rachel to carry on the obelisk's mission. Which meant she'd be one step closer to bowing out, escaping.

It seemed that the boy would turn her down. His jaw clenched. He seemed on the verge of rising, maybe running away, maybe striking her. But kneeling there, bathed in the coaxing light of her hex, he was inclined to listen and believe. Making good choices took a certain amount of good luck, after all. And making bad choices—well, bad luck and bad choices went hand in hand. Some of the people living in Shade's neighborhood could attest to that.

At the obelisk's silent urging, Rachel slowly lifted the bottom of her shirt until her abdomen was exposed. Her stomach was perfectly flat these days, with little ridges of a six-pack exposed. She was the skinniest she'd been since having Aggie, for sure, and definitely not a healthy weight—but the weird part was the dark purplish glow radiating from her skin just below her navel. The obelisk shard glowed through her, illuminating an array of veins like forks of lightning. Again, she expected the boy to recoil, to stand and back away, but instead he pivoted toward her, still on his knees. She didn't have to instruct him. Intuitively, he reached out and placed his trembling hands on her stomach. Rachel felt the power flowing out of herself and into him, like a cold wind blowing through her flesh. Shade shut his eyes and sucked a breath, and Rachel repeated the words the obelisk was saying inside her mind.

"I now declare you a Morbus, lord of death, master of contagion, digger of graves. Rise, Shade, and be my Ten of Spades."

When the power was done flowing into the boy, Rachel felt exhausted and exhilarated and wild, like she might cry and laugh and pee her pants all at once.

Shade must have felt the same way because he was grinning and jittery as he rose to his feet, staring at the new marks on his hands.

"Wait. So I can make bad luck stuff happen now? Like you?" he asked.

Rachel nodded, and Shade grinned.

"Then there's something I've gotta do," he said.

17

AGGIE

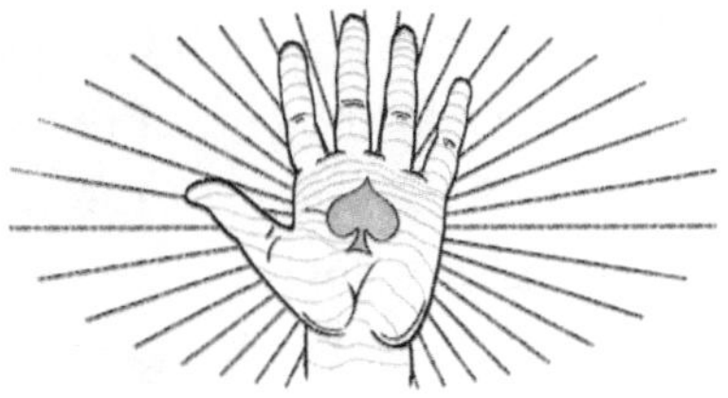

We were back on the road and Molly was looking in the rearview mirror again for probably the tenth time. This time, her stare lingered.

"Can you look forward, please?" I said. "You're stressing me out."

"Someone's following us," Molly replied.

Sure enough. We slowed down. Sped up. Changed lanes. Got off the highway and got back on. No matter what we did, a black sedan remained behind us, trailing like a distant shadow.

"Maybe Jack sent someone to protect us," Molly said, sounding a little dreamy.

"Maybe it's my sister's murderous goblin ex-boyfriend." Lorcan glared at Cleo.

"You dated a goblin?" Seemor sounded aghast.

"Obviously, you don't know my sister," Lorcan grunted. "Nothing's too depraved for her."

"*Obviously*," Cleo replied, "you've never seen a goblin's—"

"Okay," I interrupted. "We could banter all day, but it's not going to get us any closer to finding out who's following us."

"What do you suggest, queenie?" Lorcan said.

I looked at everyone in the car—Molly. Lorcan. Seemor. Cleo. My crew. Could I trust them? If it came to bullets and blood, would they have my back? I guessed I might find out sooner than I'd expected.

"I suggest we confront them," I said.

❧♡♤◇♧❧

At the next rest area, we laid our trap. It was a simple plan, and I was the bait. Molly drove to the end of the lot and parked. I got out alone and walked back toward the restroom. Seemor was to follow just behind me, invisible. Once I'd gone a good distance, Lorcan and Cleo would also get out of the car and lurk by one of the picnic tables, pretending to vape while keeping lookout for the black car and its occupants. Once I was in the bathroom and our pursuers had followed me in, Cleo would enter so I wasn't alone. Lorcan would charge in, too, if he saw signs of a fight. Molly, our non-fighter, would stay in the car with the doors locked, ready in case we needed to make a quick getaway.

As I walked toward the restroom, I scanned the rows of cars for the black sedan. It was twilight, and even though we weren't in the deep south, the air already seemed warmer, tinged with the flower-blossom scent of late summer rather than the bonfires-and-pumpkins smell of Michigan in late September. In this moment, under a lavender sky with a warm breeze brushing my cheeks, it seemed as if everything might be alright. I might succeed. Mom might be okay. Jack and I might live happily ever after. I might even enjoy being queen. Optimism bloomed until I remembered the danger I was in. If I didn't stay sharp now, I might get myself killed before any of my daydreams had a chance to come true.

The interior of the rest stop consisted of high, beamed ceilings with tiled floors and wood-paneled walls. Posters reminding drivers to wear their seatbelts and yield to construction workers lined the walls, along with a map of Southern Ohio with a little star telling visitors *you are here*. I lingered near the map, pretending to study our route. If I hadn't been listening for it, I would never have heard the shuffle of Seemor's feet behind me.

"Hey," I whispered. "I have to actually go to the bathroom. *Do not* follow me inside."

The disembodied response came from the empty space just to my right.

"Don't worry, I've watched you guzzling coffee for the past two hours. I have no desire to see what happens next."

I entered the bathroom and sat doing my business, a dagger in hand in case an enemy vaulted over the stall door. In my other hand, I held my phone. No texts from Mom. No texts from Jack. That was fine, I told myself. I needed to be focused on keeping alive anyway, not texting. Still—

A footstep. Slow and cautious, the ball of someone's foot gritting against the dirty bathroom floor. I held my breath, then clenched my dagger in my teeth, wiped as fast as possible, and listened. Another footstep. This wasn't the gait of someone walking into the bathroom to pee. It was the measured tread of a hunter stalking their prey, and the only prey in here was me.

I pulled up my pants, then readied myself, drawing my gun to brandish it along with my dagger. I slid back the lock, then shoved the stall door open and stepped out, scanning left, toward the entrance, for enemies. Nothing. I scanned right, toward a tiled wall with a mirror on it. Nothing. I walked down the row of stalls, kicking each one open in turn. All were empty.

"Seemor, if you're in here, I swear to God…"

No answer.

I gave a shuddering sigh and rubbed the back of one hand over my eyes. I was just tired, wound too tight. When I got back in the car, I should try to get some sleep.

I stepped toward the sinks—and a figure glitched and wavered into existence in front of me, startling me so that I almost screamed.

The figure wore a midnight blue hoodie pulled up to cast a shadow over their face. Camo-patterned cargo pants ended at a pair of high-top basketball shoes. The figure was a few inches taller than I was, too tall to be a sprite and too short to be a sylph. There were other luck beings besides those beyond the rift. Goblins, leprechauns, jinn, and dozens of others whose names I'd read during my studies in the Valentines' library but didn't remember now, though not all of them had the ability to shift invisible. The only thing that really mattered was whether this person was friend or foe—and from the way they'd snuck up on me, I thought I had my answer. Flaring charm, I aimed my gun at the intruder's heart—but when I saw they held no weapon, my finger hesitated on the trigger.

"Who are you?" I demanded. "What do you want?"

"Those are the wrong questions," the figure said. I couldn't tell whether the voice was male or female.

I tilted my head. "Alright," I said. "What question should I be asking?"

"Who can you trust?" The hooded figure's words echoed faintly in the tiled room, seeming to hang in the silence. "You're heading for a trap."

It took me a second to find my voice. "Okay. Who can I trust, then?" I said. "You? A peri who snuck up on me in a rest area bathroom?"

The person's hands shifted slightly, and I saw that their palms were glowing—but the light there wasn't the purplish black of the dark suits or the red of the diamonds and hearts. This glow was an eerie blue-green. But I couldn't see what shape the pip was, if there was one.

"Watch out for your husband," the intruder said in a hissed whisper. Then whoever it was moved and glitched out of existence at the same moment. Spooked, I stumbled backward. My back hit the wall, and the gun in my hand went off. The mirror in front of me crackled into a disjointed spiderweb of cracks.

I braced myself for a strike from my now-invisible attacker. But even over the sound of my heart pounding and the gun's report still ringing in my ears, I could hear their footfalls retreating out of the room.

A moment later, Seemor burst in, with Lorcan and Cleo a step behind.

Lorcan cast around, seeing me safe but spooked, then noticed the broken mirror. "Bollocks. What happened?"

I opened my mouth to explain, but the stranger's words echoed in my mind: *Who can you trust?*

"I... thought I saw something," I stammered, still catching my breath. I shouldn't have been so shaken up, but something about the confrontation had the quality of a nightmare—being trapped like that with a stranger who could blink in and out of existence at will... it was creepy. And those glowing blue-green hands... Plus, there was something else. I couldn't quite put my finger on what it was, but it bothered me. The figure had been familiar somehow. And powerful. Whoever it was, I could sense their power, a roiling disturbance tugging on my own charm— but whether it was charm or hex the stranger exuded, I couldn't tell.

I thought of the person who'd been watching me at the school, who'd hexed the tree branch down onto my head when I tried to follow. Could this have been the same person? If so, who were they? Why were they following me? What did they want?

"Well, you managed to kill your own reflection," Lorcan muttered, gesturing toward the mirror. "Congratulations. The queen trial should be a breeze."

"Shut up," Seemor told Lorcan. Then, to me: "The black sedan didn't show up. We must have lost them."

"Or they smelled our trap and stayed hid," Cleo added.

I nodded lamely, still too jittery to trust myself to say much.

"Let's get out of here before the cops come and arrest us for vandalizing the place," Seemor said, shuffling back toward the door. Lorcan followed. Cleo paused, giving the place one last, narrow-eyed inspection before she left, as if something didn't quite add up and she was trying to figure out what.

"Be right there," I said, slipping the gun into the holster at my back.

And I washed my trembling hands twenty-three times.

18

RACHEL

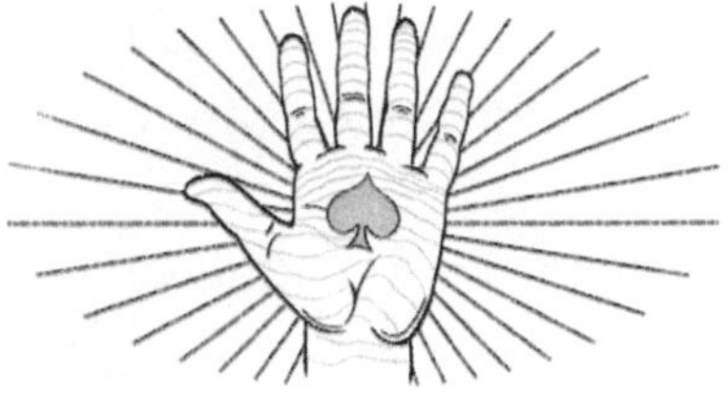

Araucous greeting met Rachel and Shade as they stepped into the restaurant. The shouts alarmed Rachel for a moment, until Shade started receiving hugs and claps and handshakes and pats on the back from the restaurant's many smiling patrons. It was a hero's greeting if she'd ever seen one.

The place was called Pico's, a fact Rachel had learned from the faded sign out front, which featured a large cartoon hamburger. Inside, the décor was straight out of the late 80s, with brown woodgrain tiles on the floor, Formica tabletops, and rattan lampshades hovering above booths of dark wood. Dated as it may have been, the restaurant was well lit and meticulously clean; its energy held the effervescence that seemed to permeate any well-loved hangout. In other words, it was a good luck place.

A small man with a long, thin beard wearing chef's whites emerged from a pair of swinging doors and clapped Shade in an embrace so fierce Rachel was afraid they might both topple over.

"Who's this? Your parole officer?" the man asked, breaking free from Shade and side-eyeing Rachel.

Shade laughed. "Nah. This is Rachel. Rachel, this is my cousin Moses."

"Miss Rachel. A pleasure," Cousin Moses said with a winning smile. "Not a parole officer, then you must be...?"

"A queen," Shade supplied.

"Oh ho! Your queen?" Moses was clearly amused by the idea.

"Everyone's queen," Shade said. "Y'all just don't know it yet. Hey, get us some of that poutine. Extra gravy. And a couple of orange pops."

"You know where the soda machine is," Moses said, but he bustled away all the same.

Shade gestured to a counter and he and Rachel both took seats on stools. Their view was a rack that held about three dozen fresh pies and a window into the kitchen where Moses was busy with a deep fryer.

"So," Rachel prompted, glancing around.

"This is my place," Shade said, gesturing proudly around the room. "Well, it's half mine, half Moses'. I put up the money to buy the business and the startup cash, plus I provide security, and Moses puts in the day-to-day work."

"You provided the cash," Rachel said. "From your other enterprises?"

Shade nodded.

"Drugs?" Rachel asked, keeping her voice low.

Shade snorted and shook his head. "Hell no. Anyone slings

anything harder than weed around here, we bounce them straight out. My favorite auntie died from that shit. I don't put up with it. Nah. Our hustle was car parts."

Rachel was surprised. "Car parts?"

"Some of the car companies based here are supposed to have a certain percentage of their cars made with American parts, right? So they buy from American suppliers. But it's expensive to make parts in the US, so some of these suppliers actually get their shit from China, slap a US label on it, then pass it along. Sometimes they can make more money buying the part from China and relabeling it than they can by making the parts here. So my crew and I act as middlemen, helping them move their product without drawing attention."

"So you're an auto parts smuggler?" she asked.

"You got it," he said, sipping the pop Moses had set in front of him.

Rachel sipped hers, too. It was delicious.

"This is all top secret, now," Shade said. "I mean, you don't seem like the type to go and talk about a guy's business model, but..."

"Of course," Rachel agreed.

Moses bustled back over and placed a plastic basket in front of them. It was stacked high with French fries topped with gravy and white cheese. The first fry Rachel put in her mouth tasted amazing. For a moment, she was surprised by how hungry she was, but when she tried to remember the last time she ate, she drew a blank.

For a long time, the two were quiet as they devoured the gravy-drenched fries. When the basket was nearly empty, Shade glanced around. "This place is Moses' dream. The guy's got six kids to feed. And we provide scholarships, too. Anyone working here, we match their wages with money toward college tuition."

"Sounds perfect," Rachel said, though she had a feeling there was a *but* coming.

"It was," Shade said. "Until last year, when our new neighbors showed up across the street."

He stood and walked toward the exit. Rachel followed. As she went, the feeling of *the work* rose in her, that sensation of restless need that was both exhilarating and frightening—frightening, because it usually meant she was about to do something terrible.

They emerged into the night and regarded the fancy new chain fast-food restaurant across the street. Cars wrapped around the building in a serpentine line, waiting to access the drive-thru. Through the plate-glass windows, Rachel could tell the place was stuffed with people. Though not empty by any means, Pico's was dead in comparison.

"Our sales dropped by sixty percent when they went in," Shade said bitterly. "That was our profit margin, gone. And our landlord raised the rent on our building by ten percent because he said the neighborhood was coming up. You believe that? Damn gentrification. This place is our livelihood. Our future. Not just for us, but for our whole family. And our workers."

Rachel nodded, then glanced back across the street. *The work* was calling to her now, a yearning as delicious as any she'd ever experienced. *Give in,* it whispered in her bones. *Give in, and enjoy.*

"If they suffered some bad luck, though..." Shade said, nodding across the street. "How does it work?"

She stepped up next to him. "Open your hands and face them toward the restaurant over there. Like this..." She opened her hands and showed him. The spade pips on her palms pulsed with mischievous light. "Feel the power inside you. Then look over there and imagine fire in the wires. The fuse box won't trip. Fire bursting from the stoves. Gas lines breaking."

Shade set his focus on the restaurant across the street, then shut his eyes—a good student.

"Imagine it, then let your hex go," Rachel instructed. "One, two, three..."

Power throbbed from Rachel's hands—a delirious relief—and she saw light pulsing from Shade's palms, too.

"Damn. It feels good," he muttered.

For a moment, nothing happened. Shade opened his eyes.

"Did we do it right?" he asked. "Or—?"

"Just wait," Rachel said, and she glanced at the time on her phone. They had more to do tonight. So much to do. But it was all in a night's work for a queen.

Seconds ticked by, and across the street, nothing seemed to happen. Then, the screams began. First one, then two, then a half dozen patrons spilled from the doors of the restaurant, shrieking and yelling. The last few to emerge were on fire, and they dove to the ground, rolling to extinguish themselves while others tried to smother the flames on their bodies with T-shirts or hoodies. Thirty seconds later and the whole restaurant roared like a funeral pyre, its towering flames licking up toward the night sky, smoke billowing faster and faster, making Rachel think of a massive archjinni.

Shade chuckled and shook his head, then went serious again, looking almost reverent as he stood there, bathed in firelight.

"So that's what bad luck can do," he whispered in awe. When he looked at her, Rachel saw a flash of little-boy vulnerability, even desperation, in that hard, man's face of his. "Queen Rachel, there's one more thing I need to do. I'd be forever grateful if—will you help me? Please?"

19

AGGIE

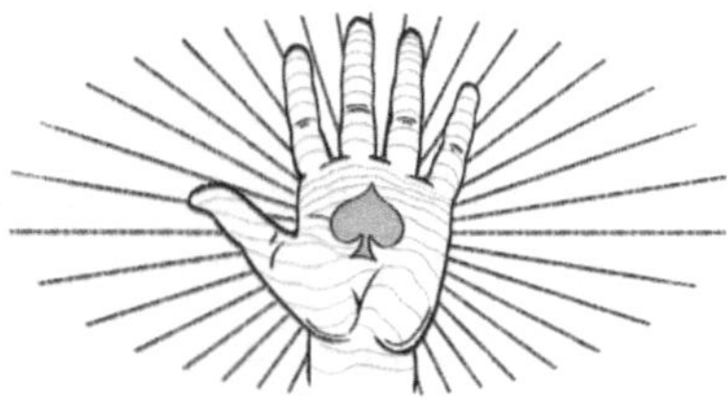

It was dark when we rolled into Nashville. That sounded like a song lyric, and there was something musical and poetic in the way the streetlights and the neon bar signs lent a pink illumination to the gray clouds scudding by above. Despite the fact I'd come here to face what might be a deadly challenge, some momentous energy hung in the air. It was a good luck city, I decided. Maybe all the young musicians drifting into town upped the charm of the place. Whatever it was, I felt the pips on my hands burning with a restless energy.

"So what's the plan, Ip Man?" Molly asked as we pulled up to a stoplight in front of a honky-tonk bar.

"Ip Man?"

She shrugged. "He's a martial arts guy. I've been watching kung fu movies with Braden and his friends," Molly said.

"Ah, Braden." I arched an eyebrow. "Are you and Claudette going to have a kung fu showdown over *him* one of these days?"

Molly flushed. "No," she scoffed unconvincingly. "We're just friends."

"As entertaining as your little girl crushes are, do you two have any idea where we're going?" Cleo said from the backseat.

"Actually, I do," I said, smug. The ace had given me three pieces of information about our destination. One: it was in Nashville. Two: it was a castle. Three: it was located on a river. So on the drive down, I'd used real estate websites to stalk properties that fit the description. I held the phone up now to show everyone the results.

"Whoa," Molly said, glancing at the picture on my phone screen. "That is indeed a castle."

"And it's on the Cumberland River," I pointed out. It would be extrapolating too much to say this *had* to be the place, but the odds seemed good.

"Is it for sale?" Molly asked.

"Not anymore." I scanned the data on the site. "Looks like it sold two years ago. For twenty-one million."

Seemor gave a low whistle. "Who bought it?"

I scanned the site some more, then shook my head. "It doesn't say."

"Well," Cleo said. "I guess we'll find out."

We were all hungry and tired, but also eager to scope out our destination. So we made our way through a series of stoplights and out of the city center, passing industrial areas then suburbs before finally making our way into an area where the lots and the houses got progressively larger. Gated communities. Estates. Horse ranches. Then forest.

"Are we close?" Molly asked, craning her neck to get a glance at my phone.

"I'm *close* to roasting this little sprite over a spit and eating him," Lorcan grumbled. He'd been complaining about being hungry for an hour.

"Watch out," Seemor said. "I'd give you indigestion. I'd also stab you in the face before you got a hand on me."

Lorcan grunted. "You couldn't beat me in a fight if I had both hands tied behind my back and a bag over my head."

"Someone should put a bag over that ugly-ass head," Seemor said.

Cleo laughed. "I'm starting to like this sprite," she said.

"He'd be an improvement, given your taste in men," Lorcan said.

Cleo smoldered for a second, then lunged, reaching over Seemor's head to grab her brother by the throat.

"Hey," Molly pointed through the windshield. "What's that?"

The backseat battle ended as everyone leaned toward the nearest window to get a look.

Ahead, spotlights pointing up into the sky waved and criss-crossed. We rounded a bend in the road and found ourselves suddenly in a traffic jam. Shiny, fancy cars—Bentleys, Mercedes, Maybachs and Rolls-Royces—were all lined up to turn down a driveway then pass through a security checkpoint manned by half a dozen burly men in sequined sport coats. Behind them stood a wrought-iron fence and gate, and beyond that loomed a massive stone castle. The front yard was probably four hundred feet long, and even from here I could tell the place was festooned with lights and flowers, its grounds studded with fountains and populated with string quartets, bronze sculptures, and ornate marble gazebos.

"Whoa," Molly breathed.

We inched forward in the line of luxury cars, and I was glad that our Escalade didn't stand out too much among the other shiny, new vehicles.

"Should I turn? Should we try to get in?" Molly asked.

"No," Seemor, Cleo, and I all said at once. They were probably eyeing the burly security guards, just like I was.

As we rolled past, the wrought-iron gate swung shut, and that's when I saw it: at its center was a huge red-enameled diamond.

❤ ♠ ◇ ♣

"The Diamantes? My queen trial is to steal a treasure chest from *the Diamonds*?" I demanded—of no one in particular.

We'd holed up at a steakhouse a few miles away from the castle to reboot, and my crew was collectively demolishing a gigantic fried onion. I turned my attention to Lorcan, who'd been suspiciously quiet ever since we'd arrived in Nashville.

"Lorcan," I said his name slowly and reproachfully. "You know the Diamantes. Whose house was that?"

He shifted in his seat as if suddenly uncomfortable, then took out his phone.

"Are you texting me the answer?" I asked irritably.

A second later, strumming acoustic guitar and twangy Telecaster wafted from the phone speaker, then a voice broke in, strong and lovely with just a hint of honey-sweet country accent.

> *We were so young*
> *That lost summer*
> *We were both sure*
> *It would all last forever*
> *We were so wrong*
> *Everything changed*

"Ugh, I hate this song," Cleo muttered, chomping a bite of fried onion.

I wasn't a big fan of country music either, but when the chorus kicked in, I couldn't help but break into song—and Molly did too.

> *The country fair left town*
> *The rides shut down*
> *You were my funnel cake*
> *My sweet summer lemonade*
> *But the Ferris wheel's gone*
> *And you moved along*
> *My carnie boy*

By the last line, Molly and I were both belting it out at such an embarrassing volume that our waitress chuckled as she brought our plates of food.

"Y'all big Diamond Queen fans too, eh? You know, she lives right down the road." She smiled at us, then bustled away.

I turned back to Lorcan, fiery. "Wait—you mean Diamond Queen is—?"

"*The* Diamond Queen?" Lorcan said dryly. "My, you should've been a detective."

Diamond Queen was one of the biggest country stars in the world, and bar none the world's most famous drag queen. Her latest single, "Carnie Boy," had reached the top of the charts and had achieved that love-hate level of ubiquity where everyone was sick of hearing it yet felt compelled to sing along whenever it came on. It was so catchy and over-the-top that it flew way past *cheesy* and orbited all the way back around to *cool* again. She had her own reality show, her own line of fashion apparel, and her own record label, which, last I heard, had become one of the largest in Nashville. It was impossible to watch TV or scroll through a social media feed without seeing Diamond Queen's smiling, glammed-up face. I was generally oblivious to pop culture except for its most nerdy permutations, so the fact that I even knew who Diamond Queen was said it all: she was everywhere.

"I thought luck gods liked to keep a low profile," I said.

"Not DQ," Lorcan said. "It irritates the other Diamantes for sure, but what can they do? She's the queen."

"Why isn't she in Detroit, with the rift?" I asked. The rift was an energy nexus, a portal between the worlds of the peri—luck beings—and humans that could only be seen by peri or by luck gods. It tended to shift every year or so, and when it did, the luck gods migrated with it, because they were at their most powerful when they were near the rift. No one knew why, exactly; it was just the way it had always been. It had manifested in Detroit a few months before, and that's why the luck gods were there. When it moved again, they would move too—something I didn't like to think too hard about.

"Luck gods like to be near the rift," Lorcan agreed. "But they don't *have* to be. The Diamantes, especially, have to spread out to oversee their multinational corporations. DQ has an entertainment business to run, and she needs to be in Nashville to do it."

He stuffed another large glob of fried onion into his mouth.

"She's not just a performer, she's the head of a business empire and the high commander of the Diamantes," Lorcan went on, chewing. "She's also the most powerful and ruthless luck god alive."

Given the luck gods I knew and how ruthless and powerful they were, that was a pretty bold claim.

"Most powerful... What about the king?" I asked.

Lorcan shook his head. "The Diamante king was named

Tanner Edwards, but no one's heard from him for twenty years. Speculation is, DQ killed him, or sent him into exile."

"That makes Diamond Queen a high queen," I said. Traditionally in the luck god hierarchy, kings ranked higher than queens and hence were more powerful. But several times in the history of suits, queens had ascended to the more powerful position. Normally, it happened when a king died; the ace would elevate a more experienced queen and the less experienced new king who came in would be subservient to her. It wasn't unheard of, but it was unusual. And it meant that we wouldn't just be facing off with a queen—we'd be up against a queen with king-level luck power.

This was a lot to take in. I'd anticipated that there might be some sort of baddie guarding the chest the ace had sent me after. Queen trials were supposed to be a *trial* after all, not some easy-breezy road trip. But I never imagined I'd be up against another good luck god, especially one so much more powerful than I was.

And how many sycos did she have lurking around that gargantuan estate of hers? We'd seen at least a dozen just driving past. Breaking into a normal celebrity's house would be crazy. But a celebrity who also happened to be a luck deity? It seemed decidedly dangerous, even suicidal. And yet we had to pull it off somehow.

"Helloo?" Molly waved a hand in front of my face. "Your gigantic steak isn't going to eat itself there, missy."

I shook myself out of my reverie and tried to eat. But when I cut the steak, its juices ran red, and my stomach clenched. Inevitably, that was not the only blood that would flow before this was all over.

I glanced up to find Lorcan typing away on his phone, and my heart stuttered inside my chest. Lorcan worked for the Diamantes. He would warn them—of course he would!— unless I stopped him, fast.

Acting on impulse, I reached out and slapped the phone out of his hand, charming as it flew so that it landed right under the heel of our server's boot as she walked past. *Crunch* went the screen.

"What in the hell?" Lorcan blustered.

The server bent down, distraught, and picked it up.

"Oh no!" she said, bringing the phone over to our table. "I am so sorry."

"No worries," I said, quickly snatching it from her hand. "Really. It's under warranty."

As soon as she turned away, I dropped the phone into my water glass. Lorcan glared at me and crossed his arms over his chest.

"Really, you think that'll keep me from ratting you out to the Diamantes if I want to? There's a phone store on every block in this town."

"Not one that's open after eight PM."

Cleo huffed a sigh and stood. "I'm going to the little girl's room while you two work this out. I'll be right back."

"Look," Lorcan said when she was gone. "Unless you're willing to kill me with that steak knife, you're not going to stop me from warning the Diamonds. If you're smart you'll give up, head back to your suit, and tell them you changed your mind about being queen. DQ is powerful as hell, and she's got more guards than Fort Knox in that estate of hers. You have no chance of stealing from her. Zero."

"And she's got *leeeegs for miles!*" Molly said, breaking into another Diamond Queen song—one about a plucky young stripper putting herself through community college with her pole dancing skills. Molly drank the last of her water until the straw gurgled, then stood. "Sorry. I've gotta make a tinkle, too. Care to join, Aggs?"

"I'm good," I said. I did have to pee, actually, but I was loath to let Lorcan out of my sight. I definitely couldn't kill him with a steak knife, but I had to find some way to keep him from tipping us off to the Diamond Queen.

"I'll bring Seemor his food," Lorcan said, scooting out of the booth and grabbing the takeout box for Seemor, who was waiting in the car—since we didn't think the residents of Nashville were ready to dine with a sprite.

I flared charm in a generalized way, just hoping it would somehow stall things until I could figure out how to deal with Lorcan.

And sure enough, at that moment, the family of five sitting next to us stood to go, blocking the aisle. In the traffic jam, Molly and Lorcan were forced to pause for a moment. As they stood there side by side, the solution to my problem came to me in a stroke of evil genius.

I aimed my hands at them, palms out.

God, forgive me, I thought. But it wasn't divine forgiveness I'd need; it was Molly's. Because there was only one way I could think of to cement Lorcan's loyalty, and that was to make him fall madly in love with someone loyal to me. And so for the second time, I released my charm and used Cupid's Arrow on Molly—binding her to Lorcan. The effect was instantaneous. They paused, looked at one another, then started making out right there in the middle of the restaurant.

20

RACHEL

The Queen of Spades and her newly minted Ten stood watching *Wheel of Fortune*, the TV's colors flashing across the otherwise dark bedroom of the residential care facility. It had been a somewhat long drive—they were on Eight Mile near Botsford Hospital—but the obelisk had urged Rachel to indulge their recruit. Rachel remembered what an emotional process taking the mark of spades had been for her, so she understood. She also felt the itching, restless burn of *the work* in her hands, calling to her yet again. Burning down the restaurant had left her flush with hex, but there was no mistaking the feeling that there was more to be done.

"He needs a vowel," Shade muttered, nodding toward the TV.

"True love never dies," Rachel said, finishing the puzzle.

Her mind went to her husband, Kevin. Aggie's father. Her true love who had, in fact, died. Bad luck.

Shade's attention shifted to the woman lying in the hospital bed. She was large, her body an indistinct blob among the hospital gown and sheets. She had a breathing tube down her throat and another tube up her nose, both affixed with tape, but despite all that, Rachel could still see the resemblance between Shade and his sister.

"Nat was smart. Beautiful. Funny," he said. "Now she can't even get up and go piss. My auntie used to come here and talk to her for hours, but they'd scanned her brain. She wasn't hearing nothing. Talking to her was just a waste of breath. Still, I'd come here sometimes after school, too, and just hold her hand."

Shade approached the bed and took the woman's hand, his thumb rubbing the back of her knuckles.

"But that was for me, not her. I knew she couldn't tell I was here. All she could do was breathe and hurt. I talked to my aunt lots of times about taking her off the machines and letting her go, but she wouldn't do it. And the doctors wouldn't listen to me." He shook his head.

Rachel stepped up next to Shade and saw tears glistening on his face. He held up his hands, aiming the pip's dark lights at his sister. Then his face crumpled into a sob, and he hid his eyes with his hands.

"I can't. I can't do it," he said, falling to his knees and leaning his forehead against the bed as if it were an altar. "Will you do it, Queen Rachel. Please?"

Rachel placed a comforting hand on his head, then turned her attention to the unconscious woman. The work thrummed in her now, a delicious, urgent need.

Bad luck, to have your organs fail you, sister. And yet sometimes bad luck could be a mercy.

Rachel reached into herself, searching for some reticence,

some qualm, some impulse to hesitate. Disturbingly, she found none. Had the obelisk erased her conscience? Did she feel nothing because of the months of sleep deprivation, hunger, and depravity the obelisk had subjected her to? Was she brainwashed? Or was this who she'd been all along underneath it all, a sociopath waiting for the stone to come and give her an excuse to be the empty, remorseless person she'd always been, deep down? Or had losing Kevin done it? Did the loss of a soulmate leave a person with only half a soul? Whatever the answer, she felt nothing more than she would have at the prospect of crushing a bug underfoot. That was probably bad. And yet, she felt no guilt either. She felt nothing but *the work*, and *the work* felt good.

Next to her, Shade sobbed, great, wet-sounding heaves wracking his whole body. *I can set two people free tonight,* Rachel thought. *The obelisk was right about the good that bad luck can do.*

"Please, Queen," Shade sobbed again. "Please, Mother."

And so Rachel raised both her hands, bathing Shade's sister in the eerie, unnatural light of her spade marks. And with just a slight twist of her will, Rachel extinguished the tenuous flame of the woman's life.

21

AGGIE

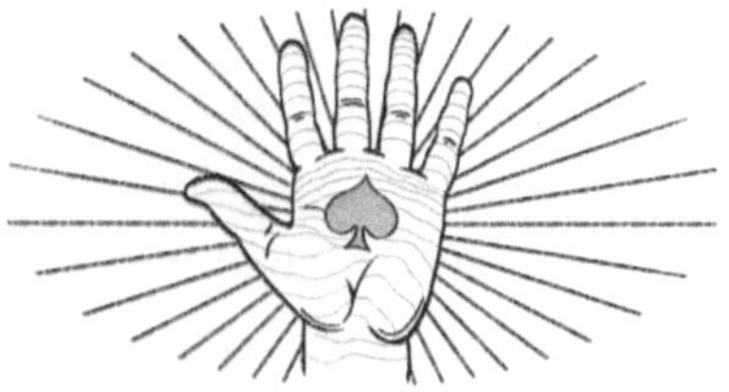

"Excuse me!" I snapped at Molly and Lorcan for the third time. They stopped tickling one another but continued holding hands, their pinkies linked like they were a couple of twitterpated freshmen. We'd made it to a hotel in a touristy part of the city and booked ourselves a pair of adjoining rooms. Since Seemor was the only one of us capable of turning invisible, I'd sent him to go and swipe some acceptable disguises. I was trying to play criminal mastermind with Cleo and come up with a viable plan for breaking into Diamond Queen's mansion, but it was awfully hard with Lorcan and Molly's constant canoodling.

Yes, I felt terrible for Cupiding my best friend for the second time, but the more she and Lorcan fondled and smooched, the more my guilt was replaced with annoyance. Charm notwithstanding, neither one seemed to be resisting their role in the least.

"We're attempting to plan a death-defying heist here," I reminded them.

"More like a suicide mission," Lorcan agreed. "But I'd die a thousand deaths if it would make my fookie-wookie happy."

"It *so* does," Molly beamed. "I really appreciate you helping Aggie like this. You are seriously the sweetest guy in the world."

They drifted in for another kiss, Lorcan's gold front teeth glinting.

Cleo leaned into me. "You magicked them with some of your hearts voodoo, didn't you?" she accused.

"Uh," I started to deny it, then realized Cleo was far too clever to believe any other explanation. "Yes, okay? I didn't want him to go to warn the Diamantes. It was the only way I could think of to ensure his loyalty."

"What about my loyalty?" she said. "Are you going to magic me in love with the mutt Seemor when he gets back? Or you?" She drifted toward me until our faces were awkwardly close.

"I don't know," I said, leaning back slightly. "Are you going to warn the Diamantes?"

She held my gaze for a long moment, then shrugged. "Nah. I don't have much love for those pretentious misers, myself. Just kick me another mil in gold and I'll keep your secret."

"Just another mil." I rolled my eyes. But I didn't have much choice, did I? "Fine."

I glanced again at the couple on the couch, making out.

"You're not mad?" I asked Cleo, nodding toward them. Molly had thrown a leg over Lorcan's, and his hand was creeping up her thigh.

Cleo snorted. "Mad? Hell no. Lorcan was so hung up on that stupid queen of yours—he needs some nookie. Let them go into the other room and have a go, I say. Get it out of their system."

"No!" I said, aghast.

She shrugged her indifference, which I supposed was better than being mad at me.

I clapped to get the attention of my star-crossed lovers.

"Hey! Guys, please. Eyes forward." I tapped the hotel stationery on the table in front of us with the pen. On it I had drawn a rough sketch of the mansion based on information from Google Maps and the real estate site, which helpfully had a 3D floorplan listed.

We'd done some research and found out that a big country music awards show was coming up in two days. Diamond Queen always threw a massive, three-day party ahead of the event, inviting a cross-section of famous music stars, Hollywood actors, and music industry executives. The party we'd witnessed earlier was night two. That made tomorrow the final party night. The plan was obvious. Disguise ourselves as guests, get into the party, and use the crowd as a cover to search for the chest. But as the saying goes, the devil was in the details—and we were trying to hammer those out now.

"So, you were saying?" I prompted Cleo.

She pointed to the paper. "Seemor goes invisible and climbs over the wall here. He opens this back gate and lets me and Aggie in. We split up and start searching for the chest. Seemor gets a hold of a party invitation and brings it out to the two of you. You come in by car, dressed as a glamorous rock 'n' roll couple."

"Why don't we just sneak in with you?" Lorcan asked.

"Because we need you to bring in the car," Cleo said, "so we're ready for a quick getaway. Pay attention."

"Besides," I added, "we don't know how big or how heavy this chest is. We might not be able to get very far carrying it on foot. This way, we just have to get it into the back of the SUV."

"Aggie is so smart," Molly said, turning to Lorcan. "Isn't she so smart?"

"Not as smart as you, my sweet cream pie," Lorcan said, and the two rubbed noses.

"Jesus in a trench coat," Cleo said, rubbing her forehead as if staving off a migraine.

"Guys, no more PDA. I'm serious," I said, then turned my attention back to the floor plan. "I'll search the house systematically, starting with the basement and working my way up to the top floor. Cleo will search the outbuildings, and the two of you will search the grounds and keep an eye out for—"

I heard a sound in the hallway outside and paused, my hand on the hilt of my dagger. My thoughts snapped back to that hooded figure in the rest station bathroom. *You're walking into a trap.*

Maybe I was. The ace who'd burned down my house wasn't exactly the most trustworthy person. And yet she'd burned the house down to get me into the suit. And she'd picked me as queen over all the other Valentine women. It didn't make sense that she'd done all that just to send me off to die, did it? If she wanted me dead, there were lots of simpler, more convenient, and more reliable ways to make it happen. Besides, why should I heed the warning of a mysterious stranger who was stalking me?

Whoever was walking by in the hallway passed, and I exhaled. When I looked back at Molly and Lorcan, they were nuzzling cheek-to-cheek.

"Come on. You guys have got to be maxed out on oxytocin by now," I griped.

"We're paying attention," Lorcan said. "You search the house, Cleo searches the outbuildings, we come in by car and search the grounds, Seemor stays invisible and keeps lookout."

"We keep in touch via text," Cleo said. "Those of us who still have a phone, that is."

"Aw, poor Lorcie," Molly said, pooching out her lip. "Don't worry. I'll share mine with you."

I sighed. "If we get caught because the two of you are hiding out in some bedroom of that mansion, I swear—"

But who could I blame but myself? I was the one who'd made my friend fall in love against her will—again. I remembered all those times people had warned me about Jack, saying he was ruthless. Wouldn't they say the same about me? If I kept on down this path, what would I become? A good queen and a terrible person, probably. But there was no point in second-guessing myself. If I hadn't done something about Lorcan he'd have certainly ratted us out, and the Diamantes and their sycos would be planning an ambush for us. I'd done what I had to do.

"So what do we do if something goes wrong?" Molly asked.

I stared at the floor plan, chewing the end of the pen. "Get out however you can. Stick together. Leave me if you have to."

"Right," Cleo agreed. "We both have leprechaun keys—since my dumbass brother gave our people's most sacred treasure to this... *young lady*."

"Careful," Lorcan rumbled.

"...so we can evacuate out any door, if necessary," Cleo finished.

"If you can get out in the car, that's best," I went on. "But if not, you can escape on foot by going out this back gate, here."

Having presented our plan, Cleo and I paused. I was proud of what we'd come up with, but instead of applause, Lorcan gave us a smirk.

"Anything to add, Lorcan?" I asked. "You're the one who knows about Diamond Queen and her estate."

He snorted. "I already said, it's a suicide mission. They'll have electronic surveillance. Tons of syco thugs. Sharpshooters. Sprites. Guard dogs."

"So going in through the back gate...?" Cleo prompted.

He shook his head. "Don't think for a second they'll leave it unguarded. Go in or out that way and they'll know. The only way in will be through the front door. And they'll never let us through without an invitation."

We all lapsed into a sullen silence, thinking. After a moment, I perked up.

"Oh," I laughed, pulling out the golden leprechaun key I had in a chain around my neck. "Why didn't we think of this before. If it can get us out, it can get us in, right? We'll just—"

Lorcan and Cleo were both shaking their heads.

"Leprechaun doors create an energy signature," Cleo explained. "The Diamantes have developed ways to detect that energy. Got tired of being robbed blind by our people, I imagine. We walk in there through a leprechaun door, we'll set off so many alarms the place will light up like a Christmas tree. It's a no-go."

I shut my eyes in exasperation, resisting the urge to pick up my floor plan and crush it in my hands. *Okay, think. Logic. Simplicity.* The only way in was through the front, Lorcan said. To get in through the front, we needed an invitation.

"We have to get an invitation," I said. "How do we get an invitation?"

"Forge one," Molly suggested.

"Right..." I said. "But we don't know what they look like."

Everyone mulled for a moment. Chins were rubbed.

"We could send Seemor in invisible," Lorcan suggested. "He could pick a pocket and bring an invitation back out to us."

Cleo frowned. "It's not a terrible idea, but it's risky. Picking pockets is tricky, and if he gets caught, they'll lock the place down, go on high alert, and we're done."

"Probably true," I said.

"Me, I'd just slug someone in the nose and take their invitation," Lorcan shrugged.

"Someone might notice you punching another guest

outside the mansion's front gate, snookums," Molly said, kissing his ear.

"So we don't do it at the front gate," I said excitedly. "We hide out in the forest down the road from the house, wait for a fancy car to come by, stop them, and take the invitation."

"Like highwaymen." Lorcan grinned approvingly.

"Like highway *women*," Cleo amended. "I like it."

"We waylay a guest in the forest, take their invitation, and walk straight in the front door," I summarized, feeling satisfied. It was a good plan. The best we had, anyway.

The door lock clicked, and the door swung open. We all tensed, and I snatched my gun off the table and aimed it at the door, feeling impressed by my gunslinger-like speed. But it wasn't my invisible stalker or a Diamond spy. Seemor waddled into the room, his arms laden with clothing store bags. His eyes widened at the sight of my gun barrel, and I lowered the weapon quickly.

"A tad jumpy, are we?" he carped, dumping the bags on one of the beds.

I was excited to see what disguises he'd stolen for us, until I saw what the bags had written on them. "A thrift shop?" I said.

He rolled his eyes. "It was all I could find. The mall nearby is out of business. You may have heard of a little thing called the internet? Retail is in decline."

"Yeah, I've heard," I said, holding up a hideous tie-dyed sheath dress.

Molly brandished a pair of bell-bottom jeans studded with rhinestones and giggled. "Oh my God."

"You said flashy party clothes," Seemor huffed.

"These are flashy, alright," Lorcan held up a fishnet crop top, holding it gingerly between finger and thumb.

"No, this will work," I said. "Musicians dress crazy. You saw the people going into the party tonight."

"We're going to look like an Abba cover band on crack," Molly laughed.

"Maybe," I said. "But we don't have time for another shopping trip."

"Right," Cleo said. "Tomorrow is going to be all reconnaissance and planning. I want to know every inch of those grounds before we set foot there. It's late. We better get some rest."

I pointed to the door leading to the adjoining room. "Lorcan and Cleo, you take the other room. Seemor, you take the other bed in here. Molly, you're with me."

She and Lorcan shared a pining look.

"Don't even think of sneaking into bed together," I warned. "I have a gun and I'm willing to use it."

❦

By the time we woke, bright sunlight was slanting in through the gap in the curtains. I stretched out and found the bed next to me empty. I sat up with a start and headed into the adjoining room to find Molly and Lorcan fast asleep, spooning in his bed.

I grabbed a pillow and bludgeoned them awake.

"I told you two to stay—*in—your—own—beds!*"

They sat up, blinking and fighting off my blows. Lorcan called me a few explicit names while Molly grabbed my pillow and tried to disarm me. We both collapsed onto the bed, laughing.

"Nothing happened!" she said once we'd reached a truce.

"I told you. I'm a gentleman," Lorcan sniffed.

"Maybe," I said. "But Molly isn't. Let's get some breakfast."

We ate and coffeed at a waffle joint across the street from the hotel. Then, at Cleo's suggestion, we made our way back to the Diamond Queen estate for another round of recon. The sun was bright, the sky blue, the music Molly DJed on the SUV's sound system was folksy Americana fare far more pleasant than the heavy metal ear-bleeders she usually chose. Despite the danger hanging over us, the love songs made me think of Jack, and I wondered for the twentieth time that morning what he was doing. But he hadn't texted me yet, and I wasn't going to be the one to break the seal. The last thing I wanted was for him to think I was a needy girlfriend or that I didn't trust him. So I pushed thoughts of him aside to concentrate on the mission ahead.

First, we looked for a location where we could waylay a party guest to steal their invitation. About half a mile down from the estate, we found a place where the road s-curved through a patch of forest. Off to one side was a sandy dirt road that led to a parking lot for a hiking trailhead. We could lurk on the side road then pop out when a car was coming, block the road and snag their ticket.

"Fine, but what's to stop them from backing up and turning around?" Lorcan asked as Cleo and I sketched out the plan.

I looked around for something to blockade the road with, and my eyes ranged up to the huge tree branches arching over-head. I pointed. "Seemor can be up in the tree and can cut off that big branch. We'll have our car in front of them and the tree branch behind. They'll be stuck."

"Why do I have to be in the tree?" Seemor grumbled.

"Because you're the one who's half squirrel," Lorcan said.

Seemor gave him a deadly glare, but I was actually glad that Lorcan was starting to act like his old snarky self again. Maybe that meant Cupid's Arrow was starting to wear off slightly.

With phase one of our plan figured out, we moved our attention to the estate itself. As we approached the castle, I wished we had a less conspicuous vehicle than the cruise ship–sized red Escalade. But if there were any guards keeping a look-out, we didn't see them as we slow-rolled past.

The estate looked even more impressive in the daylight.

The diamond gate was shut, but through it we could see the vast, parklike grounds, its emerald lawn unfurling for hundreds of yards until it reached the castle itself, which rose from low hills like a country western Avalon. No guards were visible, but we noted several guardhouses where they were probably stationed, as well as at least six security cameras. We drove past and proceeded about a quarter mile up the road, where I asked Molly to turn down a side street and park.

"What are we doing?" Molly asked when we were stopped.

"You'll see." I rummaged in my bag and got out Deuce's drone. Because it looked like a bird, it was inconspicuous enough to avoid drawing attention even in daylight, so it was perfect for surveillance missions like this. I launched the thing and piloted it over the trees. After a few moments, the estate came into view on the drone's controller screen. The bird easily cruised over the fence, then circled over the roof of the house.

"What's this thing going to show us that the satellite view of the online map can't?" Lorcan asked.

"Excellent question," I said. "Nothing—right now."

After circling the mansion's roof a couple of times, I found what I was looking for—a dormer. I carefully steered the bird down and landed it in the corner where the dormer met the roof. The bird would be safe there, and it couldn't be seen from the grounds below.

"The satellite view isn't detailed enough to let us see individual people," I said. "So we'll park the drone here for now, then tonight we can use it to scan the grounds again and map out where all the guards are. Having it in place early will save us time tonight—and there's also less of a chance of it being spotted and making someone suspicious," I finished.

Cleo actually looked a little impressed. "Nice thinking," she said.

"And all this time I've been wondering what Jack sees in you," Seemor grunted—but he was smiling.

"Duh," Molly threw an arm around my shoulders. "My girl is highly intelligent."

"As are you, Molls-Balls," I smiled. "As are you."

We definitely had plenty of intelligence on our side. But we were up against an army of syco thugs, an unknown number of peri and luck gods, and a powerful Diamante queen. I just had to hope our smarts would be enough.

22

RACHEL

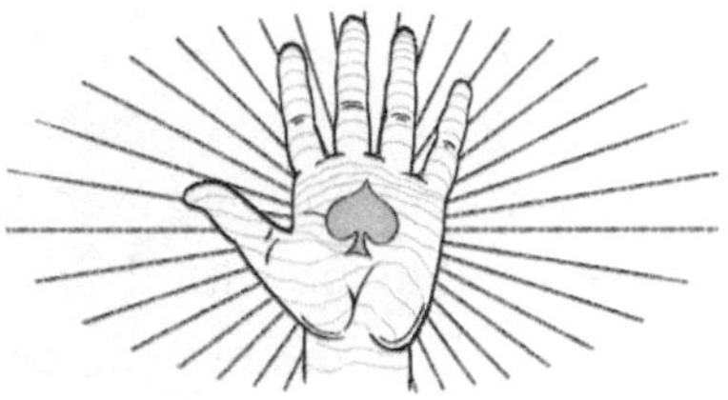

It was mid-morning by the time Rachel turned the key and pushed her apartment door open. Coming home after several days out on Morbus business with no sleep and little food felt disconcertingly similar to returning home after a bender. The feelings were so similar to what she experienced during the worst of her drinking days, in fact, that she was struck with a sense of déjà vu so strong it stopped her in her tracks. She was exhausted, but also brimming with a jittery feeling that was equal parts relief and dread. Relief because being home felt wonderful, and dread at the thought of lying to her daughter again.

"Aggie?" she called and steeled herself for a response. When none came, she walked down the hall and peered into Aggie's room. It was filled with its usual pleasant clutter of class folders and paperback books, pizza crust–laden plates, and Dr. Who bobbleheads. But no Aggie.

She sighed with relief so hard she almost slumped to the floor. She probably could have slept right there, leaning against the doorframe. But the shard of obelisk living in her belly didn't like to let her sleep. Any time she was almost out, it would disturb her—with a susurration of whispers, a sadistic chuckle, a painful jolt, or a new command. Even without its interruptions, she wouldn't have been able to sleep much, anyway. The demands of *the work* were so urgent they kept her running day and night.

She'd thought the demands of alcoholism had driven her actions, that constant need to get tanked, then hide the fact that she was tanked, then awaken from being blacked out and scramble to fix everything in her life she'd broken the day before— while also getting tanked again. But that cycle, harrowing as it was, was nothing compared to this. *The work* was like being covered head to toe with the worst rash imaginable; it was impossible to think of anything else but the desire to scratch, scratch, scratch. Except in this case, scratching her itch meant bowing to the compulsions of *the work*. Recruiting sycos. Following the obelisk's strange and often illogical commands. And making bad luck things happen.

That was another reason she couldn't sleep these days. Any time her eyes shut, a grotesque slideshow played through her mind depicting all the horrible things she'd made happen to people—and animals—since she'd received the mark of spades. The only silver lining was that most of the time, those memories were blessedly blurred by the haze of sleep deprivation. Perhaps that was one of the reasons the shard kept her from sleeping, she thought with a yawn. It wanted her disoriented. Off balance. Mad. Weak. And part of her was weak. But another part of her—the new part—the dark goddess—grew stronger every day.

Something touched her ankle and she gasped, reaching for the obsidian dagger at her belt. But it was only the cat.

"Oh, Hadron," she knelt, stroking him. "Where's Aggie? Has no one fed you?"

His plaintive meow worked as well as begging, and Rachel walked into the kitchen with him adoringly tripping her all the way. She popped a can of wet food and set it on the floor next to a bowl overflowing with dry food. It was a sign that Aggie might not be back for a while, if she'd left the cat extra cat food in the bowl, Rachel thought. She was too exhausted to wonder where Aggie was and what she was doing; she felt only relief that her daughter wasn't there to ask questions, that she didn't have to come up with more lies.

Hadron was easier company. He required no explanations, she thought, as she watched him nibble ferociously at his food, scraping the can across the floor with each lick. Sweet Hadron... Suddenly, the pips on her hands began burning and aching. She imagined a vase sitting atop the fridge tipping over on Hadron, smashing on him in a burst of blood and broken glass. She imagined him stepping out a second-story window. Sticking his little claw in an electrical socket and frying.

Bad luck, Hadron, the obelisk inside her crooned darkly.

"I will not kill my cat," Rachel growled, and thumped herself in the stomach with her fist. It hurt, but she doubted the obelisk felt a thing—if a stone could feel at all.

For Hadron's protection, she left the kitchen and found her way to the bathroom. As she stripped, she wrinkled her nose in revulsion. The clothes stunk, and her skin beneath them was streaked with filth. Just how long had she been out there roving the streets? She couldn't remember.

Just a little longer, she reminded herself. Then the suit would be rebuilt, the obelisk's task would be complete, and it would let her go. It had promised to let her go.

She had no choice but to trust in that promise. The alternative was that the stone would drive her mad. It had proved it could do it. If it drove her insane, her only escape would be death. So if she wanted to stay alive, she had to do what the stone said, just for a little longer.

She tossed the clothes in the trash can rather than the hamper.

In the shower, water ran down her skin like scalding fingers, so hot it hurt. Burning a little was the only way she could begin to feel clean, as filthy as she'd become. She closed her eyes, breathed in the steam, shampooed her hair with luxurious slowness, shaved all the parts that needed shaving. Loofahed herself until her skin was red and shiny. When the hot water began to turn cool, she got out, dried herself, wrapped her hair in a towel, and put on her robe. Then she padded on bare feet to her bedroom, her eyes already drifting shut. The stone was quiet. Maybe it would let her sleep this time, after all. *Please,* she thought. *Just an hour.*

She stood over the bed and let all her joints give way, collapsing face-first onto the bed like a broken-necked crow.

She took a deep breath, then let it hiss out slowly, sinking into the duvet as if into a warm, calm sea.

"I promised Aggie I'd keep an eye on you," a voice said.

Rachel shoved up onto her hands and knees, her muscles suddenly taut, her hands already burning with hex.

A boy sat in a chair in the corner of the room. Aggie's handsome Valentine crush. He had a cocky smile on his perfect young face, and he was pointing a gun at her.

Kill him, quick, hissed the voice from inside Rachel's stomach, but she ignored it. Aggie had tried to keep her relationship with this boy a secret, to make Rachel believe she'd steered clear of the luck gods and their dangerous world. She thought Rachel was oblivious—and maybe Rachel had been oblivious to a lot of things over the last few months. But even in the throes of her dark queenhood, Rachel couldn't miss the change in her daughter. Aggie had started paying attention to her hair and makeup. Sneaking out at night. Wearing *perfume*, for heaven's sake, when just a few months ago Rachel had had to remind her to shower. It all spelled one thing. A secret, forbidden, irresistible boy. This boy. And Rachel would not kill the one her daughter loved—unless she absolutely had to.

"Well, well," Rachel said, regaining her composure and settling back to sit against the bed's headboard. "Jack, isn't it? Is that your name, or your rank?"

"Both," he said.

"Ah," she smiled. "Then I guess you can call me Queen."

The boy smiled. "Alright, Queen."

Rachel rose from the bed, pulling her robe more tightly around herself. "Can I offer you something to drink? I'm afraid I only have water and pop."

Jack shook his head. "I don't drink with queens anymore," he said. "Bad experience."

She tilted her head. "Then what can I do for you, Jack?"

"The question is, what can we do for each other?"

"I can't imagine we have too many overlapping interests," Rachel said. "You're a red suit, I'm a black."

"Aggie is a red suit as well. Don't the two of you still have overlapping interests?"

His words sent a subtle stab through Rachel's heart. "Not as many as we used to," she admitted. "But all this is temporary."

Jack's eyes narrowed. "Is it? I'm not sure you read the fine print. Being a luck god is a lifelong gig, Queen. And we tend to live a pretty long time—unless someone shortens our life for us."

She crossed her arms, growing impatient. "What do you want?"

"I'd like to expand those overlapping interests you and Aggie have." He leaned forward in his chair. "Red suits and black suits don't have to be enemies. They don't even have to be separate."

Rachel cocked an eyebrow. "What? You want to join forces?"

His glimmer of a smile told her she'd guessed right. Forbidden boy indeed. The obelisk had whispered of this, of this boy and his ambitions. The Morbus might peddle bad luck, but at least they had an identity. They had a role, like predators in a well-balanced ecosystem. They culled the weak. Humbled the proud. But this boy wasn't trying to fulfill his role. He was trying to change it, to outgrow it, to gather more power for himself. That's what the obelisk had warned her of. Though he might have his uses, this Jack was dangerous. To her. To himself. To all the suits. And perhaps most of all to Aggie. Rachel's anger flared.

"You've seen what being a Spade is," she said. "My castle is an abandoned hospital. My army is sad, lost, sick people. I've spent the last few weeks eating crows cooked over a fire in an oil drum and making people die. That's the bad luck life. Is that what you want? You think I'd let Aggie suffer like I am?"

"All the more reason to combine suits," Jack said. "Our chefs at the Valentine house are pair of sprites who trained in Paris. Their food is exceptional."

"Don't be glib with me, little boy," she said.

"Don't be dismissive of me, old lady," he shot back, smiling.

She might have been offended except she'd noticed his eyes wandering. He didn't find her *that* old. She stood and pulled her robe tighter around her body.

"Last time we met, you barely escaped," she said. "I'd be careful if I were you."

The smile widened on that face of his, that glistening, roguish face, beautiful as an angel's. A dangerous face for a dangerous boy.

"You really think I couldn't have handled your little ragtag band of newbies at the hospital?" Jack snorted.

"So you pretended to let them chase you away?" she scoffed. But the stony look in his eyes told her he wasn't bluffing. "Why would you do that?"

"Your daughter has an aversion to power," Jack said. "The only way to get her to accept more power was to show her that she needed it—to defeat you."

Rachel felt suddenly confused. "What power?"

Jack's eyebrows went up. "Oh, she didn't tell you? Aggie is going to be Queen of Hearts. Think of that. The two of you, a pair of queens."

Rachel felt as if the breath had been knocked out of her lungs. The obelisk hadn't warned her of this. Aggie... a queen. This luck god's life was like the mob—or a tar pit. The more you struggled to get out, the deeper it pulled you in, until— until what? Until you were either corrupted or smothered. A mixed metaphor to match her mixed-up thoughts.

"I know neither of you would want to hurt the other," Jack went on. "But that doesn't matter. The work is a powerful thing. As long as you're on opposite sides, sooner or later it will pull you together and the two of you will have to deal with each other. When that happens, there'll be blood. Yours or hers."

"And you have a solution?" Rachel said.

"I have the only solution," Jack said. "End the dichotomy. Blend the suits."

"And how would you propose we do that?" she demanded.

"Easy," the beautiful boy said, his dangerous smile returning. "By making me your king."

23

AGGIE

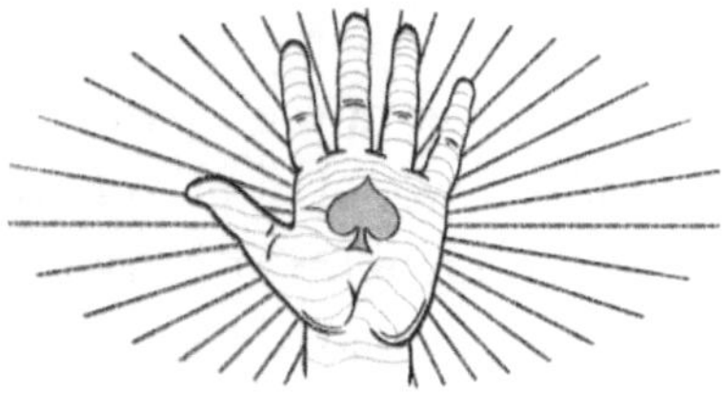

The night of the heist arrived, creeping in like a shadow at sunset. The day had flown by in a tense whirlwind of planning, discussion, gathering materials, and chaperoning Molly and Lorcan, who tried to sneak off and make out every two minutes.

I must have been more nervous than I realized, because not only was I counting everything, I was also looking at ordinary things as if it were the last time I'd see them. I drank a root beer and thought *my last root beer.* I ate my last chili dog. Played my last round of Sudoku on my phone and sent my last texts to Mom and Jack. They were identical, at first—*I love you*—until I changed Jack's to *wish me luck* with a kissy-face emoji. After each of these *lasts,* I added the mental amendment: *before I become queen.* But that didn't seem to matter much to my subconscious; a nagging feeling of melancholy had seeped into my bones, too deep to shake off. I was more of a mathematician than a language person, so it took me a while to name what I was feeling, but I came up with it eventually. *Foreboding*, that was the word for it. Foreboding.

At last, there were no more plans to work out, no more preparations to make, no more research to do or equipment to gather. Thinking was my wheelhouse, but for the moment, the thinking was done. It was time for action. And so we left the hotel room (*for the last time*, my melancholy whispered) and took forty-six steps to the waiting SUV.

As darkness settled in, we were once again rolling into the neighborhood where the Diamond Queen's estate sat.

We returned to the side street around the corner from the mansion and I fired up Deuce's drone. It was still early in the night, not even 9 PM, but through Lorelei's digital bird's-eye view, we saw guests already arriving, a parade of sequined gowns and flamboyant suits, fancy hats and dark sunglasses. I piloted our bird, making broad laps around the grounds while Cleo watched over my shoulder, marking *X*'s on our makeshift map in all the spots where guards were stationed.

There were two by the side gate, two guarding each of the five entrances to the house, three near the pool house, ten by the front gate, and four or five scattered around the perimeter of the grounds, patrolling the fence line. No doubt there were many more inside the house, but of course our drone couldn't see them. I also noted that we hadn't located Diamond Queen yet, but she was probably inside, visiting with her guests.

When we'd finished staking out the place, I piloted the bird back to us, caught it, and climbed back into the car, where we debriefed. Lorcan and Molly had found their way into the backseat together, along with a disgusted-looking Seemor, so Cleo sat in the driver's seat.

"Lorcan was right. The back gate is too heavily guarded," I said, studying the map Cleo had marked up.

"I'm always right, queenie," Lorcan said. "You'll learn that."

"Lorcie's a clever boy." Molly playfully swatted him on the chest. He responded by tickling her, and they collapsed together against the door of the car, a riot of arms, legs, and giggles.

Seemor rolled his eyes. "Can we please drop Romeo and Screwliette off somewhere before we do this? They don't seem entirely focused on this extremely dangerous mission."

"Hey!" Molly protested.

"Screwliette," Cleo snickered.

"Guys, seriously," I snapped, and the two lovebirds sat up and unhanded each other, at least momentarily.

Cleo was studying the map again. "The back gate is a no-go, but the back of the property is still a vulnerable spot. If things go south and we can't get back to the car, we should meet up there to fight our way out and escape up the river on foot."

Everyone nodded, sobered by the scenario Cleo had described.

"The biggest problem is going to be finding the chest once we're inside," Cleo went on. "That place is huge; it could be anywhere."

That was bothering me, too. "It might take all night to search that place," I agreed. "Fortunately, from what I read online, it seems like the DQ's parties go late, so hopefully we'll have enough time. If we haven't found the chest by the time the party is winding down, meet back at the car. We'll get out and make another plan. Got it?"

Everyone nodded.

I made Molly resume her spot in the driver's seat, and she chauffeured us to our next stop: the ambush location. To get here, we had to drive past the DQ's mansion again, and I reflexively held my breath as we passed. But the guards were busy with the growing lineup of cars they were checking in, and nobody seemed to notice as we passed. After a few moments, we'd left the bright lights of the estate behind and passed into the dark forest beyond, where I could breathe again.

"There." I pointed out the sandy turnoff of the trailhead parking lot. "Let's back in."

Molly did, swinging the car around and then reversing down the side road that was nearly obscured with thick underbrush and trees. As we backed up, she clicked off the headlights. It felt a little disorienting for a moment, drifting backwards in the sudden darkness. The dirt road was narrow, and branches screeched against the car's paint, making me wince. When we were far enough back that we wouldn't be noticed from the road, Molly put the car in park.

Seemor climbed out, opened the back hatch, and hefted the small electric chainsaw we'd bought earlier from a big-box hardware store. He slung it over his shoulder with the rope we'd tied around the handle, which would hopefully allow him to climb a tree with it.

"Give me at least ten minutes to get up there and get situated," he said. "I'm going to saw partway through the limb so it will be ready to drop fast when we spring our trap."

"It's going to be a big climb, little sprite," Lorcan said. "You need a boost?"

"Boost this," Seemor grabbed his crotch. Then he slammed the door on Lorcan's laughter and waddled away into the woods.

"Lorcie, I told you, play nice with Seemor," Molly said.

"Sorry sweetkins," the leprechaun said, reaching to rub Molly's neck.

"Mmm. Feels good," she moaned.

I tried not to bury my face in my hands. *Don't complain too much,* I reminded myself. *It's your fault they're in love.*

We waited. Out on the street, a car zipped past, then a second. After a while, we heard the chainsaw starting up.

I took a deep breath and when I released it, it came out shaky. This was the first real mission I'd led as a Valentine. Sure, I'd been involved in battles. I'd charged into danger, put my life on the line. But this time, people were putting their lives on the line *for me*. To be honest, it was a level of responsibility I didn't feel ready for. Molly would be staying in the car, but even as our getaway driver, she was at risk. Why had I brought her along? I suddenly wondered. Just for my own comfort, so I had someone with me I knew I could trust? And what about Lorcan and Cleo and Seemor? Seemor served the Valentines and was used to danger, but how was it fair to ask him to go on a mission led by someone as new and inexperienced as me? Lorcan had also gotten into plenty of scrapes serving the Diamonds, I was sure, but I'd had to tinker with his mind to keep his loyalty. I'd basically brainwashed him into serving me, which was completely unethical. Cleo was here purely for the money, maybe, but she still didn't deserve to die if I messed up. And besides, she had that kid to take care of. If things went wrong and something happened to any of them, it would be all my fault.

I shut my eyes and released charm from the marks on my hands, willing it to infuse Molly and Lorcan and Cleo with good luck. The warmth and the giddy, ecstatic feeling of *the work* filled me, but when I was done, I only felt a little better. Good luck was helpful, but it could only get you so far, especially with a mission as potentially dangerous as this one. I suddenly wanted to send them all away, to find the chest myself. This was my queen trial, after all. Why had I thought it was okay to involve all of them?

I found myself breathing fast and doing what I did every time I had an anxiety attack: counting. I touched finger to thumb, first on my right hand, then on my left, working my way down, forefinger, middle, ring, pinky, forefinger, middle, ring, pinky, and counting with each touch, *one, two, three, four, five, six, seven, eight...* until I reached the magic number of twenty-three, then I started over again.

Once, I'd thought I was cured of these sorts of compulsions. That I'd charmed myself into wellness. But OCD was like being a luck god, I was coming to realize. It was a part of me. Not some limb I could simply amputate, it was a vital organ. All I could do was try to master it and not let it master me.

All remained silent out on the main street. The chainsaw's whirring whine had finished. Seemor was ready. But no cars passed.

Waiting. I always hated waiting.

"There were like fifty cars going by before, now there's nothing!" I complained.

Lorcan was still rubbing Molly's neck. She groaned again.

Last backrub, I thought. Then I gritted my teeth, willing my inner pessimist to shut the hell up.

"You two are going to have to stop that, honestly," I said. "Hands to yourself."

Grudgingly, Lorcan took his hands off Molly's shoulders and leaned back in his seat. "Fine." He stuck a toothpick in his mouth, clenched it between his gold teeth, and folded his arms in defiance.

We sat. Still no cars.

This was getting ridiculous.

We'd eaten barbecue for dinner, and it sat like a brick in my stomach. We'd also drunk a bunch of peach tea, and my bladder ached. Should I pee now, or wait? Did I truly have to pee, or was this just that needing-to-pee feeling I got when I was nervous? Did Jack ever worry about this sort of thing before a mission?

A sudden light lanced through the tree trunks. Headlights.

I sat up and thumped Molly on the arm. "This is it. Go. Go!"

Molly put the SUV in gear and punched the gas. We shot forward, bounding ahead and bursting into the road. With trembling fingers, I typed out my text to Seemor—*now*.

My heart was pounding so hard I could barely breathe. In response to my adrenaline, maybe, the pips on my hands flared, filling the inside of the car with red light. I touched my weapons. Gun. Dagger. I'd seen Jack do that before battle. But this would be no battle. Just stop the car. Demand the invitations. Tie up our victims, take their cell phones, and leave the prisoners in their car on the side street. Later, when we'd safely nabbed the chest, call the police with an anonymous tip so they could come and untie our poor prisoners. Easy.

We rolled into the middle of the roadway and stopped. The approaching car rounded the corner, and its headlights blazed, filling the driver's-side window with blinding light. Growing bigger, brighter, bigger, brighter. Coming too fast. They wouldn't have time to stop. They'd kill Molly. Why hadn't I thought of that? They wouldn't have time to stop... *Twenty-one, twenty-two, twenty-three, twenty-three, twenty-three...*

Screaming breaks. I shut my eyes. Balled my fists. Clenched every muscle. Flared charm so hard I felt feverish.

Then silence. My eyes snapped open. The car barreling toward us had stopped.

"Go!" I shouted, shoving my door open and jumping out. Drawing my gun, I made my way around the front of the Escalade. Lorcan had burst out of the backseat and had his gold-plated .45 leveled at the car. Cleo ran toward the car at a crouch, one golden dagger in each hand. Molly was staying in the SUV like she was supposed to.

Good. All according to plan.

The acrid smell of burned rubber filled the air, and I rushed through a wisp of smoke to the car's driver's side. It was a black sedan, long and luxurious. Definitely going to the party. Perfect.

The window slid down as I approached, and I trained my weapon on the driver.

"Hands up!" I shouted, trying to sound as commanding as possible. "Just give us your party invitations, and nobody has to get—"

The tinted window lowered, revealing the driver's face. I froze.

It was Marley Blackover.

"Somebody always gets hurt, Kindergarten," he said.

Then he shot me.

24

DEUCE

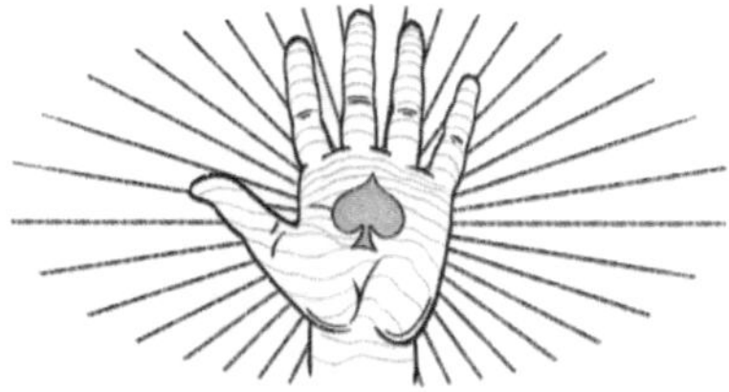

Deuce found Jack sitting at the end of the Valentine mansion dock, silently regarding the night sky and the dark water. Deuce had planned to regale Jack with his and Mina's exploits watching the leprechaun's kid. So far, the boy had broken Deuce's computer screen, tried to steal Mina's cell phone, and spilled about a quart of Fruit Punch Hi-C all over King Michael's throne. Deuce had a soft spot for mischievous boys; some might say he was one. But this kid was bordering on full nightmare status, and Mina seemed on the verge of tying him up in a rowboat and shoving him out into Lake St. Clair. All this Deuce had been about to tell Jack, but something about his friend's vibe gave Deuce pause and killed the amusement he'd been feeling a moment before.

Jack hadn't even turned as Deuce approached, which was

unlike him. Usually, Jack was taut as a bowstring, snapping his attention to every possible threat instantly. But a lot of things about Jack were different lately.

His devotion to Aggie was one of them, Deuce thought. Maybe he was truly in love with her; that could change a person, supposedly. (Deuce didn't know anything about love firsthand—except the lame, unrequited kind.) Jack had lost people, too. There was Queen Aubra, who Jack had been close with before she betrayed him. And Carlotta Blackover, who'd betrayed him, too. Jack had lost his best friend, William. Before that, they'd lost another Valentine, Horus, in Siberia, opening the way for Deuce to join the suit. All those losses could affect a person.

But Deuce couldn't help feeling something more was happening with Jack. It wasn't just that Jack had been spending less time with Deuce, or that he seemed even more distant and moody when they were together. Those changes had been creeping up for a while. But in the last day or so, Jack wasn't just acting different, he *was* different. Cold. Alien. Like someone had opened him up and tinkered with his soul.

Deuce sat next to Jack and gave his friend a rough pat on the back.

"What's up, buddy. Dipping your toesies in the water?"

"It's a little cold for me," Jack said without looking at Deuce.

"Yeah. I'm more of a hot tub guy myself," Deuce said before lapsing into an awkward silence.

He gazed into the lapping, shimmering void below, then to the phone in Jack's hand. *He's worried about Aggie. That's all.*

"Any word from her?" he asked.

He wouldn't have thought it possible, but Jack's expression darkened even further. His hands clenched tighter on the phone as he shook his head. "Not in a couple of hours. The chest is in the possession of the Queen of Diamonds. They're going in tonight."

"The Queen of Diamonds? Who's that?" Deuce asked. The highest-ranking diamond he'd ever heard about was Danusia, the Jill. There had been speculation about whether higher-ranking Diamantes simply didn't exist or whether their identities were just secret.

"Diamond Queen. The country music star," Jack said.

Deuce gaped in amazement for a moment, then laughed so loudly that a couple of ducks nesting on the shore took flight.

"*Carnie booooooy . . .*" he sang loudly.

"Please. Don't sing," Jack said.

"Jeez, talk about hiding in plain sight," Deuce said.

The silence that followed was broken only by the lapping of the water. A feeling of tension crept back into Deuce, along with the nagging worry. *Jack's not alright. And it's not just that he's worried about Aggie.*

Deuce followed his friend's lead and gazed out over the dark water.

"She's going to be okay, you know," he said. "She was trained by the best."

Jack nodded vaguely.

"And you helped, too," Deuce added, giving his friend an elbow. Normally, this would have elicited at least a smile, but Jack remained stone-faced.

"This whole luck god life," Jack said slowly. "Do you ever feel like you're just a pawn? Like the world is just this big game, this power struggle, and we're all... I don't know. Expendable?"

Deuce considered this. "I think a playing card analogy is better than a chess one," he said. "But if we're pawns, who's moving us around?"

Jack didn't answer immediately.

"The aces? The obelisks, I guess?" Deuce said.

He had only seen the ace and her glowing crystal tower once, on the day he was inducted into the Valentines. In his memory, the scene felt more like something from a weird fantasy movie than real life. But everyone knew the aces were the highest-ranking members of the suit, and they derived their power from the obelisks. If the luck gods were all puppets, like Jack seemed to be implying, then the aces and their obelisks were pulling the strings.

"Right," Jack said. "The ace and the obelisk. But what is it they really want? Just to gather more and more luck power? Or... I don't know... to balance the world's luck supply some-how? And to do it, they're willing to sacrifice us? To sacrifice..."

The words fell away behind Jack's clenched teeth.

"Aggie?" Deuce supplied. He shook his head, sighing. "I don't know, man. I mean, you know the ace better than I do. And you said she promised you an end to the bloodshed between the suits, right? Isn't that what she told you? That she'll end the fighting, and you're going to be the one to help her do it?"

Jack nodded. "That's the idea. Gain enough power, and we can ensure peace. But what I'm worried about is: what's the price? I know what I'm willing to sacrifice, but what is the ace willing to sacrifice? If it's Aggie..." He shook his head.

Deuce paused. This might be a good segue to something he'd wanted to talk to Jack about for a while. But now that he stood on the precipice, nerves tightened his throat. Jack already felt so distant, he didn't want to risk pushing him away further. Still, he swallowed hard and said, "Speaking of Aggie... when did you first start getting feelings for her?"

Jack stood, suddenly seeming impatient. "I don't know. What does it matter?"

"I was just wondering," Deuce said. "The night we met her, you said we should try to keep her out of this life."

"Yeah, but the ace ordered me to bring her into the suit," Jack said. "And now she's risking her life doing god knows what."

"Right," Deuce said. "But when did you go from thinking

she was some mortal girl you didn't want to bring into the suit to... you know, falling for her? Is there a specific moment? Do you remember—?"

"What does it matter?" Jack said again, his voice rising. "She's in danger and I can't help her!"

Deuce fell into a frustrated silence. He wanted to tell Jack what he suspected—what he'd suspected for a while about Jack and Aggie's relationship. But he didn't know how to do it without sounding jealous or petty, or—

"I see what this is about," Jack said, cruelty edging into his voice. "You've always had a crush on Aggie."

"I—no—" Deuce stammered. "I mean—"

"And now that you know she's going to be queen, you think I ought to step aside so you can make your move and get in good with her."

For a second, Deuce was too stunned to respond. Then his own anger drew him to his feet. "I don't care if Aggie becomes queen. I don't even care if she's a luck god. Even if she were a regular person, I'd—"

"You'd what?" Jack demanded.

The truth of what Deuce wanted to say, what he'd always felt about Aggie, bubbled up in his chest like magma. It burned. It hurt. But he couldn't tell Jack.

"I'd be her friend," Deuce finished. "Just like I'm your friend."

Jack held his gaze for a moment, challenging, implacable. Then he exhaled, some of the fire going out of his eyes. "I know you are."

Jack ran his hands through his hair. For a moment, it looked to Deuce like one side of his head was illuminated with red light from his pip, but the light from the other side was strange. Different. It was only a flash, an optical illusion, then Jack's hands were back at his sides, fists clenched again.

"Are you alright, Jack?" Deuce asked quietly. "You used to

take me with you on patrols. Lately, you haven't been. Where are you going?"

"Jesus. You're really full of questions today," Jack said with a cold laugh. A breeze swept toward them across the surface of the lake. It rippled the water as it came, like some unseen hand disturbing the stillness.

"I'm worried about you, man," Deuce whispered, feeling more vulnerable than he'd expected.

A moment passed, then at last Jack turned to him.

"You should be. You should be worried about all of us," he said. Then he turned and walked away up the dock, leaving Deuce alone amid the lapping, black water.

25

AGGIE

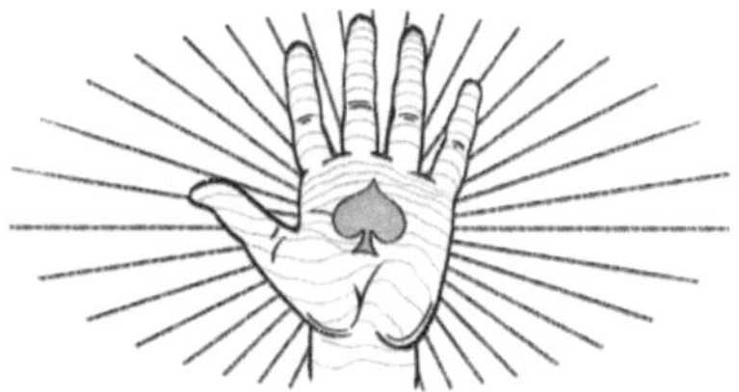

For a moment I was dead. Or I thought I was dead. Marley had fired his gun at me from just a few feet away. I'd already been flaring charm as I approached the car—it was habit now whenever I was going into a dangerous situation—and I'd charmed even harder in the instant the gun went off, as I'd been trained to do, hoping to make the bullet go astray. Then—my hand hurt. I looked down to find the 9-millimeter I'd been holding broken at my feet and my thumb already swelling and throbbing. Marley's bullet had hit my gun. Lucky for me.

I swung with my injured hand, slapping Marley's gun aside as he fired his second shot. His forearm slammed against the back of the car door's window frame, and I leaned all my weight against it, bending it backward, until he cursed and dropped the gun. More shots were popping off around us. Lorcan was cursing. Molly shouted something I couldn't understand. I shoved Marley's arm back one more time, trying to break it, but he reached through the window with his other arm, grabbed me by the hair, and hauled me through the window, into the car, thumping my head on the window frame as he did.

"Help me grab her!" he shouted to his passenger as he threw the car in reverse.

We lurched backward. At the same time, the guy in the passenger seat tried to restrain me and a woman leaned forward from the backseat to help. She had a half-shaved head of bleach-blonde hair, and I caught a flash of a glowing club on her hand as she grabbed my wrist. I lurched forward to head-butt her, but the guy in the passenger seat got a meaty arm around my neck, putting me in a chokehold.

"Go, go, go!" he was shouting. There was another sound too, like a bumblebee from hell hovering above us. In the chaos, I couldn't figure out what it was until something crashed down from above, knocking in the car's sunroof. A leafy stick tickled my ear, and I understood: Seemor had finally gotten the tree branch cut.

That was the moment I realized I still had my dagger in my left hand. Flaring as much charm as I could, I twisted my left wrist free of the Blackover woman's grasp and whipped my blade up toward the chin of the passenger who had me in a headlock. I felt it thump into skin, and he screamed and let go of me as a hot dollop of blood hit me on the forehead. In the same motion, I brought the dagger forward. It struck blondie in the hand, pinning it to Marley's headrest. While she snarled and groaned, I kicked my legs up and caught Marley in a figure-four that would have made my Valentine fight trainer, Ari, (may his memory be a blessing) proud. I squeezed Marley's neck with my legs, but I had no time to choke him out. I had to get out of the car, fast. I tilted my head back so I could see the passenger door, grabbed the handle and jerked it, but it didn't open. Locked. As I fumbled for the lock button, the passenger, his face now bleeding from a wicked gash, began trying to bring his elbow down on my face. His first blow hit my left cheek and had me seeing stars. I had no choice but to cover up my head with both arms to keep from being bludgeoned.

A gunshot, like a crack of thunder.

The inside of the car exploded with broken glass. I winced as shards rained over me, then peeked through my arms and saw that the windshield had been blown out.

Releasing Marley, I kicked my legs back over the steering wheel and clambered backward onto the dashboard, warding off Marley and his passenger (who I now recognized as Cinco, the Blackover five) with my dagger. Then I rolled out onto the hood of the car, sliding on shards of glass and smears of my own blood.

I stumbled to my feet, taking stock of the situation. Lorcan held a sawed-off shotgun with a smoking barrel, now trained at Marley. Cleo was locked in a knife fight with a wiry Blackover who must've originally been riding in the car's backseat with Blondie. Seemor was still clambering down the tree. Molly stared out the windshield of the SUV at us all, wide-eyed. But what sent a fresh pulse of adrenaline through me were the headlights racing up behind her.

Four red SUVs, spread across the road in a V formation, skidded to a halt behind Molly's vehicle. Burly men and women in sequined silver sport coats poured out of them. The Diamond Queen's army.

For a second, I froze like an animal, caught there in the road with those blazing white headlights burning into me. Shouts. Gunshots. Everything was unravelling so fast I could barely comprehend it, much less figure out what to do next. *One, two, three*—I started to count headlights, then stopped myself. *Stay present. Focus on the pain.* My injured thumb ached. My face and head stung. I longed to shut my eyes and open them again to find myself someplace else. School. Home. The Valentine mansion. Jack's bed. But reality wouldn't give up that easily.

I heard another engine revving and saw Molly barreling toward me. The Escalade barely missed my head with its rearview mirror as it shot past, the tires screeching to a halt.

"Get in!" Molly shouted.

The rear passenger window was down, and I grabbed the inside of the doorframe and hoisted myself onto the running board.

"Hang on!" Molly said as we picked up speed again, darting around the Blackover's damaged car and bounding over the end of Seemor's sawed-off limb. I threw myself into the window, worming inside just as Molly screeched to a stop again, pitching me forward and causing my head to thump into the center console.

"A little warning next time you stop, okay?" I grunted over the crackle of gunfire.

The rear passenger door opened, and Seemor and Lorcan both piled into the back with me. A second later, Cleo jumped into the front seat. Before the door was closed, Molly had already peeled off, pinballing me back into the seat again.

With a groan of pain, I sat up and peered out the back window. It looked like the big bang back there, headlights whooshing toward us like stars in an expanding universe. Muzzle-flares sparked like the explosions of colliding asteroids. All else was darkness, void. But the howling engines, the shouts and the gunshots weren't getting any quieter. The Diamonds weren't just letting us go. They planned to catch us.

I slumped, leaning my aching head against the leather seatback.

"You did your best," Seemor patted my shoulder. "We're lucky to be alive after an ambush like that."

"Helluva lot of bad luck, springing our trap on the Black-overs," Lorcan agreed. "That or those black suits knew we were coming."

I thought of the stranger who'd appeared in that rest station bathroom to warn me: *you're walking into a trap.* Was this what they had been talking about? But how could this have been a trap? We were the ones who stopped the Blackovers car, and it was completely random. If they hadn't been driving down that road at that exact moment, we'd have stopped someone else instead. We'd sprung a trap on them, not the other way around.

No, the fact that it was the Blackovers we'd run into was just supremely bad luck—which they'd probably been flaring in great amounts. But it still begged the question, what were the Blackovers doing here? Were they trying to attack Diamond Queen? Or were they perhaps after the same prize we were, the chest and whatever was inside?

There were too many variables and not enough information. I wasn't going to be able to figure out those mysteries now, especially with carloads of gun-toting sycos on our tail.

I involuntarily leaned sideways as Molly took a corner at fifty miles per hour, taking us down a side road and into a neighborhood.

"Maybe I can lose them in here," Molly said. "If I can just get back to the highway, I think I can get us home."

Home. That made me think of Mom. How could I have failed her so spectacularly? Not only had I not retrieved the chest the ace sent me after, I hadn't even made it to the estate. That meant I couldn't pass the queen trial. Which meant I couldn't be queen. Which meant I couldn't stand up to Mom. Which meant I couldn't help her. And that was unacceptable.

"No," I said, sitting up. "I'm not quitting."

Cleo gave a bitter chuckle. "No offense, queenie, but I don't think you have much choice. It will take a miracle for us to get out of this car alive, much less—"

"Get out of the car," I muttered, my hand going to the leprechaun key around my neck. I glanced at the car door, then at Lorcan.

"A door is a door, isn't it?" I asked excitedly.

He frowned. "Jesus. Riddles? She's gone full daft, this one."

"A door is a door," I repeated, clutching the now glowing gold key in my hand. I'd never been in Diamond Queen's house, true, but we'd driven past it several times by now. I'd seen the place, so I could visualize it. And I'd seen the inside on the realtor website's virtual tour, too. I had a concept of the place I could hold in my mind. But would it be enough?

"What are you doing?" Seemor asked, sounding worried as I clambered over him to get next to the car door.

I thought of the Diamond Queen's mansion and grabbed the door handle. Out the window, forest whipped past at what had to be seventy miles per hour. The pavement below was a blur. I shut my eyes, pulled the door handle, pushed the door open.

"Grab her!" Lorcan said.

Too late. I pitched myself forward, out of the car.

♡ ♤ ♢ ♧

I landed with a thud and a splash in about six inches of dirty water at the bottom of a corrugated steel drainage pipe. Instead of tumbling into the roadway out of a speeding car, I'd wound up in a culvert, and disorientation washed over me. That happened pretty often using the leprechaun underground. The odd thing this time was the tunnel size. Normally, leprechaun tunnels were large enough to walk in, but as I scrambled to my feet, I saw this tunnel was only tall enough for me to walk through bent over at the waist. Maybe because a car door wasn't the same as a normal-sized door, so the tunnel it connected to was smaller? Who knew? I'd tried to read up on my golden leprechaun key in the Valentine library, but I hadn't found much. Apparently, leprechaun magic was mysterious, even to luck gods.

I looked over my shoulder. The car door was behind me, shut now. Seemor watched me through the window, looking amazed as he muttered to the others, his words inaudible behind the glass.

Okay, so I'd jumped out of a moving car and survived. Another bucket list item checked off the list. I reached a hand toward the car door and flared my charm, giving the SUV what good luck I could. They'd need it to make it down those curvy roads with the Diamond army in hot pursuit.

My path led onward. I shuffled and splashed down the steel tube, its darkness illuminated only by the glowing key and the heart pip on my injured left hand. My right hand—miraculously—still gripped my dagger, and I was grateful I had at least one weapon with me.

My back and legs were starting to ache from walking hunched over when at last the corrugated steel ended in a wooden box, open on my side. On its bottom sat an array of strange items. Folded towels. A spray bottle of tile cleaner. Two rolls of toilet paper stacked up. Beyond these, I saw the outline of a door even smaller than the car door had been. I pushed, and it swung open easily. I half crawled, half spilled out onto a bathroom floor. *Cripes, another bathroom.*

Two women, one in rockstar leather and the other in a flowing teal outfit like a genie costume, were leaning up against a wall, passionately kissing. The genie one saw me and gave a small shriek, as if I were a rat—which I probably looked like, since I was crawling out of a storm drain.

They stopped their make-out session, and both turned to stare at me, their eyes flicking from my beat-up face to my water-stained chucks to the dagger in my hand.

"Um," one of them said, but she didn't seem to know where to go from there.

"I was just... looking for a tampon," I said, forcing a curdled smile.

The rocker arched an eyebrow. "To stuff in your nose? Because it's bleeding."

I reached up and touched a nostril with a forefinger. It did indeed come away bloody.

"Oh," I said, awkwardly reaching past them to tear off a square of TP, which I jammed into my nose. A little charm and the bleeding would stop soon enough, but I didn't want my hands glowing too brightly while these two were staring at me.

Slipping past the women, I sheathed my dagger, hiding it as best I could beneath my flowy, flower-patterned satin top (thanks, Seemor). I should probably do some special ops-type moves, knock these two women out and tie them up or something. They were witnesses, after all. But that seemed impractical and unkind, plus I had no rope. I'd just have to hope they'd seen enough weird stuff at parties like this that they'd shrug me off.

I opened the bathroom door a crack and peered out. A hallway. Marble floors. Framed gold and platinum records on the walls. I couldn't see any partygoers from here, but I could hear the din of laughter and the thump of music just ahead.

The genie put a hand on my shoulder. "Boy trouble, sweetie?" she asked. "You can stay in here with us. No boy problems here."

Her friend in the leather gave me a suggestive wink. I managed a tepid smile. "Boys are the least of my problems," I said, "believe me." And I slipped out the door.

The hallway opened into a spacious, high-ceilinged living room. The carpet, walls, ceilings, and furniture were all white. The accents—paintings, throw pillows, sculptures—were all red, many with a diamond motif.

Certainly, the Diamond Queen's charm would be off the charts here, in her own lair. I'd never fought another red suit, and it was hard to imagine how that would work. When good luck and bad luck clashed, it felt like a metaphysical arm-wrestling match. What would it be like to contend with someone else using charm? It would be tricky, I imagined. Less arm-wrestling and more judo. I'd have to be smart and careful. And lucky, especially if what Lorcan said was true, that DQ was the strongest of the luck gods.

It would be ideal if I didn't run into her at all. Get in, get out. But Lorcan had warned us about using the leprechaun underground to get into the compound. Alarm bells were probably going off somewhere, and while I hoped most of the Diamond Queen's thugs were out chasing Molly and the others, there were certain to be more here guarding the queen—and the chest. Best to keep moving.

I took a deep breath and stepped into the living room, compulsively counting guests as I went. There were two sets of twenty-three, plus eleven more. Fifty-seven. It was always nice when my OCD dovetailed with a useful task, like recon.

I didn't see any obvious Diamantes, and it was unclear from glancing around who might be a dangerous syco and who was just a random member of the music business elite. The guests were beautiful, and more high-fashion than I'd imagined for a country music party, although I did spy several ten-gallon hats, some blinged-out belt buckles, and more than a dozen pairs of cowboy boots.

Over by the door. Two huge men in sparkly sport coats. Guards. Yikes.

I stepped behind a group of tall guests and snagged a glass of champagne from a passing server's tray—not to drink it, but to blend in with the other partiers. I probably should have drunk it to dull the throbbing pain in my thumb, but the memory of Mom's alcoholic binges remained too raw for that to seem okay.

Be calm, act normal, I told myself. *It's just a party.* Not that I ever acted calm or normal at parties, mind you.

Just take a lap and search the room for the chest. It seemed unlikely that the queen would leave whatever I was seeking out in plain sight, but who knew? The Diamond Queen herself hid in plain sight, on TV, on the radio, in viral videos online. Maybe the same philosophy would hold true for her treasure.

But I saw no chests as I made my lap of the room, just an endless stream of laughing, dancing, drinking revelers. As I pressed through the masses, a disquieting thought occurred to me. What if the DQ had opened the chest already? Anything could have been inside it. That vase sitting on the hearth. The white guitar hanging on the wall. The crystal punch bowl. The treasure the chest contained could be anything, and I'd never know.

Thinking in *what ifs* wouldn't help me. I'd just have to hope that the thing—whatever it was—was still in the chest. Or, if it wasn't, that I'd know it when I saw it.

"Excuse me," a tall boy about my age touched my shoulder. He wore nothing but jeans and a red leather vest with no shirt beneath. His oiled abs gleamed, looking as defined as a carton of eggs. Sexy eggs. He smiled, displaying a prominent set of dimples.

"Hey, you've gotta be the girl from that girl punk band, right?"

I put my hands on my hips. "Why does it have to be *girl* punk band?" I demanded. "Is there such a thing as a *boy* punk band?"

"Uh . . ." The boy blinked, befuddled.

"If I were to be in a punk band, which I am not," I went on. "I would be a musician in a punk band, not a girl in a girl punk band."

"Yeah, queen! You tell him." A dark-skinned drag queen sidled up from behind the boy to clink glasses with me.

"Well damn," the boy in the leather vest grinned. "With an attitude like that, you ought to start a punk band. Let me buy you a drink."

Before I could protest, he'd linked arms with me and started walking us toward the bar. I tried to shrink away, but the drag queen came up on the other side of me and threw an arm over my shoulder, hemming me in. "And the second round is on me, girl. I like me a fierce feminist. We need to get some makeup on that face, though. You look like you got in a tussle."

I gave a shaky laugh and discreetly plucked the toilet paper, which I'd forgotten about, out of my nostril. I considered slipping away from this friendly pair, but there were guards stationed at either end of the bar. I didn't want to make a scene, and I was probably less conspicuous if I looked like I had friends than if I was skulking about alone. I stopped breathing for a second as we passed by the nearest guard, but sandwiched between guests as I was, his eyes skipped right over me—with a little help from my charm.

We sidled up to the bar, packed in among a crowd aglow with laughter and good cheer. I might even begin to enjoy myself here, I thought, except from outside the estate I heard— or imagined I heard—the sounds of roaring engines, gunshots, and shouting. I forced a smile, counting the liquor bottles lined up along the back wall as the boy in the vest ordered me a shot. The bartender poured, and the boy raised his glass.

"To new friends," he said.

"To new friends," I echoed weakly, and downed the drink in one burning gulp.

I spent the next few minutes in verbal sparring, turning questions back around on their asker.

"Where are you from?"

"I've moved around a lot. Where are you from?"

-

"What happened to your face?"

"Oh, I slipped and fell. Where did you get that snazzy vest?"

-

"How do you know our lovely Diamond Queen?"

"I don't know her that well, actually. I was surprised she invited me. How do you know her?"

-

After waiting what I hoped was a non-suspicion-arousing period of time, I excused myself and pretended to be heading to the bathroom. The two shots I'd taken left me dizzy (I'd refused a third) but they did dull the pain in my thumb, which I was grateful for. I took a last glance around the room as I darted through the archway that led into the hall, and I caught one of the guards eyeing me. *Not good. Better hurry...*

Back down the hall I went, moving fast, in search of a staircase. If I went downstairs or upstairs, I reasoned, there might be fewer people. That would allow me to search in hiding places like closets or cabinets without drawing suspicion. Several doors off the hallway led into what appeared to be guest bedrooms. I peeked into each of them but saw nothing resembling a chest. The hall dead-ended in a study filled with books and an impressive vinyl record collection. Four people sat on a leather sectional, chatting. One of them I thought I recognized as a major country music star, though I couldn't think of his name. I smiled at them politely, but they didn't pause in their conversation or even seem to notice as I made a quick lap of the room. No chest. I moved on.

I made similar perfunctory orbits through a kitchen, a music room full of guitars in glass cases, and a formal dining room decorated with life-sized paintings of the Diamond Queen herself, whom the artist had depicted tastefully and voluptuously nude. As I passed the window, I heard a commotion. My heart seemed to freeze in my chest as I peered out. Three guard vehicles were returning, their occupants pouring out like storm troopers. I counted them as they emerged, *four, five, six, seven...* I bit my lip, waiting to see a beat-up Lorcan, Seemor, Cleo, or Molly dragged out of a backseat. When none of them appeared, I wasn't sure whether I felt relieved or even more worried. They weren't captured, that was good. But it didn't mean they hadn't been shot, or killed in a car wreck, or—

I shook my head, trying to clear the dread-spiral it was descending into, and went back to counting guards. I got to twenty-two and I really wished there was one more, so I could reach my number of completion. When no more appeared, I sighed and turned from the window.

My friends weren't captured. Good. But now there were more guards around, which was undeniably bad news. I had to hurry. But the estate was massive. It would take hours—or days—to find the chest, even with my entire crew. How was I supposed to do it alone? I had to think systematically. Approach this like a scientific problem, gather information, develop a hypothesis.

If I were the Diamond Queen, where would I put an important item? To answer that, I had to break the question down further. What sort of a person was the Diamond Queen? I'd never met her, but... my eyes ranged to the massive paintings of her gracing the walls. What sort of person was the DQ? The sort who had naked self-portraits and her own platinum records hanging on her walls. She was a celebrity. A star. Someone brimming with ego and confidence. Where would a person like that hide a valuable treasure? Would they bury it? Hire an assassin to guard it for them?

No. A person with an ego like DQ's would trust their own

abilities. If my hypothesis was correct, she'd keep the treasure close and guard it herself.

Moving at a pace just shy of a jog, I made my way toward the front of the house, where I'd already glimpsed a grand staircase running to the upper floors of the mansion. I stepped into the foyer, then halted. Two guards stood at the foot of the steps and a velvet rope stretched across the bottom of the staircase. I was pondering how to talk my way through the blockade when the front doors opened, and the guards from out front poured in.

I immediately spun and started to walk away, taking out my phone as I went and pressing it to my ear to make it appear I was doing something normal. But I still heard one of the guards saying: "Perimeter breach. Spread out and search."

Crap on a stick.

Okay, in a house this size, there couldn't be only one staircase to the upper floors. There would be at least one more point of access for servants. It only took me a few minutes to find it: a small elevator located in a quiet hallway just off the kitchen. A guard stood in front of it, looking big and stoic and mean.

Probably I could charm my dagger and take him out— maybe Jack would do that, or Ten. But hurting people was not my jam, and stabbings tended to be loud and messy. What I needed was a distraction.

I glanced around the kitchen.

From the front of the house, I heard the thudding of boots, coming my way. In no time, the guards would make it here to the back of the house. They'd lock everything down and I'd be finished. I had to get into the elevator before that happened.

I flared my charm, using it on my own mind. *Think, brain. Think. Spark the right synapse. Come up with something brilliant.* Looking around. Fridge. Kitchen Island. Microwave. Stove.

Stove. Yes.

I stepped up to it, snatched a towel off the oven handle, turned on a gas burner, and tossed the towel on top. It smoked for a few seconds, then burst into flame. Moving fast, I crossed the room and hid in the pantry, keeping the door open a crack so I could peek out. In moments, a thick black smoke was rolling off the burning towel, making the room hazy. Sure enough, the guard from the elevator came in, craning his head to see where the smoke was coming from. As soon as he passed, I slipped out of the pantry, hustled to the elevator, and pushed the button. It seemed to take a week for it to groan and hiss its way down to me.

In the kitchen, a smoke alarm went off, peeping shrilly. I could hear the guard cursing, followed by the sound of running water.

Footsteps, fast and close. I punched my finger into the elevator button again and again. Twenty-three times, charming as I did.

"Come on!" I whispered desperately.

Ding. The elevator doors slid open. I shot inside and pounded the 2 button. The doors slid shut again, but just before they met, I saw several guards blur past, racing to the kitchen. The elevator hummed upward. I shut my eyes and took a deep, steadying breath.

You can do this. You have to do this.

Molly. I whipped out my phone. No texts from her. I started to type, hoping to let her know I was okay, to send her one last message in case I didn't make it out, but my thumb hurt too much to type fast. Then the elevator bucked and dinged, and the doors slid open.

I put my phone away and stepped out into the dimly lit hallway. Party sounds drifted up from below, eerily muted, as I moved down the hall on cat feet.

I passed several doors. Each was ajar, allowing me to peek inside. A guest room, the bed neatly made. A tidy study. What looked like a storage room full of boxes and plastic totes—but no chest. And then, in the middle of the hallway, I came upon a pair of double doors. They were arched and made of carved wood painted red, with a crystal diamond inset in the center of each one.

It had to be the master suite.

I reached out, grasped the ornate brass door handle, and twisted, fully anticipating that it would be locked. But it turned easily. I readied my dagger, pushed the door open, and stepped inside.

The room was exactly what I'd imagined: a world of pure opulence. Mirrors in jeweled frames. Chairs that appeared to be made of crystal with cushions of fluffy white feathers. A vast diamond-shaped rug that looked soft as cashmere. A vast bed canopy hung with gauzy, scarlet curtains.

And at the foot of the bed, ancient-looking with black and gold trim, sat a chest.

I stared at it numbly for a second, my heart skipping with elation.

I took a single hurried step toward the chest—then a sound froze me in place. The strum of a guitar. A lovely voice hummed a little riff, and another strum came, a minor, tragic-sounding chord. Coming from the bed. From behind the curtain. I glanced toward the door. Maybe I hadn't been seen. Maybe I could still get away before—

"Well," a melodic-sounding, Southern-accented voice drifted from the bed. "You've come this far. Come on over and let me get a look at you."

26

AGGIE

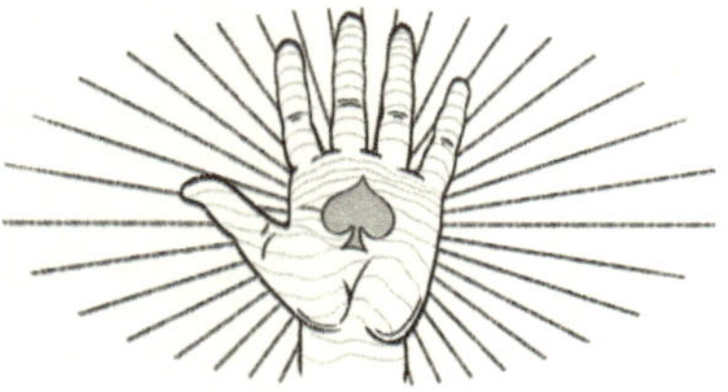

I gulped, hiding my dagger behind my back, and stepped cautiously toward Diamond Queen's bed. As I did, I glanced once more at the chest, only a few steps away now. Could I grab it and run to the door? Open a leprechaun portal and jump through? It might work. But only if the chest was light enough for me to grab with one arm, which didn't seem likely given its size, and only if my enemy didn't have a gun on me, which seemed less likely still.

I reached out slowly and whipped the curtain aside.

There she sat, the only celebrity I'd ever seen in person, looking as gorgeous and as regal as any royal imaginable. Diamond Queen. Her hair alone was epic, a mane of glittering platinum curls so vast it might have spawned its own weather system. A copious amount of perfectly applied makeup covered her face, giving her the impeccable look of an American geisha. Her fingernails and her lips were an identical shade of blazing crimson, and she wore a funky gown that was something like a red and white 1950s waitress uniform spangled with rhinestones.

"You're beautiful." The words spilled out of my mouth. It seemed reasonable to open with a compliment, and it was the truth.

Diamond Queen gave a radiant smile. "Not going to make this easy, are you?"

She set the guitar aside and picked up two items from the puffy duvet cover next to her. One was a sawed-off shotgun with a glittery stock. The other was a *main gauche* dagger with a swirly, diamond-laden guard. She aimed the shotgun at my chest and shut one eye, aiming. I raised both hands, my charm flaring.

"Wait," I said. "Hearts and Diamonds are allies, right?"

The queen looked at me askance. "That why you're sneaking around my house like a wannabe ninja holding a dagger?"

I sighed. "That... that's just because—"

She shook her head, stopping me. "I know, I know. This is your queen trial. And it's a hell of a cruel one if you ask me. You'd have been far better off if that ace of yours had sent you up against the Blackovers, or the Morbus. But the Diamantes?" She shook her head. "That's just a recipe for destruction, sweetheart."

"Yeah?" I prompted. I was sensing that the Diamond Queen liked to hear herself talk. Maybe I could use it to my advantage, or at least keep myself alive a little longer.

"Of course, girl," Diamond Queen said. "Everyone knows Diamonds are the most powerful suit. Not only do we have luck, we have money."

"The Valentines have money," I countered.

The queen gave me a look. "There's money and there's money. The Valentines may have fancy clothes and a private jet—"

Wait, there was a private jet? Then why the hell had I just gone on a road trip with a smelly leprechaun and a surly sprite? I resolved to confront Michael about it—if I lived to see him again.

"But the Diamantes buy industries," the DQ went on. "We own politicians. Small countries. And of course, people."

Her shiny ruby lips twisted into a smile at the last word.

People.

"You knew I was coming," I said. Of course, that rotter Lorcan would have ratted me out. He probably figured out what we were doing as soon as he heard we were going to Nashville and told Danusia right away, long before I'd made him fall in love with Molly. I'd been an idiot to bring him along. A real queen would have gone on her own. But then, maybe that's why I was a senior in high school and not an actual queen.

I could surrender now. Throw myself on the Diamond Queen's mercy. But what then? I'd go back to Detroit and be back to square one, watching powerlessly as Mom slipped away. I couldn't do that, not to her and not to myself. Somehow, I still had to get that chest.

"Of course I knew you were coming," the Diamond Queen said. "I've been watching you since you came in tonight." She gestured up to a bank of TV screens mounted to the ceiling above the bed, which showed live-stream security footage of the whole compound. "I was pretty impressed you made it this far, to be honest. But here you are, a little ol' fly in a web."

I glanced at the door.

"Yep, my boys are outside," she said. "One whistle from me and they'll storm in, then it'll all be over."

"We could make a deal," I said. "Give me the chest and I'll

be queen. We could be allies. You'd have an in with the Valentines. We could work together—"

From below came the sounds of commotion. Shouts. Thumping. One scream, then another. The queen and I both glanced at the door, and when I looked back at her, I saw the first tiny tremor of worry cross her painted face. Her eyes, when she turned them back to me, were fierce.

"Sorry, little girl. We have to make an example of you. The Valentines need to know that the Diamantes are not to be trifled with. You want to mess with someone, mess with the dark suits. Or sprites, or goblins or leprechauns. You want a queen trial, send the candidate through the rift and see how they fare on the other side. But don't you dare send them toe-to-toe with the Diamond Queen. Because, baby, you poke this bull, you're gonna get the goddamn horns."

The commotion outside was getting louder. If I could just delay a little longer, maybe an opportunity was coming.

"At least tell me this," I said quickly. "What's in the chest? That's what I was sent to get."

The queen's carefully drawn eyebrows went up. "You don't know? I guess your ace is just as infuriatingly mysterious as ours. But sorry, baby girl. You're never going to find out what was inside."

The queen swung her legs over the end of the bed and stood, slipping out from behind the gauze curtain and cocking her shotgun. She emerged like—well, like a goddess. She towered over me, standing at least six-foot-five in her high-heeled cowgirl boots, and her face was terrible in its beauty.

I stumbled in reverse until my back was against the wall, flaring charm.

DQ raised the shotgun, squeezed an eye shut to aim.

From just outside the door came a shout, then a gunshot. Something banged the door, rattling it on its hinges. DQ glanced at it. While she was distracted, I snatched a framed platinum record from the wall next to me and held it in front of me like a shield.

The queen looked back to me, her eyes narrowed. "Oh, hell no. You are not gonna hide behind Carnie Boy. You put that down!"

"No."

"Put it down. NOW!"

At that moment, the doors blew off their hinges. In charged Ten—my Ten, Valentine Ten—carrying a chair like a battering ram. Before Diamond Queen could react, Ten hurled the chair at her. Ten and I both charmed it in-air, and it struck DQ in the face and knocked her off her feet. She landed on her back on the carpet, and the chair tumbled to a rest on the far side of the room. For one strange second, all was perfectly still.

Then two of the queen's men stormed in. Flaring charm, I lunged forward and tripped one. Ten grabbed his head as he fell and guided it into her knee. He went to sleep with a thump. Then Ten gracefully spun in and slashed the other one's throat. His knees gave out and he landed splayed on the carpet with a splash of arterial blood. I looked to the doorway for more enemies, but that was it—for now.

I turned my attention to Diamond Queen. She had a gaping gash running down her forehead from hairline to right eye, along with one hell of a goose egg. It was definitely going to leave a mark.

Ten and I looked at each other.

"Hey Six," she said in her irritating, cocky way.

"What are you doing here?" I demanded.

"You're welcome," she said, gesturing toward the laid-out queen. She crossed to the chair, picked it up, and went back to the double doors, slamming them and jamming the chair under the handles to keep them shut.

"This is *my* queen trial," I said.

She screwed up her face as she turned back to me,

pretending to consider my statement. "Is it? If I complete it, maybe it's my queen trial."

Her eyes alighted on the chest. She crossed to it, hoisted it onto her shoulder, and headed over to the picture window.

"No, it is *not* your queen trial," I shouted after her. "I was doing fine until you came along and—"

"And saved your ass?" Ten finished. "Sure you were. Look, I'm doing you a favor. Even if you did somehow complete this trial, I'd still have killed you in the challenge when you got back to the mansion. This way, I get to be queen, and you get to live. Everybody wins."

She peered out the window then, apparently satisfied with what she saw down below, hurled the chest through, shattering the glass. The chest hit the ground below with a low thump like the concussion of thunder. Ten kicked out a few stray shards of glass then jumped onto the windowsill, ready to leap down after the chest.

Except I grabbed her by the hair and tugged her back inside. She fell back from the window, shouting in pain and shock and stumbling to keep her footing. Then she wheeled on me.

"I said, this is my queen trial," I declared, feeling equally badass and terrified. But I'd come too far to let anyone bully me out of my victory now. Mom needed me.

"Fine," Ten snarled, drawing her dagger. "Let's do this the hard way."

27

AGGIE

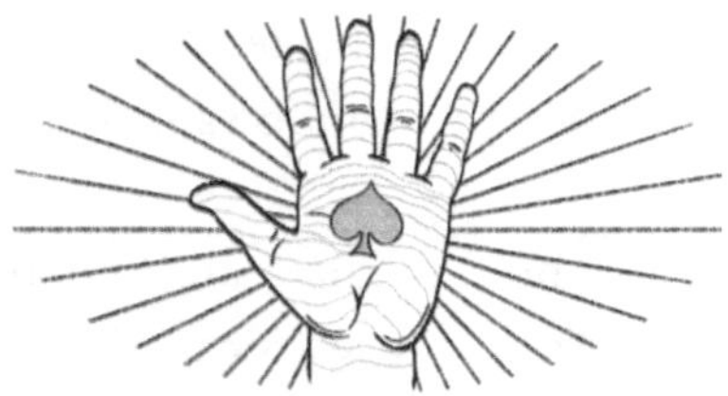

It occurred to me as Ten circled, the blade of her dagger glinting in the Diamond Queen's mood lighting, that I did not want to fight her. I mean, I had often wanted to fight Ten. She was a not-nice person. But she was also a strong, smart woman and a loyal Valentine. She also had more powerful charm than I did and was a far better fighter. There had to be some middle ground between giving up and failing my queen trial and letting Ten slice and dice me—right?

But before I could think of how to urge a truce, Ten struck. She surged forward, feigning an attack with her weapon and instead smashing me with a high kick that left my vision swimming and my head humming.

Okay, so we were fighting. Ten could take me in any fair fight. So how could I make this fight unfair?

She lunged again, slashing with her dagger, and I simply ran, sprinting across the room then swimming through the gauze curtains to end up standing in the middle of Diamond Queen's bed. I assumed a fight-ready position, bouncing—because how do you not bounce when standing on a bed?—as Ten approached. Grimacing in fury, she tried to slash her way through the tangling curtains. In that moment, the absurdity of the situation struck me, and I couldn't help but laugh. Which made Ten even angrier.

"Dammit. Grow up, Six," she growled, finally freeing herself from the curtains to join me on the bed.

This was my only viable strategy, I decided. Make things weird. Piss Ten off. Delay. And use my luck. Because I'd need a LOT of it.

I flared my charm, picking up a pillow.

"Pillow fight," I called, and winged it at Ten. She skewered it easily with her dagger and threw it aside.

I threw a second one. She knocked that away, too.

"You think this is how a queen would behave?" Ten scolded me. "You're a joke."

"Why aren't you laughing, then?" I taunted, throwing another pillow, which she hacked in two with a furious swipe of her dagger.

From the direction of the barricaded door, I heard the rattle of a door handle and the chatter of low voices. *Uh-oh.*

I'd backed up to the bed's headboard now, seeking more pillow ammunition. Except instead of a pillow, this time my hand found a remote control. I snatched it up and started mashing buttons. The TVs above the bed changed to show an episode of Diamond Queen's reality TV show, playing at a deafening volume. Ten bull-rushed me and I dove out of the way, rolling and bouncing back to my feet. As I did, I must have hit another button on the remote, because the bed began to spin in a circle. Flashing, colored lights lit up along the bed's canopy and loud calliope music began to play. I didn't know why DQ would have such a setting on her bed, and to be honest, I didn't want to know, but it was working for me now. I ran in a circle around the edge of the bed like it was a treadmill, while Ten leapt and strode ahead, trying to cut me off. Each time, I managed to duck out of her way on the uneven footing of the duvet and bound to the other side of the bed, eluding her. Her face had gone crimson with anger.

"When I catch you—" she began, but at that moment several of the Diamond Queen's thugs splintered the door and burst into the room.

The first two through the door saw their fallen leader and ran to her side. Three more entered after them and spied us on the bed.

"The window," Ten shouted as our enemies opened fire.

Flaring charm, we both streaked across the room and leaped straight out the shattered window, dropping two stories like a pair of synchronized divers, then landing in a roll in the driveway.

Even flaring charm, I got a scraped knee and a couple of cuts from shattered glass—but that was better than the bullet wound and the broken neck I'd have gotten without charm.

The party was breaking up in the chaos. Guests had gathered near the front entrance, waiting for valets to bring their cars. Seeing us, they screamed and huddled back in the house's portico. I glanced toward the road, our logical escape path, and saw that the gates had been damaged. One had been knocked down, the other hung crooked on its hinges; a car must've bashed through them. Had my crew done that? It certainly hadn't been part of the plan, but then, the plan had gone pretty sideways. Near the broken gates, a knot of sequin-coated guards had gathered. They spotted us now and began jogging our way, weapons drawn.

"Where's the chest?" Ten asked suddenly. I turned a circle, looking, but there was no chest in sight.

"You dropped it out the window. It should be right here," I said. "Unless..."

As if in answer, an engine revved off to our right. A black BMW nosed forward, knocking partygoers out of the way. Behind the wheel, Marley grinned at me, eyeing us from behind his trademark sunglasses. I glimpsed the chest in the car's trunk before the blonde Blackover slammed the lid shut, raced around, and leapt into the backseat.

"Come on!" I said, starting after them. They'd already pushed through the tangle of party guests and were accelerating down the driveway. The guards tried to block them, then saw they weren't stopping and dove out of the way. In a roar of engine and a rain of sparks, the car glanced off what was left of the gates and blazed off the estate grounds, picking up speed and disappearing from sight.

Ten and I both slowed our run.

We'd failed. The Blackovers had the chest.

"Nice work," Ten snarled, shoving me.

"Me?" I demanded. "You're the one who—"

But there was no time to argue. Partygoers were pointing and murmuring, many with their cell-phone cameras trained on us. Dozens of guards stampeded toward us from every direction. Sirens wailed in the distance, getting louder.

"Come on!" I grabbed Ten's arm and we ran along the front of the mansion, away from the swarming guards.

"Where are we going?" Ten asked.

"A door," I wheezed.

"What door?"

"Any door." I held up the leprechaun key, its golden glow increasing as it prepared to do its work. Only there was no door. Only the stone wall of the house to our right and a garden to our left. And our pursuers were getting closer. We rounded a corner of the house and barreled into a group of guests sitting around a bonfire amid a cloud of skunky-smelling marijuana smoke.

They all turned to gape at us.

Ahead, at the far end of the house, four guards swung around the corner. They spied us and pointed. One spoke into a mic at his wrist. The other two drew weapons.

"There," Ten pointed.

Perhaps a hundred yards away, across an open expanse of lawn, a guesthouse stood along the fence line. And it had a door.

"Go!"

We sprinted.

I glanced back to see three more guards appear from around the corner of the house. They all ran, trying to head us off. It was a footrace. Not my favorite thing.

I chugged along as fast as I could, charming my blood to hold maximum oxygen and my muscle fibers to fire fast. But my stupid short legs, even at their luckiest, were no match for those charging guards. So I shifted my focus. With a flare of charm, the closest guard's shoelaces came untied. I thought of Deuce as the guard tripped and tumbled. Two others bashed into him, going down in a heap. But the others were still coming. Ten, who was several yards ahead of me, shouted:

"I'm going to stall them. You get the door open. *Don't* leave me."

She peeled off and charged our pursuers, meeting them with a flare of charm and a clash of weapons.

I ran, slammed into the guardhouse door, thinking of the first *not here* place that came to mind—the Valentine mansion. The leprechaun key burned brighter, I twisted the knob, and the door opened.

Beyond lay a tunnel. Safety.

I darted through then turned back, waiting.

Waiting for what? For Ten, who'd been ready to kill me earlier? For Ten, who would probably stab me the moment we were in the tunnel together? For Ten who'd had it in for me since the moment we met?

She had taken care of two guards already; they lay motionless at her feet. Five more were trying to pen her in, but she held them off with amazing skill and ferocity, even as she hazarded a backward glance toward me. Then I saw them. Beyond her, more guards were coming, dozens of them, thundering toward us.

And I slammed the door.

For a moment, I stood leaning against it, gasping in the cool, dank air of the tunnel as I caught my breath.

Leaving Ten. I'm leaving Ten.

That was the act of a queen. Ruthless. Calculating. It's what Aubra would have done. It's probably what Ten would have done if our roles were reversed. But it wasn't me. Was it? I was pretty cutthroat in robotics club. In the battle to become class valedictorian, I planned to defeat Claudette and take no prisoners. And Mom... I would die or kill to get Mom back, without a doubt.

But this? Part of me wanted to be the badass woman who would leave Ten to the wolves. But as the seconds ticked by a pressure in my chest grew, squeezing my heart to the point of pain. Maybe I was lame. Maybe I was weak. Maybe I was no queen. But I couldn't just leave Ten.

Heaving a sigh, I flared my charm again and opened the door.

But Ten was nowhere to be seen.

A small army of guards had fanned out and were approaching the guardhouse. At the sight of me, they shouted, cracking off gunshots and rushing in my direction, a wave of brute humanity.

I slammed the door and ran down the tunnel, into the dark.

28

RACHEL

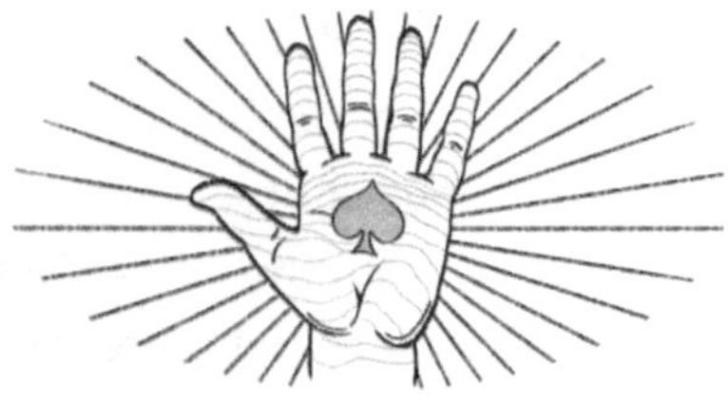

Who knew this bizarre place existed right in the middle of Detroit?

At the obelisk's instruction, Rachel and Shade had gone downtown to the Fisher building, one of the city's iconic Art Deco office towers, ridden the gilded elevator up and gotten off at a secret floor. Now, they were in a templelike place that was illogically vast—there was no way all this should fit into the footprint of the Fisher Building. The *Barth Menagerie of Fortune* seemed half curio shop, half circus sideshow, with a brimming side-helping of creepy vibes. And Rachel was pretty sure the tall, thin, bald host with the stars tattooed on his head who they were currently following down the hallway had to be an alien.

Sylph, the obelisk corrected from inside her mind. *The sylph *are influential traders among the peri, and Bartholomew Barth is one of the most powerful and well-connected of them. His ability to procure things is unmatched, and with his army of clones, he could be a valuable ally. Tread carefully with him and say only what I tell you to say.*

Clone army made Rachel think of *Star Wars*, which was good, but then the stone had told her to keep her mouth shut and be a good puppet, which was bad. Such were the ups and downs of being a bad luck queen.

"This was one of our more difficult procurements," the sylph, Barth, was saying in a low, rather pretentious-sounding voice. "But we are delighted to be able to succeed in getting it for you, my queen."

They emerged from a long, vaulted hallway into a round room. The walls were made of an odd, bluish stone. Carved marble busts sat in recesses, but their hideous faces were more Lovecraftian than human, and Rachel looked away, repressing a shiver. At the center of the room sat a car—a white Porsche— and a muscular worker in a tank top and a welding mask was cutting the hood with a plasma torch.

"This vehicle has been a prized bad luck object for over fifty years," Barth said. "Of course, we were quite surprised when your Darby told us *why* it was so unlucky. I'm eager to see for myself."

The light and sparks from the plasma torch were blinding, but shielding her eyes with one hand, Rachel was able to see that the worker was not cutting the hood itself. He was cutting *around* the hood, which had been welded shut. When the worker had completed his circuit, the hood smoldered, edged in an outline of glowing hot metal.

The worker put the plasma torch down and pushed back his mask with one muscular arm, revealing a face that was handsome, with unusually prominent cheekbones. Rachel had assumed the lavender tinge to his eyes was caused by the glow of the cutter, but as its flame went out, she saw that his irises indeed had a light purplish hue. And his smile displayed rows of disturbingly sharp teeth, a greeting that nearly made Rachel cringe.

A goblin, the obelisk narrated inside Rachel's mind. *They are a dangerous lot. I'm surprised Barth has one in his employ.*

"Well, Varsmith. Get on with it," Barth told the goblin in a bored drawl.

Varsmith got into the car and popped the hood, then came back around and lifted it.

Shade stepped back slightly in response to the wave of repulsive energy that throbbed out of the open hood, but Barth and Rachel both edged closer to peer at the car's engine. No, not the engine, Rachel remembered. Porches had trunks in the front. Barth reached in and took out an item about the size of a basketball, wrapped in black cloth. With a slowness both dramatic and reverent, he unwrapped the cloth, revealing—

Yes, whispered the obelisk.

—a black urn, of the sort used to hold a dead person's ashes after cremation.

Their sylph host grunted with appreciation as he gazed at it. The goblin—Varsmith—gave a low whistle.

"A gathering urn," Barth said, nodding with appreciation. "Quite rare. I haven't seen one of these in hundreds of turns. And never on this side of the rift."

He approached and offered it to Rachel. At five-foot-seven, Rachel was no shrimp, but the sylph stood at least a foot and a half taller, and he stooped to hand her the urn. As it settled into her arms, she found it was heavy as a bowling ball, and it exuded cold. The moment she touched it, her hands and fore-arms went numb and tingly.

"Use it well," the sylph said with an awkward bow.

"Thanks," Rachel said, "but how does one use a gathering urn?"

The sylph chuckled. "Why, to gather."

Rachel flashed back to the condescension she'd received from male colleagues in academia over the years and irritation filled her, causing her hex to flare.

"Gather what, wiseass?"

The sylph recoiled, blinking, then bowed again, lower and more respectfully than before.

"Forgive me, my queen. The gathering urns are famous. I thought you must know... but I forget that education is different on this side of the rift. The urns are used to gather living shadow. If I may?"

Barth reached tentatively toward the urn, and Rachel handed it back to him.

"I'm sure there must be a few flitters in here," Barth muttered, and tilted the lid of the urn open just a crack.

A sound like a rush of cold wind filled Rachel's ears, and for a moment she felt a spin of vertigo. Then, from all around the room, from beneath the car and behind the ugly busts and even from behind Rachel herself, little bits of shadow seemed to detach and flutter through the air to be sucked into the urn. As soon as they were inside, Barth clapped the urn's lid back on.

"See? It's for gathering jinn," the sylph explained. "When a jinni is destroyed, they are reduced to bits of shadow, which tend to gather in places with high concentrations of bad luck. The urn allows one to gather them up again. Once enough shadow is gathered, a jinni is reconstituted."

We will use it to reform Invidia, the stone within Rachel said.

She turned away from Barth. "Invidia, the archjinni who possessed me? No thank you," she whispered.

She will not be able to enter you again, the obelisk replied. *You're more powerful now. But you will need Invidia, and whatever other shadows you can gather—and you'll need them soon.*

"Why?" Rachel asked. She was almost afraid to hear the answer.

Because a battle is coming. Without Invidia, you cannot win it. And the life of your daughter hangs in the balance.

Rachel thought of the last time she was home. Aggie hadn't been there. She'd been so preoccupied with her own problems that she'd dismissed it. And Rachel hadn't been checking messages on her long-dead phone, either. She shut her eyes and gave a mighty sigh. She had more questions. Many more. But if Aggie was in danger, they'd have to wait.

She turned back to Barth. "Thank you," she said.

The sylph arched one hairless brow. "My pleasure. And now, as for the other item, Darby said you require—"

Rachel paused. "Other item?"

"Yes," Barth said. "The army."

29

AGGIE

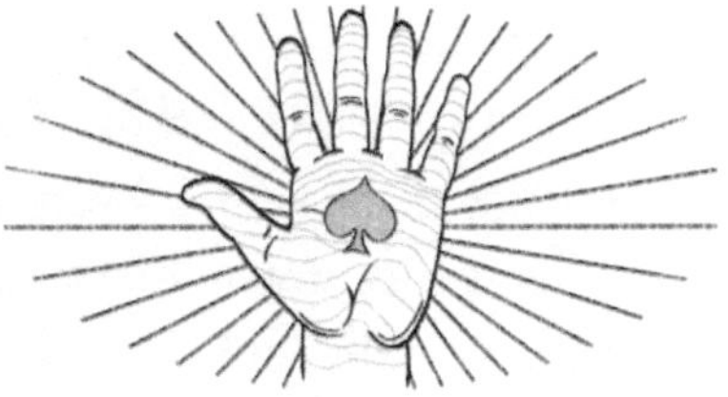

All conscious thought left me as I fled through the tunnel. All I knew was I wanted to escape from the Diamond Queen's compound, to go home. And so I was surprised and a little embarrassed when I staggered through the door and into Jack's bedroom.

The room was dim, illuminated only by the string of white Christmas lights that ran around the ceiling. Jack sat at his desk poring over something on his laptop, and when I came bursting in he looked so surprised that for a moment it seemed he would tip over in his desk chair. Then he was on his feet, catching me in his arms. His strength encompassed me, and I let go, falling into him, tears pouring down my cheeks.

"Aggie, what—?"

"I failed," I said as he half-carried me to his bed and we sat down together on it.

"What happened?" he asked. His hushed voice somehow matched his scent, which was dark and sweet and comforting, like tea sipped fireside on some cold winter night. I just wanted to wrap his whole being around me and forget everything that had happened.

Instead, I pressed my face against his chest while he held me and I told him, in one gushing sentence, everything that had happened in Nashville, finishing with: "So I didn't get the chest. And I basically left Ten to die. Now I can't be queen. And my mom . . ." my words petered out into a final release of tears.

Jack sat quietly for a moment, and though I couldn't see his face, I knew the look of determination that would be there, knew the exact slant of his eyebrows and the clench of his jaw.

"You did your best, Aggie," he said. "Given the situation you were in, I'd say you did amazing. You're lucky you made it out."

"But the Blackovers got the chest," I protested, pulling myself back from the brink of crying again.

"Forget the chest," Jack said, fire in his voice. "Whatever's in there, it can't be worth it. The ace should never have sent you into a hornet's nest like that. And I should never have let you go alone."

I wasn't alone, of course; I had a crew with me, but I knew what he meant. He shouldn't have let me go without *him*. The implication was: without Jack by my side, I was alone, no matter who else was with me. If I was being honest with myself, that's exactly how I felt. At school, I always felt invisible until I became a luck god. Now everyone noticed me, but they didn't *know* me or my secret life as a demigoddess. Molly and I loved each other, but she was always too caught up in her own drama to be very focused on me. Mom knew me, but she was so far gone down the Morbus rabbit hole that I hardly recognized her.

Jack was the only one who really saw me, knew me, and understood me.

Suddenly, I wanted him. I mean, I always wanted him, but I'd always pushed him away, too. Our nights spent in this room together had been nights of *almost*. Nights of teasing, toying, then retreating, and we'd both pushed each other away equally. I didn't need a therapy session to see that I was scared to get too close to him. There were lots of very good reasons.

But now, with him so warm against me, with his strong arms wrapped around me, I wanted to get too close. What was I so afraid of, anyway? Was this boy so much scarier than jumping from windows or dodging bullets? Was his body more threatening than a raging Blackover, or a vengeful Diamond? Was his kiss scarier than Mom in the throes of her bad luck power?

But the answer was yes. Yes, he was terrifying. Maybe that's why I was trembling.

I sat up and looked at him. Really looked at him. We were so near our breath mingled, our lips hung a blink away from touching. Then I shut my eyes and we were kissing, our mouths pressing together, tasting, searching. I pulled him closer, deeper, wanting us to disappear into each other, to forget everything. Let go. Let in. Be reckless. I wasn't even counting heartbeats anymore. And I wouldn't push him away, not this time. I'd pull him close. All the way.

Somewhere in the tangle of our embrace, our hands entwined. I felt something from his hand then, an electric chill —and he pulled his hand away suddenly, made a fist of it and cradled it against his chest. His eyes met mine again. For a second, we both sat suspended there, catching our breath. I wanted to ask him what was wrong.

But then reality caught up with me like a crashing wave, and I knew.

"It's Ten, isn't it?" I asked. "We can't just leave her."

Jack blinked, then his roguish grin made a brief appearance. "Can't we?" Then he sighed, serious again. "You're right, of course. Give me the leprechaun key and I'll—"

"No," I said quickly. "You can't just blaze in and rescue her. I'm telling you, the compound is a deathtrap. And after everything that happened, they're going to be on high alert."

Jack frowned. "Diplomacy then. The Diamantes will want to make an example of Ten, but we might persuade them to take a ransom—as long as the Diamond Queen survives."

"I should be the one to go and talk to them," I said. "I mean, all this is my fault in the first place."

Jack put his hands on my shoulders and shook his head. "No," he said. "You're exhausted. You're beat up. Besides, I know the Diamonds. I know Danusia. Let me do this for you. Please."

The mention of Danusia's name always sent a bolt of jealousy through me, but this was no time to be insecure.

"Okay. Go," I said. "Please. I'm going to feel horrible if—"

Something buzzed in my pocket. I took out my phone.

"Molly!" I said, answering the call.

Molly reeled off at about forty words per second the story of how they'd managed to evade their pursuers. Basically, they'd had a high-speed chase through about ten miles of suburban neighborhoods and winding two-lane roads. When they'd merged onto the highway, the Diamante thugs had turned back —probably because they got the call that I had infiltrated the estate.

Then, Molly and the crew had waited at a truck stop, fueling up on gas and coffee, waiting to hear from me.

"I'm back in Michigan," I said, then sketched what had happened to me as quickly as possible, too weary to go through it all again in detail. "Just come home," I finished, and we ended the call.

"Well, I didn't get them killed," I told Jack. I felt like I could suddenly breathe again.

He gave a wan smile. "I'll take care of Ten." He traced a finger along my bruised, cut cheek. "And I'll send Deuce up to give you some first aid. It's all over, okay? Everything's going to be fine."

"Right. Except I failed the queen trial. Doesn't that mean I'm supposed to die. Isn't that what the ace said?"

The steel came back into Jack's eyes. "I'll talk to the ace. We'll work it out. I won't let anything happen to you, Aggie, I promise. Just stay and rest."

I nodded. "Okay."

Sitting back on his soft bed, I watched him strap on his weapons and leave, shutting the door quietly behind him. My sweet, protective Jack.

Maybe I couldn't lead or fight like a queen, but I could lie like one. Because I had no intention of curling up in bed and giving up. The chest was still out there. The Blackovers were probably bringing it back to Detroit right now, and my queen trial wasn't over for another twenty-four hours. This wasn't finished yet.

30

JACK

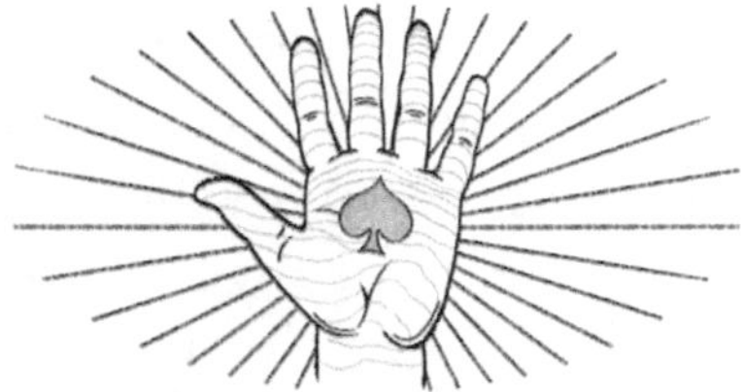

Jack paced in a posh waiting room in one of the taller and newer office buildings in downtown Detroit. He'd been there for over an hour, grumbling to himself, checking his phone, and contemplating the rather generic modern art that adorned the office's white walls. Even in the best of circumstances, Danusia loved to make him wait, but now she was certainly screwing with him. That, or planning a trap.

The place felt more or less like a normal office with its beeping phones, suit-clad workers walking busily to and fro, and a waiting area complete with a little bowl of mints. The only major oddity was the occasional shimmer as a peri drifted through, mostly invisible.

A young female receptionist arrayed in fashionable office

couture watched him with a wariness that made Jack think she probably had a pistol concealed under the desk and knew how to use it. Knowing the Diamantes, she probably did.

He paced. Jack hated waiting. Moments of inaction were when doubt and guilt and grief crept in, like water seeping into the hull of an otherwise seaworthy ship. Proud dreadnoughts had been sunk by less, Jack knew. Negative emotions were insidious, distracting. Seeing Aggie like that, beat up, injured... it made his soul boil, and he couldn't help but feel responsible. He had played a major role in sucking her into this life, after all. Perhaps in some parallel universe, she'd never met him and was just a happy high school senior with no injuries and no blood on her hands. And yet, what could he do? This was the universe they lived in, and here she was a demigoddess, with all the power and pain that entailed.

And all the restrictions. It was ironic—the more powerful he became, the more he felt like a marionette, made to dance by some unseen hand to a tune that only he could hear. And yet that melody called him, a siren song, unceasing. *Peace. You will bring peace,* the ace had said. *But you must buy it with blood.*

He would have preferred to pop in a pair of earbuds and listen to music to drown out his thoughts, but Jack didn't own earbuds anymore. He had loved music once, in an adolescence that seemed a hundred lifetimes ago. He'd even dabbled in learning to play the piano. But now there was no place he felt safe enough to have his sense of hearing blotted out by music, least of all here. If he missed the sound of a footfall, the cocking of a gun, he might be finished.

"Sir?" the receptionist said, "Miss Diamante will see you now."

Jack followed the receptionist down a long corridor lined by glass-doored offices where executive types sat pecking away at computers or talking into phones. Even at eleven o'clock at night, the place still hummed with activity.

On his left, the solid wall gave way to one of glass, and he saw Danusia inside, sitting at one end of an empty conference table. Opposite her, the face of an Asian man took up most of a large screen.

Jack trusted very few people, and Danusia Diamante he trusted less than most. Part of it had to do with the summer they spent together on Cypress a few years ago. It had ended badly, and despite sharing a few pleasant encounters since then, he was pretty sure she'd avenge herself sooner or later. That, or try to win him back. Jack wasn't sure which prospect was scarier.

Danusia was a beautiful, intelligent, savage bitch. Maybe that's why he understood her so well.

She said her goodbyes, then the screen went dark. Danusia nodded toward the door, and the receptionist opened it, letting Jack inside, then stepping over to a bureau that stood against a wall. She opened the drawer and came out with a compact machine gun. Jack watched as she expertly checked the chamber, shut off the safety, then casually walked back to take her position at the door. He'd been right about one thing. The receptionist knew how to use a gun.

He scanned the room. On the far side of the conference table, a pair of glass double doors led out to a balcony. That was one of the results of being a combat-trained guy who also happened to be very unpopular. You noted where the exits were because you often had to use them.

"Jack," Danusia said in that ever-bright British accent of hers. She'd traded in her normal glamorous attire for a business suit, but she wore it like it belonged on a red carpet, and she looked radiant as ever, all shimmering platinum-blonde hair, long smooth legs, and a face that was eerily perfect. A woman had to be very lucky indeed to look like Danusia Diamante.

Jack nodded toward the screen.

"Long-distance relationship?"

Danusia flashed a vicious smile. "Business, I'm afraid."

"It's pretty late for business, isn't it?"

"Not in China,"

"Right," Jack said. "The sun never sets on the Diamantes' business empire, eh?"

"Oh, I don't know if I'd call it an empire," she said. "I prefer a series of covert worldwide monopolies."

"Sure," Jack said. "That sounds better."

Danusia drummed her long fingernails on the glass tabletop. "I'm afraid I can't offer you any investment tips today, though, Jack. Our suits are at war."

Jack tried to keep from glancing at Danusia's friend with the machine gun as he forced a smile. "Come on. War?"

Danusia folded her arms. "Your six and your ten infiltrated our queen's house, robbed her, attacked her, and left her for dead."

"But she isn't dead," Jack pointed out. Then added, less certainly, "Is she?"

"No," Danusia replied. "But before this is over, you may wish she was. She is a performer, and your friends damaged one of her most precious assets."

"A one-of-a-kind guitar signed by Elvis?"

"Her face," Danusia said coldly.

Clearly, Jack's usual swagger was falling flat today. Time to shift tactics.

"Look, I understand the gravity of the situation," he said. "That's why I'm here to talk peace."

"Peace?" Danusia snorted. "Wonderful. Which piece of your ten would you like? I'm sure our queen has some lovely fingers she could send. Maybe an ear? Ooh, how about a tongue? You've some experience with your ten's tongue, haven't you?"

Jack couldn't help but wince. They wouldn't be torturing

Ten. Danusia had to be bluffing... he hoped. "Just tell me what to do to make this right."

Even Danusia's glare was pretty. "I'd love to, Jack. But I'm afraid this issue is above my pay grade."

The secretary shouldered her weapon. No doubt the door behind him was locked as well as the doors to the balcony. Killing him would be like shooting a goldfish in a bowl—unless he managed to get to the balcony. That was his only chance.

"Danusia, don't do this," Jack said. "You know I have big plans. You and I were good together. We could form an alliance. Hell, we could form a dynasty."

Danusia grunted. "And how many dynasties have you tried to start since we were last together, hmm? Sorry Jack. It's too late. You'll never be a dynasty. You'll just be a stain someone has to scrub off this beautiful marble floor."

The office chairs lined up along the conference table all swiveled at once. Sitting in them were half a dozen sprites who now wavered into being—each armed with a gun. Right again. It *was* a trap.

Jack had been forced to leave his weapons in the lobby, but he flared his charm now and assumed a fighting stance.

The sprites brandished their weapons, and—

"Stop!" Danusia shouted, looking aghast. She whispered, "Your hands..."

His hands, yes. Jack had almost forgotten that Danusia would be able to see the marks there. A heart on one hand, a spade on the other.

"Oh, you mean these?" Jack showed her his palms, and the power within them flared brighter. Charm and hex. It was something that hadn't been seen in centuries: a luck god with two powers. It created a strange feeling in his body, wielding both at once, a tingly sensation at once exhilarating and painful. Like being on extremely pleasant drugs while also being torn in half.

And yet he'd already learned how potent the combined powers could be. It was one thing to pull. Another to push. But when you could pull and push together, then you had true leverage, the ability to move worlds. He was only beginning to understand and control that power. To live through the next few minutes, he'd have to learn fast.

For once, Danusia's angelic face registered total shock.

"You really did it," she whispered.

Jack nodded. "That's why this is a crucial moment, Dani. We could team up. If you gave me the mark of Diamonds—"

Her shrill laugh betrayed her fear. "Then you'd be even harder to stop," she said. "You know the teachings, Jack. Since the day Uthule the tyrant was drawn and quartered by the four original aces, blending the suits has been an abomination."

"That's an old story," Jack said. "One they teach us to keep our power divided, to keep us constantly fighting one another. But if I unify the suits, I'll be able to—"

"You won't unify the suits, Jack," she said. Tears glistened in her eyes, a bad sign. "This ends now."

She nodded, and the sprites and the secretary all opened fire, a sound so loud Jack felt as if he were being punched in both ears.

He flared the charm and the hex at once, as hard as he could. Bullets zinged past all around him, some rustling his clothes or fluttering his hair. A sting of pain erupted at his right shoulder, but he knew better than to let it slow him. Instead, he streaked forward and leapt between two of the seated sprites and onto the table. Two more steps, then he jumped again, hurtling over Danusia to slam into the balcony doors with all his force. The lock held, and Jack stumbled backward, dizzy from the impact. He held both his hands up, palms facing toward the doors again. They were made of bulletproof glass, no doubt, but...

Jack envisioned one of the sprites' bullets missing him,

hitting the glass, and causing it to shatter. Bad luck for the sprites, good luck for Jack. He flared his powers, his right hand burning with charm, his left tingly with the icy flow of hex. *Bad luck for Danusia, good luck for me. Come on!* With a *boom* the glass doors shattered, shards spilling to his feet like a shower of glittering gems.

"Stop him!" Danusia shouted.

As Jack rushed out to the balcony, she lunged after him and managed to grab the back of his jacket. Jack twisted around, his back against the railing, brought his leg up and stomp-kicked her in the gut. Not very gentlemanly, but when a woman was trying to slaughter you, equal treatment was required. She stumbled backward, her face crumpling with pain. The force of the kick pushed Jack backward so that for a second, the small of his back rested on a railing, his body balanced like a lever on a fulcrum. Then he kicked his legs up and flipped backward over the rail—falling from twenty stories up.

31

AGGIE

In a movie, I'd have snagged some weapons and ammo from the Valentine armory and immediately stormed back out into the night. But this was no action flick, and I was no superhero. I was a high school girl who was battered, filthy, exhausted, and starving. Worst of all, I had no idea what to do next. I had to find the Blackovers and get the chest back, sure. But where were they? How would I find them?

To answer that question, I retreated to my favorite thinking spot, the shower. The steam and soap and pleasantly hot water did wonders for my aching body and my racing mind. But although I emerged a lot cleaner, I was no closer to a solution.

The Blackovers would likely take the chest to one of their two main hideouts in the city: the brewery or the casino. But staking out both locations would be tough. Each were large places with multiple entrances, and it would require a whole flock of bird drones or a full crew of Valentines to keep watch over both locations. I'd left Deuce's drone in Tennessee, and the Valentines weren't supposed to be helping me. If I did somehow spot the car as it arrived at one of the Blackovers strongholds, I'd then have to charge in and steal the chest away from God knew how many armed Clubs and sycos. That would be no easy task, especially when I didn't know where they were going, so I couldn't set a trap ahead of time. It would be far better to ambush Marley and his goons before they reached their destination, when they were far from help and had their guard down, but I had no clue how to pull that off.

I'd wandered out of the bathroom into the bedroom and was halfway toweled off when there came a soft knock at the door. My mind irrationally went to Ten and I snatched my dagger off the dresser before hastily wrapping the towel around myself and calling, "Come in."

Deuce's shaggy head peeked in the doorway, and I saw that he was carrying a tray of food.

"Hey," he said. "I heard you were here, and I brought you some—hot damn woman, what happened to your face?"

I laughed. "What happened to yours?"

"Touché," Deuce self-consciously rubbed the patchy beard he'd been growing out ever since becoming a three. "I think mine can be chalked up to bad genetics and poor personal hygiene. You, on the other hand, look like you head-butted an anvil."

"No," I said. "Just a few Blackovers and a country music star."

"That's what Jack said. The one who sings 'Carnie Boy,' right? I'd like to headbutt her, too. I want to hate that song, but it's so freaking catchy." He gave a falsetto rendition of the chorus with ironic gusto.

It felt so good to laugh that for an instant I forgot all the stress and danger and pressure I was under and felt like a normal, happy human.

Deuce's eyes had wandered from my face, and I glanced down to find my towel slipping. I hiked it up and Deuce snapped his eyes down to the tray, an awkward moment passing between us.

"Uh, well, I'll just leave this here, and let you rest, O exulted future queen." He set the tray down on a table and backed toward the door. "Jack asked me to give you some first aid, but I can come back when you're—"

"Wait," I said. "Stay. I need your brain."

He eyed me suspiciously. "I think the calzone I brought would be much tastier."

"Not to eat, like, zombie-style. Although I'm hungry enough that if you hadn't brought that food with you...never mind. I have a problem to figure out. Wait just a second."

I slipped into the bathroom and dressed. When I came out, I explained my conundrum with the Blackovers while Deuce ace-bandaged my thumb (it was sprained, not broken) and I ate the delectable cheeseburger he'd brought.

"...so I'm trying to figure out how to track the Blackovers down," I finished. "The clock is ticking. I have to get that chest by morning, or I fail the queen trial."

Deuce thoughtfully rubbed his beard again. Actually, I decided, it didn't look too bad on him.

"I think you're right," he said finally. "The key is to intercept the car before they get to one of their bases. Otherwise, we won't get that chest without a bloodbath." He took out his phone and pulled up a map of the area surrounding the casino. "But look at all these different approaches they could take to the casino. I mean, most likely they'll come here, straight from the highway, but... if not, you'll miss them. Not to mention, they could go to the brewery instead. They also have that fight gym up in Berkeley they might go to."

He shook his head despairingly. I sighed, too. I'd come so far, put the lives of my crew at risk, nearly killed the Diamond Queen, and lost Ten. And for what? To fail now, when the chest was going to be so close?

"We need to locate the car earlier, while it's on the highway," I said. "But finding it would be like finding a needle in a haystack."

"Or a grain of sand on a beach…" Deuce mused.

My eyes widened with excitement. "Or a flea…"

Realization dawned on Deuce's face, too.

"On a cat!" we said at once.

I whipped out my phone and pulled up my FleaSpotter app. "All we need are some images taken from above of a car like theirs," I said, breathless with excitement. "We train the app to spot it, then instead of scanning videos of a dog or cat, we use the system to scan real-time satellite videos of I-75 North."

"How long until their car should get here?" Deuce asked, looking at the time on his phone.

"Assuming they're speeding and not stopping…"

"A fair assumption."

"A little over three hours," I said.

"Can you train the algorithm and set it up to scan the satellite images in time? And do you think it will work at night?"

"Don't know," I said, thinking. "But I do know we need a picture of a big, black, brand new BMW sedan taken from above."

Fortunately, I remembered the make of the car the Blackovers drove when they'd taken the chest. They must have stolen it at the party because it was undamaged, unlike the vehicle Seemor had dropped the tree on.

I fluttered my eyelashes.

Deuce gave me a thumbs up. "I have a phone, I know where the dealership is, and I can climb a light pole."

I squinted at him. "Can you, though?"

He grunted, annoyed. "Shut up. With charm, yes, I can do it."

"Then go, and text me the pictures as soon as you have them. Get a bunch. I'll look for car pictures online and get started tweaking the algorithm."

"As her royal highness commands," Deuce said grandly. He swiped a French fry off my plate, then hustled out the door.

32

JACK

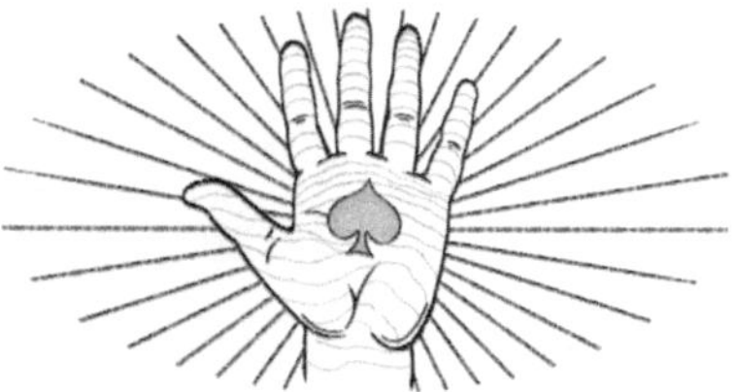

Jack backflipped off the Diamantes balcony and fell through the night. As he did, he pulled a ripcord Teemor the tailor had installed in his sports coat. A nylon membrane released, stretching between his arms and his body, effectively turning his coat into a wingsuit. As the air caught him, he flared charm so hard his hands burned, and after a moment of terrifying plummeting and wobbling, he was no longer falling; he was flying.

Danusia's furious shout and the crackle of gunfire followed him, but Jack just drifted away from them, soaring between buildings and bobbing on an updraft. He would have given anything to see Danusia's face at that moment. She'd thought she'd had him, and then—

Bad luck for Danusia, good luck for Jack. A push, a pull,

and he was free, flying through the night like... who? James Bond? Batman? Aggie would know the right pop culture analogy, but whichever it was, he liked it.

Of course, full wingsuits had a membrane stretching between the legs as well as the arms. If Jack had that, it would have given him a lot more surface area to slow his descent, not to mention more stability and control. The setup he had wouldn't have worked at all without ample charm. As it was, he shot toward Jefferson Avenue like a meteorite holding an umbrella.

A streetlight pole appeared just ahead of him, and he managed to jog left and dodge it—barely. The pavement sped up toward him. Cars roared past below, their headlights deadly white streaks. If he landed in the street and a car struck him, he'd be toast.

Charm. It was going to take a hell of a lot of it to make this landing. And it would have to be pure charm, too. Hex wouldn't help him here. There was nothing to push against, nothing willing him toward destruction except the brutally indifferent forces of gravity and asphalt and traffic. His charm seemed slightly blunted since he'd added hex to the mix, but it would have to be enough.

The road rose toward him nearer, nearer.

Tuck and roll, Valentine. Tuck and roll.

And then run.

Because in less than a minute, Danusia and her crew would swarm out of that building, and if he had so much as sprained an ankle, they'd have him, and there would be no second chance at escape.

Jack flared charm so hard he felt like his right hand might burn off. At the same time, he pushed his arms wide to maximize the surface area of his suit and tried to lean back to slow himself. He bent his knees, gritted his teeth.

Charm, dammit, charm.

Still coming in too fast…

Then something touched his feet, making him gasp. A delivery truck had come up behind him, speeding along at roughly the same speed he was, and he alighted on it as delicately as a flower being dropped into a crystal vase, dropping to his hands and knees on the truck's roof. He could almost have wept with relief. Instead, he laughed. Looking back over his shoulder, he saw Danusia and her minions in the distance, charging out of the Ren Center's entrance. Then the delivery van turned a corner, a building came between them, and the Diamonds were gone.

Jack waited until the van came to a red light and stopped, then he slipped off the back of the vehicle, landing in the street, and walked casually to the sidewalk as if he'd been nothing but a typical jaywalker.

Teemor would need to refine this wingsuit a bit, Jack thought. But then it had saved his life, so he couldn't complain too much.

He called for a ride on a phone app, then stepped into a shadowed doorway to wait. Waiting again. God, how he hated it. All sorts of thoughts flooded in, thoughts he preferred not to have. Hard memories. Pessimistic premonitions. Pangs of guilt.

Ten.

He'd failed to save her. He'd tried. He'd done his best. But he'd failed.

Still, it was possible she'd save herself. She was resourceful. She was a good fighter and a good talker, plus she had charm on her side. Of course, the Diamantes did, too.

Jack couldn't be expected to do more for Ten. Ten had been awful to him for the last three months—not that he could blame her, given the way their relationship had ended, first with the revelation that he'd been involved with Carlotta Black-over, then with his starting to date Aggie. Ten's hatred for him was valid. And Jack didn't have an obligation to save people who hated him, did he?

I owe Ten nothing, Jack told himself. *If it were me, she'd leave me to the wolves.*

Except he knew that wasn't true.

He thought then of a phrase his mother—his real mother—had been fond of saying. *No man can serve two masters.* It was from the Bible, Jack guessed, and it meant no one could chase both God and money. But the words hit him differently now as he looked down at his hands, one glowing red, the other that strange, darkish purple.

I'm not serving two masters, he told himself. *I have two powers. And they serve me.*

But already the pull of the dark work was tugging on him, wiggling painfully in his mind like a bloody loose tooth. That feeling had been steadily growing louder and more insistent ever since the spade mark had appeared on his left hand. Always, *the work* was a compulsion that was hard to resist. No drug in the world could compare to the feeling of completing *the work*, the elation, the exultant power. And bad luck work, Jack had discovered, was far more addicting that good luck work could ever be. So far, he'd resisted doing it. Hurting people. Watching them suffer. And yet if the power it gave him afterward was equal to the compulsion he felt now, it would give him the ability to do so much. Just cause a little suffering in exchange for the ability to do a lot of good, that was the trade-off. And Jack could control it, he told himself. That balance. He could make sure the good outweighed the bad.

But can you? Some deep, inner voice asked.

Jack didn't bother answering. He couldn't answer. Time was too short, the call of *the work* too strong. He lurched out of the doorway and into the night, following it.

33

AGGIE

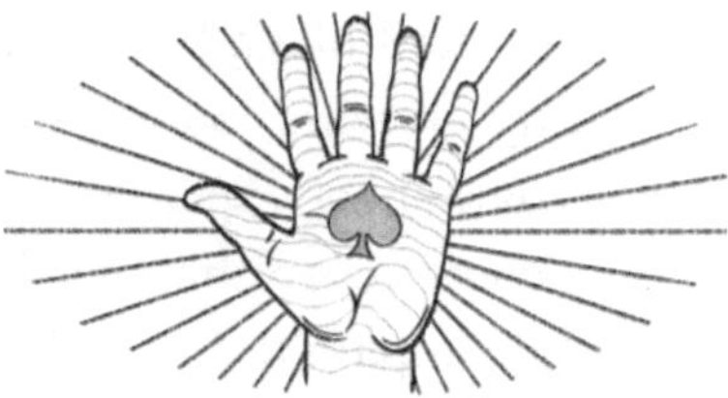

The next few hours were a blur, but there was a lot of computer coding and a lot of coffee involved. Deuce returned with seven photos of BMW sedans from above and a bruised shin he'd gotten running from the dealership's security guard.

"What if they traded out their stolen BMW for a different car?" Deuce asked. "To avoid the police or something?"

"Then we're screwed," I said without looking up from my work. "We just have to hope they were in too much of a rush to get back here to steal something different." It was a gamble, but I'd gotten used to gambling lately.

When the app was ready to test, I connected it to the traffic satellite website and hit the "scan for fleas" button. Deuce and I held our breaths, watching as the app came up with... over a hundred matches.

"Ugh," I groaned. Fleas were a lot different from cars, as it turned out. I explained the problem to Deuce, and he parroted his own synopsis back to me to confirm that he understood:

"So, the original algorithm just had to differentiate little moving specks—fleas— from the surrounding fur. But this version has to differentiate the Blackovers car from other cars. Two totally different tasks."

"Exactly," I said, already scanning the internet for more pictures of cars from above to train the algorithm on. There weren't many, and the ones there were, for the most part, didn't include the whole vehicle. Most were fancy close-ups of sunroofs, stylized sales shots.

"I'm going to have to climb another light pole, aren't I?" Deuce said.

"Several," I agreed. "Get pictures of as many different cars as you can."

He sighed, eyeing his scuffed hands. "I wish you could come with me. You know, to give my tubby ass a boost. Those poles are slippery."

I smiled, clapping him on the shoulder. "Sorry, buddy. I've got to keep working here. This pot of coffee isn't going to drink itself."

He nodded, looking determined, and headed for the door.

"Deuce," I said, and he turned back. "You're the best."

He smiled, then his look turned serious. "Aggie... Jack..."

I waited, but he didn't finish.

"Jack what?"

But instead of answering, he looked at his phone. "It's getting late. Or early. We have to hurry," he said, and left.

The pictures trickled in text by text. As each one arrived, I fed it into the algorithm's training sequence. *This, not that.* BMW sedan, not Toyota minivan. BMW sedan, not Honda hatchback. BMW sedan, not Ford SUV. Black BMW sedan, not white BMW sedan. It was tedious work, and when rain started falling around 2 AM, messing up the quality of the photos, it made my job even harder.

Worse, I was distracted. It had been hours since Jack had left to meet with Danusia. The Diamantes were our traditional allies, but after what Ten and I had done to Diamond Queen, they would be out for revenge. Hurting or killing Jack would be one surefire way to get back at me and Ten. Danusia seducing him would be another. Even though we were by no means a real, official, exclusive couple, I didn't believe Jack would do that to me. Still, whenever I thought of Danusia, I couldn't help but remember the first night I'd met her, when I found her in Jack's room, sitting on his bed with that smug *cat who ate the canary* look on her pretty face. I'd never directly asked Jack what happened that night, and I probably didn't want to know. I knew it was shallow to be just as worried about Jack hooking up with Danusia as I was about her killing him. But love can be shallow sometimes.

I texted Jack. No response. Surprise, surprise.

While I worried, I worked. After every few photos Deuce sent me, I'd run the algorithm on the satellite map of I-75 again. The number of hits I got steadily dropped, from over 189 to 144, 144 to 79, 79 to 31, 31 to 7.

Around 4 AM, Deuce returned, wet, bedraggled, and tired but still smiling.

"Okay. I think this should do it," I said, finishing one more round of algo training.

"It better," Deuce sighed. "My taint is seriously chafed from sliding down all those poles."

I grinned and yawned at once. "You want me to refer you to a doctor? I've got a great taint guy."

"Taint guy," Deuce laughed, yawning at the same time.

"I think we might have it. Here, you do the honors." I offered him my phone.

"Alright," he said, tapping the screen. "Let's find some fleas."

I stared at him and at the back of my phone for what seemed like way too long for a normal dramatic pause.

"Well?" I said at last.

"No fleas," he said. Then turned the phone around. "Just one black BMW sedan. And it's coming into the city now."

34

MOLLY

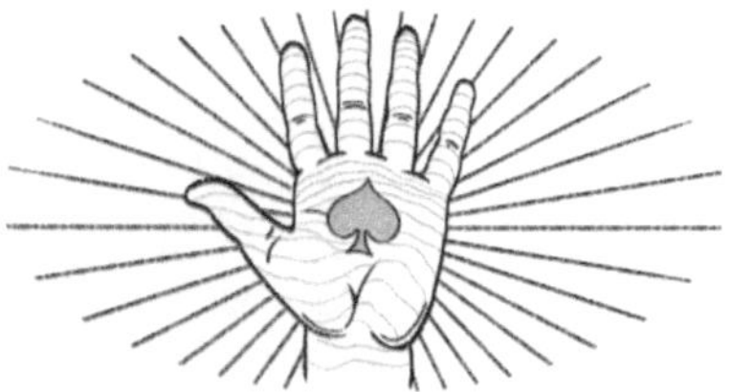

A phone charger. That's all Molly thought about as she made her way from the parked SUV (which was filled with her irritable peri friends and riddled with a shocking number of bullet holes) to her mom's town house. Her phone had died, and she wanted to connect with Aggie before the crew showed up at the Valentine mansion, in case Aggie wasn't there or there was some other drama they needed to know about. And anyway, they were going right past Molly's house; it was simple to stop in and grab it.

And so that's what Molly's mind was on—the charger—when she walked in and noticed the cardboard boxes. Dozens of them were stacked along one wall, and the house looked sparse, like someone was packing up to move. The second thing Molly noticed was her mom, James, and Mel all standing in the middle of their living room, shirtless and clothed only in red loincloths. A second woman in a red loincloth stood in front of them, reading from a binder and wearing a crown of flowers in her long, flowing gray hair. The air smelled of burning sage, and an array of candles sat flickering on the mantel. The TV was on and tuned to a satellite radio station streaming New Age music. The way everyone was standing, it almost looked like...

"You made it!" Lauren said.

Molly blinked, taking everyone in, unsure how to respond.

"Made it?" she said dumbly.

"To the wedding!" Lauren exclaimed, and her two beaus smiled. The female shaman—who was officiating the wedding, apparently—nodded.

"What in the sweet ever-loving name of balls are you talking about?" Molly said.

"I texted you all about it," Lauren sounded baffled.

Molly held up her phone. "My phone died."

"Oh, well," Lauren said, brightening again. "We had an epiphany in the desert and realized that's where we belong. Together. In Palm Springs. We already made an offer on a condo. Well, James did. And it has the cutest little bedroom for you—"

"Whoa. I am not moving to Palm Springs with you and your man harem," Molly said, her nose wrinkling in disgust.

Her mother stiffened. "Well, if you think I'm giving your father custody—"

"No," Molly said. "I'm well aware that Dad doesn't give a crap about me. I'll just... get emancipated."

Lauren folded her arms. "To get emancipated you have to be able to live independently. Pay your own rent. Your own utilities. Your own gas and car insurance. I know you're making a lot at your library job, but—"

Molly snorted. "You have no idea. It's fine. Go. I don't need you. At all."

One of the boys, Mel or James—she was still confused about who was who—put a comforting hand on her mother's shoulder. "Hey, take it easy on your mom, kiddo," he said.

"If you call me kiddo again, I will break every bone in your skinny hipster body," Molly said.

The guy blinked, stunned.

"I think if you just hear us out—" Lauren began.

"Perhaps we might all benefit from some guided meditation," the officiant suggested.

"No," Molly snapped. "No meditation. No talk. I have another family waiting for me. Another home. Another life. And all the money in the world. So *I don't need you.*"

She stormed to the kitchen island, yanked a phone charger from the plug, and stormed back toward the door through a room blurred by tears.

She opened the door and turned back. "And I have someone who actually loves me. So congrats on your wedding. And good luck with your life. Because mine is going to be better than you could ever imagine," she said, and she left, slamming the door behind her.

35

MARLEY

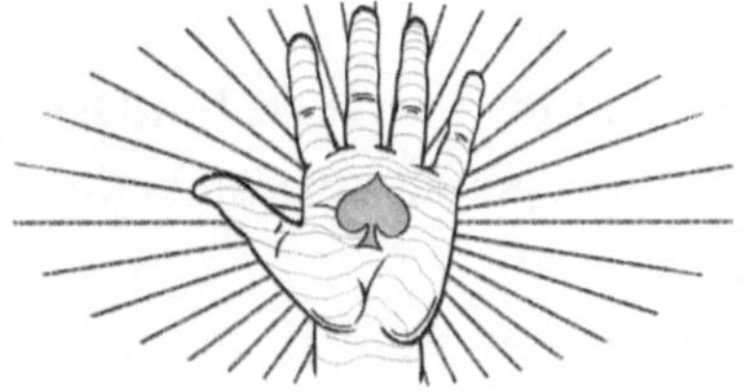

Dawn light crept into the sky as Marley and his crew rolled into the casino parking garage. Despite the coffee and the pills, Marley's eyes burned with exhaustion. Stallion, the new number two, snored in the backseat. Moira, the four, was back there as well, cracking her knuckles and humming to herself in the creepy, not-quite-on-key way that Marley found so unnerving. Moira was cute, but she reminded him of a roller derby version of one of those spooky dolls whose eyes shut when you laid them down to sleep. He would still have been happy to lay her down, however. Cinco—Dammit, Denny; it was always hard to keep track of reshuffled nicknames when someone died and everyone moved up in rank—Denny drove, his head nodding with sleepiness as they passed under the arm of the entrance gate.

"Pull around to the elevator," Marley said. "Thad is in the penthouse, and he wants to take a look in the chest before we hand it over to that witch of Spades."

"She gives me the heebie-jeebies," Moira said. "I heard she used to be a professor."

"Yep. And she's the mother of that little pain in our ass Heart, Kindergarten," Marley affirmed.

"A professor," Denny Seven slurred. He was talking funny because Kindergarten had shoved a dagger up through the soft skin under his chin when she was thrashing around in the car, and he had a bandage running all the way around his head. He was lucky the blade had hit one of his upper teeth, or it might have gone into his brain. "I'd hate to be in that woman's class."

"Don't worry, you never would be," Marley said. "You have to be smart to go to college."

Marley chuckled at his own joke, but Denny glared at him. "For your information, I got an associate's degree. With a three-seven GPA. Prick."

Marley shrugged. They were all too tired for jokes, apparently. The car lurched to a halt next to the bank of elevators.

"Fine. Pop the trunk, Einstein," Marley told Denny. "Let's lug this chest upstairs and get this mission over with. I need a bed, a Scotch, and an ice pack. Not necessarily in that order."

Denny popped the trunk, then reached back and thumped Stallion's leg with his hand. "Hey, Sleeping Beauty. Wake your ass up and grab that chest."

Stallion—Christ, what an absurd name—stirred and sat up, wiping drool from his chin. Thad had picked him up on the MMA fighting circuit. Apparently, he'd killed a guy in the ring, which lost him his fight career but made him hot shit in Thad's book. Marley didn't much like the kid. He wasn't huge —more the wiry type, with abs like an underwear model's and long arms like a chimpanzee. But he was still more brawn than brains, and Marley was getting sick of being the only intelligent person among savages. As much crap as he gave Denny, the newly minted seven actually was one of the smart ones. Carlotta had also been intelligent, probably the smartest one in the suit—much good that had done her. Marley wasn't sure what Thad had done with her, but he had the distinct feeling that if she ever did show up again, it would be in pieces.

Stallion rubbed his eyes like a sleepy toddler.

"Alright, let's—" Marley started to open the door when a car alarm went off somewhere in the parking garage, a horn blaring. Headlights flashed on one of the parked cars down the row ahead. Then, a second alarm went off, closer. Then a third.

Marley's hand went to his gun. Denny, Moira, Stallion, and Marley all opened their doors and stood, drawing their weapons. Marley took the lead, moving down the row of cars with his .45 at the ready. As he got a clear view of each space between cars, his finger tensed on the trigger. But each aisle was clear. *Clear, clear, clear,* until he came upon... a bird.

It seemed to be injured, fluttering on the concrete floor between vehicles. Denny and Stallion came up behind him and looked at it over his shoulder.

"Pfft. Just a bird," Denny said to Stallion, holstering his weapon.

Marley stepped forward and fired. The thing went still save for a few twitches—and sparks. Marley snatched it up, holding it by its head. Its body dangled by wires.

"Not a bird," he growled. "A drone."

Thud.

"What was that?" Moira whispered, her head whipping toward the sound.

It came from over by their car. As one, the four Blackovers spun toward the noise.

The chest.

"Come on!" Marley snarled, leading the charge. Gun at the

ready, he rounded the back of the car and looked in the open trunk.

Empty.

"Dammit!" he shouted, slamming the trunk lid. "Fan out and—"

Ding.

The elevator.

He looked over to see that damned Heart girl—Kindergarten—Aggie—framed up like a picture in the elevator, smiling at them mockingly. She held up a hand and waved, the heart on it glowing so brightly with charm that he almost had to look away. At her feet sat the chest.

"Shoot to kill!" Marley shouted, and his crew opened fire just as the elevator doors slid shut.

36

JACK

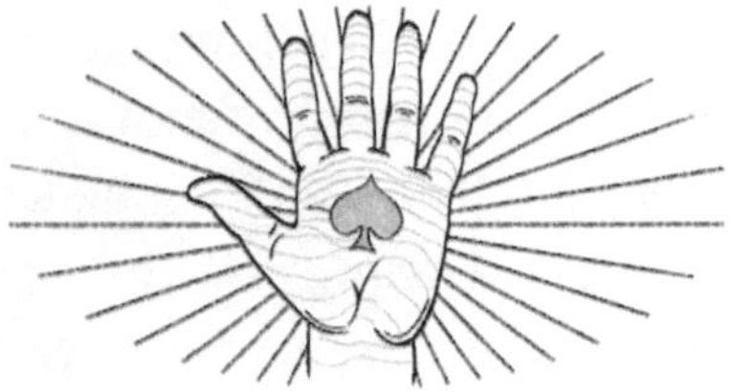

Jack had no idea how much time had passed. All he knew was there was blood on his hands, slick, sticky as syrup, and still warm. As the need to do the dark work had grown stronger, pain had built up in that black-pipped hand until it felt like a scalding brand. That pain had ebbed now that *the work* was done, fading to a faint ache. For the third time he reached down and pressed two fingers to the neck of the man splayed out at his feet, checking his pulse. He was dead, and no amount of charm would bring him back.

Sirens howled in the distance, growing louder.

I should go, Jack thought dully. But he stood transfixed by the dead man's face. It looked almost normal, as if he were sleeping, and yet there was something off about its proportions, as if the fall had cracked the man's skull and shifted his face out of shape. Jack felt he could relate to the dead man. He felt rather shifted out of shape himself.

Tilting his head back, Jack looked up at the fire escape. How high was the top? Five stories? Six?

"Move," came a voice, and a paramedic hustled up carrying a medical bag. He jostled Jack out of the way, then knelt next to the dead man. He checked for a pulse just as Jack had a moment before. A second paramedic joined him, and the two spoke in low voices, tearing the man's shirt to examine his wounds.

He's broken. Too broken, Jack thought.

"You see what happened?"

Jack looked over to see a firefighter standing at his side. Behind him loomed a huge, red firetruck with flashing red lights. In his numbness, Jack hadn't even seen it pull up.

"Uh, yeah," Jack said. "I was walking by, and he was up on the top of the fire escape, leaning over the railing. He shouted something. I think he was drunk, maybe. Then he fell."

It was the truth, though not the whole truth.

I hexed him and he fell. Though he didn't speak them aloud, the words had the ring of an accusation. Of a conviction. Of a sentence. Reflexively, he closed his hand, hiding the black mark there.

It was irrevocable. The man was dead. He'd never not be dead. Jack would never not have killed him.

No, not me, Jack thought. *Luck killed him. Just bad luck. It happens all the time.*

The painful throb in the black-marked left hand had ebbed, but a tingling, itching sensation in his right was growing more insistent. It wanted good luck work, as if yearning to make up for the bad luck the other hand had caused. Was this how it would be? Jack wondered. A constant, maddening tug of war with him as the rope? Was that the price of his power? And if so, would it be worth it?

Yes. Of course it will be worth it to end the bloodshed between the suits.

Another of his mother's Bible verses flitted through his mind. He was sure the words were wrong, but he knew the gist. *What will it profit a man if he gains the whole world, but loses his soul?*

Peace? Is that what he meant to bring about?

Even if he succeeded, it seemed there'd be peace among the suits but a war inside himself. What irony.

"...the police might want to get a statement," the firefighter was saying to him. "They should be here any minute."

Jack nodded, barely hearing the man. He was looking again at the dead man's face. So nearly normal. But *not quite.*

He turned away and began walking up the street.

"Hey, buddy—" the firefighter began, but Jack ignored him, his footfalls carrying him up the road, into the night. Suddenly, up ahead, a figure stepped out of the shadows under a streetlight.

Jack flared both charm and hex, ready to defend himself. Then, he saw who it was.

Deuce.

For a second, he nearly turned and ran. But that was silly. Why would he run from Deuce? *He has no way of knowing what just happened,* Jack reminded himself.

Jack continued toward Deuce, and they met in a halo of light. He waited for his friend to launch into one of his usual diatribes—jokes, banter, or at least an update on Aggie. But he said nothing, just watched Jack warily, his usually smiling eyes looking hard and haunted. Very un-Deuce-like.

"What's up?" Jack asked.

"You tell me."

Jack huffed with irritation and walked past his friend. "I don't have time for games, Deuce. What is it?"

"Well, I came to tell you Aggie and I figured out how to track the Blackovers with the chest," Deuce said, trailing after Jack. "And she went to retrieve it."

Jack wheeled on him. "You let her go alone?"

"Queen trial, remember?" Deuce said. "We aren't allowed to help. But I thought you'd want to be there when she gets back, so I came to look for you."

"Yeah," Jack said absently. He approached his parked motorcycle and threw a leg over.

"I figured you'd be here, talking to the Diamonds," Deuce went on. "I found your bike here and was going to wait. Then I saw you zing over me like a flying squirrel. I chased after you and . . ."

Jack saw where this was going, saw the accusation in Deuce's eyes, and he wanted to get it over with. "And?" he said, turning the motorcycle's key.

"And I saw you hex that man and make him fall," Deuce finished. "Bad luck work."

"He was drunk," Jack said. "And probably suicidal."

Deuce's silence felt like an accusation.

"There are worse things than dying instantly," Jack said, his voice rising. "Falling from that height, he could have broken every bone in his body and still lived. Sometimes it's good luck to die."

"Yeah? Good luck? Show me your hands."

Jack and his friend locked eyes. Jack's hands tightened on the grips of his motorcycle. Both hands hurt now, a maddening, buzzing ache.

"Fine." He pulled both hands off the bike and showed his palms to Deuce. The light from each—red from the right, dark purplish from the left—lit each side of Deuce's face differently, making him look strange.

"You really did it," Deuce breathed.

"Don't look so surprised," Jack said. "I told you I would."

Deuce shook his head again. "But I never thought... Spades? Aggie's mom inducted you?"

"She did," Jack agreed. A joke half-formed in his mind, something about getting on his girlfriend's mom's good side, but it died before making it to his lips. *Was* Aggie his girlfriend, anyway? Once tonight was over, she'd be married to the king. That is, assuming she made it back with the chest. And even if she weren't becoming queen, what would she think when she saw the black mark on his left hand? *She'll hate you,* some bleak voice inside Jack whispered. She won't understand. No one understands.

Deuce blinked and took a deep breath, clearly struggling to process Jack's revelation. "I'm going back to the house," Deuce said. "Aggie should be back soon, and she's going to need my support. Our support. You coming?"

For a moment, the look they shared had the feeling of a challenge, a faceoff. Jack's left hand even went reflexively to the hilt of his dagger. But that was just the bad luck work tugging on him again, he realized. He'd never draw a weapon on Deuce. He would never have to.

It irritated him that Deuce doubted that he'd return home to support Aggie. And yet, maybe he was right. Go back to the Valentine mansion and they'd eventually notice his spade mark. Or Deuce would blab. Either way, his secret would be out. Some of his fellow Valentines would understand, but most would never trust him again. Some might even attack him. Perhaps it might be better, safer, to skip all that. To just get on this bike and ride away, to do the difficult work that had to be done alone, from the shadows.

And then he thought of Aggie. Her queen trial was ending, but there would be more danger ahead. In fact, Jack suspected, the worst might be yet to come. And he would be there for her, no matter what the others thought. He would be there even if it killed him.

"I'll see you at the house." Jack fired up the motorcycle and revved the throttle, making the engine thunder. Then he dropped the clutch and fired off into the night.

37

AGGIE

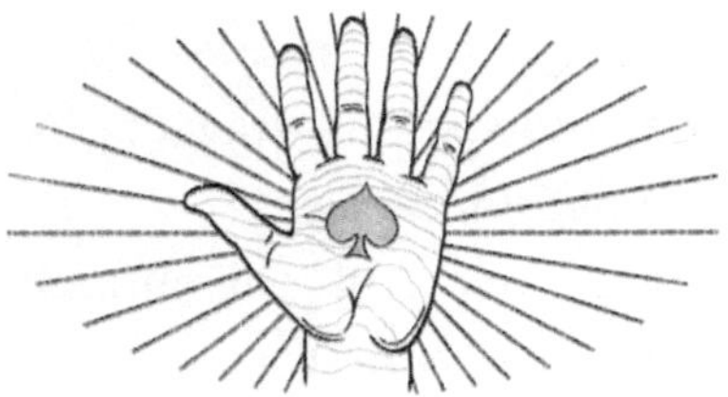

Clang, clang, clang—bullets dented the metal elevator doors as they slid closed. The last thing I glimpsed was the face of Marley, a rictus of shock and fury. Then the doors clapped shut, and he was gone.

The leprechaun key in my hand pulsed gold, and I thought of home.

Not home, I corrected myself. *The Valentine mansion.*

Why had I thought of it as home?

Maybe because I have nowhere else, now, I thought. Could our apartment really be home if Mom wasn't there? If she was living in some wrecked hospital with a flock of tortured crows and a crew of wretched sycos?

No, I had no home. Not until Mom was back to herself again.

The elevator dinged, and the doors slid open to the leprechaun underground. The tunnel they revealed this time was a long, narrow cavern. Guano spattered the floors, and cobwebs and moss caked the damp walls. I entered hunched over, trying not to touch anything. Apparently, I was more creeped out by the prospect of giant spiders than I had been by Marley's bullets. After a lot of grunting and sweating and cursing, I managed to drag the chest through about fifty yards of cavern.

The door I emerged from was my own Valentine house bedroom closet, and I had to resist the urge to flop down in my bed and sleep for the next twenty or thirty hours. But that wouldn't be the queenly thing to do, would it? I had a trial to complete. And time was very short. Already, I could see tepid sunlight peeking through the blinds.

Mina was the first to spot me dragging the chest down the stairs and into the main stairway.

"Aggie. You did it. She did it!" she announced and reached to grab one side of the heavy chest.

"No. I can't have help," I reminded her.

She contented herself with walking along beside me, bellowing: "Aggie is back! She did it!"

The rest of the suit emerged one by one, like townsfolk in the opening number of a musical, popping heads out of doors, peeking around corners. Even the sycos and sprites who usually went about their business of cooking and cleaning for the Valentines unnoticed, emerged to stare.

Dubs came to tousle my hair. "Nice work, you!"

"Jack and Deuce?" I grunted, still dragging the chest.

"Not back yet," he said. I tried to ignore the dark edge to his voice.

Jack had gone to the Diamantes. When he hadn't come back, Deuce had gone to look for him; I knew that much.

I needed to find out if they were okay. But first, I had to get this chest down to the ace to finish my queen's trial; the sun outside was getting brighter, about to break the horizon.

I lugged the chest through the throne room, toward the hallway beyond, and—backed into something at once hard and soft. Flesh. Muscle. I turned to find Cobe blocking my path.

His eyes were red-rimmed, and he looked like he hadn't slept all night.

"Cobe?" I prompted warily.

"Cobe, move!" Mina barked from behind me.

But Cobe didn't move. Instead, he reached to his belt and drew two daggers.

"Oh, come on!" I sighed, dropping the chest.

"Sorry, Six," Cobe said. "But you know how it is with me and Ten. She'll be the better queen."

I felt powerfully aware of all the eyes on us. Even the king had entered. He stood near the throne, arms folded, but made no move to help me. Some fiancé he was. I turned my attention back to Cobe.

"You might be right," I said. "I didn't choose this. And maybe Ten would have been better. But I completed my trial. I'm here. And she's not."

We glared at one another, both unyielding.

"So get the hell out of my way," I finished.

Cobe's hands tightened on the hilt of his daggers, his jaw clenched. I wanted to grab my own weapons, but I resisted. If I drew my dagger, this really would be a fight. And I didn't want to hurt Cobe. Still, his eyes bored into me. I felt the pain in them, saw the redness of spilled tears. His clenched jaw trembled. Still, he didn't move to let me pass. And I didn't back away, either.

Then from all around I felt my fellow hearts drifting nearer, drawing close behind me. Surrounding me. Supporting me.

They actually supported me.

Cobe's eyes flicked around, taking in each of the Valentines who stood against him. For a moment, I felt his confusion, the mental teetering of indecision. And I flared my charm, nudging his mind. He'd be lucky if he made a good choice and backed down now, and my charm pulled his mind gently in that direction.

Tears rose in his eyes. Finally, he sheathed his daggers and stood aside.

"If Ten asks . . ." Cobe muttered.

"We'll tell her you stood up for her, yeah?" Dubs said, placing a hand on Cobe's shoulder.

I hoisted the trunk by one handle once more. Arms trembling, I dragged it onward into the dim hallway.

As I passed, someone shouted, "Yeah, Aggie!"

Others joined in with applause, whistles, shouts. Weary as I was, I managed a smile. But there was no time to soak in their praise. The time on my trial was counting down like the detonator on a bomb; I could feel it, and I plodded ahead faster, dragging my prize behind me.

Down the steps—*thud, thud, thud*—one, two, three—I counted my way down, a sure sign that I felt nervous about confronting the ace again.

Then I was at the threshold. I paused. *Last chance to turn back,* some warning voice inside me said. I didn't want to be queen, truly. I didn't want any of this. But I'd come too far to turn back now.

And besides, what choice did I have? Without more power, I could never win Mom back. I'd end up just one more broken-necked crow.

So into the ace's chamber I went.

I'd grown to hate that strangely quavering crimson light of the obelisk. Not only did it remind me of the first time I'd ever seen it, in the basement of my burned-down house, but it also evoked something else, some ancient malevolence. Flames licking a city's walls, perhaps, while a war's survivors—the lucky ones—slipped past to safety. It was a strange thought, a vision almost, and I wasn't sure where it came from, except from the depths of my uber-exhausted and traumatized subconscious. But there was something true about it, too. Some mysterious lesson. That good luck shone most strongly in the shadow of bad, maybe. If it was a profound message, I was too exhausted and frazzled to internalize it.

The chest grated across the stone floor as I heaved it forward and dropped it with a deep and final-sounding thud at the ace's feet.

She slowly turned her red-bathed face toward me and opened her eyes. The age-milky orbs flicked down to the chest. "You did it."

"Don't sound so surprised," I said. It probably wasn't wise to be snarky to the grand leader of our suit, someone who, according to Jack, held the power of life and death in her gnarled, heart-marked hands. But if she really could see the future as Jack claimed, then she would have known how much I'd have to suffer to get this chest, and how I'd have to betray Ten. She would have known everything.

"I am surprised," she said.

"Really?" I asked, taken aback.

"You are powerful," the ace said. "And you have potential. But nothing is preordained."

I glanced around again at the obelisk's light licking the walls.

"So why did you burn down my house?" I asked. "You promised to tell me."

The ace's usual clever smile faded. "For a simple reason that a young physicist like you should understand very well. Inertia."

I frowned.

"I burned your house to set you in motion," the ace said.

"I was already in motion," I protested. "I was moving toward college. And...and a normal life."

"You were moving," the ace said, "in the wrong direction."

"It was the right direction for me," I said, my voice wavering with emotion. "And it was the right direction for Mom."

"Perhaps," the ace said patiently. "And perhaps not."

"Right, so you'd just sacrifice me and my future and my entire life just to advance your own agenda?" I demanded.

"Yes," the ace said. "That is leadership. A queen must be willing to sacrifice others. She must even be willing to sacrifice herself—if it's for the greater good."

"And who gets to decide what the greater good is?" I demanded.

"I do," the ace said. "And you will too, when you are queen. That is the price of power."

The old woman infuriated me.

"You sacrificed Ten in order to help your mother," the ace pointed out. "That was you deciding what the greater good is."

The words stopped me dead. Was that really what I'd done?

"What gave you the right to decide preserving your mother was a greater good than saving Ten, hmm?" the ace pressed.

Guilt made my stomach clench. "Nothing," I said weakly. "Nothing gave me that right. I just . . ."

"You had the power to choose," the ace said. "So you chose. That's the answer to your question, Aggie. Whoever is most powerful decides what the greater good is. The question is, who is the best person to make those choices? Who is intelligent enough? Who is morally good enough? Ten? Someone else? Or you?"

I knew the ace was playing me like a piano, but the chord she struck hit me anyway. Because she was right. I didn't want to be queen. But if I didn't take the role, then someone else would. Ten, Adelie, or Mina. Mina would be okay, but did she have the backbone to make really hard choices if she had to? I wasn't sure she did. Even if I hated the ace for manipulating me to get me to this point, the bitter truth was, she was right. There was only one person I could trust with the power of queenship: myself.

The ace seemed to sense the sea change in me because her dark smile returned. "Open the chest," she said.

38

TEN

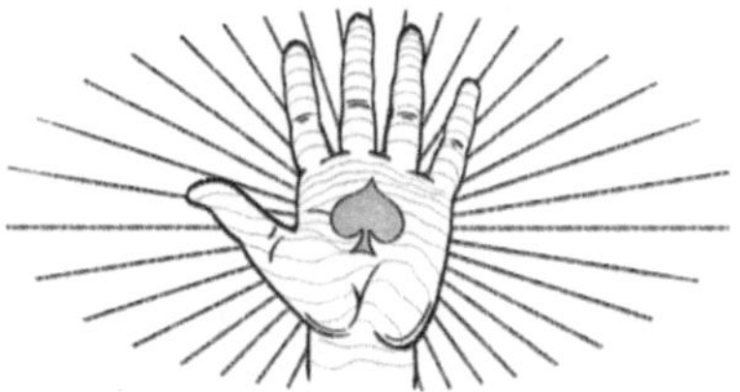

Ten sat tied to a chest press machine in the basement workout room of the Diamond Queen's mansion. Of all the things that could have been running through her mind at that moment, she was contemplating her hands, which were stuffed into oven mitts wrapped with shiny gold duct tape. Where the Diamantes would have gotten such tape Ten had no idea. From NASA, maybe. Or maybe they had it made themselves. The Diamonds had basically infinite money and controlled a large percentage of the world's manufacturing infrastructure; they could have anything they wanted made. One thing was certain: the tape had to be real gold, because gold had the property of neutralizing charm, and the luck in Ten's hands felt completely dead.

Soon enough, the rest of her would be too, unless she could figure out some way to escape.

The only entertainment to distract her from her coming demise was the antics of her jailors, a tall, ebony-skinned drag queen named Moxy Fireside and a hunky kid in a red leather vest and no shirt who'd laughingly introduced himself as Rad Chad. The two were drunkenly competing, trying to outdo one another with feats of strength. So far, Moxy had outperformed Chad by a ratio of about three to one, even wearing six-inch high heels.

Just now, Moxy had bicep-curled 120 pounds to Chad's 80.

"It's just because you're—" Chad started, by Moxy gave him a look.

"Don't say black." She wagged a finger at him. "Even positive stereotypes are stereotypes."

"I was going to say tall," Chad said. "You have more leverage."

"And you have charm," Moxy pointed out, causing Chad to put his hands in his pockets sheepishly. It was true. Ten had noticed the boy trying to use charm to derail Moxy several times during their contests, with little success. To be that ineffective with his power, Ten guessed he had to be a new Diamond, likely a two. Ten could easily overpower this pair, if only her charm weren't muffled by these stupid gloves.

"I doubt I'll have charm for long," Chad lamented. "When DQ finds out we were drinking with her wannabe assassin—"

"Oh, you're right about that," Moxy said. "DQ is going to bust out a Sam's Club–sized can of whoop-ass on us. I'd be running like hell to get out of here if I were sober enough to drive."

"You're a syco," Chad said. "At least she can't strip your rank from you."

Moxy rolled her eyes dramatically. "Sugar, I'm a syco. That means I'm expendable. I'd rather give up a pip than my life."

Chad looked disturbed. "You don't really think…?"

"Psh!" Moxy said. "I don't think, I know. There ain't a grave-yard big enough to hold the bones of every fool syco who pissed off a luck god and found out what's up."

Ten's heart beat faster at this opportunity. These two clowns needed to get away—and so did she. They could all help one another. But when she tried to suggest it, her gag made all her words sound like *mmm-mm-mmmm-mm-mmm.*

They both looked at her while she tried to speak, then went right back to their conversation.

"You really think we're just waiting around here to die?" Chad whispered.

"I didn't say that," Moxy said. "But we are going to be at her mercy. And you best believe goddesses are some fickle bitches. When DQ walks in here, you better just tuck your tail and lick her hand like a good little puppy. And if you think—"

Just then, the doors burst open, and the queen herself strode in, as grandly as if she were taking the stage for a stadium crowd. She still wore wildly high heels, but now thick gauze swaddled her entire face, making her look like a B-movie mummy, and shocks of golden hair poked out wildly from among the bandages. Her eyes were visible, however, and they burned with anger like a pair of embers. The bandages seemed a bit dramatic, Ten thought. No way they were medically neces-sary for what likely wasn't more than a massive goose-egg, a cut, and a pair of shiners. But the fury was one hundred percent real.

I'm so screwed, Ten thought.

And for the first time in years, she wished she'd taken the time to head back to Pasadena and visit her family one last time. Maybe for a Thanksgiving dinner. She could have played ping-pong with her little brother. Listened to her mom talk about real estate. She even would have been willing to take a ride in her dad's stupid vintage Jaguar, which she was fairly sure he loved more than her.

She'd been so glad to be out of their overly judgmental, controlling orbit that she'd never been back since becoming a goddess. Their only interactions had been terse phone calls on holidays and the occasional text message. They thought she was working in Detroit on a marketing internship with a big car company. When all this was over, would they know anything approaching the truth? Would the Valentines even inform them she was dead?

There wasn't time to wonder. The queen charged up to Ten, and Ten braced herself for a slap. Instead, the star stopped and snapped her fingers.

Moxy swept in, unfolding a metal chair and setting it behind the queen. DQ sat, opened a compact, and looked at her face. She groaned in disgust and snapped the mirror shut again.

Moxy and Chad, who'd taken position behind her, exchanged a worried look. With effort, Ten managed to push the gag out of her mouth with her tongue until it hung against her chin.

"Would an apology help?" she asked. "Or should we just skip to the part where you ransom me back to the Valentines?"

A ransom was the best-case scenario, but she was hoping to use a little psychology and plant the idea in DQ's mind. If she was very lucky, maybe the queen's Diamante greed would override her desire for revenge. A girl could hope, anyway.

The queen steepled her fingers, displaying an impeccable manicure, and leaned back in the metal chair.

"Ransom?" she drawled. "No. You came into my house. You ruined my party. You stole from me."

"Not to nitpick, but it was the Blackovers who made off with the chest," Ten pointed out.

"Not for lack of trying on your part," DQ purred angrily.

"Worst of all, you messed up my most valuable asset. My beautiful face."

"I think you still look lovely," Ten said, giving the queen's gauze beehive of a head her toothiest smile.

The queen sat up straighter and glanced back at Moxy and Chad. "You hear that? This bitch is still sarcastic, even though I'm about to crush her ass into jelly and spread her on toast. That takes balls. I like balls on a woman."

"Thank you?" Ten said.

"I got a question for you, ballsy," DQ drawled. "Why were you trying to steal that chest?"

Ten paused, searching for a reason she should lie. She couldn't think of any. So she told the truth.

"The other girl who was here, Aggie, was selected to be queen. Our ace sent her to steal the chest from you as her queen trial."

"And you thought you should be queen, so you came to steal it first?" DQ surmised. "So you could convince your ace to make you queen instead?"

It sounded kind of petty when she heard it explained out loud, but that didn't make it inaccurate. "Yeah, pretty much," Ten said.

Diamond Queen nodded. "Interesting. Do you even know what was in that chest?"

Ten shook her head. "No. Just that the ace wanted it."

Diamond Queen gave a dark laugh. "It sounds to me like your ace is a fool. The contents of that chest were dangerous. We bought it from a sylph—paid an incredible fortune for it, in fact—to destroy it. But the chest isn't my problem anymore. My problem is what to do with you."

"You could feed me a nice steak dinner and let me go," Ten suggested.

"Or I could pull your tits off then drop you out of my private jet onto the roof of your Valentine mansion from thirty thousand feet," DQ countered.

"Or that." Ten shrugged. Her snark had nothing to do with bravado. The truth was, her head still swam from the beating she'd taken when the Diamond thugs captured her, and she was getting too groggy to care what happened to her. She just wished DQ would untie her—or hurry up and kill her already.

"You know what? You're a bad bitch," DQ decided. "I like you. And you don't get Diamantes' money by throwing away valuable resources. I might have a use for you."

"I'm listening," Ten said.

"The chest was dangerous, but there's something even more dangerous floating around out there in Detroit."

"What?" Ten asked.

"Your Jack."

Ten blinked in surprise. She always thought Danusia was close with Jack—disturbingly close. She'd assumed the rest of the Diamonds liked him, too. The idea that he might irritate them as much as he irritated her was amusing to consider.

"He has defiled himself," the queen went on, holding up both her diamond-pipped hands. "Heart on one hand, spade on the other."

Ten recoiled with surprise. "Jack? No."

"I have it on good authority," the Diamond Queen said. "Our Jill saw both pips with her own eyes and witnessed him using them both."

"That can't be."

Ten stopped herself. Was what the queen said really so implausible? Jack had been talking for a while about uniting the suits. She'd assumed it was just that—talk. Even when he was courting Carlotta Blackover, Ten had chosen to believe he was merely playing an angle, working to make the Clubs let down their guard so that the Valentines could gain an advantage—and maybe having some fun with a beautiful woman in the process. Once he had the advantage, Jack could use it to force the Blackovers to lay down their arms and accept a peace agreement.

But maybe Ten had it wrong. Maybe Jack really was angling to get Carlotta to bring him into the Blackovers, to possess the power of both suits. Maybe he wanted the power of *all* the suits. That's what King Michael had always accused him of. Ten had scoffed at the idea Jack would try something so bold. A person would have to be an ego-maniac to attempt such a thing—it was the very definition of shooting the moon. But then, Jack had never been short on confidence.

The mark of spades, that was another question. How could he have gotten the mark when the only surviving spade was... *his new little girlfriend's mother?*

Suddenly, several puzzle pieces clicked into place in Ten's mind. She had been wondering for months why Jack had shown such interest in that plain, rather annoying Six he'd brought into their suit. Aggie was unnaturally strong for her rank, true, and she was clever, but that didn't adequately explain it. Now, Ten understood. It wasn't the girl Jack had been after. It was the mother. Somehow, he'd managed to use the girl to get to her—and had actually convinced her to give him the mark of spades. It was genius, in a sick, Machiavellian, Jack sort of way.

And now, he had two suits. The power of charm and hex inhabiting one person...

"It would make him the most powerful luck god in the world," Ten whispered. "And—"

"An abomination," the queen finished.

It was one of the most fundamental laws of the luck gods, so basic a rule that it had never had to be written down. The suits remained separate. At odds. In tension. That was the natural way, ever since the death of Uthule thousands of years ago.

"A dangerous abomination," the queen repeated. "Don't you agree?"

Ten paused, then nodded. "Yes."

"And he must be stopped."

"Yes," Ten said again, more loudly.

The gauze wrapping the queen's face shifted with what Ten guessed must be a smile.

"We're in agreement, then," she said. "And in that case, I'm willing to let you live. *If...*"

The dramatic pause irritated Ten, but the queen clearly was not going on without milking the moment for all it was worth.

"If?" Ten prompted.

"If you deliver your wayward Jack to me. Preferably dead."

Ten's breath caught. Jack was a danger. A liability, sure. He might be like a match in a dynamite factory. But could she really betray him like that—sell him to his death? She hated Jack for all he'd done, for all he was. For his lies, his betrayals, his schemes, his selfishness. But deep down, she knew it was a hatred rooted in caring. She only hated him because she loved him.

The queen's head tilted. She was getting impatient, and the subtext was clear. Side with her or die.

Sure, Ten would prefer not to betray Jack. But hadn't he already betrayed her—more times and in more ways than she cared to count? And Aggie—Ten was sure as hell getting back at Aggie. What better way than to deliver her boyfriend into the hands of the Diamonds and take the queenship for herself?

But all that was beside the point. There was no choice here, not really. The Diamond Queen was out for blood. It would be Ten's, or it would be Jack's. There was no third option. And Ten sure as hell wasn't giving up her own life for his.

DQ hummed the *Jeopardy* theme song in her sweet falsetto. "Is this a moral conundrum for you, honey? Because I was under the impression I was offering you the deal of a lifetime. Possibly a very short lifetime."

I've hesitated too long already, Ten thought. *Wait any longer, and she'll change her mind; she'll think I won't go through with it. If I change my mind about betraying Jack later, fine. But I've got to commit now, or I'm finished.*

"I'm in," she said.

The Diamond Queen gave a low chuckle. "That's good, sweetheart. Real good. But you'll forgive me if I don't trust you to your word. See, we didn't exactly get off on the right foot."

The queen opened a sequined clutch and took out a black necklace. It was made of chunky, volcanic-looking black stone and looked ancient. The pendant at the bottom had the shape of a strange glyph made of roughly sculpted copper. DQ approached Ten and clasped the necklace around her neck.

Ten immediately felt the weight of hex, like a cinderblock pulling down on her soul. The necklace was deeply cursed.

"Feels sorta like a bad hangover, doesn't it?" DQ said, feigning empathy. "Man, I do hate being around hex. Or having it around me," she added, giving the necklace a little tug. "Don't worry. I'm not going to leave you like that."

From her clutch, DQ took what looked like a large, gold locket. It split in half, and she leaned forward and closed the two halves over the necklace's copper charm. Instantly, the sickening feeling of hex dissipated.

"This is a neat little device," DQ said. "All we have to do is send a signal, and this little thing will split open. Not only does it expose you to the hex of this necklace—and this thing has about four thousand years of really gnarly hex built up—it will also shoot a tiny little dart right into your chest. The nerve agent on it ought to kill you in about seven or eight minutes, depending on your luck. Which, given the hex, won't be very good," she giggled darkly.

"At the first hint you've double-crossed us—" She drew a thumb across her throat. "So, you ready to go to war? Because we're going to need to strike before your little friend Aggie gets the power of her crown."

"She's not going to," Ten said. "She didn't get the chest."

The DQ gave her a look. "Don't be so sure, sweetie."

Ten shook her head and swore. Damn Six. She'd gotten the chest back? She really was lucky.

"So we're going in. And you're leading the charge," DQ said. "Are we clear on the deal?"

"We are," Ten said. "Except for one thing."

DQ folded her arms. "Yeah?"

"Once I deliver Jack—alive or dead—you support my bid to become the Valentine queen."

DQ laughed, glancing back at Moxy and Chad. "You see this? What did I tell you? Balls!"

"It will be me or Aggie," Ten said. "Aggie tried to rob you, too. And she won't owe you like I will. Help me take the throne, and the Valentines will always support the Diamantes—in everything."

DQ's scarlet lips twisted sideways in thought. "Deal. You deliver the Jack and I'll support you. But I'll expect you and the whole Valentine suit to be as loyal as any sycos. You give me information, allegiance, alliance. We call for backup, and y'all storm in like the damned Marines. We clear?"

Ten nodded. "Crystal."

DQ's gauze shifted in another smile. "Good. Then it appears we've got just one more piece of business, then."

She stood, folded the metal chair she'd been sitting in, and raised it over her head.

"Even is even," she said, and swung it into Ten's face.

39

RACHEL

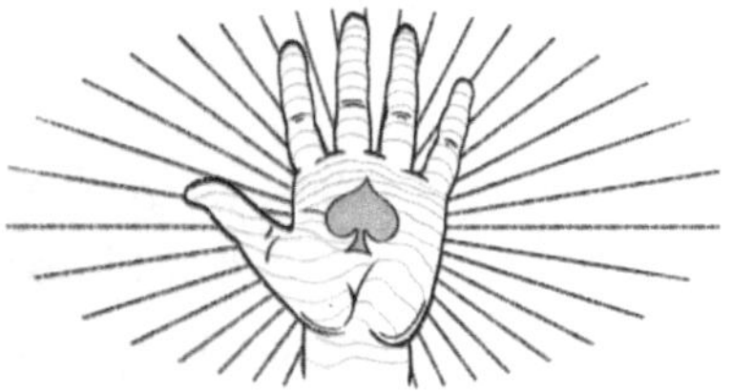

Rachel sat in a penthouse hotel room with King Thad, a handful of Clubs, and a couple of female sycos dressed like they might be go-go dancers at the casino's night club. Beer bottles littered the room, and most of those present, Thad included, had an unfocused, glazed-over sheen to their eyes, the telltale sign that they were on something. Rachel had hung out with enough intoxicated people to know. Some of those hangouts had taken place right here in this hotel, and thinking of it sent a little itch creeping up her spine. Her gaze lingered on one of the beer bottles before she wrested it away.

She'd need all her focus to make it through tonight. *But just one drink might take the edge off,* some voice inside her whispered.

Was it her own voice, or the obelisk's? It was getting hard to tell anymore.

Thad was looking at his phone, frowning.

"What's the matter?" Rachel asked him.

Thad's scowl just deepened as he slammed his phone down on the table in front of him.

"They're here," was all he said.

"I don't like this. I don't trust these guys," Shade whispered to Rachel. He was the only escort Thad had allowed Rachel to bring to the meeting. That was okay. She felt plenty secure with the black urn sitting on the floor between her feet. She and Shade had spent the last several hours hunting through some of the unluckiest spots in Detroit, and everywhere they'd gone, they gathered up flittering bits of shadow. Jinn. And some of it was Invidia. Apparently, when Jack had cut her down in that battle at Oak Hill, she'd only dissipated, not died. Resurrecting her was as simple as gathering up the pieces, which had drifted to spots of bad luck the way water trickled to the lowest point it could find. Rachel and Shade had collected enough shadow that what waited inside the urn would be powerful indeed, when it was released. According to the obelisk, Invidia would be able to absorb the other pieces of jinn they'd gathered to make herself even stronger than she'd been at Oak Hill. And so Rachel almost hoped this smug jackass Thad would try something, just so she could see the look on his face when she unleashed her secret weapon on him.

Rachel had just begun to imagine what that scene would look like when the door opened and four Blackovers slunk into the room. She guessed from their sour demeanors and their various injuries that something had gone wrong.

Thad sat up straighter. "Marley. You damn well better have a chest in your pocket," the king boomed.

The leader of the crew, a trim, handsome man in his fifties

—Marley, apparently—stepped forward. "We got ambushed. They took it."

"Ambushed? Where?" Thad demanded.

"Here. In the parking garage. We last saw her getting into an elevator. We got the whole security team to sweep the building, but she's gone."

"She?" Thad smoldered.

Marley glanced to Rachel. "The queen's daughter."

Rachel blinked, surprised. She knew her daughter was a Valentine, but could she have stolen the chest from four armed thugs? It seemed impossible—unless she had a lot of help.

"How many were there?" Thad demanded, apparently picking up her train of thought. "They must be here somewhere. It can't be that hard to find them."

Marley shook his head. "We searched everywhere. We think she has a leprechaun key. It's the only thing that explains it."

Thad growled like a bear and picked up a gnarly-looking spiked baseball bat that leaned against his chair. "And which one of you pathetic cretins is going to pay for this failure?"

The three lesser Blackovers glanced at one another in alarm, but the other one, Marley, remained cool behind his sunglasses as Thad advanced toward him.

The pips in Rachel's hands tingled hungrily, yearning for the violence that was surely coming, begging her to nudge it along. But Rachel had no desire to see Thad bash this man's brains out.

"Thad," she said in a voice so cutting the king stopped cold. "There's no need to punish them. They did their best. That's all we can ask. I'm sure my daughter is a formidable opponent."

"She's a little girl!" Thad protested.

"Maybe," Rachel said. "But she's smarter than all of you combined."

The best part about being an evil queen was the absolute

freedom to speak your mind, she thought, as she watched the men, Marley and Thad, exchange irritated looks.

"What about our alliance?" Thad demanded. "We were going to bring you the chest, you were going to be my queen."

"I would still be your high queen, if you're ready to kneel before me."

"I told you, woman," Thad railed. "The Blackovers are ruled by kings. Not women."

Rachel shrugged, rising from her seat. "Then it appears we are done here."

She knelt and picked up the urn. The thing was so heavy and cold she could barely stand to hold it, but she could feel the seething power inside, and it gave her comfort. Shade kept one hand on the pistol at his belt as Rachel led the way toward the door.

"I'm not done with you, woman. No one walks away from me," Thad said. "You *will* be mine."

Someone needs a lesson in consent, Rachel thought. But that would have to happen another time.

The four bedraggled Blackovers stood between Rachel and the exit, but when Marley's eyes alighted on the urn in her hands, she saw understanding dawn in his gaunt face.

"The urn of Jaygur," he whispered.

"Don't let her leave," Thad commanded.

But Marley grabbed his comrades and pulled them aside, out of Rachel's way.

"You coward," Thad snarled at him.

"Coward?" Marley shot back. "Do you know what that urn is? She might as well be holding a nuclear warhead."

Outside the hotel room door, Rachel glanced back to see Thad and Marley facing off, nose-to-nose. Men could be such Neanderthals sometimes. Especially Blackovers.

Thad at least had the presence of mind to glance over at

her. "Where do you think you're going, *oh mighty queen of death*?"

"I'm going to go and get the chest myself," she said, and she nodded to Shade, who slammed the door behind them.

40

___

AGGIE

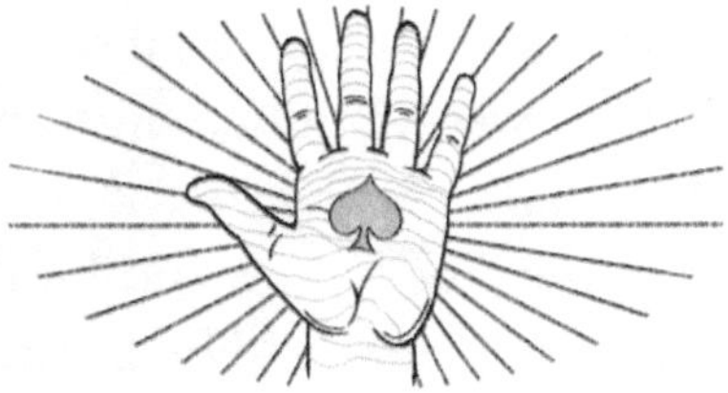

The chest was locked, of course. Because why would anything ever be easy?

The ace sent me scavenging through the house in search of charmed keys that might open it. I could never have guessed just how many keys one house could possess, but there were many. In bins in the library. Stashed in drawers of hutches. Crated in the wine cellar. The ace seemed to know where each key was, but so far none of them worked in the chest's lock. Now, I was trying a stubby, ornate silver one that I'd retrieved from a toolbox in the garden shed, but it didn't even fit into the chest's little keyhole.

I groaned in frustration and dropped the dud onto the pile with the rest.

"Maybe if I just take a little nap—?" I tried.

The ace shook her head. "There is another key in the attic. Take the narrow staircase next to Jack's room," the ace said, in a half-entranced monotone. Her hands were still pressed to the red obelisk, which pulsed in time with her words "The key is brass, and it's inside a cardboard hat box. Hurry. Your time is short."

I reeled on my feet as I trudged up the steps, trying to remember the last time I'd slept. It was the night before last in Nashville, I decided, but it felt like a lifetime ago. Adrenaline had carried me this far, but it had deserted me about half an hour ago, leaving me like a jellyfish on the beach with the tide receding. The world seemed to quaver and wink to my tired eyes, and my legs felt like pipe cleaners. My anxiety remained, but its urgency had lost its bite, and while I felt the urge to count the steps on the way up to the attic, I lost track of the numbers somewhere between nine and thirteen.

Too tired for OCD. That's a bad sign, right?

I'd never been in the attic before, and I found it alive with floating dust motes, each one golden in the morning sun. Furniture covered in drop cloths lay stacked against the walls, and all sorts of strange and random treasures were spread throughout the space in a vast jumble.

According to the history of the house I'd read, the rift had first appeared in this area during the days of the French and Indian War, when Detroit was a fur trading outpost at the edge of the wilderness, and the Valentines had built their first homestead on this spot. The rift had returned three times since. It appeared during the heyday of the Detroit auto industry from around 1938; that's when the Valentines first built the mansion in its current form. It returned at the peak of the Motown era in 1966. The relics stored in the attic were a hodgepodge that reflected these three time periods. There were muskets stacked in a corner, a trunk of fur coats that looked to be from the 30s, and a collection of dusty guitars that

I guessed must date back to the 60s. I vowed to come back and explore this place—sometime when I wasn't tired enough to puke.

It took far too much rummaging before I finally found the hat box and the tin inside it that held the key. As I hustled down the narrow staircase with it, my tired feet tangled with one another, and I tripped.

Falling—

Caught. By strong arms.

I looked up into a pair of eyes, that familiar stormy-ocean blue.

"Jack?" I breathed.

He held me to his chest, and I settled into him. That warm, hot-tea scent of his filled me. His arms surrounded me, and I relaxed more in that moment than I had in days. Tears filled my eyes, half driven by relief, half squeezed out by a massive yawn, but I blinked them back.

"You did it," Jack whispered.

"You were worried?" I asked, my inflection betraying the truth: I hoped he was worried.

"You have no idea," he said with a low laugh. "When Deuce told me you went after the chest again..." He shook his head.

"Ten?" I said. "Did you get her back?"

Jack's expression darkened. "The Diamantes weren't in a negotiating mood. Don't worry. They won't kill her, not if they can find some way to use her, and Ten is pretty useful. We'll think of some way to get her back."

"Let's hope so," I said. But I felt conflicted. I didn't really want Ten dead, and I definitely didn't want to be responsible for her death. But when she did turn up again, she'd be gunning for me. If I knew Ten, she'd never stop gunning for me —and I didn't want that either. But there was no time to discuss it.

"Come on," I said. As Jack trailed me down to the ace's

room, I explained about the locked chest and the keys, showing him the latest one I'd found.

He nodded. "Okay. Try that key. I'll meet you down there, okay?" he said, and broke off down a side hall without further explanation.

Down to the ace's room I went. Once again, her eyes were shut, and I could see them snapping back and forth beneath their lids as if she were dreaming. Still, she spoke as I approached.

"Try the key," she said. I knelt and put it to the keyhole. It slipped inside and my heart jumped.

"It fits!" I said and turned it. Or tried to turn it. It wouldn't budge. "Come on!" I snarled, twisting harder in my frustration until I heard a metallic snap.

"No," I whispered, taking out the key and staring dumbly at its jagged metal end. It had broken off in the lock.

I groaned and wondered fleetingly if all queens had so many problems.

How ironic would it be if, after everything I'd been through, I lost because of a stubborn lock?

"Time is short..." the ace said again.

"I know! You said that," I snapped.

I heard footsteps and turned to find Jack standing in the doorway. He held a massive iron war hammer with runes engraved all over it. Mjölnir, basically—Thor's hammer, for the non-nerds—but less bulky and more spiky.

"Did someone call for a charmed box-opener?" Jack asked.

"Is it okay?" I asked the ace. "Can we break in with a hammer?"

The ace shrugged. "Unlikely. It is a very charmed chest. But it's also a very charmed hammer. Try it."

Jack stepped forward, but I headed him off.

"No," I said. "Queen trial, remember? I'll do it."

He hesitated only a moment, then handed me the hammer.

It must have weighed as much as me because I nearly tipped off my feet as I took it. But I managed to remain upright as I approached the chest. With a snarl, I raised the hammer over my head with all my strength. I flared my charm, pouring every bit I had into the smooth metal handle. Then I swung. The hammer head bashed into the lid of the chest, which stove in with a satisfying crunch. I dropped the hammer, reached down and pulled aside two jagged pieces of chest lid. A darkish purplish light shone from within the chest, and we all leaned in.

Inside lay a two-foot-long chunk of dark, jaggedly broken crystal with markings scratched into it. Some of them were strange, indecipherable runes. But some of the marks I recognized.

They were spades.

A familiar voice rose from the shard of broken obelisk, so low and menacing it made me shiver.

"Hello, Aggie," it said.

41

MOLLY

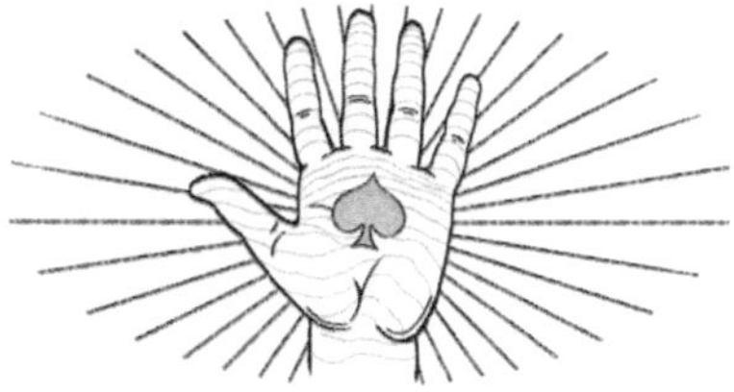

Molly sat forgotten in a corner of what Lorcan had called the Diamantes' war room. Located somewhere beneath the Renaissance Tower complex, it was a vast space, all dark granite and dramatic lighting, reminding Molly of Batman's Bat Cave. The entire Diamond suit had gathered around a conference table at the center of the room as Danusia paced up and down like a Prada-clad general. Diamond Queen sat at the head of the table, playing the role of president in a red oversized sweatshirt that Molly guessed was *haute couture*. It featured shiny plastic shoulder pads and was bedazzled with sequins in diamond patterns. On her head, she wore a veil like the one Jasmine wore in Aladdin, and the jewel-encrusted hilts of a pair of cutlasses peeked up from behind each of her shoulders.

All sorts of Diamonds and their sycos filled the room, making it feel like a meeting of Congress or the UN. Lorcan and Cleo were there too, but not Seemor. Molly had made an excuse and dropped him off at a Valentine hideout on the way here. It wouldn't do to have him running back and warning the Hearts that Molly, Lorcan, and Cleo were making a full report to the enemy, would it? All in all, Molly found being a double agent pretty exhausting, but it would be worth it in the end. It had to be worth it.

Molly knew the deliberations happening in front of her now were important and that the lives of several people she cared about hung on the choices made here and now. And yet in her sleep-deprived state, she found her eyes drifting again and again to Lorcan. Her sweet, sexy leprechaun. How had she never noticed before how perfect he was? The muscles of his forearms. That jutting, proud jaw. The way he stood, taut and wiry, like a hot, tattooed jungle cat. Even the gold teeth, which she'd found off-putting before, now held an aura of exoticness and rebellion. She was glad Aggie had taken her along on her mission because it had brought her and Lorcan together, if for no other reason. And once all this was over, when her stupid parents were out of her life and Molly was a Diamond and Lorcan was her man, how sweet life would be then. All they had to do was get through the next few hours—and make sure Danusia knew she was worthy.

"I have to believe that once they know what's inside the chest, they'll destroy it," Danusia was saying.

Diamond Queen tapped her long nails on the table in a motion that reminded Molly of a spider's legs. "My dear, why would they risk so much to steal something only to destroy it?"

Danusia frowned. "What do you think they plan to do. Use it?"

The queen gave a shrug, as if to say, *it's possible.*

"No," Danusia said quickly. "Even if Jack has the mark of spades, I can't imagine they'd try to use the Morbus obelisk."

"The promise of power can blind people, make them do a lot of stupid things," Diamond Queen countered. "Just ask their Ten over there."

Along with everyone else, Molly glanced over at Ten, who'd been placed in a seat in a corner of the room not far from the queen. She seemed pretty dazed. A gauze patch had been taped over a spot above her left eye, and that whole side of her face was puffy and purple. Molly wasn't sure whether Ten had gone rogue and started working for the Diamonds or whether she was simply a prisoner. Either way, she hoped that with one eye swollen shut Ten wouldn't notice her, and so far, that seemed to be the case.

"Jack is a lot of things," Danusia said. "But I can't believe he'd be that reckless."

A Diamante Molly had never seen before leaned forward, resting his elbows on the table. He seemed to Molly like the most elegant young man alive. He was long and lean, with prominent cheekbones and beautiful, raindrop-shaped eyes that made her think he might be part Asian. His hair was dark and slicked back and he wore a rich, perfectly tailored red suit with a glittering brooch, which Molly was sure had to be a real diamond, in place of a necktie. When he spoke, his voice sounded as rich as his clothes, like woodsmoke and wine. His accent was faintly British like Danusia's but colored with other, less familiar flavors. Could this be the Diamantes king? He seemed too young.

"In the end, their intentions don't matter, do they?" the regal boy was saying. "They took something from us. We must retrieve it. They struck our queen. We must strike back."

Danusia's pert little face wrinkled with annoyance. "You've been traveling a long time, Tristaine. Things have changed since you last graced us with your presence."

The boy, Tristaine, apparently, regarded Danusia with amusement. "I've been running our worldwide empire, D. Not backpacking around Cypress."

Danusia smiled wickedly. "Then I'm sure you can explain why our profits dropped nineteen percent last quarter."

Tristaine looked unperturbed. "Inflationary pressures caused the Fed to raise interest rates. Markets over-responded, causing a brief downturn. Plus, someone here in Detroit allowed the dark suits to rip a rift into a bad luck dimension and release a whole shit ton of jinn. Bad luck is bad for the economy, dear sister."

Danusia rolled her eyes. "Please. If we hadn't stepped in and helped the Valentines fight that battle while you were off scrubbing financial reports, then—"

"Enough," Diamond Queen barked. Silence returned, and so did her sweet southern drawl. "As much as I love hearing you two beautiful egomaniacs carp at each other, we have more urgent problems than the trajectory of the stock market. Are we going to get the chest back? Yes. But we're going to get something even sweeter. Revenge."

Danusia shut her eyes and took a steadying breath. "I agree that we need a strong response, your majesty. But I've been thinking about this all morning. The Blackovers are making moves. The Morbus are reforming, and their new queen is smart. She's cooking up something big, I'm sure of it. If we enter all-out war with the Valentines now—"

Tristaine stood, buttoning his suit coat. He was taller than Molly imagined he'd be, and she glimpsed a pair of pearl-handled pistols at his waist. "Danusia is scared," he said. "I'll lead the attack, your majesty."

"I am *not scared*," Danusia said. "I just think we need to think before we—"

The Diamond Queen stood, too. "I appreciate your caution, Danusia. I do. But this time, we're going bull riding. Tristaine and I will lead the attack. You'll stay here and protect our assets."

"But—" Danusia started, but the Queen raised a hand, silencing her.

"But nothing," she said. "I want every Diamond, every syco, every sprite, and every leprechaun armed and ready in the next twenty minutes. It's time to show these Valentines what power really is."

❧♡♤◇♧☙

As the meeting broke up, Molly watched from across the room as Danusia spoke to Lorcan. She'd dared to believe that maybe Danusia would let him out of the coming conflict, since they'd already done so much. But from the way she was talking and he was nodding, it seemed clear that she was giving him orders, and she felt a wave of jealousy and anger. As they filed toward her with the rest of the departing Diamonds, Molly approached.

"Is it time?" she asked, her hand going to the hilt of the dagger that Danusia had given her, which was now strapped at her waist.

"Time for what?" Danusia said, barely glancing at Molly.

"We warned you that Aggie was coming after the Diamond Queen," Molly said.

"Yes. You and Lorcan did well," Danusia said, checking her phone as she walked.

"So you'll do it?" Molly asked. They were in the hallway now, Danusia striding with her long legs and Molly scrambling to keep up.

"Do what?"

"Make me a Diamond."

This at last drew Danusia's full attention.

"Molly, sweetie," Lorcan admonished her quietly, reaching out to take her arm, but Molly pulled away from him.

"I betrayed my friend for you. My best friend," Molly pleaded. "You said—"

"I said I'd consider making you a Diamond once you completed a very specific task," Danusia hissed. "You have not completed it. And you won't complete it. You know why? Because you are an inconsequential little girl. Why are you even here? This is a flush, not a meeting for low-level sycos. Go."

Danusia went to walk on, but Molly spoke up again.

"You won't hurt her, will you? Aggie?"

Danusia turned back, boiling with so much contempt and irritation that Lorcan backed up a step, pulling Molly with him. "Hurt her?" Danusia said. "I won't hurt her, no. But Diamond Queen surely will. Or if you really want to impress us, you can come and use that dagger on her yourself."

The thought of hurting Aggie disgusted Molly; it hurt her even more than Danusia's dismissals, and for a second, tears rose to her eyes. Molly was used to being spurned by the cool kids. And yet at school, she'd found a way into their clique anyway. This would be no different. Molly would make sure of it. She was about to say something else, but was interrupted by a deep, melodic voice.

"Who's this?" Molly turned to find the young, handsome Diamond Tristaine watching her. Even though Lorcan stood right next to her—and she would never betray her Lorcie—the gaze of the god made her breath catch.

Danusia waved a hand at Molly dismissively. "She's just a syco."

Tristaine folded his arms and looked at Molly more intently, and she felt heat rise to her cheeks.

"The thing about Danusia is, whenever she says something

is *nothing*, that only makes me that much more certain it's *something*. What are you, an informant? An assassin?"

Molly shook her head mutely. She didn't trust herself to speak to this boy. This god.

"We're wasting time," Danusia snapped. "There are preparations to make."

"Oh, I think I have time to get to the bottom of this," Tristaine said. "What's your name, girl?"

"Molly."

Tristaine smiled, and it was like a ray of light dawning.

"Molly," he repeated. "Tell me how you fit into all this, Molly. Why are you here? Why is Danusia so intent on distracting me from you?"

Danusia rolled her eyes and huffed a sigh.

"I guess . . ." Molly glanced at Lorcan, then back to Tristaine. "My best friend, Aggie, is a Valentine. The Six. And she's maybe becoming the queen. So I'm...sort of an intermediary," she finished lamely.

Tristaine glanced down at the dagger on Molly's belt. "An intermediary with a very charmed blade."

Molly's hand went to the dagger's hilt again, her face reddening.

Tristaine raised an eyebrow. "You want to become a Diamante, like us, eh?" He leaned close. "It's no secret. All the sycos do."

Molly glanced at Lorcan to find his fists balled up and his jaw clenched with obvious jealousy, but he kept his mouth shut.

Tristaine smiled. "I think I know what Danusia sees in you, my dear. Ambition is always useful. I'm Tristaine, the Ten of Diamonds. Come. We're crashing a party at the Valentine house. You can be my plus one."

He offered Molly his arm. She glanced once more at Lorcan. Her leprechaun beau, usually so eager to fight anyone, now looked down at his shoes. That told Molly everything she needed to know about how dangerous this Tristaine was. She was afraid of him herself, afraid of the whole situation, really, and she certainly didn't want to make her Lorcie jealous. And yet this was her invitation to join the cool kids, wasn't it? So she took the ten's arm and let him lead her on—toward the coming battle.

42

AGGIE

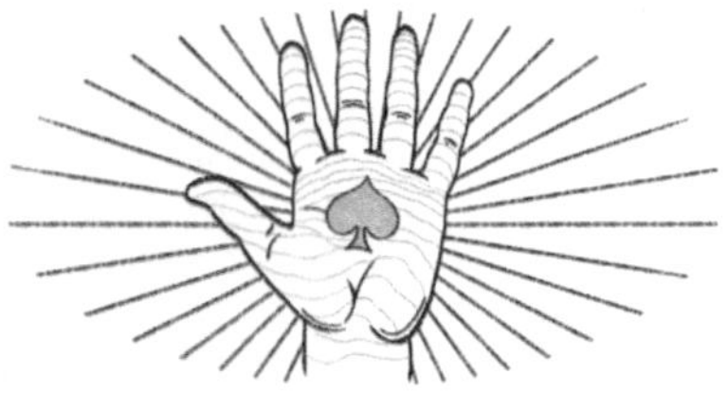

"**P**ick it up," the ace told me.

I stood staring at the broken chunk of black obelisk in the chest at my feet.

"It's . . ." *alive,* I was going to say. Or *watching me.* But the ace finished my sentence.

"It's the obelisk of Morbus," the ace said impatiently. "Part of it, anyway. Pick it up, but don't touch it with your bare hands."

With effort, the old woman peeled her own hands off the column of red crystal, shrugged a shawl off her shoulders and handed it to me. "Use this. Careful."

I draped the shawl over the black crystal, squatted, grasped the obelisk and hefted it, stumbling backwards with the weight.

You're making a grave mistake, Aggie, the obelisk said,

sounding more smug than threatening. It was hard to tell if the stone thing was speaking aloud or just in my mind, but the ace didn't seem to notice, so I guessed it was the latter.

"Now bring it here, Aggie, and press it up against our own obelisk," the ace said.

You don't want to do that, the black chunk warned in a singsong voice, pulsing with each word. I glanced at the ace, uncertain.

"Finish your task and seize your crown," the ace urged. "Quickly, now."

I hesitated for one more moment, wondering what all this meant. What would happen when the two obelisks came together?

My eyes traced the obelisk of Valentines, my mind counting each heart scratched into its surface *one, two, three...*

Queens don't count, I scolded myself, and I stepped forward. The black chunk butted up against the red obelisk, thudding into it like a battering ram. White light burst from the spot where they met, so bright I had to look away. When my eyes opened again, a ghost of the flash still hung over my vision, but I could see that the two obelisks were fused. I released the black stone and it remained in place, jutting out from our red obelisk like a limb from a trunk. But that wasn't all. With the flash, the purplish light deep within the black obelisk had gone out. And a thrill of triumph shot through me.

"Yeah! Where are your snappy comebacks now, ya paperweight?" I said, then looked to the ace. "Does that mean we killed it?"

Several questions flashed through my mind at once. If we eliminated the power of the Spades, did that mean there would be less bad luck in the world overall? Less suffering, less disease, less death? Had we only destroyed this shard, or were the others burned out as well? And what about the one inside Mom?

"Does that mean Mom—?" I started, but I saw at a glance that the ace wasn't celebrating. Her already wrinkly forehead had grown even more furrowed—and pale. She put a hand to her head and reeled. I caught her just as she began to keel over.

"Ace? Your worship?" I said, and she startled awake, sucking in a gasp. Her eyes snapped to the black obelisk.

"No," she whispered, sitting up again. I turned to see that the purplish light at the heart of the dark crystal had sparked back to life. Tendrils of its darkness seemed to be thrusting into the hearts' obelisk, just as tendrils of red reached into the blackness of the spades' crystal, as if the two pieces of stone were warring, trying to invade one another. Judging from the flow of the light, it seemed like the dark obelisk was winning.

I felt a sudden ache in my hands and glanced down. The light of the hearts in my palms flickered.

"Um, is this supposed to be happening?" I asked.

The ace looked down at her age-warped hands as well, then balled them into fists.

"No," she muttered to herself. "It shouldn't be. Unguarded, it should dissolve. Unless . . ." It wasn't until that moment, when I saw the fear enter the ace's eyes, that I felt truly afraid.

"What's happening?" I asked.

"It should be absorbing into our obelisk." Her frown deepened.

"But it isn't," I pointed out. "So...?"

The ace shook her head, a look of gray desolation crossing her aged visage. "I must lend our obelisk my strength and fight back, before theirs takes our power—or corrupts it."

"Okay, how can I help?" I said, trying not to count my pounding heartbeats.

"Go upstairs. Complete the wedding. Accept your queen power. They'll be coming to strike us while we are weakened. I can feel them coming. And you will need all the strength of your queenship to face them."

Submerged. A hollow, eerie hush. Heat on my skin. Muscles relaxed. Bruises soothed. Blood wafting away from my body in little clouds.

Maybe I can stay like this forever, I thought. King Michael couldn't marry me if I was underwater. The Diamantes couldn't exact their revenge. Jack and I would still be—whatever we were. Everything would just be on hold. But unfortunately, having no gills, I had to come up for air.

I imagined myself rising out of the bathwater like Aphrodite in her clam shell—or whatever. When my eyes opened, Mina sat on the floor next to the bath.

"I thought I was going to have to send a dive team in after you." When she saw my tepid smile, she sighed. "I'd ask what's wrong, but it's pretty obvious. So I'll just say it's going to be okay."

I looked at her, really looked at her, noticing tiny imperfections in the brown of her irises that I'd never noticed before. "Is it? Going to be okay?" I shook my head. "I always thought I'd get married someday, but I imagined I'd be like thirty-five. And it would be at *Star Wars: Galaxy's Edge*. And the groom would be…"

Mina watched me with raised eyebrows as I hesitated. "Jack?" she prompted knowingly.

But weirdly, his name wasn't on the tip of my tongue. I didn't know what I was going to say. "Well, it wouldn't be Michael," I finished.

Mina ran her fingers through a tendril of my wet hair.

"Well… you wouldn't be the first girl who took a little life detour in order to protect her family," Mina said. "Or the first to marry a crusty old geezer in order to gain some power."

"True," I sighed, stirring the sudsy water with one finger.

"You could always assassinate him," Mina said. "That would make you High Queen. Second only to the ace."

For an instant, she sounded serious, but when I looked up, I saw a little kitty-cat grin playing on her lips. At the same moment, a painful twinge shot through my hand, I turned it over and saw the pip flicker and go out, then light up again. Did I imagine it, or was there a swirl of black in it when it returned?

"I felt it, too." Mina looked at her own palms quizzically.

"You think the ace made a mistake?" I said. "Joining the obelisks like that?"

Mina grunted. "The ace doesn't make mistakes. These twinges are probably just a side effect of our obelisk absorbing the Morbus' power."

I nodded, but the knot in my stomach remained. With each twinge in my hands, it drew subtly tighter. And of course I was counting. Nine twinges so far.

Silence followed, filled only by the drip-drip-drip of water from the faucet.

I counted the drops. *One, two, three, I'm a bride to be. Four, five, six, I think I might be sick.* I suddenly laughed.

"What?" Mina asked.

"I'm just making up nursery rhymes," I said. "That's the kind of thing a Queen of Hearts should do, right?"

Mina laughed weakly, but she looked a little scared, like she thought I might be going nuts. And maybe I was. Sleep deprivation could produce psychosis, I was pretty sure.

"I think my mission has left me a teensy bit punch drunk," I said.

"*Psh*, it had to have been a piece of cake compared to my babysitting job," Mina joked. "That kid was so naughty. Every time I turned around he was stealing food from the kitchen."

"Well, Seemor did warn us," I said, and shivered. The bathwater was getting cold.

"We better get you dressed," Mina said, rising and holding a soft towel open for me.

When I emerged from the bathroom, I found Teemor the sprite tailor waiting for me. Though he wasn't my favorite nonhuman personage ever, I still felt happy to see his familiar face. At least, until he looked me up and down in my robe and grunted. "So. Michael is carrying on the classic royal tradition of robbing the cradle."

"And you're keeping up your tradition of being saltier than a bag of Fritos dipped in the Dead Sea," I countered.

"Touché," he deadpanned. "Come along."

We were in Queen Aubra's suite—my suite, now, apparently—and I followed Teemor into the dressing area. I don't know what I was expecting, but I was in no way prepared for what I saw. There on a dress form hung the most radiant gown I'd ever seen. My jaw actually dropped, and Mina squealed so loud it made me wince.

The sprite had crafted a classic wedding gown complete with a puffy taffeta princess skirt, a long train, and a stunning silk bodice. Except instead of being white, it was all red, vibrant as a ruby by firelight.

"Holy crap," Mina said.

"Seconded," I whispered.

I tried it on and seeing Mina's face told me everything I needed to know before I even looked in a mirror. She seemed in awe. And when I whirled to face the mirror, I was also in awe—of myself.

"You look like a queen, Aggie," Mina whispered.

Just feeling that crimson fabric against my skin sent a shiver of power through me that seemed to revive the pips in my hands, which had continued to gutter. My thoughts went back to the ace and the silent struggle she must be waging down in the mansion's basement. *Hurry,* a voice inside me whispered.

Next, a team of syco stylists entered, lugging case upon case of makeup and hair products. They stripped me out of the dress, clad me back in the robe, then sat me in a chair and swooped around me like electrons around a nucleus, subjecting me to a mani-pedi, a facial, a waxing, a makeup job, a hairdo. Basically, the works. The only plus was that I got a small nap in while being styled.

I awoke groggy and disoriented and was about to put the dress back on when the sounds of fighting—a thud, breaking glass, and shouting—downstairs sent us all running.

Jack and Deuce stood in the small dining room, squaring off. The glass front of the china cabinet behind Deuce was shattered and blood drizzled from one corner of his mouth, but he stood defiantly, both fists balled up. Jack rubbed an already bruising cheek, ran a tongue over his teeth, and spit blood onto the polished wood floor. The other Valentines had emerged and peered in cautiously from various doorways.

"What is going on?" I demanded, actually sounding queenly as I swept down the stairs to come between them.

Both looked away from me like a couple of kids caught fighting on a playground.

"Jack can tell you," Deuce said, glaring fiery-eyed at his friend.

I looked to Jack, who was still glaring at Deuce.

"Well, you want to be gallant?" Jack snarled at him. "Tell her not to marry Michael? Confess your love? Here she is. Go ahead."

I stopped breathing for a second. Is that what Deuce had been doing? Coming to confess his love, to beg me not to marry the king? It was ironic, because that was exactly what a part of me had wanted Jack to do—but of course, he had done the opposite.

There was no love in Deuce's dark expression now, however, as his eyes met Jack's.

"That's not what this is about, and you know it," he said, his voice low.

"Don't act holier than thou with me," Jack scoffed. "You knew what this life was when I brought you into it. I made damn sure you knew. You're no Boy Scout. If you were, you'd be dead. Every one of us has blood on their hands," he said, gesturing to all the Valentines. "And it's only beginning."

"Maybe for you," Deuce said. He glanced at me for the first time then and his gaze seemed to catch on me for a moment, like cloth snagging on a nail. "You look beautiful," he said. Then he turned and stormed out of the room. I watched, waiting for him to give me another backward glance, a word of explanation, but instead he disappeared down the hallway then left the house with the slam of a door.

The Valentines around us stirred and glanced at one another, uneasy.

"What was that about?" I asked, coming to Jack's side.

He started to touch my face, then pulled his hand away, as if my cheek might burn him.

"Uh. Nothing," he said.

I snorted. "Okay, if you're going to lie, at least make it plausible."

He rubbed his forehead, looking weary. "Aggie, I'll tell you later, okay?"

That made me mad. "Later? Like after I'm married to Michael? Then we'll finally have the heart-to-heart—no pun intended—that we've been putting off for like as long as we've known each other? That's when you'll finally explain your big plans to me?"

"Yes," Jack sighed.

One by one, the Valentines had slunk away, until only Mina and Dubs remained, watching Jack and I as if we were a fire they might have to put out. I knew this wasn't the time for a big conversation. I was too tired. Too keyed up with nerves. But somehow I couldn't stop myself.

"Well, what if that's not okay with me?" I asked, my voice rising. "What if I don't want our relationship to be a mystery anymore? What if I'm tired of being a pawn in some game I don't even understand?"

"We're all pawns in a game we don't understand," Jack said quietly. "That's life."

"Don't get philosophical." I rolled my eyes. "You're just changing the subject."

"We don't have time for explanations, Aggie. Or for Deuce's drama. Enemies are coming. The Diamantes are out for blood. The Spades will be wanting their obelisk back—"

"Right," I said bitterly. "I forgot, you know everything. You know who's coming. You know what the Diamonds are thinking. You probably knew what was in the chest too, right?"

He closed his eyes as if he might doze off and wake up later to find this whole conversation was just a dream. It was as good as a confession.

"Wait. You seriously knew what was in the chest all along?"

Jack shook his head dismissively. "The ace tells me things. What difference does it make?"

I gaped. "I can't believe this. I am so sick of your games," I said, unable to keep from shouting. "Maybe you can tell me what's happening with our pips, then? Or what the hell the Spades' obelisk is doing to ours?"

"No," Jack said. "I don't know. Even the ace doesn't understand—"

"No. Of course not," I interrupted. "Even if you knew, you wouldn't tell me. Why would you? I'm only your—" I stopped. I'd been about to say girlfriend, but the truth was I didn't know what I was to him. I shook my head, tears rising to my eyes. But I couldn't cry and ruin my wedding makeup.

There was just too much going on. Too much changing too fast. And I was too sleep-deprived to process it all.

I noticed movement down the hallway and saw my husband-to-be watching us with those gravel gray eyes. Supposed to be bad luck, wasn't it, a groom seeing the bride before their wedding? I turned my attention back to Jack, but my anger had burned down a bit, leaving a raw sadness in its place.

"Look, I'm not trying to yell at you," I said, quiet now. "The truth is, I—"

I reached for his hand, but he jerked his away, as if afraid of my touch. That was the final straw.

"I better get ready," I wheeled, hurrying away.

"Aggie," Jack called after me.

But I didn't turn back. And of course, he didn't follow.

43

AGGIE

I sat on the royal bed, in the red wedding gown, on my wedding day, and called my mom. I'd chased everyone out by then—Teemor, the stylists, even Mina. I needed to be alone with my thoughts. And when I was alone, I realized that wasn't really what I wanted. I didn't want to be alone; I wanted my mom.

Truthfully, I hadn't imagined my wedding day much growing up. I wasn't that kind of girl. My daydreams had always been more about getting into a prestigious college or hiking up Machu Picchu or having a three-story home library with a sliding ladder and a spiral staircase. But when I did think of my hypothetical wedding, of course I imagined Mom there. The face of the groom was always blurry. Molly stood among a throng of indistinct bridesmaids. The guests were a cast of nameless extras. But Mom would absolutely be front and center. She would help me get ready. She'd dry my happy tears and talk down my nerves. She would walk me down the aisle since Dad could not. And sure, this was a weird sham wedding, but it still killed me that Mom wasn't here.

And so I took out Dad's scorched rabbit's foot—his ill-fated lucky charm—and stroked it with trembling fingers while Mom's phone rang. I expected to get her voicemail. It seemed unlikely that Mom had remembered to charge her phone while sowing disaster, slaughtering crows, and recruiting henchmen, and I doubted the abandoned hospital she'd made her lair had working electricity.

And so I froze for a moment when her voice whispered into my ear, "Hey, Aggie."

"Hello, Parent," I said at last.

She sounded so quiet, so sad, so lucid, and so herself that it seemed absurd, suddenly, that I hadn't called her earlier. I'd driven five hundred miles, stormed a heavily fortified castle, and fought gods, all so I'd have the power to confront Mom— but it hadn't occurred to me simply to call and talk to her. And yet now that I had her on the line, words failed me. Tears came instead, welling up from somewhere deep inside me until I was silently sobbing so hard that I couldn't have talked if I wanted to.

"Aggie? You there?"

"I... miss you," I finally choked out.

"I miss you too, sweetie," she said. "We only have nine more months."

I sniffed. "Nine months of what?"

"Of my service. To the Morbus. The stone and I made a deal."

My forehead sank into my hand. "A deal? Mom, what makes you think you can trust the obelisk of Spades?"

"The same thing that makes you trust your Jack Valentine."

"Ha," I said bitterly. "Dumb teenage hormones?"

There was a smile in Mom's voice. "No. Hope."

Hope. The word gave me pause. I'd assumed all along that Mom was doing all this in a haze of brainwashed madness. And I knew that had to be part of it. But there might be a logic to her actions, as well. Doctors loyal to the Valentines had examined her. They'd found the shard of the Spades' obelisk in her gut to be inoperably fused to her body. Remove it, and she would die. So maybe Mom was right. Maybe the only way I could get her back alive would be if the stone let her go willingly. And the only way it would do that, it seemed, was if she did its bidding.

"For nine months?" I said.

"Our deal was thirteen months. That was four months ago. I'm sorry, I should have told you, but..."

I sighed. "It's okay. There are things I haven't told you, either."

"Such as?"

I shut my eyes, as if bracing myself to jump into cold water. "I'm getting married."

"Oh, Aggie," Mom sighed. "Jack is—"

"Not to Jack," I interrupted. "To King Michael."

A dead silence.

"Hello?" I said.

"You'd be queen..."

"That's the idea," I said, sniffling again and glancing around for a tissue, finding none.

"Aggie, no. You should get far, far away from all this. Bad things are coming. I can't stop them... If you stay with the Valentines I can't promise you'll be safe—"

Something about the frenzy in her voice, the strange cadence, the pauses...

"Wait. Is the obelisk telling you to say this?"

Silence.

"No," she said at last. Super unconvincing.

"Okay. I stay and become queen, and you can't promise I'll be safe. Fine. But what if I do leave?" I pressed. "Can you promise *you'll* be safe?"

Silence again.

"Can you promise you won't do something terrible? Something that will—I don't know—change you? Make it so you can't go back to the person you were before?"

Her sigh whispered through the phone, ghostlike. "Aggie, you know I can't promise anything. Except that I'll do my best."

I nodded. "So will I."

Another pause rose between us, swelling like a wave at sea.

"Nine more months," Mom said.

"Nine months," I agreed. "A perfect period for gestation. We'll both play our roles. A pair of queens. And when it's over—"

There was a knock at the door.

"Aggie?" Mina's voice came through the wood. "It's almost time."

"I've gotta go," I said, dabbing the corner of my eye with a tissue. An absurd laugh gusted out of me. "I have to go get married now."

"I'll be there," Mom said.

For a second, I thought I misheard her. "What? I mean... I would want you here, obviously. But you can't—"

"I told you, sweetie. For the next nine months, I'm a Morbus. And you have something that belongs to us. I'll be there," she said again, and the call ended.

♡ ♤ ◇ ♧

I walked slowly down the grand staircase of the Valentine mansion, a bouquet of red orchids and roses in my hands. Counting the steps, of course. Pausing at twenty-three. Though I wasn't to the bottom yet, I knew from counting them many times that there were thirty-five steps total. Not a favorite number.

The rest of the suit and at least two dozen sycos and sprites stood gathered at the foot of the staircase, each dressed in their finest clothes, a sea of gowns and suits in reds and whites. Strained smiles. All eyes on me.

Where was Jack? I scanned the room, but I didn't see him. *No Deuce, either.* A surge of loneliness crashed over me, but I shivered it off. Queens were never lonely. Were they? Or were they always lonely?

As I descended, I took in the foyer floor, a beautiful pattern of checkered hardwood that whorled to a glowing heart inlay at the center of the room. Beyond it stood the front doors. Just a few months ago, I'd walked into this house, into this world, through those doors. I could never have imagined everything that had happened since. If I could go back to that moment, would I enter? Or would I lock that door? Seal it shut and run?

Lock the doors. Lock the windows. Mom is coming...

No, she couldn't be. That would mean war. She had to be bluffing. I pushed the thought from my mind and brought my attention back to the present, trying to still my racing thoughts. *Be here and now, like Dr. Campos says. My wedding. The hearts mansion. This foyer.*

Ope, I stepped on the hem of my dress and nearly tumbled, but a flare of charm kept me on my feet. Strange, how second nature using charm had become. Like another sense, another appendage. A part of me. *Lucky girl. Ha.* Down, step by step, twenty-seven, twenty-eight. Piano music rang from the throne room, each note echoing through the grand halls. It was Mina, I knew. She'd learned to play during her K-pop days. She was performing again, now. At my wedding. Because I was having a wedding. So weird to think about. *Down, down, down. Surreal.*

I felt outside my body, like a spectator watching the scene from afar. Who was this girl on the steps? This girl, forcing herself to marry a wicked old man she didn't love—for power? Did I pity her? Did I mourn her? Did I even recognize her?

Jack.

I spotted him over near the door, his back pressed against the wall so that he nearly disappeared behind a table and a vase of flowers. Our eyes met, and the pain in his gaze was so real and so keen that I felt it too. It melted some part of me that I was trying to keep frozen—that I had to keep frozen, or I couldn't go on with this. And I did have to go on with it. *Protect my mom from herself. Protect the world from my mom. Protect the Valentines from my mom. Protect my mom from the Valentines. Being a queen is easy, my dear. Just smile with the world on your shoulders.*

I looked away from Jack. At the bottom of the steps, Dubs and Galen stood waiting for me, each holding a sword. My honor guard.

Dubs gave me a playful wink as I reached the bottom step.

"Your majesty," he said in that accent of his that usually made me smile. Not today.

I fell into step, and together we turned the corner and made our way toward the hallway that led to the throne room. Did I hear something? From outside? A shout? A scream? We were nearly to the arch when there came the click of a doorknob and the screek and thud of a door swinging open and slamming against the wall. I spun amid the metallic *shing* of drawing swords and the leathery *whisk* of drawing guns to see the mansion's front door flung wide. Rather than a sunny yard, it revealed a black tunnel, brown earthen walls held at bay by massive timbers. The leprechaun underground. I steeled myself to see Mom.

But the warriors who marched out were clad in red, and in the scarlet light of a flaring pip, I recognized the leader of the procession.

The Diamond Queen had come for her revenge.

Diamond Queen strode out of the tunnel, a force of at least three dozen Diamantes and sycos in her wake. An eerie, mirrored medieval helmet obscured her face, but her tall, feminine frame and the crest on her helmet—which resembled a topknot ponytail—gave her away. There were several Diamonds I'd never seen before among the throng, all of them heavily armed, including a physical specimen of a boy armed with a rapier and a 9-millimeter who moved with a smooth swagger that reminded me of Jack. Molly, Lorcan, and Cleo were among them too I saw, and they seemed to be safe. It was a relief, although how they had ended up with the Diamantes was a puzzle I didn't have time to solve just now.

"Don't mind if we crash your party, I hope?" DQ asked. "We're here for the part where you ask if anyone objects to this union."

Ten stepped out from behind the queen with fire in her eyes. "Because I object," she said.

The room seemed to contract as the Valentines—all but Cobe—drew near to defend me. Jack stepped directly in front of me so all I could see was his broad back.

"Ten, come on," he said. "You're really going to come in here with *them* and try to usurp—?"

"I'm usurping nothing," Ten snarled. "I'm a ten, remember? She's a six. The queenship should be mine. I've bled for this suit for years. She's—"

"Excuse me. I can speak for myself." I pushed Jack aside, turning to Ten. "Look, I'm sorry for what happened—"

"Oh, you apologize to *her*." Diamond Queen rolled her eyes beneath the vast fake eyelashes that poked out of her helmet's eyeholes. She turned her hands toward me. The diamond pips there blazed red, and a knot of nausea snapped taut in my stomach, doubling me over and making vomit rise into my throat. I gulped it back, wincing.

I'd never really faced off with her at the mansion, not before Ten showed up, but the fact that DQ had the power to tinker with my physiology so easily was scary. I flared my own charm and used it to calm my insides. It helped, but not much. Reflexively, I took a step back, but DQ flared charm again and my ankle twisted painfully, sending me to my knees. Bad luck for me. Good luck for DQ.

Such power. It reminded me of what Lorcan had said about her being the strongest luck god. He was right. But how was she so strong?

"Where's the Diamantes king?" I demanded suddenly. If there was a king somewhere, he would outrank DQ. I could appeal to him for peace.

DQ cocked her head, which looked pretty eerie in her ponytailed helmet. "Oh, sweetie. No one told you?"

"You killed him, didn't you?" I asked. "After you became queen, you killed him and took his power. That's why you're so strong."

DQ slowly removed her mirrored helmet. She had two black eyes. The gash on her forehead had been stitched up and was held with a pair of butterfly bandages, and a goose-egg protruded grotesquely. I wished she'd put the weird helmet back on.

"You've got it backwards, sugar," DQ said, her voice low and dangerous. "I was Tanner Edwards, the king. I persuaded the former queen to take a permanent vacation and I took her power. I'm a better queen than she ever was. And now, you're right—I wield the power of a king and a queen. That's why I can crush your little ass like a ladybug. But I don't have to get my own hands dirty, because your friend here is going to take care of you for me."

She took a menacing step closer, with Ten at her side.

"Look, I didn't want to break into your house," I said. "My ace commanded me to. And I'm not trying to fight anyone. I don't even want to be queen, really. But I'm not going to let Ten take control and then start some crusade against my mom."

DQ snorted. "The Valentines allied with the Morbus? Oh, you'll make one hell of a Hearts queen, sweetie."

"No, she won't," Ten said, drawing a rapier with a diamond-encrusted guard and stepping forward. The Diamantes had lent her a charmed weapon. Great.

As I stood again on my now-throbbing ankle, someone touched my shoulder. Mina had taken down one of the decorative swords that hung on the wall and handed it to me. It felt strangely heavy, especially with my sore thumb. At the same time, my head felt almost weightless, like I might float away at any second. Warring voices argued in my mind.

This can't be real.

No, it's super real. You're fighting Ten. Again. And no silly pillow fights will save you this time.

I glanced around, searching for some way out. My attention settled on King Michael, but he shook his head before I could even ask a question.

"Ten has a right to challenge the winner of the queen trial," he said. "It is tradition."

I wanted to tell him exactly where he could stick his traditions, but I had other things to worry about. Like staying alive. Dueling Ten felt more inevitable by the second as both suits drew into a circle around us.

Jack stepped in front of me again. "Ten, come on. We both know what this is really about. You're mad at me, so take it out on me. Leave Aggie out of it."

Ten's laugh sizzled with fury. "Some things actually aren't about you, Jack."

The tall, handsome Diamond I'd noticed earlier elbowed Danusia teasingly. "Maybe *you* should duel their Jack," he said.

"You always had a thing for him, right? We could make this a double-header."

Danusia refused to look at him. "Shut up, Tristaine, or I'll be dueling you."

Ten took a threatening step toward Jack. "This is about Six, not you. I don't like that she left me to die. I don't like her superior attitude and her sense of entitlement. I don't like her smug little face. And I sure as hell won't be kneeling to her as my queen."

"Fine." Jack stepped into a fighting stance. "But you want to get to her, you're going to have to get past me first."

Ten brought her rapier into guard position, ready to oblige, but I tugged on Jack's sleeve. "Jack."

He turned to me, looking surprised.

"I have to do this," I said.

He blinked. "What?"

"This is my fight. If you kill her or she kills you—"

"She won't—" he started, but I interrupted him.

"I'll always feel guilty about it. And if I don't stand up to her, she's always going to be gunning for me—and my mom. I have to do this."

Jack's jaw clenched as he looked from me to Ten and back again.

"You wanted me to be queen," I pressed. "So let me become queen. Our suit will never respect me if you fight all my battles."

Finally, he nodded, then he leaned in and whispered in my ear.

"She circles to her left. You circle to your right. Cut her off. Disrupt her pattern. And if things go wrong—" He stopped, as if unsure what to say next.

I went up on my tiptoes and kissed him. It was just a quick meeting of our lips, but it was enough to erase the frown lines from between his eyebrows and send a jolt of longing through my belly. Then we were apart again. His eyes lingered on mine, an unspoken reassurance flowing between us. He gave me a single nod and stepped back to join the other hearts in their semicircle.

I hefted the sword Mina had given me. It was too heavy. Awkward. What was I even doing? I had no business fighting Ten. It was a terrible idea. I'd let my exhaustion and confused emotions take the wheel and steer me into deadly territory. But I saw no way to back out now.

And the truth was, maybe some crazy part of me wanted to do this. To test myself. To see if I could win. To see if, just maybe, I really did deserve to be queen.

One, two, three... I started counting dark squares in the hardwood floor, then stopped myself. Let counting distract me now, and I'd be dead. I sent a bit of my flared charm into my mind, nudging the anxiety to lessen. There were limits to how much charm could influence human biology, I'd learned, especially when it came to my own raggedy brain, but at least I stopped counting.

I can do this, I told myself.

Ten was a badass, but no one was invincible. There had to be some clever way I could use charm to defeat her. The question was, in my exhausted, confused, bruised, and emotionally frayed state, would I solve the equation before Ten slipped her blade into my chest?

The red suits formed up around the edge of the round room, Diamantes on one side, Valentines on the other. Between them spread an expanse of open floor and two warriors: Ten and me.

Tactician that she was, Ten understood that striking fast was to her advantage, and she was already circling, blade ready, drawing closer. *One, two...* I started counting her footsteps, then stopped myself again, making my eyes focus on her blade rather than her feet. I brought my sword up, took one step, and immediately stumbled. Oh, right. I was wearing a ginormously puffy wedding gown. How convenient.

I whipped my sword blade down, cutting loose a flap of taffeta, and began tearing it free, circling clumsily away from Ten as I did. But the skirt was thick and layered, and it was only half torn loose before Ten was on me, her blade flashing a wicked red in the light of many glowing hands.

I brought my own weapon up and blocked her strike with a *clack*, then stepped backward, outside the deadly arc of Ten's second slice.

I glanced at our audience. The Diamantes all had their pips up and pointed at us. I could feel the tiny nudges and tugs of their luck on me. A twinge in a hamstring. A slight slip of my foot on the floor. DQ's power was the worst. Even with my charm flared, hers felt like a noose around my neck, trying to drag me to my knees.

"Not fair!" Jack shouted.

The one who reminded me of an Asian Jack Valentine—Tristaine, Danusia had called him—gave a roguish smile. "You know what they say, Jack. All's fair in love—and war."

Mina was the first of the Hearts to put her hands up. A second later, they'd all followed suit, pun intended, and I felt their power supporting me like a rising tide.

Ten and I circled again, our blades clashing and scraping, and with every step I felt the influence of luck—luck pressing me forward, luck pulling me back. Luck making my feet sure, luck making me stumble. Luck making my sword arm strong and luck making it cramp. It was like being buffeted by a wind that gusted from a hundred different directions. The result? Every step was unsteady. The sword felt constantly about to slip out of my grip. I had no idea whether each swing of my weapon would be powerful or weak, accurate or errant. Even my emotions and thoughts roiled from the luck gods' meddling. Was I confident or terrified? Focused or distracted? The push and pull made me feel like I was going crazy. Maybe I *was* going crazy. But one thing I never lost sight of was Ten's blade, always a single mistake away from impaling me.

I tried to take Jack's advice. Each time Ten tried to circle to her left I stepped right, cutting her off and forcing either a clash of weapons, a retreat, or for her to circle in the other direction. The problem was, I also preferred to circle to my left. Breaking that pattern was awkward for me, too. And Ten was vastly more experienced and more adaptable than I was. Her frown might have deepened a little when I cut her off, but her defenses remained impenetrable, her attacks relentless. The one struggling was me.

Soon, my arms trembled with the labor of swinging the heavy sword. My hand hurt from the vibration of the clashing blades. My legs felt wobbly, like they might give out at any second.

"Truce? Co-queens?" I panted, half joking, too out of breath to make complete sentences.

Her only response was a snarl and a strike so hard it sent my sword whirling out of my hands. I ran to retrieve it, but was jerked to a stop like a dog on a chain. I fell to my knees and looked back to see Ten standing on the end of my taffeta tail, grinning ferociously. She snatched up the fabric and gave it a mocking tug.

"Time to reel you in, little fish," she said, moving toward me and wrapping the fabric around her arm with each step. "Reel you in—and gut you."

Desperately, I flared my charm, but it felt wrong, cold where it should have been hot. I looked at my hand to find the pip dark. Dead. It glitched bright red then fizzled again, like a dying neon sign.

The obelisk. No...

The other Valentines were noticing, too, looking down at

their hands then glancing at one another in alarm. Jack had closed his hands into fists and gone pale.

The Diamantes pointed at their rivals and whispered to one another, wonder and worry in their faces. Ten felt it too, pausing to glance at the palm of her non-sword hand—the arm with the taffeta wrapped around it.

Something—the swords, maybe—made me think suddenly of my seventh-grade science fair project. I'd won by making a working model of a medieval siege weapon, the trebuchet. It consisted of a counterweighted arm that acted as a lever. A stone in a sling sat at a channel at the bottom of the trebuchet, which was attached to the long arm of the lever by a rope. When the lever swung, it would whip the stone up and over the top to throw it.

Although I found myself in a medieval-style duel, I had no trebuchet now, and no stone. But I did have a lever.

In one swift motion, I grabbed my taffeta leash with both hands, twisted to face away from Ten, placed the taffeta over one shoulder, and threw myself down and forward with all my weight, charming as I did. I somersaulted away from Ten, tugging the taffeta behind me. The force and the surprise were enough to jerk Ten forward. She stumbled, dropping her sword, and fell. I rolled to my feet, turned, and leapt onto her back. I'd lost my sword too, so I grabbed the only weapon I could—the wedding dress fabric—and wrapped it around Ten's neck. She clambered to her hands and knees, but I locked my legs around her waist and cinched the fabric tighter around her neck.

Red-faced and snarling, Ten rose to her feet while I still clung to her, then threw herself backwards onto me like a falling tree. I hit the ground with so much force that the breath blasted out of my body and my vision sparkled with stars—but somehow I held on. And the taffeta around Ten's neck had only gotten tighter. Her face was turning a frightening shade of purple now, her eyes bulging and bloodshot. Her fingernails raked over my arms, carving bloody gouges in my skin. I felt the tug of charm on me, DQ's the strongest of all. But my grip was too sure to break. The charmed dress fabric too strong to tear. I held on until Ten stopped clawing me. Until she stopped thrashing. Until she went still.

The Diamonds and the Hearts slowly lowered their hands.

I looked at Jack, but his expression was unreadable. He looked pale, and he still held one hand up, the heart pip glitching in and out.

Tentatively, I released the fabric wrapped around Ten's neck, half expecting her to lurch awake and attack me, but she didn't. I nudged her. She didn't move.

"Well, I'll be damned," Diamond Queen said in a low voice. "The little bitch did it."

There were murmurs among the Diamonds. Someone clapped for me. But my eyes stayed on Ten as I charmed her. *Breathe,* I willed. *Be alive.* Suddenly, she took a long, shuddering breath, and I could have melted with gratitude.

Until Mina's voice cut through the silence.

"Uh, guys." She pointed out the window. "We have a problem."

44

AGGIE

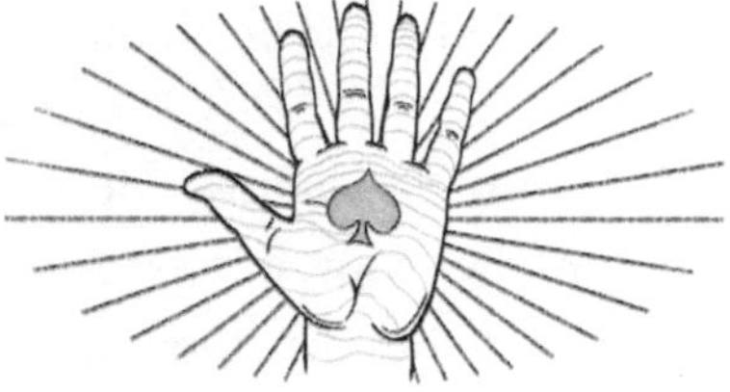

The mother of the bride had arrived, and she'd brought an army with her.

While the red suits crowded in to watch out the tall picture windows, Mom's Morbus troops advanced across the green lawn. I counted thirty-six raggedly dressed sycos and, arrayed behind them, a surreal sight: what had to be a hundred young men wearing identical faces. For a second, I thought I had to be losing my mind, then I understood. They were clones, exactly like the ones Bartholomew Barth had at his menagerie, with their puffy brown hair and pale blue eyes—although why they were following Mom, I had no idea.

Mom's followers were black-dressed, pallid, and somber as a battalion of ghosts. They moved toward us with aching slowness, weapons glinting, and I watched Mom at their head. Her hair was longer than ever, black strands whipping across her too-pale face.

"Well, I guess that's our cue to skedaddle," Diamond Queen said.

"Are you serious?" Jack demanded. He knelt over Ten, I saw, and had a hand pressed to her forehead, feeding charm into her. The sight of him like that sparked some cold part of me back to life. He was my Jack. Our loyal leader. A man who wouldn't let Ten die, even if she hated him.

"We're red suits," he told Diamond Queen. "We're allies, no matter what differences we might have. You're just going to leave us?"

Diamond Queen's smile was wicked. "Revenge is a bitch, Jack. And so am I." She looked to her fellow Diamantes. "Let's roll."

Lorcan stepped up to the coat closet door and activated his leprechaun key. When the door opened, it revealed a long, stone-walled hallway, and the Diamonds began disappearing down it, single file.

"We'll remember this," Jack called after them.

DQ only waved goodbye and kept walking. Moments later, the door slammed shut behind them. Our allies were gone.

Only Molly and Lorcan remained behind, holding hands. I wished they'd left too, gone back to safety with the Diamonds. But of course, Molly's loyalty kept her with me, and Lorcan's enchanted love kept him with her. I made a mental note to quit meddling with people's emotions—if I survived long enough.

King Michael had stepped forward to stand over Ten and Jack, his severe face etched with worry.

"Cobe, take her upstairs," Michael said. "Ten doesn't need to be in the middle of another fight."

Cobe obeyed, scooping Ten up in his arms.

"There's not going to be a fight," I said. "I'm going out to talk to them."

"I'll go with you," Jack said, standing.

Our eyes met, and there was a moment of tension between us, that old repulsion-attraction, that alternating current. But when I looked into his eyes, I felt like I saw a bit of the real, deep-down Jack I sometimes glimpsed. Not the hardened warrior—the boy who cared, maybe too much. Seeing Ten hurt had bothered him, I could tell.

"You're not going alone," he told me firmly.

I nodded. "Let's go."

Mina handed me the sword once again, and Jack and I walked out to meet Mom and our enemies.

I heard the door shut behind us. *Lock the windows, lock the doors.*

Except instead of cowering inside, I was out with the monsters now. Would Dr. Campos be proud of me? Or did this mean I'd reached a new and exciting level of mental illness?

"Remember, she's not quite your mom," Jack whispered as we moved down the walkway. "They'll want you to think she's herself, but their obelisk has been working on her for months. She's something else now. Don't let them manipulate you."

I nodded, not trusting myself to respond in that moment without my voice breaking.

As the Morbus drew near, I saw that Mom was carrying a large black urn, the sort that usually contains ashes of the dead. Just seeing it sent a shiver through me, and I knew by now what that feeling meant. Bad luck. Lots of it.

When perhaps twenty feet separated us, we all stopped. I felt like I was in some medieval movie, the leaders of a pair of armies riding out into the center of the battlefield to talk terms. Which is sort of what we were.

The breeze rustled the torn remnants of my wedding dress. A gull called over the lake.

"Hey, Parent," I said.

"Hey, Aggie," Mom replied. "I'm here to collect the piece of obelisk."

When I didn't respond right away, she pressed: "Your ace thinks she can absorb its power into her own, but she's making a mistake. Trying to absorb it will only poison your own obelisk and ruin its charm."

Automatically, I glanced at my hand. The pip there was glitching worse than ever now. I closed the hand into a fist.

"But if we give it back to you, it will increase *your* power," I said. "Isn't that right?"

And make you even harder to stop, I thought.

Mom looked at me, and I tried to decide if it was really her behind those eyes. Was she herself? Or some other consciousness, some perverted hybrid thing, like what she had been when we faced off at Oak Hill? I couldn't tell anymore. And that was almost scarier than knowing.

"There needs to be bad luck and there needs to be good luck, sweetie," Mom said. "A balance. It's your ace who is trying to mess up that balance, not us. Just give back what's rightfully ours, and no one has to get hurt."

"Someone always gets hurt with hex," Jack said. "You know that."

Mom turned to Jack slowly. "And so do you," she said with a hint of a smile.

I looked at Jack, wondering if he understood what Mom meant, but his expression gave me no clues. He merely met Mom's stare, implacable.

A young man with a spiderweb tattoo around his left eye, who I guessed must be Mom's second in command, spoke up. "I'm getting bored with this. Let me take care of this fool, Your Majesty."

In the space between one breath and the next, Jack's dagger was in his hand.

"Relax, Shade. There doesn't have to be bloodshed," Mom said to her lieutenant in an icy monotone. "Let us take what's ours, Aggie, and everyone lives to fight another day." Her attention shifted to something behind me. "Don't you agree, King?"

All heads swiveled to face King Michael, who had come out to stand on the front stoop, arms folded. The rest of the Valentines and their sycos were spread out behind him.

"I don't want bloodshed," he said. "But I can't let you near our ace."

Mom's eyes bored into him. "Too bad."

She set the urn down between her feet and took off the lid. As one, the Hearts drew their weapons and braced themselves. I held my breath, uncertain what to expect. At first, nothing happened. Then black smoke began to billow from the urn, gushing forth as if from the top of a factory smokestack. It rose and swirled, tattered whisps braiding and melding, coalescing into a shape long and serpentine, like a Chinese dragon.

"Inside! Now!" the king commanded, and the Hearts retreated back through the front door of the charm-fortified mansion. Only Jack and I stood our ground.

The dragon of smoke continued building, its tail forming first, then its body, then finally its face. But to my surprise, it wasn't the face of a reptile. It was a woman's face. A familiar face.

"Invidia?" I whispered, and the beast swimming through the air gave an eerily human laugh in response. Jack had killed Invidia back at Oak Hill—at least, I thought he did. But maybe beings made of shadow and bad luck didn't die like humans and gods did.

Jack had a hold of my arm and was tugging me back toward the mansion.

Mom called after us. "You're outgunned, Aggie. Tell your future hubby and your boyfriend there to give up the obelisk—before they both become dragon food."

She strode forward, and her Morbus advanced with her. I took in the flashing spears of the clone legion, the guns and baseball bats and knives of all those sycos. Way too many potential killing blows there to charm them all away.

Jack dragged me up the steps. We stumbled inside and slammed the door behind us. Jack's fingers had just reached the deadbolt when a massive BOOM rattled the whole house. The door blew off its hinges, leaving it in pieces, and sending Jack skidding across the floor on his back, blood seeping from a gash on his head.

"Jack!" I took a step toward him, but I was pushed back by a rush of air. The dragon Invidia flowed through the doorway like a freight train made of fog and soot. In her wake, Mom's army poured in. The clones at the vanguard spread out, their spears bristling to keep the Valentines pinned near the walls of the room while Mom strode up the middle, toward the hallway that led to the staircase and the ace's lair.

"No," I said, stepping in front of her. Anger and charm flared in me, and I impulsively reached out and shoved Mom back a step.

"No one touches the queen," the young man Mom called Shade leveled his 9-millimeter at me. Jack was there in a rush of motion, stepping between us, grabbing the Spade's arm and wresting it so the gun pointed up toward the ceiling. I expected Shade to be taken out of action instantly, as most people did when they fought Jack. Instead, he moved like a striking snake and headbutted Jack in the face. Blood gushed from Jack's nose as Shade brought up his knee, planting it in Jack's gut. Then he wheeled to point the gun at me again.

"Shade—" Mom started to speak, but before she could, the gun tumbled from Shade's hand, hit the floor, and went off. Shade went down to one knee in a shout of pain, blood already pooling around his right foot.

I'd felt the icy throb of powerful bad luck that made him drop the gun, but Mom's hands were down. I scanned the room and found no one flaring hex.

Until I saw Jack.

Both his hands were up. On one, the heart mark burned. On the other, a spade.

For a second, everything stopped. The earth seemed to reverse its spin as I stared at those two glowing symbols. Other Hearts gasped.

"Jack?" I whispered.

Before I could even form a question, two clones leapt forward and grabbed the wrist of my sword hand, pushing me back, out of Mom's way. I resisted, using charm to keep my balance, but the clones were too strong. They toppled me and I fell backward, the back of my head cracking against the floor. Pain, dizziness, and nausea washed over me, and when the blurred world came back into focus, several Spade sycos were holding me down. Hearts shouted and ran, fleeing the Invidia dragon, which had come down from the rafters to rampage. Dubs screamed as the dragon latched onto his forearm with its vicious smoke jaws and jerked him out of view.

"Dubs!" I shouted, trying to buck out of my captors' grasp.

"Hold her!" one of the Spade sycos shouted, lunging toward me with a knife.

Out of nowhere, Jack flew in again, shoving the clones off me. His charm and hex both flared as he grabbed a clone's spear, slung him to the ground, and slammed his head into the floor one, two, three times. When he was upright again, he had the clone's spear. Two clones tried to get in front of him, and he impaled them both in one thrust, like meat on a skewer, then pivoted and dumped them both to the ground.

Jack had been powerful before. With charm and hex at his disposal, he was downright scary.

He stalked toward me now with fire in his eyes and blood on his hands—and I felt very glad he was on my side.

Two more clones approached me but shied away when they saw Jack barreling toward them.

"Jack, they have instructions not to hurt her," Mom was saying.

"They already did," Jack snarled, snatching his dagger up from where it had fallen.

He was right. I touched my ringing head to find my hair sticky with blood. A Morbus syco tried to intercept, but Jack cut him down without breaking stride. A second was trying to stand when Jack stabbed him through the chest. The third Jack hacked down before he even got to his feet. I sat up, my head spinning, and found myself surrounded by bodies and Jack standing over me, his chest heaving, his face twisted into a snarl.

"You okay?" he whispered, helping me to my feet.

Mom stepped toward him, onyx sword in her hand. Jack brought his blade up and faced her.

"Any of your goons try to touch Aggie again, and they're dead," he said with deadly calm. "And that goes for you, too."

Mom's eyes narrowed. "You seem to forget, Jack. She's my daughter. You are one of my goons."

Jack stood taller, rising to his full, impressive height, towering even over my mother. "I think you forget, Rachel. I'm the highest-ranking male spade. Which makes me the king. I outrank you," he said. "And in the absence of an ace, I am the highest-ranking Morbus. Which means they are *my* goons. And I will cut them the hell up if they touch Aggie again."

Despite everything, Jack's protectiveness kindled a giddy warmth in my chest. But there was no time for emotion. I hazarded a glance around the room. The other Valentines had been chased back and cornered by Invidia. The Spade sycos and the clones had formed a semi-circle around us, cutting us off from our fellow Valentines. We were on our own.

Now, Mom squared up to Jack. "You have miscalculated, Jack. We do have an ace."

Jack shook his head, but his eyes glazed with doubt as he considered her words. "No. In Siberia, we blew up the house containing the obelisk. The ace died."

Mom tilted her head. "Did he?"

Jack shook his head. "Of course. All that was left were pieces. An ace is never far from their obelisk, and we had the place surrounded. He had to be there. He couldn't have gotten out."

"Didn't find a body, though, did you?" Mom teased.

I was confused. What did it matter if the Spades' ace had survived?

"No," Jack agreed. "We didn't find a body. But it would have been obliterated in the blast. There was nowhere else he could have gone. Except…"

I thought of the voice coming from the black shard of stone in Mom's gut.

The Hearts' obelisk didn't talk. The Spades' did.

"Except *into* the stone," I finished. "That's what happened, isn't it? Somehow, the Morbus ace got absorbed *into* the obelisk."

Jack looked at me like I was crazy.

"Occam's Razor," I said. "The simplest solution is the right solution. The stone itself can't talk. It talks because the ace is inside it."

"Correct," Mom said, taking a step closer. I couldn't keep glancing at the menacing sword in her hand. "Unguarded, an obelisk's power can be absorbed by another obelisk. But that's why aces remain so close to their obelisks. To guard them. To protect their power. And that's why your obelisk will never be able to absorb our obelisk. Because our ace is within ours, fighting, keeping it from being absorbed. And slowly corrupting yours."

I glanced at my hand. The pips were glitching again. Going dark then red then dark again.

"Our obelisk is going to poison your suit. Ruin your charm. But I can help you," Mom said. "Just let me take our chunk of obelisk back, and all this will be over."

I stepped in front of her. "No. Maybe we can't absorb the obelisk's power, but I'm not giving it to you, either. I'm not letting you get stronger."

Because if I do, I'll never get you back. That's what I was going to say, if a lump hadn't formed in my throat.

Mom's expression darkened. She turned to Jack. "And you. You are the King of Spades, yes. And in the absence of an ace, you would automatically ascend to the highest rank because of your gender. But our ace lives, and his will supersedes that order. He has made me high queen. Your superior. And I order you to go, get the piece of obelisk, and bring it back to me now." He started to answer, but she interrupted him. "And remember, wayward Valentines might get a slap on the wrist, but disobeying, among the Morbus, means death."

Jack's eyes got that glint in them that sometimes scared me. "You'll find I'm very hard to kill," he said.

The Invidia dragon growled, causing my fellow Hearts to cower. I saw Mina cradling Dubs. He was pale, and blood pooled around him like a red shadow. His lips moved, but no sound was coming out.

"Invidia craves blood and luck, Aggie," Mom said. "She's going to start devouring more Valentines if we don't leave soon."

I felt a sudden heat in both hands and looked down. The pips were burning a pure red now, as bright as ever. I waited a second for them to glitch, but they didn't. Something had changed.

I reached out and touched Jack on the hand. "Maybe you should do what she says," I suggested.

"What?" he hissed.

I showed him my unwavering pip. "They're not glitching anymore. Maybe it's a sign from the ace."

Truthfully, I wasn't sure if it was a sign or not. But the longer we stood here facing off with Mom, the more Valentines were going to get hurt. We couldn't let that happen. Besides, if our pips were pure now, maybe it meant that our obelisk had defeated theirs. Maybe the shard we'd be returning to Mom would be like a burned-out lightbulb, useless. Regardless, we couldn't hold Mom's archjinn and her army off forever.

"I'm waiting." Mom swooshed her sword blade through the air impatiently.

Jack gave me a rueful look, as if to say, *you'd better be right*. "As my future queen," he whispered to me, "of course I am yours to command."

He turned back to Mom. "Fine. I'll go down and bring back the obelisk."

"I'll go with you," she said.

"No," Jack replied. "No Spades are allowed in the presence of the ace."

She gave him a look.

"Except me," he amended.

Mom glared at him, then relented. "Fine. I'll send four clones along to help you carry it. You and your ace should be able to handle them easily enough if they try any treachery, and they'll be able to report back if you try any tricks." She nodded to the clones, four of whom broke off from the others and joined Jack. He eyed them appraisingly, then gave a grudging nod, turned, and led them into the darkened hallway.

There came an awkward moment of waiting, stasis, and stalemate as the two suits stared at one another. No one spoke. I tried to think of something to say to Mom. There was so much to catch her up on. The college essays I'd completed, the work I'd done converting the flea spotter into a car spotter. Once upon a time, we'd really have nerded out about that. But now the words wouldn't come. We just stood looking past one another like a pair of strangers. Even after everything I'd lost, that somehow felt like the biggest tragedy so far. But I was too walled off to cry. Tears might come later, but something told me the fight wasn't over yet.

Finally, footfalls sounded in the hallway, and every head turned to watch Jack and the clones reappear. But they carried no obelisk. No chest. Mom's expression was scary.

"Where is it?" she demanded.

"It wasn't there," Jack said, and the clones all nodded their agreement.

"It couldn't have been absorbed," she muttered. She paused, listening to the obelisk in her belly, I guessed. Then she wheeled on Jack.

"You had someone take it. A double-cross," she said.

Jack frowned, looking confused. "What? No. Who would have taken it? We're all in this room."

"We'll have to teach all of you a lesson now." Mom sounded genuinely regretful. "Today, you'll all learn to respect the Morbus."

She flared hex so powerfully my stomach contorted with nausea, doubling me over. She swung her obsidian sword, striking a vase off a table. It shattered, sending shards flying across the room like shrapnel. Someone cried out, and I looked to see Lorcan, over by the wall, wailing and falling to his knees. He had a hand over his eye, and blood was already weeping down his cheek.

"Lorcie!" Molly howled, cradling him as he slumped.

I had no chance to help them, because just then the clones gave a battle cry, lowered their spears, and charged the Valentines in a terrible clash of arms.

Invidia snarled and lunged for the Valentines. Galen was the first to challenge the dragon, but the beast of smoke simply headbutted him sideways, sending him windmilling across the room to land in a heap.

"No!" Jack shouted, stepping toward our attackers.

But Mom said, "Stop," and Jack froze, grabbing the wrist of his spade-pipped hand and falling to his knees in agony. "You will be obedient," Mom commanded. "Or we will break you."

She wheeled toward the hallway. "I'll go visit your ace myself. She'll tell me where she's spirited our obelisk off to."

Once more, I stepped in front of her. I had no idea what was going on down in the ace's chamber, no idea whether Jack and the ace had stashed the obelisk to try and trick Mom or whether perhaps the obelisk had actually been absorbed. But I knew that if Mom killed the ace of Hearts or somehow destroyed our obelisk, it might mess up the balance of luck worldwide—not just for me and the Valentines, but for millions of people. I couldn't let her do that.

Mom sighed. "Aggie, don't do this. Just let me pass."

"No," I said.

She moved toward me, *one, two, three,* measured steps. My grip on my sword tightened as my gaze shifted to the blade in her hand, glinting and deadly sharp. But she wouldn't use it on me. Last time we'd fought, she'd been possessed by Invidia. That's what had made her so bloodthirsty that she was willing to hurt her own daughter. Now, when I looked in her eyes, I saw that it was really her. A strange version of her, maybe, but her.

And yet she still brandished her sword as she stepped toward me, and instinct made me flare charm.

"Move, Aggie."

"No," I repeated.

Mom's teeth went on edge, tears of frustration filling her eyes. "For the last time, move," she snarled.

"Or what?" I asked.

I saw the pip on her non-sword hand flare, and I knew what it meant. It was *the work*, calling to her. Urging her to do something bad. To cut me down. And a hypothesis came to me. What if Mom could prove to herself right now that she was strong enough to resist *the work*? Wouldn't that end everything? Because if the Morbus obelisk couldn't compel her to do terrible things, her power would diminish, along with its hold over her. She'd go back to herself. In theory, at least.

"Aggie," she warned.

I threw my sword down at her feet.

"I won't move," I said. "And you won't hurt me."

For a second, her expression softened. It was full of all the tenderness and love I'd always known from her. I expected her sword to clatter to the floor next to mine, for her to pull me into a hug. But then, like a black curtain being swept closed, a wicked snarl returned to her lips. She raised her sword.

And I knew in that terrible instant that my thesis was disproven. I'd been wrong. Tragically, pathetically wrong. All our lives, we're taught that kindness is more powerful than hate, that good can overcome evil, that love conquers all. I saw now how horribly flawed and simplistic that thinking was. Brains are chemical machines, susceptible to influence, doomed to change. And forces are forces. You might have the wings of an angel, but if the gravity is stronger than the lift you generate when you flap, you'll never fly. You'll crash to the ground. Like I was crashing now.

I looked for Jack, but he stood frozen, his spade-marked hand trembling, his teeth bared in pain.

Mom stepped toward me, her obsidian blade raised over her head with both hands, a snarl on her face. Her muscles tensed for the killing blow.

I winced, cowered, flaring my charm one last desperate time with no objective, no hope in mind.

Mom let out an inhuman wail of fury and began her down-swing—then she froze.

She blinked. Tears welled in her eyes. She sank to her knees, reaching back over her shoulder with one hand, as if trying to scratch an unreachable itch. Then she fell forward, face-first, onto the floor.

A dagger hilt protruded from her back. And standing over her was Molly.

45

AGGIE

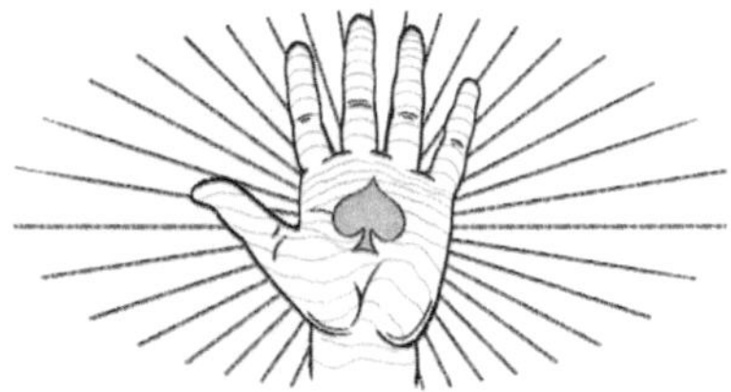

olly just killed my mom.

The thought passed through my head like a neutrino, ungraspable. *Molly just killed my mom.* No. Impossible. Yet there she stood, saucer-eyed, trembling hands going to her mouth as Mom, at her feet, writhed in a soup of her own blood, reaching in vain for the blade that stuck out of her back.

"That was for Lorcie," I heard Molly say, but the words seemed to come from some far-off universe. They had nothing to do with me.

I realized I was screaming some unintelligible string of sounds. Then I listened and I deciphered what I was saying. "*...seven eight nine ten eleven...*" Numbers poured out of me. Usually, numbers meant control, and I was counting something tangible, but not this time. This time, they were gibberish, x-rays pulsing around the rim of a black hole.

Am I going crazy? I wondered. I must be. Because Molly did not kill Mom. How could she? Why would she? It made no sense.

In a rush of air and roiling smoke, Invidia landed over my mother, the force of her arrival making me stumble back. The monster gave a wince-inducing roar, half dragon bellow, half human scream. Before anyone could react, she snatched Mom up in her front claws, pumped her great wings and rose into the air, bearing Mom with her.

"Mom!" I shouted, but it was too late. The creature was already out of reach, and Mom was, too. It winged upward and smashed through the glass dome above us. I cowered in a hail of glass, and when I looked up again, the cloudless morning sky was empty.

Shade, Mom's second, had taken command. "To the cars now. Move!" he shouted, staggering out the door on his injured foot. My fellow Valentines watched, too dazed to counterattack, as the Spade sycos and clones fled. Out the window, I saw our enemies spill out the broken gates, pile into cars, and tear off down the road.

One by one, the Valentines emerged from their defensive positions, crunching through the glass shards and taking in the damage with glazed eyes. My gaze lit on a thick smear of blood near the center of the floor. Mom's blood.

Mina was the first to reach me, and she swept me into a hug, which I received numbly. The others milled about, weapons in hand, checking corners and nooks for any stray enemies who might still be lurking nearby—but it seemed they'd all retreated.

I looked around. "Molly—?"

"She took off," Mina said. "I saw her help Lorcan up and the two of them went into the coat closet—er, the leprechaun underground."

God, I should never have hooked Mol and Lorcan up. But I never could have imagined it would lead to this.

I turned to see Jack standing before me. "Your mom," he started. Then he stopped, as if no words could encapsulate everything he had to say.

"I feel like," I paused, fighting to take a breath. My chest felt heavy, my whole body weighed down, but I didn't feel the impulse to cry. That had to mean something, didn't it? That I wasn't feeling grief? I was no mystic, but there was no question Mom and I were two quantum-entangled beings. If she were dead, I'd know it. I'd feel it. Wouldn't I?

"I feel like maybe... she's not dead," I finished.

Jack nodded, putting his good luck hand on my shoulder. "The Morbus will do all they can to keep her alive," he said. "They may be black suits, but they still protect their own."

"I should go to her," I said, taking a step toward the door, but exhaustion caused me to waver on my feet. Jack tried to catch me, but I automatically shied away from his spade-marked hand. He noticed my reaction, and his already mournful expression grew darker.

"I'll go," he said. "If you go, it will just mean another battle, but... I'm one of them."

There seemed to be so much feeling in Jack that no words could contain it all. Sorrow. Regret. Apology. Even longing. And I—I felt completely depleted. Empty.

"Where will they take her?" I said. "Do you think they'll go to a hospital, or...?"

"I'll find her," he said.

"Jack," the king's voice boomed, and we turned to find him standing under the archway, glaring. The rest of the Valentines hushed, watching, as Michael shook his head slowly. "I didn't think you'd really do it, Jack."

Jack shrugged tightly and unclenched his hands, letting the red light and the dark light shine equally. "I always said I'd unify the suits," he said. "That's what I'm doing."

"You have become an abomination," Michael said. "You are no longer welcome in this house."

The king did have the authority to banish people from the suit. But he wasn't the highest-ranking Valentine.

"The ace—" I began.

"The ace favors Jack, yes," King Michael interrupted. "That only makes him more dangerous."

The other Valentines glanced at one another, and I knew what they were doing: silently choosing sides.

"You're dangerous, Jack," the king went on. "You know you are. If you're as gallant as you pretend to be, you'll protect us all —by leaving."

The moment grew long and tense as King Michael and Jack stared at each other, and the rest of the Hearts held their collective breath. Then Jack stepped forward, jaw and fists clenched. He seemed about to speak, then paused to glance down at the spade mark on his palm.

"You're right," he said quietly.

"Jack," I whispered.

Murmurs rippled through the other Valentines.

Jack took a few backward steps, then turned to me. He came close, and despite everything, I still felt alive enough that my heart fluttered when his good luck hand touched my cheek. I took in that warm, honey-and-tea scent of him. *For the last time,* that morbid part of me said. But that wasn't true. I knew it wasn't.

"I will find your mom," Jack whispered. "And I'll protect her. I promise."

I nodded, but I could find no words. I was thinking too many thoughts at once. Of my mom, off bleeding somewhere. Of my gratitude that Jack was going to help her. Of the warmth of his hand on my cheek. Of the cold hex that I knew waited in his other hand. And what should I say, anyway? Thank you? Goodbye? I love you?

His fingertips slipped down my cheek, brushed across my trembling lower lip, his touch tender, gentle. But when I glanced down, I saw he still had blood on his fingers.

"Aggie..." He leaned in, his lips close to my ear.

And I leaned into him, too, feeling somehow that these would be words I'd have to cherish, that I'd have to remember them, hold on to them for a long time before I would hear his voice again. "Yes?" I said.

"Be queen," he whispered. And he left.

46

AGGIE

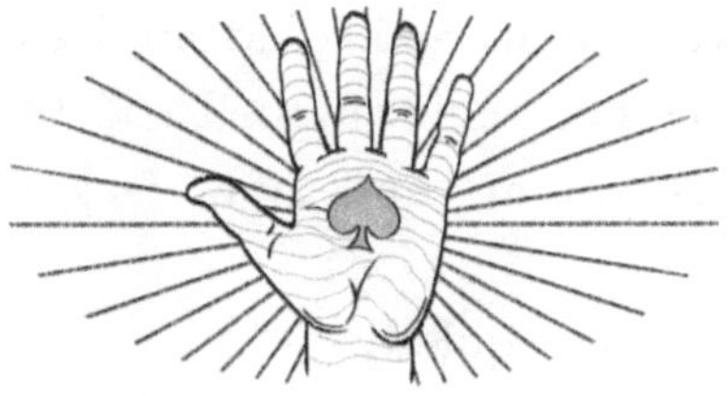

It was as if the world were one of Mom's vintage VHS tapes and someone had pressed *rewind*. I was washed again. Made up again. Stuffed again into the red wedding dress, which Teemor had managed to cobble back together with amazing efficiency.

Then I was walking into a throne room lit by flickering gaslight. Everyone was there, some of them beaten or scraped. Or—not everyone was there. Dubs and Ten had been rushed to a syco-owned medical clinic. Jack was gone. And Deuce. *Deuce!* He'd left after his fight with Jack, so he'd missed the entire battle. But here he was now, sitting in the back row wearing a red suit and a black tie, like a regular guest at a regular wedding. Seeing his face flooded me with warmth that almost brought tears to my eyes. When he saw my grateful smile he rose, stepped forward, and took my hands.

"You're here," I whispered.

"About your Mom—I'm sorry I wasn't here."

I shook my head. "I'm glad you weren't. I'm glad you're safe," I said.

He nodded gravely. "I was ready to keep on driving. To leave forever. But I decided I couldn't miss this," he said. "I mean, if this is what you want?"

I looked down the makeshift aisle, a red carpet running down the center of the throne room. At its end, the king stood, looking stern. Behind him, where an officiant would normally be, stood the ace and her obelisk.

Did I want to do this? No.

But did I have to do it? So I could survive in a world where friends literally stabbed people in the back? So I'd have enough strength to wrest Mom—and now Jack—back from the darkness?

"Yes. I have to," I said quietly.

A mix of emotions washed over Deuce's face, a series of glyphs too quick and complicated for me to decipher. Then he seemed to steel himself and nodded. "Then I support you," he said, giving my hands one last squeeze before letting go.

I offered my arm. "Walk me down the aisle?"

His eyes widened, then he smiled and took my arm.

Together we strode down the carpet with the eyes of gods and sprites and sycos following our every step. As we reached the dais where the thrones stood, Deuce let his hand slip down my arm and gave my hand one more quick squeeze.

"By the way, you look incredibly hot. I mean beautiful," he whispered. Then he stepped away, leaving me to stand alone.

With a deep, tremulous breath, I stepped up to where King Michael and the ace waited.

"Let us begin," the ace said in her crackly, ancient voice, and the wedding guests took their seats.

"Wait," I said suddenly. "I'm sorry, but what happened to the Morbus obelisk?"

I just realized I'd been whisked upstairs to dress so fast I'd never found out the real story. All I knew was that my pips were glowing normally again.

"Did our obelisk absorb it?" I asked. "Or did you and Jack hide it? Or...?"

The ace and the king shared an awkward look.

"I was deep in my trance state, fighting to protect our obelisk..." the ace began. "And..."

"It disappeared," the king finished.

I frowned. "Wait. It just... like... went poof and vanished?"

If after everything I went through to get that stupid obelisk, the Morbus got it back, I'd be pissed.

As usual, the ace seemed to read my thoughts. "The Morbus did not get it," she said.

"We don't think," the king amended with a note of foreboding.

I shook my head, perplexed. "Then who...?"

"We don't know," King Michael said irritably. "Can we get on with the wedding, please?"

I was pissing my future husband off already. Not a great sign.

King Michael and I turned to face each other. He took my hands in his. Even with his king-strength pips burning brightly, his skin was cold against mine. And after that—well, I don't remember. There were words. Responses. Promises. Mental counting. I had to remind myself to breathe. I kept expecting a wall to cave in and an archjinni to burst through, or the doors to blow off their hinges, or the windows to shatter as the Clubs stormed in like an evil SWAT team. These daymares flashed through my mind in a never-ending carousel, but no real terrors appeared.

And then a ring with a huge ruby on it slipped onto my trembling finger. Someone handed me a platinum band, which I slipped onto Michael's finger. The ace said, *man and wife*, and it was over.

I realized in that moment that I'd never actually expected this to happen. But here I was.

I'm married to a man I don't love. And I haven't even graduated high school yet.

Michael took my arm and we turned to face the assembly to a tepid round of applause.

"Tomorrow morning," Michael whispered, "we'll have your coronation."

My only response was a gulp, my throat so dry it clicked. *Five, six, seven…*I was counting the guests, but there were too few of them. Not twenty-three. Most of the sycos had fled when the attacks came. And the others who were missing? Jack. Mom. Molly. I couldn't even process that now. It was all I could do to take one step at a time as Michael and I processed down the aisle.

Gods knelt as we passed.

♡ ♧ ◇ ♧

There was a feast, but I couldn't eat a bite.

There was entertainment, dancers from some fancy ballet company, but I couldn't keep my eyes on them. I kept watching the door, waiting for the next calamity to wander in.

At some point, I took out my phone and checked the results of the Michigan Girls in Science awards. Of course, with everything going on, I'd never even had the chance to submit my project. The name next to *first-place winner* drew out my only smile of the night, a bitter one: *Claudette Dodson*. Of freaking course.

The king and I had our first dance, and I floated through it, feeling like a ghost. "Your demeanor is quite regal tonight," Michael said, his dank old man breath on my cheek redolent of red wine. He sounded surprised, but clearly intended it as a compliment. Of course, he was complimenting the fact that I was silent. Emotionally destitute. Too wrecked and numb to speak or be myself. *Is that what history wants in a queen?* I wondered. *A girl crushed flat, like a flower in a book?* The thought angered me, and the anger woke me up—a little.

Before I knew it, the party—if you could call such a somber affair a party—was winding down. Everyone gave another round of applause as Michael took my hand and led me from the room and up the grand staircase to the royal bedchamber. *Oh, God.*

We both retreated to our respective bathroom areas without a word. A satin nightgown had been laid out for me, something far more sensual than I ever would have been comfortable in, but someone—Mina, I guessed—had brought a pair of flannel jammie pants from my room. I put them on beneath the nighty, grateful that I didn't have bare legs. When I emerged from the bathroom, the king sat on the bed in a pair of red cotton pajamas, a pair of reading glasses perched on his nose, reading something on his phone. He glanced up as I entered and must have noticed how pale my cheeks were.

"Aggie." He took off his glasses. "Tradition requires us to spend the night together to seal our marriage ahead of your coronation tomorrow—where you will receive the full power of your queenhood. But as I told you before, we need not touch."

"No, that sounds great, thanks. Let's not," I said, all in one rushed breath. The king nodded, still looking at me.

"You don't like me very much," he observed. "That's fair. You came into the suit under difficult circumstances, and I wasn't very welcoming. But I want you to know, I have come to appreciate your virtues, Aggie. You're young. Impulsive, perhaps. And not without your personal flaws."

"Is there a *but* coming, or do you just plan to roast me all night?" I asked.

The king snorted a laugh. "You see, I doubt anyone else in our suit would talk to me like that. I've begun to understand what the ace sees in you. You have strength, Aggie. A surprising amount of strength. I hope one day we might be friends. And I think with time, you just might become a very good queen."

A compliment was the last thing I was expecting, but it didn't make me feel much better.

"Honestly, I just want to get my mom back, so we can go back to—" A lump rose in my throat, choking off the words. I swallowed it down but left the sentence unfinished.

King Michael gave a slow nod. "If that is your wish, then with the ace's permission, I'll do all I can to help you."

He patted the bed next to him.

"Come, lie down. You look dead on your feet. There's plenty of room in this huge bed for two to sleep quite separately. I won't touch you. You have my word."

I hesitated, but the king was right. If I didn't lie down soon, I was likely to fall over. And the massive bed with its red satin sheets and its puffy burgundy duvet looked heavenly. Casting caution aside, I flopped down. I ran my hands over the cool, smooth sheets and then looked at my pips. They burned brightly, as if just lying in bed with Michael were an act of *work*. That was good. Because I didn't know what lay ahead of me over the coming weeks and months, but if the past was any indication, I'd need a heck of a lot of luck to get through it.

"Good night, Aggie," the king said and then clicked out the light.

I'm not going to be able to sleep, I thought. I'd be up all night, dreading the feeling of the king's cold hands on my body. But the gravity of my exhaustion was far stronger than my anxiety. I usually counted my way to sleep. Now, I only made it to three before sleep took me.

47

CLEO

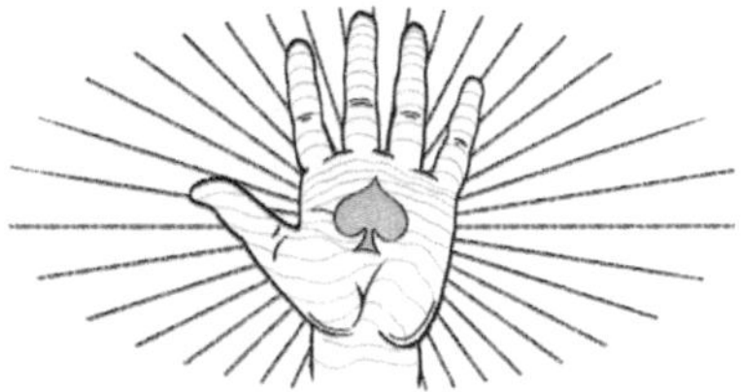

Cleo was sitting in a booth at the Coney Island diner, picking at a greasy omelet when the boy approached on his silent little feet and dropped her leprechaun key onto the table. She wiped her mouth and tossed the napkin onto her plate.

"You get it?" she asked.

The kid gave a silent nod.

"Good boy."

Cleo whipped out some cash, let it flutter onto the table, then stood. Grabbing the key by its golden chain, she took the boy's hand, and together they went down the hallway that led to the restrooms and the kitchen. She shoved the kitchen's double doors and they opened into what looked like the tunnel of a stadium, illuminated by the key's golden light. Inspirational sports posters were taped to the tunnel's concrete walls. Stenciled onto a header above them were the words GRIT – GRIND – GLORY.

"That might make a good tattoo," Cleo quipped, but the boy didn't respond. He wasn't much of a conversationalist. But he was a hell of a little thief.

The double doors at the far end of the tunnel opened into Cleo's lair, with its familiar smells of laundry detergent and microwave pizza. With the doors shut and barred behind them, Cleo stepped into the living area.

The prize sat upon the coffee table, its jagged crystalline surface glowing with a vaguely malevolent, purplish color in the dim light.

"The obelisk of Spades..." Cleo said reverently. How much could she sell a powerful, one-of-a-kind relic like this for? She wasn't sure, but she knew it was a hell of a lot. Wars had been fought over lesser objects. And the buyers? Dark suits, red suits, sylph—all would be clamoring to get their mitts on this. And that would mean a pissload of gold for Cleo.

She put a hand on the boy's head and mussed his hair. "You did good, kid. We'll make a thief out of you yet. Those idiot Valentines didn't expect a thing, I bet."

She chuckled, then glanced at the boy, suddenly unnerved by his silence.

"You didn't touch it with your bare hands, right?"

When the boy didn't answer, she turned to face him, crossing her arms. He hid both hands behind his back, a sheepish expression on his pale little face.

"Goddamn it, Gallo Jr., show me your hands," she commanded. Tentatively, the boy held out his hands—palms down. Gently, Cleo took both his hands and turned them over.

Just as she suspected. The mark of Spades glowed evilly from both the boy's little palms.

"Aw, crap," Cleo said.

48

AGGIE

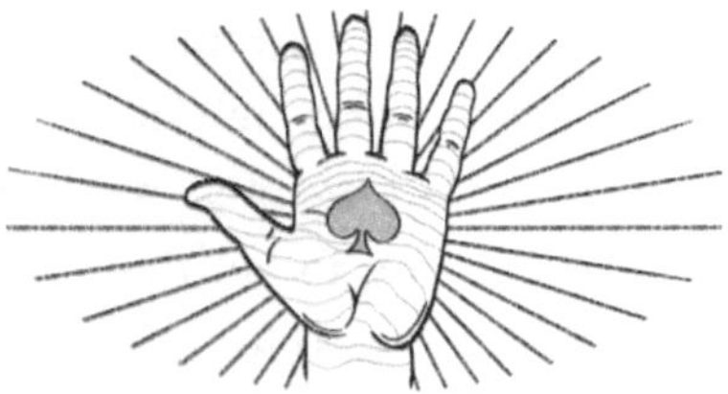

Everything was pleasantly warm. Morning sunlight bathed my face. My feet were cozy under the thick blankets. My hands were warm, too. Warm and wet.

Eyes still shut, I rubbed my forefinger and thumb together. Slick liquid greased my fingers. With effort, I forced my eyelids open.

King Michael was here. He had the duvet pulled up to cover the side of his face and he was staring at me.

Creepy—had he stared at me like that all night?

Wait...

As my sleepy vision focused, I realized what I had at first thought was the red duvet pulled up over Michael's head was in fact glistening red liquid—blood.

And his staring eyes did not blink.

I screamed, scrambled out of the bed, and stood, backing up.

Automatically, I scanned the room for danger. For a second, I thought I saw a shimmer over by the window, but when I looked hard at the spot, I saw only the wind-fluttered curtains. The window was open. Had it been open when we fell asleep?

I looked down at my trembling hands, both soaked with blood. *Not good.*

Footsteps approached, and a second later the door swung open, and Valentines spilled into the room. Mina. Then Cobe. Then Adelie and Galen.

"What? What is it?" Mina was asking.

I pointed a trembling, bloody finger at the bed. At Michael. My husband.

"Th-the king," I stammered. "The king is dead."

❦

The adventure continues! Get the ebook version of Daughter of Diamonds, Luck Gods Series Book 3 from Amazon and Kindle Unlimited. Or get the paperback wherever books are sold!

*One more thing! I have a FREE Luck Gods book for you. **The Thief and the Lucky Boy** is a novella that takes place in the Luck Gods story universe just after **Girl of Hearts** and before **Mother of Spades**. It's a really fun story, and it tells how Cleo met her little kleptomaniac protégé. Sign up for my e-newsletter and grab your free ebook copy of **The Thief and the Lucky Boy**.*

And if you enjoyed this book, please take a moment to review it on Amazon.

Did you notice any typos, errors or omissions in this book? Let us know by emailing them to: j@jgabrielgates.net.

Thanks again for reading, and good luck.

• *J. Gabriel Gates*